RHYLLA'S SECRET

Genre: Historical Fiction /Romance/Adventure

Cover design created by Cat Petersen

Kite Hawk photo by David Vickers

Rhylla's Secret

Published at Ingram Spark
by Elizabeth Rimmington. 2021.
Queensland
Australia

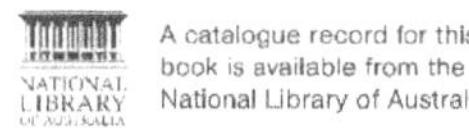

A catalogue record for this
book is available from the
National Library of Australia

ISBN
978-0-6485257-7-6 (Print)
978-0-6485257-8-3 (Epub)

Disclaimer
This novel is entirely a work of fiction. While some of the names, characters, and business places mentioned may have existed, their interaction with the story characters is pure fiction. All incidents are either the products of the author's imagination or have been used in a fictitious manner. The opinions expressed or beliefs held are those of the characters and should not be assumed to be the opinions or beliefs of the author.

RHYLLA'S SECRET

Written by

Elizabeth Rimmington.

ABOUT RHYLLA'S SECRET:

What was to have been a wonderful year for Rhylla MacBurnie
disintegrates into heartache and secrets.
After a moment of fury, her husband Robbie MacBurnie stares at
his brother Greg, lying in a widening halo of blood while Rhylla
and Robbie's daughter, Kirsty, lies unconscious and in disarray.
To protect his family, Robbie, disguised as his brother Greg, hops a
train to Mount Isa. The police want to arrest Greg while a Sydney
razor gang seeks to silence him forever.
Rhylla is left to cope with the challenges of Kirsty's pregnancy, not
knowing if her husband is alive.

APPRECIATION

To Caroline, Margaret and Denise for your polish.
To Bob and Cilla for solving the drilling conundrums.
To Joy and Kaye for sharing their knowledge of Blue Water Creek.
To the fellowship and support of good friends within the local
writing groups.
To the staff at the Gympie Library for their support.

Previous Books by Elizabeth Rimmington:

Shadow of the Northern Orchid – 2019
And the sequel
Shadows on the Goldfield Track – 2020
Burdekin Heartbeats – 2020
And now
Rhylla's Secret – 2021

Elizabeth Rimmington

Elizabeth is an Australian author living in a rural area of South-East Queensland. During a career in nursing followed by several years driving a taxi cab, Elizabeth has met many and varied people from all walks of life. A storehouse of memories from which to plunder and develop story characters able to infiltrate the reader's heart by osmosis. Their laughter, their heartbreak, and their pain will fill the book lover's soul with happiness, tears, fear, and empathy.

Visit Elizabeth Rimmington at her website
www.elizabethrimmington.com.au
Her FREE monthly newsletter includes a new short story every time.
Find her on Facebook – elizabethrimmington.author

One punch thrown in anger can cause repercussions to echo through a family for generations.

PART ONE

Nefarious Deeds

1933

PROLOGUE

Hazel highlights within the pupils of his eyes glinted in the lantern flame. His mouth hung partly open. The crust-coated tongue slowly lapped at the dollop of drool gathering on each corner of his lips. Unaware of the attention, Kirsty sipped on the mug of hot cocoa he had prepared for her while she worked on the last maths problem of her homework. The whistle of the rising wind in the trees outside was now only a background noise on the periphery of her mind along with the irregular burping of the innards of the kerosene refrigerator behind her.

She rubbed her eyes and lifted the mug to her lips again. The slight tremor of her hands ruffled the surface of the dregs as she drank. A satisfied smile curved the man's thin lips. She was oblivious to his rough hand on hers as he steadied the placement of the cup onto the kitchen table beside her books.

The wooden slats on the back of his chair creaked when he leant back to admire the view of innocence. The strawberry-blond hair draped her body as her head hung awkwardly from the neck. Her groomed hands twitched several times before falling from the table – one to her lap and the other to hang loosely at her side.

His smile stretched to a lecherous grin. He would have liked to further inhale this vision with his every breath, but time could be limited. He hated to rush these things. This had been an unplanned pleasure and the family might return within the hour.

The curtain of hair now draped his shoulders while her arms swung loosely with his every step as he climbed the staircase. At the top, he hitched her body into a more comfortable position on his broad shoulders before making directly towards the one room from which a dimmed light's glow announced the open doorway. By chance, it happened to be Kirsty's own room.

CHAPTER ONE

A satisfied smile rested on her lips as Rhylla MacBurnie placed the last of her files into the tan briefcase and secured the catch with a faint click. Her sigh filled the sleeper compartment. She leaned back to peer through the open window – away from the reach of the soot smuts streaming back from the train engine's fires. When the train slowed as it approached the city, she caught occasional glimpses of the glow of the Flinders Street electric lighting ahead. Peace flowed through her body with the soothing balm of the swaying carriage and the music of the steel wheels on the railway track. The southern Townsville suburbs passed by unseen as her mind filled with anticipation of her reunion with her beloved husband and their only child now living at home, Kirsty, the youngest.

This trip to Brisbane as District Manager of the northern branch of her family's company had proved not only successful from the business point of view but also thoroughly enjoyable with the visit to her cousin Leonard and his family. Her smile deepened as she recalled the dinner with her two eldest offspring, Tim and Bronwyn, both studying at the University.

All the signs were there – this was going to be a wonderful year. Idly her long fingers twirled a strawberry-blonde curl behind her ear.

Thin streaks of smoke and steam from the engine drifted in under the roof of the Townsville platform adding to the night's darkness reducing the already dull lighting. When the train came to a halt, Rhylla's heart pounded with excitement. She felt like a teenager again. Her breath caught in her throat at the sight of her dark-haired husband waving and grinning like a schoolboy himself. Not for the first time, wonder filled her soul. They were forty-six years of age and parents of three grown children. Where had all those years gone and so quickly? She jumped to her feet and with eager arms swept up her belongings.

Their laughter drew stares from the people around them as Robbie helped her down from the carriage. He struggled to relieve her of the briefcase and overnight bag while endeavouring to envelop her in a warm hug at the same time.

"My darling, Kitten, I've missed you so much. These past ten days have seemed like an eternity." Robbie whispered into her ear.

Rhylla stretched up to squeeze him with all her might. "Oh, Robbie, I missed you too. It's wonderful to see you again."

"You wait right here and don't move while I fetch your suitcase from the porters' trolley."

"Kiss me once more before you go and I won't move an inch."

Robbie pecked her lips before his gaze wandered up and down the length of the train. "Is your father not with you?"

"No, darling. You know he never misses the opportunity for a plane ride. He flew back yesterday. Give me a comfortable sleeping carriage on the train any day. I cannot understand his attraction to those noisy flying machines bouncing along just above the countryside. Once was enough. It left my stomach in my throat, in my boots, or on the floor. They are nothing but the devil's playthings."

The new moon and stars hung over them when they exited the station. Robbie wasted no time loading his wife and the luggage into the car. Before he settled behind the steering wheel, they hugged each other again.

"Don't suppose it'd do if we hitched ourselves into the back seat and began the preliminaries? No one would see us in this light."

Rhylla giggled. "Old man, you are a dreamer. These days, neither of us has the flexibility to achieve anything trying a stunt like that." She thrilled at the sight of his pale eyes deepening to an almost violet shade seen even in the feeble lights of the station and passing vehicles. After more than twenty years of marriage, she recognized this sign of his raised emotion. The match to light the fire of her own ardour.

"Well, old woman, let's get home, pronto."

Once Robbie had guided the vehicle through the traffic, Rhylla asked, "How have things really been while I was away? How's your accounting business been doing? Did you have the time to finish drafting the next chapter of your latest book as you wanted to?"

"The business is growing in leaps and bounds. Several new clients turned up last week wanting our firm to do their bookkeeping and their taxes. We acquired a young fellow not long out of Sydney University."

"You'll be happy with that."

"I'll say. I still can have a few days off a week to keep writing." Robbie threaded the vehicle around two Clydesdales pulling a dray of kegs from the brewery and continued his report on the week gone. "After Mrs. Barnes left for her father's funeral, Kirsty and I coped alright. Your mother had us over to dinner a few times. If it's possible, I think her domestic help cooks better than our Mrs. Barnes. I narrowly escaped food poisoning on those occasions when our daughter insisted on cooking for me. Mr. Evans showed me how to make a damper. We didn't starve."

Rhylla laughed. "Starve – indeed! I didn't know our gardener knew how to cook? I thought Mrs. Barnes cooked most of his meals."

"I am starving though, my darling. Not for food, my love. I'm starving for you. To share my body with you. To kiss you and hold you and become one with you, Kitten."

"Hmmm. That I do understand. Maybe Kirsty will retire early tonight and we can disappear into our bedroom."

"Fat chance of that. She's been looking forward to your arrival for days. We'll be lucky to see our bedroom before midnight."

It was Rhylla's turn to grin. "Will that be past your bedtime, dear?"

"Never."

CHAPTER TWO

Strong arms pressed her down. Leaden limbs offered a feeble struggle in response. The pull of clothes down her legs set up a scream in her throat but it faded to nothing before a sound exited her mouth. Merciful blackness engulfed her. When he rammed himself through the virginal gateway, a muted squeal was unheard or unheeded. Blue-grey eyes opened wide but without focus. They closed as the rhythmic pounding ravaged her body.

"Honey, you do the cocoa. I'll run up and see if Kirsty is going to join us." Robbie MacBurnie kissed the top of his wife's head after he closed the back door. "It's great to have you home again – did I tell you?"

"Only ten times since you picked me up at the train station. I really missed you too."

Robbie's feet clattered up the polished timber staircase to the bedrooms. He bounded through the doorway with his mouth open in preparation to call fifteen-year-old Kirsty. It shut on a gasp of shock to see a man struggling into his trousers beside his daughter's bed. Robbie's head lifted and his eyes widened further when a second shockwave hit him. He recognized his older brother, Greg – the dark secret of his family – the black sheep, Greg.

Disgust and hatred deepened the colour of his blue eyes to a dark violet – almost black. They fuelled Robbie's right arm. It swung of its own volition. He held nothing back. The clenched knuckles caught his brother under the receding, unshaven chin. Greg's salt-and-peppered ungroomed hair flew up into the air as his head snapped back. A sickening thud filled the room when the head connected with the corner of the solid chest of drawers. Blood sprayed forth from a gash on the skull wound. After a fleeting glance of surprise, the facial expression sagged as the large body slithered down the side of the furniture and onto the dark timber floor – painting a blood stain from the top drawer to the bottom drawer. Within seconds of his entering the room, Robbie stared down at the dead body of his brother. Unconsciously, his left hand massaged the bruised knuckles of his right hand.

A raised voice whipped at Kirsty's consciousness. She hauled herself up through the abyss of blackness. Exhaustion dragged her back as glutinous mud sucked at her feet when on the riverbank.

A nauseous sensation nestled inside her belly. An odour of stale sweat clung like limpets inside her nostrils. Hot rocks of weariness lay heavy on her eyelids. Through the slit gained by determination alone, a scuffle appeared as a blurred shadowy scene to her right. To investigate the reason why was beyond her. Her eyelids fell completely shut only to snap apart for a brief second at the sound of a sharp yelp followed by a crash. Her mind retreated into the black void.

Rhylla's call as she raced upstairs did not penetrate the fudge of Robbie's mind. Her forward propulsion sent her crashing into his back. Her pink lips opened to speak but only a squeak intruded on the tension of the air.

She stared at the unmoving body. Her blue-grey eyes fixated on the sight of the red halo of blood.

"Is he dead, Robbie? What's happened? Who's this?" She whispered the erratic questions bouncing like balls inside her head. The thought of her daughter in danger swung her around to find the partially clothed body of her youngest on the bed. "Oh, good heavens, what's happened?" She rushed across to cover her daughter's body with the sheet. She grasped the unresponsive hand. "I think she's asleep. How can she sleep through this?"

Robbie's power of speech had deserted him. His head swung left and right struggling to find words. He drew Rhylla into the protection of his arms and croaked, "He's raped our baby. That evil piece of rubbish has raped our baby. He's dead."

"Oh, God, NO!" Rhylla wailed and looked upon the face of her sleeping daughter on the bed. "NO!" Her hands flew to cover her mouth and suffocate the threatening scream. Again, Rhylla stared at the body on the floor and asked in a hushed tone, "But who is he?"

Robbie's mouth twisted into an unpleasant grin. "Rhylla, meet my older brother, Greg. He has sunk lower than I thought he could ever do. Meet the rapist, Greg MacBurnie."

"I thought he was away with the Merchant Navy."

"So did we all."

"What are we going to do? Robbie, if he's dead, then you have murdered him."

"Pity I didn't do so a dozen times in previous years. Now he has damaged my pure little angel. Will she be okay do you think, Rhylla?"

They both moved across the room to stand over Kirsty who lay with eyes closed. Facial expressions changed like rain clouds drifting across the sky. Intermittent groans escaped softly from her throat.

"I'll clean her up in a minute." Rhylla's hand soothed the girl's furrowed forehead. "What are we going to do about this body? Can your solicitor friend, Jim Sullivan, or maybe your copper mate, Doug Hampson, make this all go away?"

"I'm not sure what to do for the best. I want time to think. Can you help me get the body downstairs and out to his truck? I presume that's it I noticed out in the yard when we drove in. I thought it belonged to one of Mr. Evan's friends but he's away this weekend." He bent to straighten the man's limbs. "What about Kirsty – will she remember anything? What do we tell her? He must have given her some kind of drug."

"You could be right. She certainly appears doped. Firstly though, we'll get this dreadful man out into his car. I'll have to get towels to wrap the wound. We don't want blood throughout the house."

Robbie stood in deep thought for some moments while Rhylla went to retrieve towels from the linen press. He helped lift the head as she used the towels to contain the red ooze.

"We can't have her taken through the courts regarding the rape." Robbie pondered aloud.

"No, they still treat any rape victim, foolish enough to go to court like they're to blame, even now in 1933 – it might as well be 1833. There's little improvement in the attitudes over the last one hundred years."

"You know, Rhylla, I'm not sorry I killed him. It's probably best the beggar's dead. I've probably done the world a favour."

The pair held each other tightly. Both hearts pounded as one. Tears stung their eyelids. Neither could speak another word.

For the remainder of her life, Rhylla was to remember the bump, bump, bump of the man's head on the staircase and the resulting jarring felt in her arms as she struggled to help her husband drag the body downstairs. Whenever a door slammed, her memory recalled the crashing of the back door against the wall when caught in the winds of that night. The pain of the strain down the length of her spine as they dragged him up into the back of the utility truck was to torment her for years.

Her teeth caught her lips as she watched her husband cover the body with an old canvas from the coach-shed. Deep down, she knew life would never be the same again. She did not know how exactly, or even the why, but life would change.

When he jumped down beside her and held her closely the tears fell. "Oh, Robbie, what are you going to do with him?"

"I'm going to dispose of the body and the truck in the old unused quarry out towards Davidson's place. I'll get Jim Sullivan to drive out and collect me from near our fishing spot – I can walk there from the quarry tonight. I won't get back until about lunchtime tomorrow I shouldn't think."

"But, Robbie, will Jim do this for you? He's a solicitor after all and can't be seen to be covering up a murder."

"Jim's a good sport. He won't forget I saved his life from the croc when we were kids. I won't tell him more than he needs to know." He leaned back. In the moonlight broken by the dancing shadows of the tree branches whipping in the wind, his hands travelled around the periphery of her face – treasuring familiar places. "Will you be alright looking after Kirsty on your own until I get back? It's a blessing Tim and Bronwyn are away at University."

For the first time since the drama started, Rhylla realized she had not given a thought to her two elder children. "Yes, of course, I'll be fine. Just you take care." She pressed another firm kiss on his cheek. "Now go, my dear."

Rhylla stepped back, sheltered from the wind by the trunk of the tree near the coach-shed. She wanted to start bawling and never stop but the thought of her daughter upstairs needing comfort set her feet in motion. As she went to pull the backdoor of the house closed, she glanced firstly to one of the two flats above the coach-shed where the gardener resided but it was his weekend off. He would not be home until tomorrow. Rhylla's glance panned that part of their property she could see, given the cloudy night. Not for the first time she appreciated their large property with its bushy perimeters. Never had she appreciated the privacy of her house setting so much. After she closed the door behind her, she leant back with a deep sigh. Relief quietened her beating heart knowing privacy dwelt inside the house also. Mrs. Barnes, the housekeeper, was away in Bowen until next week.

With the bloodied towels and cleaning rags soaking in a bleach solution in the laundry tubs, Rhylla climbed the steps once again. This time she carried a bowl of water from which a pleasant aroma of lavender drifted.

Sweet perfumed water teased Kirsty's mind to the surface of consciousness. Lead sinkers weighed down her eyelids and her tongue lay thick and swollen in a dry mouth. Soft hands along with soft words from her mother's lips comforted her as the warm sponge freshened an unclean body.

Movement when the soiled bed linen was replaced with fresh sheets, stirred Kirsty.

"Mum, I must have had a terrible nightmare. Did I wake you?"

"No, my dearest. Do you want to talk about it now or in the morning?"

"I feel so tired." She lifted herself onto her elbow and leant over the edge of the bed. "I think I'm going to be sick."

Rhylla reached down by the bedside and held up the waste receptacle.

Kirsty dry-retched several times but expelled nothing of her stomach contents.

"Can I bring you a cup of tea and a Bex powder?"

"No thanks, Mum, I just want to close my eyes."

Rhylla sat on the stool by the bed holding Kirsty's hand while her daughter drifted back to sleep. The fingers of Rhylla's other hand stroked Kirsty's strawberry-blond locks so like her own, but without the odd grey hair hiding within. Her mind wandered fitfully drawing up random thoughts of her family rather than addressing the main issue of the night's events.

Her eldest, Tim had it all with the dark, wavy hair and chiselled features of his father. The boy's pleasant nature, easy intelligence and sports prowess made him a favourite with teachers.

A frown marred Rhylla's features as her thoughts drifted to Bronwyn – the first daughter. A strong-willed child with whom Rhylla found it hard not to clash. Bronwyn could not be called a plain child. She had been saved from plainness by thick, wavy, dark hair like her father's and high cheekbones like her mother's. Her fathomless eyes looked out from a highly intelligent brain marred by a fierce streak of ambition. Was she ever likely to find a husband? It would need a strong man to take on a woman as strong-willed as Bronwyn. Rhylla struggled not to have favourites but Bronwyn could be hard to like at times.

She watched her baby, Kirsty. Not such a baby at fifteen years of age. This daughter was as angelic in her nature as she was in looks. Not the academic like her siblings – more the artist. Tears rained down Rhylla's cheeks. Kirsty did not deserve this. Will she ever find a man willing to accept damaged goods? And what if she were to become pregnant after this? What would be the future for her sweet daughter and the baby?

Once Kirsty's breathing indicated her daughter was asleep, Rhylla stood up and moved over to part the drapes a little. She settled into the deep armchair in the corner of the room and listened to the whistling winds as they sent the clouds streaming across a slim crescent moon.

"Please, God, keep my husband safe and help us all through this."

After a short stop-off at the house of his friend, Jim Sullivan, to ensure he'd have a lift back to town in the morning, Robbie fought the steering wheel of his brother's rattling, farting utility truck for what seemed like a lifetime until he thought he must be near the turn-off to the old quarry. Between the one dull headlight and a reluctant windscreen wiper attempting to clear the water of the occasional light rain sprinkle, everything appeared as an alien landscape. He slowed down. Even so, he almost missed the exit which had been overgrown with bushes. They were new since he last drove past this way. With his head stretched forward in the hope of seeing the sky, he fervently prayed the threatening storm might hold off until he had completed his chore. It would never do to be found with a bogged vehicle containing a dead body. He guided the utility towards where he believed the quarry cliff-face should be. It was a slow journey as he dodged around the re-growth of stunted trees. When the vehicle stopped at the lip of the cliff drop-off, he dragged on the brake and opened the door.

Having played cricket and tennis since a youngster his body was in reasonably good physical condition despite his age, but Robbie still found hauling a dead weight from the back of the truck to the front seat extremely exhausting. He rescued the sheet of canvas – not being sure if it had been tattooed with his name or not. With the body sagging across the steering wheel, Robbie put the gear stick into neutral and released the brake. Regret, or was it remorse, held his hand for a short moment before he shut the door firmly and walked to the back of the vehicle tray.

He leant his weight against the tailgate and pushed hard. The utility did not budge. Not a wheel moved. Robbie stretched upwards and took a deep breath before trying again. He grunted as he felt every muscle in his limbs and back protest. There was some forward movement of the vehicle but very little. He leant in harder and groaned louder. His boots scratched into the dirt seeking purchase. Had spending so many hours as an accountant and part-time author sapped his strength? As a young man, he had manually relieved bog holes of many horses, drays, or suchlike on his parent's property without all this effort. He ground his teeth, growled and threw everything he could at the task. Slowly the wheels inched forward until the vehicle toppled almost taking the unprepared Robbie with it.

Robbie stood bent with hands on his knees straining to catch his breath. He listened to the crashing and snapping of undergrowth as the falling truck careered down the cliff-face. His heart quailed at the noise. What if the damn thing caught up on a tree before it reached the lake's water? Then he heard it – the splash followed by a gurgle of the waters below where he stood.

Tears of relief filled his eyes to mix with the sweat as it ran down his body from head to toe. His heart rolled over in his chest. Nausea hit his gut once again. It struck him that he had no idea if the vehicle had indeed been his brother's and if so, had he driven it all the way up from Sydney. Perhaps he should have taken time to check to see if there was any paperwork in the car. Knowing Greg's loose morals, it could quite easily have been stolen. Once Robbie accepted it was too late now to worry about those things, his breathing returned to normal. He rolled up the canvas sheet and broke a leafy branch off the nearest stunted bush. In the intermittent light of a moon shy behind the clouds, he began to erase all evidence of his and the vehicle's tracks as best he could.

He had not been at this chore for more than ten minutes when the skies opened and a deluge of rain flooded the area. Despite throwing the folded canvas about his shoulders, runnels of water streamed down his hair and into his collar where they saturated his shirt and cooled his body. The temperature plummeted. But Robbie knew it was not only the sudden cold that set his teeth chattering and body shivering but the result of after-shock on the filthiest of filthy nights.

He forced one foot in front of the other. Rolling thunder beat the drum. With only the occasional streaks of lightning to guide him, Robbie backtracked to the graded road which he then followed to the fishing hole further on. The graded road might add five miles to his journey but would be much easier to navigate in the poor light. If he stuck to the bush, he might end up walking around in circles.

To distract himself from the discomfort of his quivering body and stumbling feet, he allowed his thoughts to drift back home. He worried how Rhylla and Kirsty might be coping. He tried to think of what he could do to lighten the burden for them both. At times his mind wandered to his friend Jim Sullivan. Had he asked too much of the man to risk his reputation to help a murderer – even if a vindicated one? This thought set him worrying if Jim's car would make it over the road after the cloudburst. Jim was not known to be a practical person. Jim Sullivan, Doug Hampson and himself had been brought up on neighbouring dairy farms on the Atherton Tablelands in the north. They had attended primary school together before going on to boarding school. As youngsters, they had spent many hours riding their horses around the neighbourhood searching for more excitement than the monotonous work of helping their fathers milk cows. He and Doug Hampson managed to get the trio into numerous fixes but they also managed to extricate themselves by resolving most of the problems encountered. Jim was always happy to follow their lead. Would Jim think to put the chains on the tyres to help him through the slippery mud?

The rain had ceased and the clouds were fast disappearing when he arrived at the meeting place near the creek. Only a faint glow of the morning could be seen on the distant horizon. Robbie spread the canvas out to form a makeshift tent when he noticed the blood. He washed the light canvas as fast as he could all the while keeping a lookout for any sign of a crocodile in the area. Before leaving the water's edge he quickly washed his own body. Hanging the canvas over a branch well back from the water, he settled in underneath with his back against the tree trunk. He dozed on and off but the trouble he found himself in now did not allow a restful sleep. His mind boiled with clashing thoughts.

After a cup of tea, Rhylla dragged her feet up the stairs in the glow of early morning to check on Kirsty but the girl remained asleep. She watched her daughter's chest rise and fall regularly. Aimlessly she returned downstairs and wandered into her office. This room always brought her peace with its dark timbered walls. Her father's large desk took up centre place in the room. A bookcase ran the full length of one wall. It held many of her father's tomes alongside the novels Robbie had written. The opposite wall held several cabinets in which she stored many of the files from her work. The third wall held several large photos. One showed her grandfather and family taken in front of the first office he opened in Australia, at Brisbane. "McNeven Property and Investment Family Company" was inlaid on the front of the building above the doorway. Another photo on prominent display was of the office her grandfather had opened for the company here in Townsville in 1890. Her favourite picture was one taken in 1892 of her parents, older brother Maxwell (who was later killed in Europe during the Great War), herself aged 5years, her three-year-old brother, Sean (who drowned before his twenty-first birthday) and their baby brother who died with scarlet fever when he was three years old. Rhylla sat at her desk and stared out through the lace curtains as they danced on a light morning breeze in front of the glass windows in the fourth wall. How did her parents cope with losing all their children but one – herself? Amongst her own feelings of the loss of her siblings, she would never forget the pleasure she had felt when taken under her father's wing and trained in the running of the family company here at the Townsville office.

She drew some papers towards her and attempted to settle to work but her mind was not on the task. She pushed them aside and began to doodle with a pencil on the wide blotter. Weariness burnt in her eyes. An aching neck, unable to hold her head up any longer, carried her head forward to rest upon the pencil marks. She dozed.

The heat of the sun streaming through the window stirred her to wakefulness. Visions of the previous night's events flooded her mind. A night never to be forgotten for all the wrong reasons – the 28th of April 1933. Rhylla lifted her head to look at the clock on the photo wall. A quarter to eleven – still an hour to midday. Was that really the time? It seemed so much later. How the time dragged. Maybe she forgot to wind the timepiece on Monday. Her chair scraped on the floor as she stood to open the glass door of the clock, insert the key and give it a twist. But it had already been wound. Rhylla sat and doodled some more, but after a few moments, she scraped back her chair again and made her way to the staircase.

Her heart lifted to see Kirsty sitting up on the side of the bed.

"Hello, darling, are you feeling any better?"

"I feel more awake, Mum, but I don't know what happened to me last night. Did I have a nightmare or what? It was the strangest thing."

Rhylla sat and held her girl close. "What do you remember of last night?"

"That's the strange part. I don't remember anything."

"Do you remember your dad leaving to collect me from the station?"

"No, I don't think I can. I remember our dinner. We had bread and sugar."

Rhylla smiled. "Your father knows you shouldn't be eating too much sugar. It will bring out the pimples on your face."

Kirsty gave a short giggle. The sound lifted Rhylla's spirits.

"When Mrs. Barnes isn't here, Daddy always feeds us bread and butter and sugar on the last meal before you return from your meetings in Brisbane." She giggled again. "He always tells us not to tell you but we always do."

Rhylla hugged her tighter.

"What else do you remember from last night, dear?"

Kirsty's forehead wrinkled and her blue-grey eyes, replicas of her mother's, narrowed as she searched her memory. "The next thing I vaguely remember is you sponging me with lavender water sometime in the middle of the night." They sat in silence as each attempted to organize their thoughts.

Kirsty asked again, "Did I have a nightmare?"

"It seems so, my child." And Rhylla said no more. She struggled with the arguments on whether to tell Kirsty everything and upset the young girl unnecessarily or wait until time dictated the need to tell – should the worst happen and she was left pregnant. "How do you feel in yourself?"

"Only tired. I feel a bit sore below, you know, my private parts – where I hurt myself when I had the accident on my pushbike yesterday, or was that the day before?" She rubbed her pubic bone and stood up. "I think I'll come downstairs and have a shower now."

Rhylla stood up also. "A good idea, my love. Now I'm off to make a pie for lunch. Will you manage your shower by yourself or would you like a hand?"

"No, Mum, I'll call you if I feel wobbly."

Rhylla turned and made her way to the kitchen downstairs berating her cowardice at every step. Trembling hands began the mindless task of preparing a meat pie for their lunch when Robbie returned – if he returned by lunchtime.

After placing her pie in the oven, Rhylla shut the stove door with a soft clunk. Her head lifted at the sound of a loud knocking on the front door. She adjusted the vent on the firebox. Her mind ran amok. *Why would Robbie be coming through the front doorway?* Her feet almost ran along the carpet runner in the hallway. She swung the heavy timber door inwards ready to throw herself into his arms but held herself short when she found Doug Hampson standing on the top step twisting his hat in his hands.

"D-D-D-Doug," she stuttered. "Sorry, you're in uniform – Senior Sergeant Hampson." But at that point, her throat clamped shut. She could not get out another word.

"G'day, Rhylla. Sorry to barge in like this. Is Robbie here?" He drew himself up to his full six feet six inches height and used a hand to smooth his oiled brown hair.

Rhylla stood with her mouth agape and her mind racing.

CHAPTER THREE

Robbie threw the dry canvas onto the back seat of Jim's car.

"Thanks, mate." He nodded at Jim sitting behind the steering wheel of his Chevrolet with the motor running. "Glad to see you remembered the chains. Did you have any trouble getting here?"

"No problem, Robbie. Now, are you going to tell me what all the mystery's about?"

Robbie jumped into the front seat and pulled the door shut with a slam. He sat tapping his fingers on the ledge of the door. Jim glanced over to see Robbie clench and unclench his jaw.

Jim raised his eyebrows. "You okay, mate?" He asked as he released the clutch and made a five-point turn avoiding the muddier patches in the road.

Robbie nodded and eventually began to speak.

"If I did something illegal and I told you, my solicitor, about it, do you have to tell the coppers?"

The car nearly went into a culvert when Jim's head swung towards his friend. "What the hell are you saying?"

"Look out!" Robbie yelled.

Jim dragged the car back on track and looked again, more slowly this time, at Robbie twisting uncomfortably in the passenger seat. "What sort of crime are we talking about here? I don't know anyone as honest as you, Robbie." He grinned. "Well, maybe a few misdemeanours as a kid."

"I'm talking murder, Jim."

The car veered to the side of the road again. Jim straightened the wheel before replying.

"You! You're hard-pressed to kill a beast for food." Jim glanced to the passenger's side and gave a half-grin. "You're having me on, aren't you?"

"Geez, Jim, if only I were."

Silence laden with disbelief, tension and horror filled the cabin.

"As your solicitor, I would be obliged to advise you to confess to the police. I would accompany you of course. You would not say a word to them without me present." He looked again at Robbie. "Not even to Doug Hampson – especially Doug, probably. It would put him between a rock and a hard place if you did, him being a copper and all."

"Is there a 'but' coming?"

"On the other hand, speaking as your friend, a very close-lipped friend, I think you'd better tell me what's going on."

Robbie's struggle to speak repeated itself but once the words began to flow, they poured out like water from a broken faucet. He did not stop until the whole story was told. He sat staring out through the windscreen – drained.

Once more silence fell inside the cab but this time it was laden with compassion.

After Jim mentally digested everything, his questions began.

"This is that older brother of yours we're talking about – this Greg?"

"Yes, the very same."

"The one that looked the spitting image of you when we were younger. The one who your dad threw out of the house on more than one occasion."

"That's him."

"I'll be damned. I thought he'd disappeared to the other side of the world."

"He had but he came back."

"What was he doing coming to your place?"

"How should I know. I didn't stop to chat with him. The last time I saw him we weren't even on speaking terms."

"What does your daughter say about everything?"

"She was still passed out when I left the house."

"When you say passed out, do you mean she was drugged?"

"We think so."

"We … Is Rhylla home?"

"That's where I was when he came to the house – collecting Rhylla from the train. I presume he talked his way into the house. Kirsty would not have known the circumstances between Greg and me. She would have seen it was indeed my brother; we are so alike."

Robbie watched through the window when the signs of civilization made an appearance. His guts somersaulted. Nausea threatened. When was he going to wake up and find it had all been a bad dream?

Back at the MacBurnie house, Doug watched the flow of changing expressions on Rhylla's face and wondered what he had interrupted. *Had the perfect married couple had their first argument?* The short-lived jealous streak prodded again. *No wonder it was so long in coming with the McNeven money to smooth troubled waters. A full-time housekeeper and live-in gardener must have made life a lot easier on them.*

"Doug," Rhylla searched again for words. "Robbie is not in at the moment. Can I help?"

"That's too bad. I wanted to warn Robbie his brother, Greg, might be heading this way. We had a report from the Brisbane boys late yesterday. They're pretty keen to get Greg in their interview rooms. Apparently, he's been mixing with some bad company in Sydney."

"Oh," Was all Rhylla could manage. She coughed and then couldn't stop coughing until it seemed like she was going to choke.

"You alright, Rhylla?"

A head nod was the best answer she could do.

"Okay, well tell Rob I called and ask him to come to see me when he can. I'll bring him up to date. I won't be at the tennis tomorrow, the missus has me mowing the lawn."

"Thanks, Doug, I will." Rhylla forced a strained smile.

As Doug made his way along the front path, Jim Sullivan's new car pulled into the driveway. Doug deviated in that direction.

Robbie paled. "Geez, Jim, he's in uniform. What's he doing here in uniform. Has he found out already? How could he?"

Jim was first out of the car. He stood up and grinned over the bonnet. "Hey, Doug, how's things going? Are you looking for Robbie? I found him out running. The team should never have told him he was getting a poddy gut. Now he's running miles a day to lose the lard. He'll end up killing himself." He grimaced at his own choice of words.

While Jim was talking, Robbie climbed out of the car and shut the door quietly.

He nodded towards Doug Hampson and walked across the lawn to shake his hand. "How's things?"

Doug had not failed to notice the haggard face nor the pale brow on which sweat beads gleamed in the sun. *They must have had a real ding-dong argument.*

"Good, Robbie. You?"

The men stood talking over the car engine bonnet. Rhylla slipped quietly back inside the house.

The meat pie sat in the middle of the table. Three small helpings had been taken and each sat on their plates, hardly touched.

"Kirsty, you usually love meat pie. Darling, try to eat a little more."

The young woman looked across at her father with a wry grin on her face. "The same might be said about you, Dad." She lifted her fork and rearranged the food on her plate. "Is it true, what Uncle Jim said outside earlier? Have you taken up running because your mates say you're getting tubby?"

Robbie's smile was hard come by. "Enough cheek, young lady. I'll be the next Clarke Gable, you'll see."

Rhylla reached across and held his hand. "You've always been my Clarke Gable and more, dear." The smile reached her eyes. She turned to Kirsty. "What are your plans for this afternoon, darling?"

"I think I'll sit on the back verandah and try sketching the mulberry tree again. I'm not happy with my last effort. Can I help you wash these dishes first?"

"No, off you go. Your Dad and I will manage."

Rhylla stood and placed the left-over pie in the refrigerator for the evening meal. The kerosene motor rumbled its complaint at the extra workload. She pulled the kettle over to the heat of the stove and turned to Robbie.

"Can I make you a fresh cuppa, dear?" Rhylla opened the firebox door and pushed in another log. She opened the flue a tad.

"Hmmm. Yes, Kitten, please."

Rhylla returned to sit at the table while waiting for the kettle to boil. With their daughter out of earshot, she returned to speak of the events earlier in the day.

"I guess Doug told you he had word from the Brisbane police who said your brother was mixing with bad company in Sydney."

"Yes, he did. Doug also mentioned some gang from Sydney was after him too. Greg had a way of mixing with disreputable people." Robbie sat in deep thought for some time. The rattling lid on the steaming kettle brought his head up. Rhylla rose and made a fresh pot of tea for them both.

"It set my mind thinking. If I could dress as Greg and be seen climbing on the train for Mount Isa, people – witnesses – if asked, would say they had seen Greg MacBurnie board the train for the Isa. We are so alike physically it would be easy to pass myself off as him. And people who know me would be thinking of the clean-shaven accountant-come-author, not a vagabond."

"Why on earth would you want to pass yourself off as him?"

"Think about it, Rhylla. The police will not look locally for Greg if they have witnesses putting him on the train to Mount Isa."

Rhylla sat thoughtfully sipping her tea before speaking. "Won't it look suspicious if you've disappeared?"

Robbie's finger traced the rim of his teacup back and forth before he looked up. "I really need to leave this area until things blow over. Who knows how long before the body is found? It might be days or weeks or months – hopefully never." Robbie added two spoons of sugar to the cup of tea Rhylla poured for him. "You can tell folks I'm away up at Cape York or Tasmania or somewhere with poor communication channels."

Rhylla sipped at her cup of beverage. "Why would you want to do that?"

"I'd be out researching my next novel while I have the chance to take time off from the office. Besides, if I were to be captured and charged for Greg's murder, I'd rather it was done away from here and not in front of you and the children and our friends."

"But you wouldn't be in the Cape you'd be in Mount Isa passing yourself off as your brother, Greg? Is that what you're saying?"

"Yes, that's the idea."

"And what about those gangland people from Sydney who are out for Greg's blood? Won't they be happy to find Greg in Mount Isa and put a bullet through your skull or knife through your belly in place of your brother?"

"It will take them several weeks or months even to find me in Mount Isa. I'll get a job in the mines, maybe call myself another name – that's what Greg would do. After a few weeks, I'll disappear into the night. Change my appearance back to me, Robbie MacBurnie, and come home again."

"Sounds very complicated to me – and dangerous. You'll have both the police and the thugs after you."

"Maybe, for a little bit, but the police won't be looking for the body of Greg, here, will they?"

"I don't know, Robbie."

"Can we think about it? The goods train doesn't leave for Mount Isa until tomorrow night. I'll travel on that. They always have one passenger carriage pinned on to it."

"It doesn't sound like pleasant travelling to me."

"No, but then Greg would be unlikely to travel first class, would he?"

"No, I suppose not."

CHAPTER FOUR

Kirsty sat on the front verandah of her grandparent's house situated on the Townsville waterfront looking out towards Magnetic Island. She watched with interest, the folk strolling by; gentlemen accompanied by their ladies all dressed in their best afternoon wear. Most of the women held onto broad-brimmed hats which threatened to take a shortcut across to the island on the brisk breeze. Tree branches swayed in the sunshine. Some ankle-length dresses were still to be seen but most of the females chose the latest calf-length skirts worn with pastel blouses. The majority of the men wore lightweight dark suits and well-brushed felt hats. Their shoes all gleamed having been polished vigorously before leaving their homes.

Down on the sand at the water's edge, children laughed and squealed as they joined in a game of cricket.

In the distance, the ferry could be seen ploughing through the waters on its return trip to the mainland. Coloured hats and umbrellas of the weekend picnickers stood out against the white timber and blue sea. From her seat, Kirsty imagined the rumble of the new motorized engine, which only last year had replaced the old steam engine, and now would be drowned out by the singing of the passengers. It had been some months since her family had taken a trip to the island. She promised herself to ask her parents to do so again in the not-too-distant future.

"It's lovely to see you again, Kirsty. You grow more like your mother every day, I think." Mrs. McNeven selected an iced fairy-cake from the plate of dainty temptations the housekeeper had placed on the afternoon tea tray. "I wonder where your grandfather has disappeared to?"

As she spoke her husband appeared through the hall doorway. "Are my two best ladies talking about me when I'm not here to defend myself?" He removed his hat and tossed it on the hat-stand near the door. Old knees creaked as he bent down and kissed his wife's cheek before walking around to Kirsty's chair and offering his hand. Kirsty jumped up and hugged her grandfather tightly.

"Oh, granddad, you know I could only say nice things about you."

"We have a sweet-talker here, I think, Beryl." He pulled out his chair and sat. "So, what's to eat? These little cakes will barely fill the hole in my tooth. I've been out doing man's work. I need something substantial."

Beryl McNeven rolled her eyes. "Firstly, Andrew, you don't have any teeth left in your head so you have no holes to fill. Secondly, the man's work you talk of has only entailed watching the handyman help unload the wood delivery for the kitchen stove."

Kirsty laughed. Dimples flashed in her cheeks.

Andrew McNeven tried hard to look offended. "Well, I can inform both of you ladies it takes brains for such a task. The size of the logs must be examined to ensure they'll fit into the firebox and the load must be examined to ensure we are getting the correct quantity and value for money. Some types of gum-tree timber will burn away in minutes producing little heat and some of the iron-bark timber produces too much heat and may crack the walls of the fire-box."

Beryl McNeven looked up at her husband with suspicion. "When and where have you learnt that from? You've never had to chop a piece of wood in your life."

"I deny that charge. Chopping wood was my father's favourite punishment for me and my brothers when we were younger – chop enough wood to keep the stove and the fireplaces going. Remember, in Scotland, we had many fireplaces that hardly stopped burning wood."

"I thought you said your ancestral home burnt coal in the fireplaces."

"Well, maybe that was another story, or maybe we used timber before the coal. It's so long ago I can't remember."

Kirsty could not stop laughing. The dimples danced.

Andrew McNeven grinned. "Everyone's a Doubting Thomas."

At that moment, Rhylla arrived driving her recently purchased Model A Ford coupe. She pulled the car up on the street outside the garden fence.

"Ah, here's my little star, Rhylla. She believes everything her father tells her."

Half an hour later, after they had waved their daughter and granddaughter off, Beryl turned to her husband. "I was so worried this morning when Rhylla warned us Kirsty had been peaky lately – and she was right. The girl was not at all her usual self when she arrived. By the time she left, her colour had returned along with her usual happy smile."

"She was probably just feeling miserable because her father's going away on another research trip for his latest book – that's what Rhylla said, isn't it?"

"Yes – tomorrow, I understand. I don't know why he goes off on these trips alone. Rhylla is left with a lot of responsibility." A frown added to the lines of Mrs. McNeven's aging face.

"Nothing that girl can't cope with. Besides, she has plenty of help in the house with Mrs. Barnes and then her gardener doing the outside work. There's only Kirsty at home these days with the other two at university."

"Yes, but Rhylla is away at the company office most days."

"Not so much these days. She does a lot of work from home and besides, she thrives on work."

"Just like her father."

"I'm hoping to convince her to take on my role as Chairman of the Board when young Tim finds his feet in the business. And Rhylla was saying she's sure young Bronwyn will want to have a place in the company too. Rhylla's workload will decrease once that happens."

"Maybe she'll be able to travel with Robbie when he goes off on his research trips."

"Now, dear woman, don't pick on Robbie. He has to do the research if his writing is to shine and if he wants to be able to give up the accountancy work and dedicate his time to full-time writing he'll need to shine."

"Yes, you're right, Andrew. They seem to be so much in love. I just want them to be happy."

The weakening sun hung on the western horizon when Rhylla walked into the house. She paused. Everything seemed so quiet – too quiet. Robbie must have had to go out for something. He had been racing around in such a dither all day in Kirsty's absence, getting himself packed and prepared for his journey tonight. Together they had searched the coach-shed for his old kitbag. He pulled all his things out of his cupboard in the bedrooms looking for his oldest fishing clothes and a cap to wear.

"It would never do for me to wear my best suit if I'm trying to look like my brother," he had forced a laugh before holding her tightly. "My darling, I'm so sorry to have put us into this situation."

Standing in the sitting room, Rhylla recalled the desolation which had swallowed her at the time. Despite her promise not to, her tears had fallen in abundance. "Robbie, none of this is of your making. Only one person is to blame and that is your brother Greg. Please remember that."

Now there was just this heavy silence. Kirsty had disappeared into the music room to finish some theory work for her class the following day. Rhylla ran up the stairs and into their bedroom. Robbie was not there, only untidiness remained. She went to every room on the top floor but there was no sign of her husband. In the bathroom, she found evidence of the cream and powder she had suggested he use to grey his hair and his early beard. Neither Robbie's hair nor his beard was nearly as long as Greg's had been but it was a start. Both the jar and tin were gone so he must have decided to take them with him. She turned towards the sink and searched. His razor and strop were missing. The kitbag was gone. Fear gripped her chest. It was becoming impossible to breathe against the pounding of her heart. Had he gone without saying goodbye?

She went down the stairs slowly. Her feet dragged as she opened each room, every time with her hopes high only to have them crash into the pits of her belly. She stood at the open doorway of the music room where Kirsty's supple fingers now danced along the keys as she practised her scales, but Rhylla did not hear a note.

Her eyes brightened. Maybe he had left a letter under her pillow. They had often left notes for each other under their pillows over the years. She turned and stumbled upstairs again. And there it was – a large envelope with her name scrawled on the outside. Impatient fingers tore at the package. A single page fell out onto the bedspread followed by a smaller envelope with Kirsty's name printed across the front of it.

Her eyes squinted as she read in the dim evening light.

My dearest, my heart, my Kitten,

I am sorry I did not have the courage to say goodbye to you knowing these current circumstances. You will find included here an envelope for Kirsty asking for her forgiveness – I only mentioned I had been offered a lift to Brisbane and took this opportunity to follow up on some research on the Darling Downs.

I will hide in the shadows near the station tonight until I catch the train, as planned, to Mount Isa. With any luck, it will all go without a hitch and I'll be back before you know it.

This will be the worst trip by far that I can imagine and I will miss your company, terribly – more even than I do on my routine research absences. Kirsty will very much need your attention in the next few weeks especially if recent events produce unwanted complications and I regret absolutely that I may not be there to support you in this.

Rhylla – my love, my heart, know I will be with you every day from the time you rise until the time you go to bed and also through each night. My heart melts at the thought of your arms about me. Keep well my darling, keep safe.

Your friend, your admirer, your husband, your lover, and everything in between.

God fill you with strength and courage until I return.

P.S. I will send word of my progress to you through Jim Sullivan. I do not want anyone tracing this new persona back to you or the family, my love.

P.P.S. You'd best burn this, just in case. It would not do to be seen by anyone else, my darling.

Rhylla's Secret

The tears fell as Rhylla curled up on the bed soothed by the gentle melody flowing up the staircase from the music room below.

CHAPTER FIVE

Robbie felt the nudge of the boot but took some moments to orientate himself. The last thing he had meant to do was fall into such a deep sleep.

"Ya can't sleep 'ere, Mister."

His bleary eyes opened to see, in the darkness, a railway porter swinging a dull lantern.

"Gotta ticket for the goods train heading for Mount Isa." Only just in time, Robbie remembered he was supposed to be his brother, Greg MacBurnie. He altered his speech to fit the persona.

"Well, ya best stir ya bones, cobber. It'll be in the station very shortly and it won't be stopping for more than five minutes to collect any passengers."

Robbie stood up, remembering to sag his shoulders as he did so. He hoisted his kitbag over his back.

"Thanks, mate." He slouched off walking beside the railway track in the direction of the station-platform light. Before he had gone halfway, the rumble of the goods train passing at his side hastened his feet. Some flat-bed wagons carried machinery and equipment for the mines of Mount Isa or sheep and cattle stations en route. Stores and supplies were secured in closed wagons. The bin wagons were empty – returning to be filled with mineral ore from Cloncurry and Mount Isa. Several stock rail-crates added to the long line behind the coal-smoking engine upfront. The one passenger wagon was second-to-last in this line with the guard van last of all.

Several people stood mid-platform waiting for the passenger carriage to come to a stop in front of them. A man with his family, a wife and four children, one asleep in the mother's arms, climbed up into the carriage first. After them, two men climbed aboard, one holding a Gladstone bag and one with a rolled swag. Robbie, as Greg, slunk into the carriage seeking a gloomy corner away from everyone. He pushed the window up to allow any cool breeze entry. With his cap dragged down low on his forehead and the kitbag between the wall and his body, he settled in. This railway car held two lines of double seats with a passageway down the middle. Every second row of double seats was turned to face the double seats behind. The man and his family were seated near the front of the carriage and the two men halfway along. The swaying of the carriage and the clickity-clack of the wheels on the railway track lulled Robbie/Greg back into another deep sleep.

The sun on his face and whining children brought him to the surface of consciousness. One man fussed with the contents of his Gladstone bag. The snores of the man sleeping with his head on his swag filled the wagon. Two children aged about seven or eight both dressed in navy shirts and trousers with unbrushed hair and bare feet could have been either girl or boy. Their mother's head drooped to swing with the movement of the train as she dozed while the baby slept on her lap and a toddler slept on the other seat beside the father. Beneath the father's hat which had been pulled over his eyes, snores, every bit as loud as the man on the swag roll, shook his fair moustache. Robbie/Greg pulled himself upright and sat staring out through the open window. He squinted his eyes against the occasional coal smuts of soot flying back from the engine's fires.

A clatter at the rear of the carriage heralded the arrival of the railway guard from the guard van.

"Good morning, folks. We'll be at Charters Towers in ten minutes. There'll be an hour's rest-stop for you. This carriage and my guard van will be dropped off at the station while the engine takes the remainder to unload freight at the goods shed. When that's completed, they'll be back to collect us. If you're lucky the Church Guild ladies will be in the servery selling a plate of porridge, a cup of tea and toast, all for sixpence. Don't leave the station because the train won't wait for you."

Robbie/Greg lingered until everyone else left before he climbed down from the carriage. After eating his breakfast, he was glad to climb inside again when he found the three eldest children running in and out of the seats and trolleys on the platform, squealing all the while.

"Hopefully they'll let a bit of steam off before they're confined inside again. Hope they're not too noisy for you." The father apologized for his offspring. "We'll be getting off at Hughenden so that should be about mid-afternoon."

Robbie/Greg nodded, in passing. Back in his seat, he drew a notebook from his bag and a pencil from his pocket. Briefly, he considered how this would not be a trait of his brother but it was something to relax his tortured mind. The world around him retreated into the background of his conscious thoughts as he began to write. The shunting of their train back into place and the thump and clanging of the connection with the passenger carriage brought his head up briefly. He noticed the Gladstone-bag-man was not on board but a station hand, by the look of his hat, boots and clothing as well as the saddle and bridle hitched over his shoulders had now claimed the seat opposite Robbie/Greg.

"Gudday, name's Jack." His brief introduction.

"Good morning, I'm R … Greg." *Not a good start in this new role,* passed through his head.

But it seemed the newcomer was not too concerned as he tossed the saddle on the floor by his feet before he curled up in the corner and shut his eyes.

Robbie/Greg's occasional glances through the train window presented a country where firstly cattle either enjoyed the grasses, a result of recent rains, or rested in patches of timbered country. As they approached Hughenden, sheep were added to the stock numbers. Each time the train stopped at a siding to top-up the water wagon he joined the men stretching their legs on the ground beside the tracks. The mother had been given permission to use the toilet at the end of the carriage but the men and children relieved themselves outside in the shelter of the wagons.

As the train shuffled its way into the Hughenden station, the commotion of the children preparing to exit the train caught everyone's attention. The door from the guard van rattled and banged when the guard entered.

"Hughenden, folks. Once again, we'll be shunting the main train onto the freight-shed's line to unload while you'll wait at the station. The ladies from the church guild usually have tea and sandwiches for those who're hungry. They will charge fourpence. Again, don't wander too far. The train won't wait for laggers."

Now he thought about it, Robbie/Greg realized he was hungry. He wasted no time lining up for sandwiches and a cup of tea. After drinking another cupful of tea, he wandered out to the front of the station from where he peered along the almost deserted street. A fresh breeze sent dust billowing down the dirt road between the timbered buildings adding another coat of dust to cover any paint that may have once graced the walls. It layered the three cars parked in front of the few shops. Four brown horses hitched to the hotel rail neither noticed nor cared as they stood with their heads bowed.

The shunting train drew him from his meandering thoughts and sent him racing back to the carriage.

"What time'll we get another feed, fella?" Jack asked the guard checking their presence.

"Richmond will be the next main stop. It should be just going on dark when we haul into there. Most of the time they have tea, sandwiches and soup prepared."

"Thanks," Jack replied before he moved off to sit and talk with the fellow further down the carriage. The man, leaning on his swag, rolled a thin cigarette using strands of tobacco from a bent and dirty tin. The smoker's eyelids narrowed at the quick flash of burning sulphur when he struck the wax match on the bottom of the match-tin. This man dragged out a pack of cards from his top pocket and began to deal using the swag roll as a table. Mumbling voices of the pair occasionally broke into bursts of laughter or groans of disappointment.

After their stop at Richmond, the makeup of his fellow passengers did not alter. At Julia Creek, in the middle of the night, the card players said farewell and left Robbie/Greg all alone to travel on to Cloncurry. The guard came in and they talked for a bit but Robbie/Greg did not say a lot given that he had little idea of what his brother may have been up to in the latter years.

Breakfast at Cloncurry provided the option of steak and eggs which Robbie/Greg accepted not knowing what the day ahead may present him with. He enjoyed two cups of tea strong enough to chew. A tall rotund man dressed in a business suit carrying a small case climbed in through the front door of the carriage and slipped into the first row of seats. Two young men with blond hair and unlined tanned faces, wearing denim trousers and flannel shirts each tossed their canvas bag onto the seats across the walkway from Robbie/Greg. Their bodies landed beside the bags. The last passengers to arrive were a pair of short muscled men with unkempt brown hair poking out from under grey felt hats. They may have been twins given the identical corduroy trousers and black shirts topped by soured expressions on their faces. Each carried what appeared to be an almost full rum bottle in hands of thick fingers ending in tatty dirty nails. Robbie/Greg noticed immediately the shortened shillelaghs hanging from their belts. Instinctively he knew they were looking for trouble. *Hopefully, not before the Mount Isa stop*, he thought.

The guard's head poked through the front doorway of the carriage. His eyes took in the last two arrivals. A frown disappeared as quickly as it had arrived when he heard the pair arguing loudly in a thick Irish brogue over their choice of seats. Every point was accompanied by a bit of argy-bargy. He'd seen them all – the different characters who landed in this carriage.

"We should be in Mount Isa in about four hours." He then slammed the door before he backed outside to make his way to the guard van.

Robbie/Greg sat with his notebook in front of him. He listened with interest to the men in denim trousers and flannel shirts as they talked in the seat nearby. They were on their way to get work in the mine at Mount Isa. One offered advice on the process of application, job description and accommodation. At first glance, Robbie/Greg had not thought him old enough to have acquired this experience.

During the journey, the hopeful miners leaned across the passageway and introduced themselves: Steve Whittle, the taller of the two, and Billy Jackson, his cousin, with the bluest eyes

Robbie/Greg had ever seen. This time the pseudo name flowed from Robbie's lips more easily.

"Gudday, I'm Greg. Greg McInroy. I'm hoping to get work at the mines too."

The one offering all the advice, Steve, grinned. "They'll be as pleased as punch to see three of us walk in together. I heard they've been a bit short lately." He then turned his head to the pair in the middle of the carriage where the voices were raised and the bottles were being swigged with a regular rhythm. He rolled his eyes at his mate. The pair grinned. He lowered his voice so only Billy and their new friend, Greg, could hear. "Let's hope they pass out soon."

But the argument went on for an hour before the pair chose to look for additional opponents. Steve and Billy were their first targets. While they were just throwing insults the younger men mostly ignored them but when the aggressors made their way towards them, the closest, Billy, jumped up to take them head-on. With the swing of a meaty paw, Billy was sent flying over the seat to land two rows forward. He lay still. Steve, a wiry lad, was out of his seat before Greg had time to take in what had happened. Steve's clenched fist caught the first assailant between the eyes. The man fell like a fallen tree to land silent in the passageway. Steve walked over the prone figure to take a swing at the second bloke but this man was ready. He caught Steve on the side of the head sending him into the next row of seats. The young man did not stay down for long and while he was scrambling upright, the man known now as Greg was able to send a couple of punches to the side of the Irishman's head sending the hat flying into the air, but doing little to subdue the man. The man batted Greg like a fly off his arm and went for Steve again. Steve was jammed against the frame of the open window with his midriff being pummelled in an attempt to make it fold. The drunk was in the process of stuffing the young man's body through the opening but

Steve clung desperately with one hand while throwing punches into the aggressor's face. Greg strived to pull the man off Steve. He noticed the shillelagh sticking out at right angles from the Irishman's belt. Greg dropped his hand and dragged the short thick stick with its heavy end from the man's trouser belt. The weapon landed with a crack behind the man's right ear. Blood sprayed out in all directions. The man shook his head and stumbled. A yell echoed from outside the window. When the man fell forward, his weight had sent the top half of Steve's body out through the window. Steve's hands and fingers whitened on the window ledge. Nails scratched the timberwork. The wind of the train's passage threatened to peel him off the outside wall of the carriage. Greg had no choice but to bring the shillelagh down once more onto the man's head rendering him unconscious. He ran across the seat to the window shoving the man out of the way. Greg caught hold of Steve's one visible hand and hauled his new friend inside where the young man with a very pale face attempted to catch his breath.

"Geez thanks, Greg. I sure thought I was a gonna that time. How's Billy?"

"I'm fine." A shaky voice spoke as he climbed over the seat in front. "Have we got anything to tie these two rogue bulls with?"

At that moment, the guard entered warily through the back doorway from his van. In his hands, he swung two pairs of handcuffs. "If you can help me drag these two codgers into my van there's a steel ring in the floor to secure troublemakers. Firstly though, we'd better put the bracelets on the pair of them."

When the man, calling himself Greg McInroy, jumped from the carriage to the ground at Mount Isa, the afternoon heat slammed into his body nearly taking his breath away. He looked at Steve and Billy but they did not appear to have even noticed the life-sucking, melting, dry heat.

"Is it always this hot?" Greg asked.

"Not always, it's much worse in the summer when the monsoons threaten," Billy said with a grin.

"You'll really know it's hot when the humidity's added to the recipe," Steve laughed. "You coming with us? We're heading to the Isa Pub for a cool beer before we go see if Mrs. Bonanno has a couple of spare beds at her boarding house."

CHAPTER SIX

Rhylla sat absorbed in the paperwork spread across her desk at home. Assisted by the pencil she twiddled in her hand while pondering the numbers in front of her, strands of hair escaped from the roll at the base of her neck. At first, she did not hear the soft knock on the door but when Mrs. Barnes, the housekeeper, spoke, Rhylla looked up, sighed and dropped her pencil.

"Oh, dear, I'm sorry. Is it morning tea time already?"

The soft wrinkles multiplied when the elderly lady smiled. "Sorry to interrupt, Mrs. MacBurnie, but it has gone well past ten. Do you wish to have your break here or in the kitchen?" It was usual for Rhylla to join Mrs. Barnes in the kitchen at this time of the day. The observant lady often spoke of family issues Rhylla may need to know about or snippets of local gossip she thought might interest her employer. Since the children were all grown up now, it was usually current affairs they spoke of – local or far-reaching.

"No, no, Mrs. Barnes, I need to get away from this desk and clear my head. The kitchen will be fine." Rhylla pushed her chair back and stood up. The hair-roll rocked dangerously when she rolled her head on her shoulders and her hands went to support the muscles in her lower back as she stretched.

"How many times have I told you, you need to have a break more often. It can't be good for you sitting at that desk for hours." Mrs. Barnes tried to frown but her smile was too wide.

"I'll get a change of scenery when I pop into the town office after lunch."

They made their way to the other end of the house and into the kitchen.

"I suppose it's too early to expect a letter from Mr. MacBurnie just yet. Where did you say he was away doing his research this time?" Mrs. Barnes made small talk as she removed the boiling kettle from the stove and rinsed the teapot with the hot water. When satisfied the pot was hot enough, she dropped in the tea-leaves and filled the pot with steaming water.

"Robbie was expecting to be in south Queensland and maybe the fruit district of Victoria. I expect it will be at least a week or two before he gets to drop a line." Rhylla chewed her bottom lip and attempted to keep her face blank of emotion while her memory struggled to recall what she had been told to answer to this question.

Mrs. Barnes opened the cake tin. Taking up a sharp knife, she cut three slices of the Madeira cake and placed them on one of the plates on the table.

"Have you noticed how Kirsty seems to be missing her father more this trip than ever before? She is quite withdrawn. Not the usual sparkle at all."

Rhylla looked up, startled. Had she been so wrapped up in her own worries she had not noticed her daughter's altered mood? She sipped her tea before speaking.

"I forgot to tell you, Mrs. Barnes, Kirsty wasn't very well last weekend. Just a mild fever that passed over in a few hours. Maybe it will be her time of month too, I think." Rhylla took a bite from the cake; not that she felt like eating, but in an endeavour to appear calm.

"I will speak to her tonight if she has not improved today. Thanks for letting me know."

"You're most likely right – nothing to worry about."

"Now tell me, how did you leave your family last weekend? It can't have been easy after losing your father. We've had no time for a chin wag this week, at all."

Mrs. Barnes went into much detail about the family and her father's funeral but Rhylla's mind was not really at the table. When the stories began to wind down, Rhylla offered her and Robbie's condolences once more before she stood and thanked the woman for morning tea. She made her way back to her office.

After a lunch of cold meat and salad, Rhylla tidied herself and left for town. "Goodbye, Mrs. Barnes," she called before she pulled the back door closed. Mrs. Barnes's reply was heard coming from the kitchen when Rhylla made her way along the path to the coach-shed. As was part of his daily routine at one o'clock on a weekday, Mr. Evans, the gardener and handyman was in the process of backing her car out of the shed. As usual, he parked it under the large camphor laurel tree near the driveway ready for her arrival.

"Thank you kindly, Mr. Evans."

"You're most welcome, Mrs. MacBurnie. Have you heard from Mr. MacBurnie yet?"

"Not yet, Mr. Evans. He may be a great author but he's a shocking correspondent." Rhylla's laughter sounded feeble even to her own ears.

"Send him my regards when you do write."

"I will."

Once in town and she was able to close her office door behind her, Rhylla moved swiftly to her desk taking up the pile of mail waiting for her attention. Her fingers trembled as she shuffled through the business letters. Her sigh filled the room when she discovered nothing from her husband either directly or through Jim Sullivan, his solicitor.

The clock on the wall above the door declared it four o'clock when Kirsty slipped into her mother's town office. Rhylla looked up and smiled. Kirsty waved her fingers before sitting herself at the small desk she used most afternoons to commence her allotted homework or to sketch her latest project.

"I'm just going to the boardroom for a quick meeting with the mayor and our local manager. After we have finished you and I can go home, darling."

Kirsty looked up, nodded her head, and smiled.

Rhylla noticed the small smile – not Kirsty's usual wide grin and hushed comment about how the mayor does not know what a quick meeting is. She gathered up her papers and headed out into the hallway.

Late in the evening when the night had fallen and the house settled, Rhylla took time to sit in the cool breeze drifting in through her bedroom window and contemplate her day. She had to admit Mrs. Barnes might be right – Kirsty definitely had withdrawn this week. Maybe her daughter remembered something of last Friday night's assault. Rhylla could not decide whether it might be a good thing or a bad thing. *If that piece of garbage has left her pregnant then maybe Kirsty needs to remember,* she thought, *but then, should the poor girl be told her father killed the man responsible and is now evading the law, trying to protect the family? But if Kirsty isn't pregnant, wouldn't it be better if she doesn't know a thing? Oh, God, it's all too much to think about. Please keep Robbie safe.* She stood and made her way to her bed – her lonely bed where she lay for what seemed like hours before her eyes began to close.

"Mummy, Mum, are you awake?"

Rhylla felt the heavy weight of her eyelids. It seemed to take forever to swim to the surface of wakefulness before she realized it was her daughter kneeling on the floor beside her bed shaking her arm softly.

Her dry tongue attempted to form the words. "Yes, Kirsty, darling. What's wrong?"

"Mum, can I sleep with you? I think I've had another nightmare. I don't feel safe in my room tonight."

"Of course, dear." Rhylla's arms reached over to lift the sheet aside inviting Kirsty to lie beside her. As she did so she felt her breath catch in her throat. Her heart pounded in her chest. This did not sound good. "Can I get you a drink or something, dear?"

"No, thanks. I just need to go to sleep."

Rhylla wanted so much to question her daughter on why she felt her bedroom was unsafe but soft snuffles heralded the arrival of sleep for Kirsty. Rhylla was not so lucky and lay again for what seemed hours pondering her best move.

When Rhylla woke in the morning to the birdsongs in the garden, Kirsty was gone from the bed.

At the entrance to the Isa Hotel, Steve, Billy and the man they knew as Greg stomped the road dust from their boots. From inside a shout of laughter split the babble of voices. The three new arrivals made their way into the bar. When the barman served their first beer, it disappeared down their throats in record time.

Greg looked to his friends. "Same again? My shout this time."

"Thanks," replied Billy and Steve in unison.

The three men threaded their way around the drinkers to stand and peer through the open window. Their drinks rested on the window ledge, their kits on the floor at their feet. Outside, irregular swirls of dust lifted on the erratic breezes to spin down the main street. Two men loaded a dray with bags of produce while the dark horse in the shafts stared in boredom at the dust around its feet. Standing in the doorway of two adjacent shops, the shopkeepers held a desultory conversation.

By the time the remnant froth of their third beer lay at the bottom of their glasses, the men had made their plans to apply for a job at the Mount Isa Mines Office in the morning.

"We'd better head over to Mrs. Bonanno's and check we've got a bed for the night." Steve made the first move. Billy and Greg followed him out.

'Board – Single Men' in white paint filled the sign written on the plank as it rattled each time the gate opened. Hinges squealed in complaint when Steve pushed the gate back against the straggly grass at the side of the dirt path lined with river rocks. Billy followed him through. Greg looked up at the unpainted timber structure of two stories. Someone had made a valiant effort to grow a few dispirited geranium flowers in front of the lower floor along the edge of the awning provided by the open verandah on the top floor. In the distance, the rumbling Mount Isa Mines complex provided an enterprising backdrop to this dismal residence.

"Come on, Greg, don't be shy. Mrs. Bonanno won't eat you."

It was the Chinese man shuffling his way at speed around the corner of the house who pulled the three men up in their tracks.

" 'Ello, 'ello. I, Mr. Ling. You want Mrs. Bonanno, yes?" The short, skinny man in dark trousers and shirt with sandals on his feet and a conical, woven-straw hat on his head bowed. As his body became erect again his face lit up but his eyes squinted. "Mr. Steve is that you?"

"Good to see you again, Ling Too." Steve turned to his friends. "Billy and Greg meet Mr. Ling Too. He and his brother Mr. Ling are handymen and gardeners for Mrs. Bonanno."

A torrent of bastardized Australian-Chinese gushed from Mr. Ling's smiling mouth. Ling and Ling Too were mentioned several times and one bony arm protruded from long sleeves to point repeatedly towards the back fence. When he noticed the vacant look on the faces of the three visitors, he made motions as if taking off his pants and squatted. The two arms now waved frantically towards the back fence. The word dunny now joined the repetitions of Ling and Ling Too.

Like a sunrise escaping a dark cloud, comprehension eventually dawned on Steve's face. He started to laugh. Holding his sides, he turned to Billy and Greg.

"It seems I have ballsed that up. This gentleman is, in fact, Mr. Ling. Mr. Ling Too is currently enjoying the comfort of the dunny out the back." Steve's bare arm beneath rolled-up sleeves pointed aimlessly, "You'll find the small outhouse placed halfway down the back yard beside a sizeable vegetable garden."

"Yes, yes, Mr. Steve right. I, Ling. Welcome. Welcome. Mrs. Bonanno in kitchen."

Ling led the visitors along a narrow, dusty track beside the house to where smoke rose from a chimney sticking out at an angle from a galvanized iron walled kitchen separated from the main house by a wide awning. A rough-hewn timber table accompanied by a long wooden form on each side stood under the awning. In the kitchen, large push-out iron windows had been opened to their full extent. A woman's resonant voice called from inside.

"Ling, who's these men you're taking on a conducted tour?"

Not understanding exactly what his employer had said but getting the essential gist of the question, Ling called back. "Mr. Steve back, Missus. Mr. Steve."

Sophie Bonanno's knowledge of the Chinese language was minimal at best but she understood the name, Mr. Steve – one of her favourite past tenants.

"Well, don't leave him out there melting in the sun. Bring him and his friends in here."

Greg followed Steve and Billy into the kitchen where the heat from the stove along with the heat from the late afternoon sun stirred the sweat into a frenzy over his body. He was surprised to discover the voice belonged to a beautiful woman in her late twenties – thirty, maybe. Beneath a shapeless grey dress, he could not help but notice the hint of a well-proportioned female body.

She turned to Mr. Ling with a smile. "Thanks, Ling. Clothes finished boiling. Ling and Ling Too carry to washtubs, please." The woman stood an inch or two taller than her handyman.

The Chinaman bowed and backed out through the wide-open doorway just as Ling Too appeared at his side. Greg stared at the pair. He spoke to no one in particular. "One's a carbon copy of the other, aren't they?"

Mrs. Bonanno smiled. "There has to be two of them to make a shadow. It's amazing what they can do together, though. If the world had more workers like them, things might get done a darn sight quicker." She held out her hand. "Hello, I'm Sophie Bonanno, the owner of this establishment."

"Er … Greg ... er ... McInroy, Missus."

Greg and Sophie shook hands before she then turned to the other two men. She shook Billy's hand and asked, "And who is this bloke with the baby-face?" Her gentle smile softened the blow.

"I'm Billy Jackson, Missus." A crimson flush rushed to his face and neck as she held his hand longer than necessary.

"Take a seat out at the table. I'll bring you all a pannikin of tea and cake to be going on with until mealtime. I presume you're here looking for a bed, Steve?"

"Yes, please, Mrs. Bonanno. We're hoping to get work at the mines tomorrow."

"You do know they've completed the single-men's quarters over at the mines now. I think the rent is a little cheaper. Not that I want you to go – I need the business. I just want to make sure you're aware."

"They told us that at the pub when we got off the train but it's worth the extra couple of quid here to have our washing included and much better meals," Steve assured their hostess.

"I see you have an outhouse down the back. Does the council provide a collection service then?" Greg did not know why such a gauche question popped out of his head but there it lay on the table in front of him along with the black thick tea and a fruit cake to die for.

Steve's laughter coloured his answer. "Yes, the council do a dunny-round once a week but they have very little to take away from this house."

Billy's curious gaze added itself to Greg's. Billy looked up at the house beside them then turned his eyes towards Mrs. Bonanno. "Surely you've enough guests living here to fill a dunny can and more in a week?"

Her eyes twinkled and a grin split her lips. "I'll let Steve finish this tale."

"Billy, lad, don't you wonder how the only patch of green within a hundred miles is the Lings' vegetable garden. Mrs. Bonanno's meals have no rival in the district. Each meal comes with a full complement of fresh well-fertilized and watered vegetables. Much of the water comes from the endless clothes washing happening every day plus encouragement from an overfull dunny." Billy's expression of horror and dismay set Steve's laughter off again. Once he had it under some control he went on, "The trick is not to think about where the ingredients of the food you eat actually come from. Just savour the flavour. Believe me, after a full day down the mine you'll be too tired and hungry to even worry about the origins of your food."

The snores and snuffles of his friends asleep in the next room penetrated the partition wall as if it was made of nothing thicker than cardboard. Greg let his mind meander through his day. His meeting up with Steve and Billy had been fortuitous. Their accommodation was clean and ample. Mrs. Bonanno and her husband, Vince, who he met at teatime, were pleasant enough hosts. Vince did not speak a lot but he did seem friendly. He provided information for their first day tomorrow.

It was Robbie's thoughts, not Greg's, which drifted back to his family in Townsville. A deep ache filled his chest as he considered the possible worries Rhylla and Kirsty might have to face without him. His lips whispered into the night.

"Goodnight my darling girl, Rhylla. Goodnight my little princess, Kirsty. Please, God, keep you both safe."

CHAPTER SEVEN

The butter maker behind his rib cage churned as soon as Robbie, calling himself Greg, stepped into the cage at the head of the mine shaft. His jaw clenched with the click of the gate latch. The four-hour induction course held this morning mentioned nothing about this overwhelming fear with its ability to suck all the colour from his face and the courage from his soul. It darkened to violet the iris in each of his eyes.

The clunking of the giant wheel and the rattle of the chains above his head did nothing to offer encouragement. Robbie attempted to divert his attention by glancing around at the faces of his fellow passengers. Steve stood nonchalantly in the corner of the cage. Billy wore a grin as wide as his face. Was he covering up a somersaulting gut also? Two other inductees returned his wary looks. Their instructor, with his clipboard tight in his left hand, did not lift his gaze from the floor of the cage.

Two miners dressed in soiled canvas trousers and flannel shirts shared the journey down into the depths of the earth. An involuntary grunt exploded softly from Greg's throat when he noticed the picture of a skull and cross-bones on each side of a small wooden crate they had placed on the timber floor between their feet. DANGER and EXPLOSIVES were lettered beside each drawing. Black dirt ingrained the miners' clothes which appeared not to have seen a boiler for a long time. Their conversation on the subject of a racehorse they were in the process of purchasing never missed a beat from the time they entered the cage until it landed with a thud, a clang and a rattle at the bottom of the mine shaft. It was at that moment Greg remembered – too late – the warning they had been given in the lecture room earlier.

"On some occasions, the descending or ascending shaft cages have been known to trip for some unknown reason. They'll bounce. Men have been known to be hurt when not prepared for this event. Remember to always keep relaxed with your knees slightly bent. Imagine you're standing in a moving boat."

As the memory flashed through his brain, he strived to release the tensed muscles throughout his body. Fortunately, today was not the day for this particular cage to bounce.

Fear clenched Robbie's gut tighter when the darkness closed in around them and a polluted shawl of stale air slipped over their bodies.

A single dull light shone from a pole on the edge of the landing platform. As one, the group of inductees stepped back to let the two miners and their delicate cargo out first before they stepped from the cage into the unknown. A hushed stillness descended upon the group as they watched the miners disappear towards the far end of the drive-tunnel. But this was soon shattered when the cage rattled off up the shaft to the daylight once again. Robbie struggled not to throw himself at it in the hope of escape.

The instructor led his charges to the nearby Crib Room where the lights glowed like a sentinel in a world of blackness. Before they left this area, the novices were instructed to check their battery-operated lamps were attached securely to their belts and to ensure they worked.

"And don't go whinging if you think it all too fiddly. Only twelve months ago the miners were running around with candles."

As sheep will follow the leader, the men plodded behind the instructor into the black abyss. Like trained fireflies, each man's lamp-light danced along the drive in a single line. Rough walls of hacked-out rock hemmed them in on all sides. Their lights reflected dully off the rail tracks used by the shuttle locomotive hauling the ore bins.

Greg listened to his thudding heartbeats in his chest. They echoed in his ears. After they had walked an estimated three hundred yards, the men were called to a halt.

"Now, men, I want you to stand just where you are. Don't move. Turn off your lamps. All together."

Sudden darkness, blacker than any imagined bowels of hell, swallowed everything and everyone. Greg seemed to need all his effort to drag breath into his lungs. With it came the sensation of hot, dry dust. He could not be sure if the thumping in his ears was the echo of his heartbeat or the noise of workers further up the drive-tunnel or maybe on one above or below them. After a few moments, the shock settled to reveal an eeriness – an emptiness – a hushed quietness in their little hot black cocoon.

"Lights back on," the leader called. "As you have seen, the darkness is nothing to be feared." He swung about and began to lead his inductees further along the drive-tunnel.

The noise of voices interspersed with the clanging of crowbars on rocks and the scraping of shovels by a working team indicated they were nearing the drive-face. The closer they approached the louder the work. Without warning, the scream of the drilling rig threatened to burst their eardrums. Even the instructor jumped backward when a shuttle train with its snaking line of bins rumbled along beside them.

After visiting the crushing plant and the smelter earlier today, Greg had thought nothing could make more noise than the jaw crusher, the drag classifier and the Genter Thickener, but now he began to think the heat of the smelter might be more easily suffered than this noise and the suffocation of the underground. His eyes took in the superstructure shoring up the drive-tunnels. Their instructor had proclaimed earlier in the day how this was the best system one could see in any mine in the world, but to Greg's baleful glance it looked little better than a lad's attempt at building a wooden house. Sweat poured down his face and inside his clothing. He had a sudden urge to tear at the unfamiliar long growth of hair and beard on his scalp and face until his nails drew blood.

"Right, you blokes, we'll head back to the office now and you can collect your assignments for tomorrow." The man's voice strained to be heard above the noise.

As much as he wanted to see the sun and breathe fresh air again, Greg struggled to make his feet step into the cage for the return journey to the surface. He hardly took a breath on what seemed an unending journey upwards. Only ingrained good manners prevented him from brushing everyone aside and jumping forwards to be out on the solid ground. Jellied legs felt as if they were not going to hold him upright when eventually he stood on the surface with the sun and its burning heat searing his body. Pretending an indifference, he most certainly did not feel, he stood for some moments looking out past the railway line and the Leichhardt River at the reassuring sight of the township of Mount Isa in the distance. How much longer will he need to keep up this charade as his brother Greg? How long until he will be able to return to Townsville and his wonderful family?

Rhylla's fingers hovered above the handpiece of the office telephone. Had Robbie made it safely to Mount Isa? The thought of Sydney criminals searching for her husband as well as the possibility of the police wanting to ask him questions about a body disposed of in a local quarry, sickened her. She picked up the receiver but quickly replaced it on the cradle. Robbie's words of warning whispered in her ears. "We mustn't use the telephone to communicate, my dear. We don't want everybody knowing our business. I'll write to you through Jim Sullivan."

Pale fingers tapped out a slow dirge. A frown marred her forehead. With a push to her chair, she stood – then paused. Her weight leant forward onto her hands gripping the edge of her desk.

"Are you alright, Mrs. MacBurnie?" Alice, the secretary, spoke from the doorway.

"Yes, yes, Alice, I'm fine. I just remembered I have to go out for a few minutes." Rhylla stood erect and moved over to collect her hat, gloves and purse from the stand.

"Was there something you wanted, Alice?"

"No, Mrs. MacBurnie, nothing that can't wait."

Rhylla followed Alice out into the corridor.

When the cool breeze channelling along the main street of Townsville whipped over her, a calmness soothed her ruffled temperament. Her footsteps settled into a more ladylike pace instead of the striding gait of a man. At the bottom of the three steps leading up into the solicitor's imposing chambers, Rhylla stopped. Was she doing the right thing? Would Jim think she was panicking just now when Robbie needed her to be calm and rational? But her swirling stomach would not allow her to let go. She climbed up to the entrance and into the deep shadows of Jim's outer office.

The Head Secretary stood and moved out from behind her desk on which the sign declared loudly who she might be. In a hushed tone, she spoke. "Good morning, Mrs. MacBurnie. May I help you?"

This tall woman with the ankle-length black dress and dark hair pulled back tightly into a knot had always tended to overawe Rhylla, but today she stood her ground.

"Would Jim Sullivan happen to have a minute for me please, Mrs. Bacon?"

"Oh dear, Mrs. MacBurnie, I'm so sorry but Mr. Sullivan is in court today. May I leave a message for him?"

As hope for an immediate answer to her questions lay slaughtered on the air between them, Rhylla felt her innards collapse upon themselves. The struggle to speak exhausted her.

"No thanks, Mrs. Bacon. It can wait."

Heavy legs carried her out into the street where she stood – her stare vacant. Never had she felt so disinclined to return to her office. She moved out to the pavement edge to view the town clock. It was only three-thirty in the afternoon. Kirsty had said she was going to vigoro practice today and would not be at the office for a lift home until five o'clock. The hour and a half wait seemed an eternity to Rhylla.

On the slower journey back to the company office, Rhylla pondered on their current circumstances. It had been two weeks since Robbie had departed on his hair-brained scheme. No word had been forthcoming from him to date. Kirsty awoke each morning pale and despondent but within an hour she was ready to leave for school smiling and enthusiastic about her plans for the day. Rhylla's suspicion her daughter had been left pregnant by the damned Greg MacBurnie chewed at her insides.

Later that evening, as darkness fell outside the quiet house, Rhylla stood peering through the kitchen windows. Her mind did not register the sound of a car on the cul-de-sac outside the front of the house. Her thoughts filled her head. Kirsty had disappeared upstairs to Robbie's library where she hoped to find information for her latest project.

A small yelp escaped her throat when a voice spoke from the garden path outside.

"Hi, Rhylla, can I come in a moment?"

"Jim Sullivan, you nearly gave me a heart attack. What are you doing out there?"

"I saw the light on. I didn't want to knock on the door and wake up the housekeeper or the gardener. Both are capable of beating me to a pulp with their slippers."

Rhylla chuckled. "You're such a sook. Come around to the back door."

She led her visitor into the kitchen and walked over to move the kettle to the heat of the woodstove. "Can I make you a cup of tea? Or would you prefer something a little stronger?"

He grinned. "Tea's fine. I can't go home with the smell of whiskey on my breath or Mabel won't let me hear the end of it."

As much as she wanted to blurt out her questions, Rhylla did not speak until they both sat with their cups of tea in front of them. She offered Jim the tin of oat biscuits freshly made by Mrs. Barnes earlier in the afternoon.

"I'm starving. I do hope Mabel keeps my dinner hot for me." He smiled. "The secretary, Mrs. Bacon, left a note to say you called this afternoon. Sorry I missed you."

"Oh, Jim, I'm becoming concerned about Robbie. He has been gone for two weeks and we've not heard a word from him. He did say he'd send all correspondence through you. I hoped something may have arrived."

"You must have missed the afternoon mail by minutes." He reached into the inside pocket of his suit coat and dragged out a brown envelope. Rhylla's name was printed in the handwriting she desperately wanted to see again. "This came inside a package for me. I thought you'd be wanting it as soon as possible. Robbie scribbled me a note too. It sounds like he has landed on his two feet – no need to be too concerned."

Rhylla had to summon all of her self-control not to tear the paper open but the good manners installed in her from babyhood prevailed. She received the letter gently. "Thanks, Jim."

"Now, remember, Rhylla, any communication to Robbie must go through me. I'll ensure your envelopes are added to the packages I send to him as his solicitor."

"Yes, of course. I understand."

"How are you and Kirsty managing? Is there anything I can do for you?"

"Thanks, Jim. No, we're well looked after by Mrs. Barnes and Mr. Evans."

"Good. Well, you let me know if there's anything I can do. Just give me a call when you have a reply to send. Be careful what you say over the telephone line."

Rhylla thanked Jim as she walked him to the door.

With flying feet, Rhylla hastened along the hallway to her home office at the other side of the house. Impatient hands shut the door quietly behind her. She had to return to the doorway to flick the recently installed light switch. At the desk, she took up the paper-knife and slit the envelope with a single slice. Two further envelopes landed softly on the desk. The one with "Kirsty" in bold letters on the front, Rhylla set aside. The one with her name received the paperknife treatment also. She recognised immediately the pages torn from his writing notebook. In the dull light, her eyes squinted to read the pencilled writing. What appeared to be dusty smudges of fingerprints were scattered across the wording as if it had been written by a labourer at work.

She smoothed the pages and held them closer to the light.

My very dearest Rhylla,

I'm sure my adventures will one day make a fine novel but at the moment all I can understand is the regret I feel at having left you in Townsville with such a responsibility, the ache I feel in my heart with such a distance separating us, and the hate I will always feel for my brother who has been the cause of everything.

My darling, I will wait anxiously for your communication.

The trip on the train was hot, long, rough, and at times noisy but these issues are minute compared to the worries I have about my loved ones at home. I met two other chaps heading to Mount Isa with the plan to take up work in the Mount Isa Mines. We three have found board with a nice couple originally from Sydney, a couple named Bonanno. This town is a hotchpotch of nationalities. I do wish things were different and I was researching a book here. At first, it appears an unattractive corner of our country but when one looks more closely, it is full of helpful and friendly people. It has the feel of an exciting undercurrent somehow. Not like a city usually has – more subtle. I think it is the continual background hum of the mines perhaps.

After a day of induction, I'm working underground in the mines. Only one thing to be said for this job; I'm glad I'm planning short employment.

There has been no sign or word yet relating to the other issue but I'm keeping my ears and eyes open.

Rhylla my love, my world, my heart is breaking and it is only the hope everything will be normal again in the not-too-distant future that keeps me going. I have to believe this effort will protect you and Kirsty. All my love to you both.

Robbie. (Travelling as Greg McInroy at the moment.)

Rhylla stood to turn off the light. She returned to her seat in the darkness. Her fingers stroked the letter now nestled safely back in the envelope. The sound of Kirsty's call from the kitchen set Rhylla in motion once again.

"Mum, where are you?"

Rhylla rose and flicked on the office light once more. "Here, dear."

"What were you doing sitting here in the darkness?"

"Come in, little one, I have a letter for you here, from your father."

"Oh, all right." The younger woman took the letter without even looking at the front of the envelope. "I'm heading off to bed now, Mum. Good night." She walked over to give her mother's cheek a peck. "I'll see you in the morning."

Rhylla stood still, trying to absorb what she had just witnessed. Kirsty and Robbie had been so close. It was abnormal for the girl not to be jumping for joy at receiving her father's note. Surely Kirsty did not hold resentment against Robbie for going away without saying goodbye. She chewed on her lip at the thought.

CHAPTER EIGHT

After a month of riding the cage to the bottom of the shaft, Robbie MacBurnie, still known to everyone in Mount Isa as Greg McInroy, found his heart did not pound so loudly nor did his guts threaten to spray the cage and other miners on each journey up or down. Even the dark shadows within the drive-shaft did not rate a sudden intake of breath. He did still envy Steve and Billy their casual acceptance of the idiosyncrasies of underground working though – especially the difficulties of working in shadows and flickering lights.

Today he was going to begin work as an offsider to Vince Bonanno – husband of their landlady, Sophie Bonanno. Vince was a driller working on the drive-face. Usually, the man only drilled the short holes used to pack the dynamite – fracture, the miners called it. When it was fired, it broke the drive-face into large boulders. Once the echoes of the explosions and the dust settled, the miners moved in to further smash up this ore before loading it onto the dollies or carriers. The noise of the engine and rumble of the wheels on the railway tracks then bounced off the drive walls when the shuttle locomotives collected the dollies full of ore and hauled them off to the processing plant.

A wry grin broke through Greg's usual tense expression as the cage descended. Vince had asked to have Greg allocated to offside for him on the drill. He had told Greg he believed the older men had more sense and were less likely to do things without thinking. Greg was not sure if this was a compliment or not. Did it mean he was seen as an old fuddy-duddy?

Once Vince began explaining what the drill was to do and how it was set up to do its task, Greg forgot where he was and concentrated on the job before him.

"We're gonna drill the holes along the top of the drive-face, down the sides, down the middle and across the bottom – these bottom ones they called the lifters. The powder-monkeys they blow the holes one after another starting with the top, then the sides, then the middle and then the lifters. This break up the face nice."

The drill itself lay at forty-five degrees to the floor of the drive. It had been attached to a steel leg – thicker than a man's leg – holding the weight of the drill's body. Air hoses and water hoses snaked their way to the drive-face alongside the railway tracks. These provided the power for the drill and the water to clean the drill-bit and lubricate the drilling surface. At the commencement of each shift, Vince and his offsider checked every piece of the machinery and metal connections to ensure nothing had vibrated loose or had weakened the steel.

"The powder-monkeys they fire the drill-face twoa times a day," Vince instructed Greg from his position on the floor as he inspected the footing of the leg brace, "at the end of the shifts."

At first, Greg was sure his eardrums were going to burst but as the day wore on, he managed to put the sound of the drill and the pain in his ears out of his mind. The core contents removed from the inner tubes of the drill were laid out in specially designed core boxes to be inspected by a geologist on each shift. After inspection, they were sent to the surface in the supply cage.

In the ascending cage at the end of his shift, Greg's mind swirled with all he had learnt during the day. He was stepping out of the cage before he realized it had started and finished the trip to the surface without him being aware. His hands itched to write down everything he had seen and done. Another novel was certainly to be found down in the dark pit he had feared so much on his first day.

Perspiration dripped from the tendrils of dark hair bordering her face. Sophie Bonanno picked up the damp cloth from the back of the chair at her side and swabbed her face before returning to fold the dried clothing now piled high on the work table. Her quick fingers checked each item for the colour-coded wool threads tied into buttonholes or added with her darning needle. Her establishment held three double rooms on either side of the downstairs hallway. She looked up at the sound of the sharp knocking on her front door.

"Oh, damn." She considered sweeping the clothing back into her laundry basket but decided not to. The only people who ever knocked on her door, other than hopeful tenants, were either a man of religion determined to save her soul or the mailman with an ongoing complaint about the broken letterbox. Mr. Ling, the handyman-gardener, or Mr. Ling Too, the laundryman, only ever knocked on the back door. She removed her apron and swept her hands down the front of her dress in rhythm with her footsteps as she strode along the rough-hewn timber floorboards leading to the door.

Sophie swept the door open, ready to move unwanted visitors along smartly. A gasp held her rigid in the doorway.

"Hello, Sophie."

His ginger hair had greyed in the past four years and another scar sat proudly upon his left cheek. His swollen belly threatened the endurance of the buttons on his shiny suit from beneath which polished shoes peeped. But she recognized him immediately.

"Uncle Mat, this is a surprise." Sophie swallowed. The presence of Matt Cockburn here could only mean trouble. "What could ever have tempted you from the fleshpots of Sydney?"

"Well, girl, if you ever invite me in out of this hellish hot sun, I'll tell you. I hope you've a cold ale in the house. My throat's as dry as a dingo's fart."

"Of course." Her trembling hands opened the door further. She examined the balding patch on the top of the man's head as she followed him through the house to the kitchen out the back. He entered the room ahead of her. Sophie pointed to the chair at the end of the long table with forms down the length on either side.

"I'll just get you that drink."

On the house verandah outside, in the shade of the camphor laurel tree, she uncovered her supply of ale bottles resting under a wet hessian bag. Back in the kitchen she opened the bottle and took a glass from the bench and delivered it to her guest. To hide her anxiety, she walked to the tap over the washtub and poured a drink of water for herself. With a resigned sigh, she turned and sat at the other end of the table.

"So, Uncle Matt, you've not told me what you're doing way out here. I presume you arrived on today's Qantas flight?" A brief smile came and went along with the vision in her mind of her squat uncle riding all the way from Sydney on horseback. Even if he had travelled in a car, he would have arrived with a never-ending list of grumbles. "I do hope Aunt Molly is well."

"Hell, lass. She's as strong as a bullock, still." He gave a rumbling chuckle. "There's not a man or woman in Sydney game to test her right hook." The glass at his elbow was pushed aside and he drank a long swallow direct from the bottle. "I'm here at her request."

Sophie gave a short cough. "I don't remember Aunt Molly ever making a request, Uncle Matt. What does she want with me? Please don't say she wants me to come back to Sydney. She agreed I should leave that way of life. It was her idea, actually." Sophie chewed at her thumbnail. "Vince and I have made a good life here. I don't want to go back to Sydney."

"Oh, yeah, Vince Bonanno. How is lover boy? What's he doing here? Running a few brothels and gaming parlours then, is he?"

"No, Uncle Matt. I told you, we've made a new life for ourselves here. Vince works hard underground at the mines."

"I have to admit I find it hard to believe. You've made the boy soft, Sophie. I think your aunt sometimes regrets letting him leave with you. It's hard to find an enforcer as good as he was."

"No, Uncle Matt. Vince only did that work because he had no other choice. He's doing fine here and makes good honest money."

"Anyway, your aunt sent this note for you and a few dollars to tide you over." Matt struggled to remove a wadded envelope from the inside pocket of the suit coat he wore. "As you can see, I haven't touched a bob of it. Geez, my life wouldn't be worth a sneeze if I did. She'd slice me open quick smart, from throat to gizzard with that pearl-handled razor of hers."

"Thanks, Uncle Matt." Sophie was in two minds whether to accept the gift, knowing as she did, it had come by graft of one kind or another. She also knew it was Matt who would suffer if she refused to take the money. On the other hand, a few extra quid never went astray out here. Everything costs a lot more here than on the coast.

Matt drank the last drop from his bottle before pushing his chair back. He stood. "Lass, I'll say goodbye. Will you tell Vince to come by my room, Room 4, at the Mount Isa Hotel at nine tonight. I need to see him before I leave tomorrow."

Sophie's mind was not on her work for the rest of the day. She was tempted not to forward the message on to Vince but then this would put him in trouble and alienate her from Uncle Matt and from her benefactor Molly Lynch.

Damn, damn, damn. Why can't Sydney keep out of my new life – especially now?

Work-hardened hands rubbed at her arms as a nervous tremor raced through her body. A sense of nausea filled her stomach.

In the dull hallway light, the scar across his forehead almost disappeared into the folds of his frown, as Vince Bonanno paused with his hand lifted to knock on the door of Room 4. The hand dropped to his side. He rolled his body sideways to lean against the hallway wall. The thought of what Matt Cockburn might be about to tell him or order him to do did not sit well with him. He and Sophie were doing quite nicely here in Mount Isa away from the Sydney underworld. They'd been foolish to think they could ever be completely free of the tentacles of Molly Lynch or whatever she was calling herself these days. His first instinct was to slip in quietly and choke the life out of the woman's messenger-boy but Sophie had warned him caution would be the best approach. No one knew Molly better than she did. The woman had favoured Sophie since picking her up off the streets as a child. Vince knew he'd never really be forgiven by his previous boss for removing her protégée. He believed Molly's love, twisted though it may have been for Sophie, along with Molly's awareness of her fast-collapsing enterprise due to the law changes being administered by the government, contributed to her final approval for Sophie and himself being released from her clutches. Molly's stint in the nick for cocaine possession three years ago had certainly been a shock to them all. Now here Molly was sending the man Sophie had called Uncle Matt, with a message for her previous enforcer – an occupation Vince had been pleased to escape. He acknowledged Molly had only released him willingly because Sophie had begged her to allow them to bring up their children in a different environment from that which they had both known. After an early miscarriage, it seemed he and Sophie were never to have any children – this broke his Sophie's heart. Seeing the one person he loved saddened, had broken Vince's heart too. Now, with another infant on the way after so long, they did not want to tempt fate. Were Molly and Uncle Matt between them, going to destroy their hopes? Vince drew himself upright, his jaw clenched. Not if he could help it.

The calloused knuckles rapped at the door.

"Come in." Fed back through the timber.

Vince turned the knob and pushed the door inwards moving through the gap as he did so.

Uncle Matt sat at the small window drinking from a glass of whiskey. He set it back into the wet ring on the window sill before standing to shake the hand of his visitor.

"So, Matt, still delivering the messages for our Molly, I see." Vince's sneer was barely contained.

"Don't be like that, boy. You know you're only here and not in Sydney slicing up bodies on her orders thanks to the grace of our Molly."

"Yeah, I know. What you want then, if you're not givin' the instructions from the boss?"

"Don't be so hard on her, Vince. Molly has mellowed in recent times."

"I find that hard to believe."

"Seriously, she has. Molly mostly uses the press as her choice of weapon these days. She's happy for the papers to write articles about her philanthropy activities towards the unemployed – when the mood takes her."

"What brought on the change then?"

"Who knows. Maybe it's something she learnt while in the clink recently or as I said maybe she has just mellowed."

Disbelief was written in capital letters across the expression of Vince's face. "So, what's the message you bring today?"

"There's a bloke, Greg MacBurnie, who she wants sent to his maker. He came in on the train from Townsville a couple of weeks ago as far as we can gather. Most likely planning to hide in the mining community."

Cynicism hardened Vince's expression further. He fell into a broken ethnic accent to add emphasis to his thoughts.

"Ah, si, si: so mucha for the mellow eh. What's Molly doing putting a hit out on this poor sod?"

A mocking chuckle filled the room. "He's the one she fell for – hard – but he slipped out of her clutches. Molly said there were reports the bloke was heading north and then news came back through her usual convoluted channels. He'd caught a train from Townsville to Mount Isa. Molly wants you to find the bloke and pay her respects – final respects – if you get my drift."

"Yeah, I know what you mean. Mellowed you say, eh."

"Molly says mines are notorious places for fatal accidents."

"She donna give up, never, eh?"

"No, boy, she don't, and don't you forget it." He swigged from his glass again still not offering Vince a drink. "Remember, you're only on remand while ever you keep young Sophie happy. If that stops happening, Vince, you too will be dead meat."

With his shoes in one hand, Vince opened the door without making a sound but Sophie had been anticipating his return.

"She wants you to snuff some poor beggar out then, doesn't she?"

"You should be asleep, Sophie. You've a big day tomorrow."

"Well, does she or not?" Not waiting for a reply, Sophie answered the question herself. "She does, I just know it. Can't she keep out of our lives? Who is it she wants dead way out here miles from Sydney?"

His clothes landed where he tossed them before Vince slipped in under the sheet and held Sophie close. She snuggled into his side.

"It's a bloke called Greg MacBurnie but as far as I know we've had no one by that name employed at the mine lately. He's supposed to have arrived at the Isa a couple of weeks ago." Even as he spoke, the face of Greg McInroy filled Vince's mind. His arrival time fitted and he did arrive by train from Townsville. Vince was not happy about this assignment. Greg McInroy, if it was the same man, was a good worker and quick to learn. Vince had requested the man work as his offsider on the drilling rig. Why, the man even boarded right here in his own home. For some moments his thoughts deafened him to Sophie's next words.

She nudged him. "What has this Greg MacBurnie done to earn her venom?"

Vince gave a short chuckle. "Molly fell in love with him but he flew the coop. She's anything but happy."

Silence lay in bed with Vince and Sophie for some time while their thoughts followed similar paths.

"Vince, did you consider our very own Greg McInroy might be Molly's errant lover? He'd be the right age and he's a good-looking man. He's been here four weeks or more now. He's such a nice man too."

Quiet filled the dark room once more until a barking dog interrupted the background hum of the mines. Vince had thought Sophie was asleep but she had only been thinking.

"You'll have to do it, Vince. You know that, don't you? Molly won't give up on something she's set her mind to."

"Yes, Sophie, I know that. Now can we get a bit of sleep? It'll be time to wake up before I even get to shut my eyes."

As usual, the nights of Townsville in early June featured less oppressive heat and humidity. Rhylla looked forward to a peaceful sleep without tossing backward and forward in an attempt to relieve the discomfort of a hot night.

"Mum, can I talk to you?"

"Yes, of course, Kirsty. What's on your mind?" Rhylla sat on the edge of her daughter's bed. She refused to think of how her eyelids ached to fall shut and her head throbbed after a long day working through office papers.

"Can someone get pregnant if they don't have … you know … with a boy?"

Rhylla's headache and tired eyes were forgotten immediately. The question landed like the kick of a horse in her stomach.

"Why do you ask that question, darling?"

"My periods should have come last week but they didn't and they still haven't. Can I be pregnant even though I've never done that with a boy?"

Rhylla held her daughter tightly. Her mind swirled like one of Mrs. Barnes's cake mixtures under her wooden spoon and powerful arm. Nausea overwhelmed her. She swallowed several times but her mouth was empty of saliva. She wanted to cry but her eyes were dry. Her brain told her it was time to tell all to Kirsty but her tongue refused to obey.

"Honey, I think a cup of cocoa is called for if we're to discuss a serious matter such as this. You stay here while I make some and bring it up." Rhylla was going to ask if Kirsty wanted a biscuit with her drink but changed her mind. Once she was told the events of that night, the girl would be as nauseous as she was herself just at the thought of the telling.

While Rhylla waited for the kettle to boil, she tried to recall some of the many scenarios she had considered in the past weeks to cope with this very situation. Her mind drew a blank and here she was hiding out in the kitchen while upstairs, God alone knew what thoughts tormented young Kirsty.

After climbing the stairs with the tray, she stopped at Kirsty's doorway.

"Come into my room, dear. We'll be more comfortable."

With Kirsty sitting cross-legged at the foot of the bed sipping her cocoa, and herself propped up against the pillows, Rhylla started at the beginning.

"Do you remember the night when I last returned from the Brisbane meetings on the train? Your father drove into town to collect me at the station."

"Of course, I do. That was the strangest night I've ever had. I must have had a dreadful nightmare because I was exhausted for two days after. I still can't remember anything much."

"Darling, I can clarify some issues for you. Your father and I had agreed not to tell you this earlier out of our love for you and our wish to protect you."

"My father! What has he got to do with the night in question? It was then he left us to go on his precious book research." While Rhylla paused to sip her cocoa, Kirsty went on in a hushed whisper, "Protect me from what, Mum? What haven't you told me? Why did you need to protect me?"

Rhylla took a deep breath. She reached over to remove the empty cup from Kirsty's hand and place it on the bedside table. Her insides trembled like a leaf in a storm as she took the smooth hand in her own, now showing early signs of arthritic knobbles. She looked deep into her daughter's eyes. Aside from the missing wrinkles, it was like staring at herself in the mirror.

"Kirsty, when your father and I arrived home that night, we found you unconscious and a partially undressed man removing himself from your bed."

"What was he doing? Who was he? Why was I unconscious? How did he get into the house?" Her voice climbed in decibels with each question. Horror poured from every pore in her face. Her hands rose to clamp across her lips.

Rhylla jumped up and moved to the end of the bed to hold her daughter tightly. "Oh, my darling, hush. I am so sorry." She drew her daughter's face towards her and looked deep into her eyes. "When your father went to collect me, he left you finishing your homework at the kitchen table. Your books were still there when we returned. We think the man talked his way into the house. Probably someone who convinced you he was a friend of your father's and wanted to wait, maybe. The man poured a drug into your night cocoa. The cup had been rinsed out and left in the sink. He must have taken you to your room and he raped you."

"Raped me?" Kirsty's face whitened. She drew in a sharp noisy breath. "You mean he put … his thing … it's too horrible? How could he? I would have screamed the place down. I would have fought him tooth and nail."

"Darling, with all the will in the world, the drugs he had given you made it impossible to put up any struggle. In fact, he had given you quite a strong dose because, as you say, it took two days for you to recover."

"Why haven't the police caught him?"

Rhylla took refuge from this question by lifting her cup from the bedside table. She finished the dregs of her drink – not because she was thirsty but because she desperately needed time to think.

"Kirsty, we didn't call in the police. To do so would have meant putting you through a barrage of questions. It's a known fact, women who've been raped find it quicker to recover if they're not put through the courts where they're treated like they're the criminal. The system is run by men. Somehow things are twisted until it's the girl who is found to be at fault. This happens, not only because few men have empathy for the woman, but many women themselves believe it's the woman's fault if she has been raped. One day, hopefully, this will change. Some things in our world are improving but we still have a long way to go. Your father and I were not willing to put you in this position."

"So, where is my father in all this. Has he run away? Does he think this has been my fault?"

"Absolutely not, Kirsty." Rhylla squeezed her daughter's hands tight. "Absolutely not."

"Well, why did he go away – almost the day after it all happened. What's he going to do about this?"

"Your father will make the guilty man pay for what he has done to you. I can promise you that. He will do whatever it takes to protect his family. He loves us more than he does his own life. He is all about protecting his family at this very moment."

"Does he know who raped me?"

Rhylla released her grip on Kirsty's hands and returned to her pillows. She took up the flowered silk concertinaed fan from her dressing table and fanned her face. Rhylla knew it was beyond her to place the murder of the rapist by her husband and Kirsty's father on the young girl's shoulders. Sitting there at the end of the bed she looked so vulnerable and Rhylla was not going to shatter her daughter's hopes and beliefs any more than necessary.

"I think, while your father is out doing what he feels he has to do for us, we need to concentrate on what the immediate issue is right here – your lack of a period." Her mouth felt as dry as an unmoistened flannel. "This may mean you are pregnant but it could be from the stressful situation your body has endured." As those dreaded words flowed from her lips, Rhylla gulped. She swallowed and struggled to continue. "Even though your conscious mind cannot remember the event maybe deep down your unconscious mind does." Rhylla silently gave thanks for having gathered her own courage to talk to the family doctor only last week when she had discussed the situation and asked for information and guidance. She fought to draw another deep breath before going on. "But it is a distinct possibility you may be pregnant and if this were to be the case what do you – you, Kirsty – want to do?" She reached across the bed and touched her daughter's knees. "Your father and I will go along with whatever you wish to do. There is a test available these days to confirm if you are really pregnant. Abortion is illegal but you and I could go away, maybe interstate or, if you wanted, overseas." Rhylla felt her voice fading. Her breath almost deserted her. "Abortions can be had in other countries. If that is not what you want, we could leave here before the baby-belly shows and stay away for many months. When we return, we can pass the child off as mine. We'll bring it up here together. You'll be able to get back on with your life. Or if you chose not to hide this from the world your father and I will support you in that decision also." Rhylla sucked air into her lungs.

Unattended tears now fell down Kirsty's cheeks. Rhylla reached over and wiped them away. "Darling, this is not a decision to make on the spur of the moment. This will take many days or even weeks to think about. What you decide will affect you and maybe your baby for life. Please feel free to talk with me at any time. If you want, we can both go to discuss your questions with Doctor Gleeson. He has known you since you were a baby yourself. You'll find him a great support, I'm sure."

"Oh, Mum, why can't we just turn the clock back and I would go with Dad to the station to collect you from the train and none of this would have happened?"

"If only we could, dear, if only we could. But you and I are strong; we can do this together. Now would you like to snuggle in here beside me to sleep tonight?"

'Yes, please, Mummy."

CHAPTER NINE

Robbie woke early. With the cooler nights, his hands dragged up the sheet from the foot of the bed. He knew Billy and Steve were awake when he heard the soft cadence of their voices in the next room. Since arriving he had been lucky not to have had a roommate at the boarding house.

A shiver ran down his body, but he was not cold. For the sixth time this week, the hairs lifted on the back of his neck. Robbie wanted to laugh it off and blame his Scottish heritage but with the guilt of killing his brother still fresh in his mind, he was not so sure. He recalled his decision made before he had received the letter from Jim Sullivan yesterday. It was time to finish this farce of being Greg MacBurnie and Greg McInroy. If asked he could not have said what had spooked him but he knew it was time for Greg to disappear. His hand reached under the bed to retrieve his notebook. From within its covers, he drew out the letter from Jim Sullivan which confirmed his decision.

Dear Robbie,

I hope this letter finds you well and safe. Before you even ask, yes Rhylla and Kirsty are well – though obviously missing you.

A short note to let you know Doug Hampson dropped by this morning. He tells me the word on the police grapevine is Greg MacBurnie has taken the train west. They are now following up the stops along that line to find out where he got off. No doubt they will discover "he", is in Mount Isa. A quick retreat on your part may be advisable.

Your solicitor and friend

Jim

As he tore the letter into tiny pieces, Robbie contemplated his options. At end of shift today he planned to visit the Mine's office and pull the plug. He took up his pencil, opened the notebook and began to write. After fifteen minutes he tore the pages from the book and folded them into an envelope. His constant companion, Guilt, again stirred in his gut knowing how he had left the love of his life to cope with the awkward circumstances at home. A sigh of relief rose into the sluggish air of his room. The thought of being able to ditch the false names lifted his spirits. Robbie threw his legs off the bed. His bare feet landed with a soft thud on the bare floor; one last shift to work in that black mole hole.

The large hands of Vince Bonanno clenched the steering wheel. Sophie stood beside the car door with her hand resting on his shoulder.

"Sophie this just ain't right. We've known the man for over a month. We know the fellow. He's not a bad 'un. Molly's just pissed off at been thrown over and for that this good man must die."

"I know, Vince, I know, but we've little choice. If we don't, she'll be sending her latest muscles after us. We now have a little someone of our very own to protect, remember."

Vince's hard expression softened. He lifted a hand and held Sophie's wrist. "You're right, lass – you're right. No matter how far we run, Molly'll find us." Once more the veil of anger mixed with a dose of determination filled his expression. He slammed his hand on the horn.

"Come on, you blokes, hurry up. It'll be time to come home before we even leave at this rate," he grumbled.

The utility bounced as the three men threw themselves and their cribs into the back of the vehicle.

"Sorry, Vince, Greg commandeered the dunny and we had to line up." Billy's words could hardly be understood within his laughter.

"I nearly dislocated something having to wait so long." Tears of laughter ran down Steve's face.

"Geez fellows, one day you'll be getting old and things just don't happen so quick then," Greg protested.

Vince poked his head out of his window. Sophie bent her head and dropped a swift kiss onto his cheek.

"Come home safe," she whispered her daily mantra.

For two days the tunnel leading from their drive-shaft to the stope had echoed with the footsteps of mining engineers, management staff and drilling consultants from surrounding exploration companies. Vince Bonanno had attended these meetings, standing silently in the background listening to the discussions.

The stope was blocked. The stope was a perpendicular shaft passing through all the other drive-shafts ending on the lowest of all the drive-shafts. On each level, the dollies filled with the ore were transported by the shuttle locomotive back along the drive-shaft before diverting into the tunnel leading to this single stope-shaft. The contents of each ore-dolly were then tipped out into this shaft to fall hundreds of meters landing into large skips at the basement shaft.

These skips were hauled by another locomotive to the largest supply cage and transported to the surface on its way to the crushers, classifiers and smelting plant.

On the first day when the blockage became apparent, the shift miners working the drive-shaft had been employed in attempting to release the blockage with their picks, sledgehammers and shovels but all to no avail. Now it was time for serious contemplations to resolve the issue.

Eventually, the decision had been made. Vince was informed when he started his shift. A hole was to be drilled at an angle through the floor of this shaft and into the blockage within the stope-shaft. Once that was completed, dynamite would be packed down the hole and fired to release the jammed ore. Vince and his off-sider, the man he knew as Greg, were given the delicate job of drilling this angled hole.

Unnecessary personnel was removed to the surface; only the shift boss and his miners on the shift were left in the drive-shaft. Once the drill and its support leg were set up, Vince began the work with Greg's assistance. Vince's mind was totally absorbed in the delicate task. The thought of his assignment to kill Greg, forgotten. After several hours, the screech tone of the drill changed. Vince slowed the drill. He signalled his offsider – nearly there.

But at that moment, the vibrations of the drill triggered the blockage to stir. Small rubble of ore fell away down the stope from below their level. It gathered momentum. Vince felt it in his machinery and lifted his head sharply. He turned to warn Greg to get out. The warning was never delivered. With a tremendous roar, the blockage gave away completely and barrelled down the stope-shaft. A large rock smashed into their tunnel floor ripping the leg from under the drill. The handle end of the drill swung up sending Vince's jaw up into his brain. Blood sprayed a halo around his head which in turn spun one hundred and eighty degrees, snapping several cervical vertebrae in the process. Vince flopped lifeless onto the floor. A wall of rubble bounced into their tunnel and buried the driller.

At the same time, a large plate of rock broke away from the roof of the tunnel above Greg's head. It began to fall. The top edge of the rock plate jammed itself into the corner of the tunnel roof and tunnel wall. The body of the plate swept downwards and like a mother hen tucking its young into the protection of her body the rock plate collected Greg and slammed him into the wall. The rock swept down until it jammed its base into the floor less than three feet from the wall itself leaving a secure cocoon for the man's body. Blood ran from a large wound in Greg's head. More blood poured out from a wound hidden under his body. After being flung over his head, Greg's right arm tucked his face into his armpit.

The rush of ore and rubble falling down the stope ceased. A thick cloud of dust spewed through the tunnel and settled over everything – choking, suffocating dust. Despite the huge ventilation shafts throughout the mine, the dust hung around those areas where air circulation was poorest. Men rushed into the tunnel from the drive-shaft all wearing handkerchiefs or similar cloths tied across their faces. Steve and Billy were first to the accident site. They slid to a halt in front of the small hill of ore and rubble where the drilling rig had once stood.

"Saints preserve us," Steve whispered.

"Where the hell are Vince and Greg?" Billy's voice was no stronger.

"I'd say they're both under that hill with the drilling rig. No one will be alive under that."

Steve began to climb the hill avoiding the loose rubble, choosing to trust his footing on the larger boulders. "I see a gap near the wall over here."

"Wait there, Steve, I'll come give you a hand."

The two men edged their way to where the large plate of rock formed a gap between the rubble and the wall. Steve felt his foot slipping in the loose soil. He discovered where a narrow track of shallow rubble had formed close to the wall.

Steve aimed his lamp-light into the gap below the rock plate.

"Hey, there's a body lying in here – in the gap. I can see black boots. I think they're black – it's hard to tell. It must be Greg. Vince wears brown boots and Vince ties up his laces to the top of the boot."

As soon as Billy heard this he turned around and yelled to the approaching men. "Has someone called the rescue team? We've a body here."

At that moment, the unconscious man jerked in a feeble cough. Even with his face under his armpit, the dust had penetrated his lungs.

"He's alive," Steve screamed. "Get those first-aid boys down here fast."

In unison, Billy and Steve backed off and began clearing the path towards where the feet stuck out from behind the rock plate. Three other miners joined them in the effort. Soon a relatively smooth path led into the gap where Greg lay.

"Hey, you fellows, don't shift that man until we've checked him over. He may have a broken neck or back – anything." A large man with the white cross displayed on the front of his helmet approached the newly made track.

"Mate, you'll be hard-pressed to check anything but his toes. He's jammed in a very narrow gap."

At that point, Greg coughed again. The top arm moved a fraction. The coughing persisted. Steve redirected his light inside the gap again to see Greg's head lift a few inches before it fell back into the dirt. The body issued a grunt. The legs were seen to move.

"If the man can move his head, arm and legs can we assume he's alright to shift?" Steve called back to the first-aid man. "I can see a pool of blood near his head and another coming from under his left shoulder."

"I'd like to come and check myself."

Steve looked at the size of the bloke. "Mate, you're a few sizes too big to get near the fellow here. I'm small enough, I think, to drag him out into the open. If we muck about too long the whole lot's going to disappear down the bloody stope." Steve moved to the exposed rock plate. "Slide your stretcher along that bit of a track near the wall. I'll see what I can do. Can someone help with the legs?"

"I'm here," Billy spoke up from behind Steve's shoulder.

Steve bent double with his hands and feet on either side of Greg's legs. He stopped when he realized his hard-hat was an impediment.

"Here, Billy, catch this." He took the brim and spun the hat outside the cramped enclosure.

"Fella, you can't go in there without your hard-hat – it ain't safe."

"If this rock plate collapses on us both, a little tin hat ain't going to be worth shit." Steve's voice faded away as he turned his concentration to the job at hand.

Steve then found he needed to bend to his knees. Trying not to let any of his weight rest on Greg's twisted body, he crawled further along the gap until he was over Greg's shoulders. The rock above pressed his head down onto his own chest. It was a struggle but eventually, his right arm slid under the shoulders and chest of the wounded man. Only a dull glow of light suffused the confined space. His own body and clothes now partially covered the lamp attached to his belt.

"Billy, can you take the weight of the legs and drag them your way a bit. I'll try to bring his body after you. Only an inch at a time. It's very awkward here and I can't get a good grip."

"Gotcha, mate."

"Right … ready … pull."

The three men groaned at the movement. Steve felt pain tear through his shoulders and back. His knees felt like they were grinding on broken glass.

"Okay … again … pull."

Another inch gained. Without removing his right arm, Steve moved back a fraction.

"Again … pull."

Two inches at least. Steve renewed his grip. His arm slipped further under Greg's chest.

"Again … pull."

Nearly three inches this time. The man they knew as Greg groaned and struggled to move.

"Steady, Greg, you've been hurt. You're jammed under a rock. We're dragging you out. Can you stay still?" But Greg did not answer. He began coughing again.

When the coughing ceased, Steve checked with Billy. "Everything alright at your end, Billy? You ready to go again?"

"Go, Steve."

"Right … pull."

Billy had the legs halfway out of the enclosure.

Steve called back to him. "That was a good pull, Billy. Can the first-aid man take the legs now and you move nearer to me. I want to see if I can support Greg's head and neck a bit this time." Steve looked at the blood dripping from his hand and forearm when he removed it to alter his grip under Greg's body. In a softer voice, he whispered, "Oh, Christ."

Only two more pulls and they had Greg's body out enough for the first-aid man to perform a cursory examination. The rescuers gasped at the sight of the two deep lacerations bleeding profusely on the right side and the back of Greg's head. The first-aid man applied a thick dressing. Another wad of wool held by gauze bandages staunched the blood flow from the torn flesh on Greg's left shoulder.

"This bloke's gonna need a lot of sewing up. Okay, fellas, we'll lift him onto the stretcher and get him up to the surface as soon as we can." The big man stretched as he stood upright. "They said there's another wounded man here. Where's he?"

Steve looked back at the hill of rocks and rubble. "Under all that lot. I think we'll be getting the undertaker for him."

Steve took the wooden stretcher pole on one side of the head and Billy took the opposing pole at the head. The first-aid man carried the two stretcher poles at the feet of the patient.

They had just turned the intersection into the main drive-shaft when an almighty crash and shudder shook their bodies almost upsetting their balance.

"What's that?" the first-aid man called.

"I'd say, at a guess, poor Vince has disappeared down the stope to the bottom drive-shaft along with half that tunnel."

They met the shift boss and other miners near the crib-room.

"Thought we'd lost the lot of you when we heard that last fall." The shift boss growled.

Not a man of the recovery team noticed the normal rattle and clang of the supply cage carrying them to the surface. They stood in a line on either side of the stretcher resting on the floor. Restless eyes strived not to look at the dusty, bloodied body of Greg McInroy. It was a miracle the man was still alive at all. The men held out little hope for his future. The imagery of the driller disappearing into the bowels of the earth amidst the dirt and rocks which had swallowed him was clear in all their heads.

The moon lit up the white faces of the daisies in the garden where Rhylla and Kirsty sat out the back of the house – looking out across the parkland.

"I love the full moons, don't you, Mum? They bring out the magic in everything."

"Yes, Kirsty, my dear, they are special."

"Oh, Mum, look, a falling star." Her bare arm glowed white in the night's light. "Make a wish."

Rhylla had just finished wishing for her Robbie to be safe when a sudden wave of goosebumps accompanied by a sense of fear ran down the length of her body. She jumped up from the squatter's chair. Her gasp filled the air.

"Mum, whatever's the matter?"

"It's only the night air cooling off. Look you're shivering too. Come, we'll go inside."

But later, as she lay in her room with the moonlight streaming in through the open window, Rhylla felt a warning had been given. Her mind drifted back to her Irish grandmother who was said to have the second sight. Rhylla had always laughed it off as nonsense yet something held her back from such cynicism tonight. She curled up into a ball. Fear gripped her mind soothed by the stroke of her fingers back and forth along the scar on her right leg. She could have been killed that day when she fell while they were rock climbing. It was Robbie's quick action that saved her life. Instead, she was left with only a six-inch wound. Now she felt so helpless not being able to maybe save his life.

"Please, God, keep my man safe."

CHAPTER TEN

Unaware of the gossip humming around the streets of Mount Isa, Sophie sweated at the bench beside the woodstove in her kitchen. The Mr. Lings had spent many hours teaching her to cook in her early days in Mount Isa. Her heart was not really on her task as she chopped the pork and vegetables in the preparation of Vince's favourite dish – a Chinese meal he had favoured during their days in Sydney. Vince was known to sink into a pit of despair after completing Molly Lynch's orders to kill anyone. Sophie hoped to cheer up the father of her unborn child as best she could.

Her dark eyes lifted from her work when Mr. Ling and Mr. Ling Too shuffled at speed into the room coming to a sudden halt at the end of the table. She lifted a hand to push back her damp hair. At the sight of the expressions on faces where expressions of any kind were rare, her early smile disappeared leaving no trace of its existence.

"What's wrong, Mr. Lings?"

"Missy Sophie, we sorry."

"Oh – what disaster have you fallen into this time?"

"In town. They talk." Mr. Ling Too spread his arms wide. "Everywhere all talk. Mine killed man."

Even though she had been prepared for such news, she sucked in a sudden intake of air. Her hands felt cold. She swallowed twice before she was able to speak. "Oh, dear, I'm sorry too. Who died?" She stood, still waiting for them to tell her Mr. McInroy had been killed in a mining accident today. Her conscious brain refused to hear the words they spoke.

"Sorry, Missy Sophie, they talk it Mister Vince killed in mine collapse."

Her body landed with a thump onto the chair behind her. Tears ran unchecked down her cheeks. Sophie stared at the two men staring back at her from eyes as black as night.

"We sorry, Missy Sophie." The pair reiterated for the third time. "What we do to help?"

Even the sound of knocking at the front door did not penetrate Sophie's state of fugue.

"We go, Missy Sophie." In unison, Mr. Ling and Mr. Ling Too moved swiftly out of the kitchen to follow the track around the building to attend to the visitor at the front door.

As they rounded the corner, the sight of a large company vehicle parked in the dust at the front gate slowed their steps. The Chinese men bowed low before the two men standing at the front entrance; one of whom was in the process of lifting his hand to knock again on the timber door.

Mr. Ling and Mr. Ling Too stepped back a pace when they recognized the taller of the two men as the local police sergeant. A Mount Isa Mine's badge on the coat pocket of the shorter man identified him as a man of importance at the mine.

"We help you, Sirs?" Mr. Ling bowed again as he spoke.

"We wish to speak to Mrs. Sophie Bonanno. Is she in?"

With their heads nodding furiously, Mr. Ling and Mr. Ling Too turned to retrace their steps to the back of the house.

"Come please, Sirs."

Mr. Ling directed his brother Mr. Ling Too, to prepare a pot of tea for the visitors. He moved over to where Sophie had not moved from the chair at the end of the table.

"Missy Sophie." The woman did not stir. Mr. Ling spoke a little louder. "Missy Sophie, man from mine and policeman here."

Dull eyes draped with untidy strands of dark hair looked up and gave a brief nod.

It was Mr. Ling who sat the gentlemen at the table and poured cups of tea.

"I'm sorry, Mrs. Bonanno, I'm Mr. Talbot from the office at the Mount Isa Mines." Receiving no encouragement, he looked closer at the woman. "You've heard the news already?"

Sophie's internal struggle played itself out on her face. She attempted to speak but her tongue could not make the words in a mouth as dry as the desert land outside the door. Sophie sipped from the cup Mr. Ling had sat in front of her.

"What happened?"

Mr. Talbot brushed down the front of his suit then began to speak at some length explaining the events of the day which had left Mr. Bonanno dead and another man fighting for his life in the hospital.

Sophie's dark eyes gave no sign of having heard a word spoken. She remained still and silent. The men at the other end of the table glanced at each other seeking strength in numbers. Reporting bad news to relatives was never an easy job as the policeman was fully aware.

Mr. Talbot went on again offering the condolences of the Mine's Management and assuring Sophie a representative would communicate with her further regarding monies owed to Mr. Bonanno and herself.

When silence had sat for five minutes the men rose to leave, relief already flooding across their faces. Sophie's voice halted their retreat.

"Who was the other man – the man you said was fighting for his life?"

Behind the grey eyes, inside his head, Mr. Talbot shuffled the files in his mental filing cabinet. "A Mr. McInroy, I understand."

"Thank you." Sophie lowered her head to seek solace in the depths of the black tea on the table in front of her.

"Cor, look at him. Someone's been at him with a razor." Billy stared at the hairless patient. He turned to Steve and whispered. "Are you sure this is Greg? His mother wouldn't recognize him. What have they done? I've seen a pool ball with more hair than they've left on his head and face." Billy and Steve peered through one of the many gaps in the canvas stretched around the outside posts of the lower half of the hospital building. A lantern shone at the nurse's desk but the woman herself stood to attention behind the matron and the doctor as they discussed the condition of the patient in the bed marked number four. The men had only escaped outside by a hair's breadth thanks to the warning of their friend, Nurse Bates. It was way past visiting hours and if the matron had caught them standing by Greg McInroy's bedside, they had every chance of being patients themselves. The matron had a fearsome reputation that had everyone, townsfolk and miners alike, in awe.

"How have Mr. McInroy's observations been this afternoon, Matron?" The doctor turned as he spoke.

"The man has shown no signs of waking, Sir. The pulse, blood pressure, breathing and pupils have not changed since he was admitted earlier."

"And the wounds?"

"There appears to be no further haemorrhaging since three o'clock. We have marked the bandages around the bloodstains on the head wounds and the shoulder wound as you requested."

"Looks as if I've managed to catch all the bleeders when I sutured him up then."

"Yes, Sir."

"Well, Matron, we can do no more here for the moment. Will we have a look at your maternity case now?"

As the doctor and matron disappeared around the line of beds to the far side of the building, Nurse Bates flung a deep frown at the two faces reflected in the light of her lantern where it shone out through the canvas gap. She relented and walked their way.

"The signs are good. Your friend hasn't deteriorated since he came in. Tomorrow morning will give us a better indication of his prognosis. Now you fellows get on home and catch some sleep. You've had a long day." The severe expression dissolved into a warm smile. "Garn, get off with you. If you drop by about five o'clock in the morning, I'll still be here and I'll tell you how he spent the night."

Pain stirred every nerve in his body. A moan drifted up from the bed. The sounds of a baby squalling bored into his skull. He groaned but there were no other patients nearby to hear. Sluggish leg muscles stretched out in an attempt to turn his body onto his back but a pillow had been tucked in behind him and left little wriggle room. Bruised eyelids flickered. Pain fired another groan up into the night air when he attempted to lift his left arm. The patient rolled his head. Further blinding pain spun his mind back into the peace of blackness.

When next the patient Greg McInroy, woke, his eyelids lifted to expose the pale blue eyes beneath. He looked across to see an angel sitting at a desk nearby under the glow of light. It seemed like he watched for hours but it may have been only moments before the vision developed into a nurse in a white uniform. He coughed.

His angel looked up. She placed the pen with which she had been writing, onto the desk. Her feet made no sound as she approached her patient.

"Mr. McInroy, are you awake?" A groan was her only reply. She placed a thermometer within his armpit. A slight frown flickered across her face when she read the patient's temperature before she wrapped the blood pressure cuff around his good arm. "Mr. McInroy, can you hear me?" A little louder this time.

"Where am I?" He slurred.

"Where do you think you are?"

"Some sort of sickbay. How did I get here? Where is here?"

"What is the last thing you remember?"

The man thought to be Greg McInroy opened and closed his mouth several times. He struggled to reposition his body but groaned again when pain messages like lightning strikes zapped his body.

"I don't know. I don't know anything. I can't remember anything. Who am I? What's happened?"

"You were in an accident at the mines. You've two wounds on the back of your head and one on your left shoulder. The doctor has sutured them all. You must lie still now and recover."

"How can I lie still? I have to know who I am. I don't think I work in any mine."

"Hush now." Nurse Bates took up a small cup of water and teaspoon and drizzled fluid drops down Greg's throat.

The morning sun still clung to the horizon when Billy and Steve turned up at the gap in the canvas, they found Nurse Bates offering fluids and talking to their friend. A mutual grin of delight passed between the visitors.

"He's awake then, is he, Nurse?" Billy hissed through the gap.

Her smile was as wide as those of the illegal visitors. Her soft tread approached.

"Your friend has regained consciousness but I never told you, okay. The doctor won't do his round until after breakfast." She saw no reason, at this time, to tell them of her concerns about the rise in temperature overnight. There was every chance the cool sponge she was about to perform would reduce the fever.

"Tell Greg, Billy and Steve said 'Hello', will you?"

Nurse Bates grinned, "Now be off before Matron arrives."

"You're a trooper, Nurse."

It was late in the afternoon after their work shift had ended when Steve and Billy learnt Greg had no memory of who he was or where he had come from.

"The doctor said that his memory may return in a day or two," Nurse Bates offered as she shushed them back through the gap in the canvas.

It was three days later at the hospital when Greg McInroy took his first steps with the support of Billy and Steve. They learnt then Greg's memory showed no sign of returning.

"But will he be able to do things again?"

"Yes, once these wounds have healed, he'll do everything he was doing before." It was the fearsome matron who offered this information.

For five days at the boarding house, the guests walked on silent feet. Mr. Ling and Mr. Ling Too maintained a smooth running of the establishment. Occasional sobs were heard drifting down the stairs from Sophie's room. Mr. Ling delivered meals and drinks to her but most of the trays had hardly been touched when they were returned to the kitchen.

Two days previously, what they could find of Vince's body had been recovered from the bottom of the stope along with a concertinaed drilling rig. The coroner instructed they have the remains placed in a box and stored in the cold room of the single men's kitchen which was powered by the Mine's electricity power plant.

Officials from the mine's management arrived twice to assist Sophie with planning her husband's funeral. The sweltering day was cooling rapidly into a pleasant June evening when Sophie returned from burying her husband in a simple funeral attended by herself, the Misters Ling and one mine's official. On her return, she made it no further than the kitchen where she tipped a generous topping of rum into her hot cup of black tea. Her dark eyes lifted at the sound of footsteps on the path outside.

"What do you think you're doing, Uncle Matt, just walking in here like you own the place?" At her words, a hurt look filled his expression but Sophie was not impressed. As he stepped into the kitchen, she stood up her eyes blazing.

"Steady on there, Sophie. Molly Lynch sent me back to see how you are. She heard Vince didn't finish the job and Greg MacBurnie or McIntyre or whatever he's calling himself, is still alive." His eyes pleaded for understanding. "You know how Molly has spies everywhere. I have a message from her, she wants you to finish the job – preferably before the police catch up with him."

Sophie collapsed onto the form near the kitchen table. Her voice, though little more than a hushed whisper carried a load of venom.

"She what! It's barely a week since you were here giving my Vince orders to kill a man guilty of nothing more than bruising the ego of Molly Lynch. Underground in a mine is not a place to tempt fate and now my Vince lays a mangled mess buried in a coffin no bigger than a butter box and an innocent man will unlikely live through another night." Sophie sucked air into her lungs. Her hands swept over the material of her mourning weeds. "I'm a widow and our child won't have a father." She paused trying to control the temptation to clobber her visitor with the chopping knife sitting on the board near her hand.

"Get out, Matt Cockburn. Get out of my house."

Matt Cockburn's eyes narrowed. His lips pressed together until they were nothing but a thin line under his nose. "That's no way to talk about our boss, Sophie. You'll need to take over where Vince left off and make sure the fella doesn't see it through the night. Don't let Molly down. She's depending on you. We know the cops are looking for him too. He knows too much about the business. Molly would not be best pleased if he were to end up in their tender hands."

Sophie stood and slammed her hands upon the edge of the table. "You can tell Molly Lynch she may be a big crime boss in Sydney but she cannot do me any more harm than I have been dealt this week. Tell her to send her hitmen if she wishes. Do you think for one minute I've any wish to live with my Vince gone?" Sophie hung her head as she struggled to contain her weeping. After a few moments, she took a deep breath and threw her head back. "Now I have a man to mourn so get out of this house and don't you ever show your face here again. And you can tell your Molly I said so. My life and my baby's life would be better ended than to face life without Vince to look after us. I'd be happy to die with him."

Out in the shower room attached to the kitchen, Steve froze with his hand upon the tap. Even with the voices tuned low the content still drifted into the shower through the gap above the iron walls and the galvanized iron roof.

After the argument had ended, and heavy footsteps sounded on the track near the house, he remained immobile trying to make sense of all he had heard. Had Vince tried to kill his friend Greg? It would seem so. But worse still, whoever wished Greg dead was not happy and wanted the job finished – tonight. Somehow, he and Billy had to get Greg out of the hospital and to somewhere safe – but where? Slowly he turned the water on. His mind worked at the problem while his hands scrubbed the grit and grime of the mines from his skin.

By the time he was dried and dressed an idea percolated in his head. The central issue would be how far could Greg walk? He had been sitting out on the bench under the trees near the hospital each day since his first walk outside the ward but the walk Steve had planned could be quite a bit further. He just needed Billy to be back here soon.

Matthew Cockburn felt like a target board on a firing range. Walking down the darkened streets and alleyways of the sleazier areas of Sydney left him feeling less exposed than out here in this God-forgotten place without the covering protection of shrubs, buildings, or trees. With the difficulty of having to peer around the protuberance of his large abdomen, the ground under his feet remained a mystery. He stumbled over any rough patches as he made his way towards the hospital in the light of a feeble moon. Even with the sun long since disappeared over the horizon the sweat continued to pour from his skin. Once polished shoes now remained dull with dust. The smart suit of earlier in the day hung moist and limp with sweat and heat.

After shuffling into the dubious shelter of the trunk of a slim gum tree he paused to catch his breath and ponder his reasons for being here. Molly Lynch would not be too happy if he was to report that her fellow, Greg MacBurnie, was still alive. Matthew's heart thudded in a fat-padded chest at the thought of her temper but also at the attraction she held for him when she was on fire. Would Molly send someone else to do the job if Sophie didn't finish what Vince was to have done? He had no doubt such a person would certainly be instructed to remove Sophie at the same time. With a handkerchief drawn from his top pocket, he wiped his forehead smoothing the frown in the process. He always believed Sophie to be his child and the thought of her demise pricked his conscience enough to set out to do the chore himself. His stomach swirled at the idea – Sophie and her unborn child – his grandchild maybe. But he had not counted on the uncooperative conditions of nature itself.

At the sound of a grunt near his feet, Matthew jumped. A koala, bent on climbing the tree behind which he hid, had stopped its approach. With its head turned on the side, the marsupial analyzed this threat but hunger drove it on and with a speed Matthew had no chance on equalling, the long claws grasped at the tree trunk. Within moments the small furry body hauled itself upwards to disappear in the leafy canopy above. Matthew's heart pounded even more than earlier but for a different reason. What other dangerous animals were out here in the dark with him? As that thought passed through his head, the thump, thump, thump of a kangaroo moving off in its search for green pickings or a more comfortable resting area echoed from off to his left. Instantly he recalled the conversation he had overheard at the pub whilst having dinner earlier in the evening. Two bushmen were discussing the increase in crocodile numbers in the area since the last large flood had brought the Leichardt River down. Two of the reptiles had been shot right here on the edge of town.

While considering the option of retreating from this dangerous mission, Matthew's attention focused on the laughter of two nurses descending the stairs of the hospital only thirty yards away. He knew the staff was accommodated upstairs and the patients were treated in the downstairs area surrounded by a wall of hessian. After the nurses disappeared under the house, he realized one side of the downstairs was in darkness. Lantern lights and voices drifted out into the night from the other side of the building. Matthew's reluctant feet took him across the open ground to where he sheltered under the tank stand. From here he was able to see into the light more clearly. Four beds held women patients, judging by the sleeping bonnets covering their heads. One bed was hidden behind a folding screen around which the nurses moved in and out as their duties dictated. Keeping within the shadows, Matthew moved off to the other side of the building, which he knew from information gleaned earlier from the publican over a glass of ale, to be the men's ward. With his back to a post beside a gap in the hessian, he paused while his heart and breathing returned to a quieter rhythm. Easing his head around the house-post, he peered inside. In the glow of the light emanating from the other side of the building, he observed five beds with all but one empty. A white sheet covered the form of a sleeping patient. This had to be Greg MacBurnie. Even the hushed voices heard from the woman's ward did not seem to disturb the man.

Right, I'm going to do this. It had been a while since Matthew had snuffed out the life of another human being but slipping a pillow over a sleeping man's head, especially when the man was an invalid, should not be too arduous. His hand patted the coat where his folding razor rested snugly within his pocket. *Perhaps I'll not need this tonight.*

PART TWO

Empty Memories

1933

CHAPTER ELEVEN

With surprising quietness from the feet of a man so weighty, Matthew Cockburn moved to the bed next to the sleeping patient. He bit down on a curse when there was no pillow to be had on the bed. At the fourth empty bed, he felt the welcome pad of a head support. He snatched it up and returned to the sleeping body. With gentle hands, he lifted back the sheet. In the filtered lamplight from the other side of the building, Matthew stood transfixed when he realized he had discovered the missing pillows. Greg MacBurnie or McInroy, whatever his name, was gone.

"You alright, mate?" Steve helped his friend to sit on the ground against the bole of the tree.

Greg felt the rough bark through his thin hospital pyjamas. "Yeah, I think so." Curiosity filled his gaze as he watched Steve sitting on his haunches beside him. "Want to tell me why on earth you had me leave a comfortable bed wearing nothing but my boots and a pair of pyjamas to bring me on a hike out here with a shabby moonlight to lead the way?"

"Sorry, mate. I should have thought. With no memory, you'll have no idea that you're in mortal danger. We had to keep moving or I'd have explained earlier."

"What on earth are you talking about?"

Steve stood up and rummaged around inside the sack in which he had tossed all Greg's belongings before they had left the hospital.

"Before I tell you anything, you'd better at least put on your coat and cap. We can't take any chances of you catching a cold especially with your head and face like a shorn sheep. Your clothes and other stuff from the lodging house are in your kitbag with Billy. You do remember who Billy is ... your friend ... my cousin ... the bloke we lived with at the boarding house? He was with me at the hospital earlier today."

Greg grunted in an affirmative.

"Do you want a pair of socks on your feet?"

Greg was about to grunt another affirmative when he remembered the visit from the Mount Isa Mines Paymaster who had delivered a pay packet to him at the hospital yesterday – or was that the day before? It came accompanied by the promise of further monies owing for compensation in the future. Greg remembered stuffing the envelope inside one of the only pair of socks he had at the hospital.

"My feet are fine in my shoes, thanks, Steve."

Even in the poor light, Steve noticed the unsteady hands and shortening of the breath of his friend as he struggled into the coat. When Greg once more sat with his back to the bole of the tree, Steve, with a grin, pulled the cap down over his face.

"Got to keep that shaven head of yours warm."

Greg readjusted his cap and asked again, "So, what's this all about?"

"I happened to overhear a conversation at the boarding house. The long and the short of it is your name is MacBurnie, not McInroy. You must have been running from something or someone when you arrived here in Mount Isa then swapped names when you got here. People from Sydney are out to kill you. It seems the cops are after you also. Billy and I figured we'd best get you out of here tonight. We owe you for saving our lives remember – no, of course, you don't remember. We met on the train coming here from Townsville and you prevented a heavyweight sifting me through the train window."

"Why does anyone in Sydney want to kill me? I don't even know if I've been to Sydney?"

"That's something you can ponder on for the next few months. In a few minutes, Billy will arrive with his older brother, Trevor, and his truck. Trev's a Boss Drover working out of his father's property. He has been in town getting supplies for his next muster and droving trip. We'll head back to my Uncle William's place south of Cloncurry tonight where you can rest up for a bit. Billy and I will help Trevor and my uncle with the muster, drafting and branding of the cattle. It will take us about two or three weeks. If you've recovered enough by then, you can join the droving camp as cook's helper while we move stock down to my father's place on the Darling Downs. My father is Billy and Trevor's mother's brother."

"It all sounds very complicated. Can I ride a horse?"

"I don't know – can you? Those mugs from the big smoke will never find you and neither will our own coppers either, with a bit of luck. Billy and I packed up your gear at the boarding house. Billy will have your kitbag with our bags in Trev's truck."

"So, is my name Greg or what?"

"Who knows. At the boarding house earlier today, the fella from Sydney called you Greg MacBurnie. But it might be a good idea if we change your name altogether tonight. Just to make it a bit harder for anyone to follow your trail."

"As none of the names you mentioned have sparked my memory, I'm not going to be too worried if you make up another name, am I? What do you suggest?"

"Hell, I don't know. Billy always said you looked more like a Robert than a Greg and with the faint echo of Scottish burr in your voice you'd better stick with a Scottish surname – maybe something like Bains might suit you. Robert – Rob – Bains – there you go – a good Scottish name."

A shiver ran down Robbie's body. His heart beat faster. Was that a tremor of recognition like a flash of light he felt in his brain? There was something about the name Robert but nothing gelled in his memory.

"You sure you're alright?" Steve reached over to touch the shoulder of the man now named Rob Bains.

"Yeah. Sure. Rob Bains, it is then."

"Rob Bains sounds good." Steve's arm reached over his knees and shook the fingertips of the newly named man. White teeth were all to be seen in the shadowed faces of the men as they grinned.

A frown rode across the newly-named Rob's forehead.

"Steve, do you think you should be taking this risk? You know, helping me like this? I mean, I could be a wanted murderer or anything. I don't want to place you or your family at risk."

Steve smiled. "I may be relatively young compared to you but I've met a lot of men in my travels and many have been a lot more wicked than you have shown to be; I can tell you. Billy and I discussed this with Trevor in the pub earlier. We'll put our money on your honesty."

Tears shone in the eyes of Rob Bains. He struggled to choke out a thank you.

Both their heads swung in the direction of an approaching vehicle. A small truck loaded high with boxes, bags, swags and drums of fuel rumbled towards their position raising the soft dust which then engulfed around them as the vehicle came to a halt. In the faint moonlight, a blue-coloured dog seated on top of the luggage jumped to its feet. The hairs on the back of its neck lifted and a soft growl sounded in the dog's chest, but she offered no other sign of hostility.

Billy climbed out from behind the steering wheel and ran around to the other side of the cabin. The door screeched as he hauled it open.

"Here, mate, you jump in front where it's more comfortable." He pointed Rob Bains to the open doorway. "I've left your kitbag in there as padding for your head and shoulder."

Steve scrambled up the mountain of supplies. He patted the dog. "G'day, Blue. Shove over a bit, will you?" His reward was a slobbering lick down his cheek.

With his hand on the driver's door, Billy spoke softly to his cousin. "Did you pair figure out a new name for Greg?"

"Yeah, he'll tell you. Let's get out of here – fast. It must be nearly eleven o'clock. Where's Trev?".

"Saying goodbye to a lady friend."

"Geez, he'll be pissed off."

After stuffing the smaller bag containing his things from the hospital into the kitbag at his side, the newly named Robert Bains shuffled his body into a comfortable position as Billy guided the vehicle back into town. When Billy brought them to a gentle stop in the street across from the pub, Rob Bains noticed a tall slim man with a felt hat dragged low on his head move out from the shadows.

"Turn the bloody lights off, Billy." A deep timbered voice spoke through the window near Rob's head. "I'll drive." With light feet, the man in Cuban-heeled riding boots made little noise as he walked around the front of the truck now in darkness and opened the almost silent driver's door.

As Billy unfolded himself from behind the steering wheel, he grinned up at his brother, "I see you've oiled this door then, any reason?” Billy was quite aware that on his infrequent trips to town, Trevor's nightly visits to some of the more amorous ladies were better not advertised with screeching doors.

“Garn, get out of there. You can ride up the back with Steve and Bluey.”

With only a nod to the passenger, Trevor settled in behind the steering wheel. Within a few moments, a hand banged twice on the roof of the front cabin letting the driver know they were ready to go. It was not until the vehicle was well out of town before the driver turned his head towards the man at his side.

“Trevor Jackson. Just make yourself comfortable; it's a long rough road ahead.”

“… Er … Robert … Rob Bains.” Rob only just remembered the newly chosen name. “Thanks for your help.”

“No trouble, mate. Billy said you saved their lives on the train some weeks ago.”

“Nothing more than anyone would do, I'm sure.”

“Hmmm.” Trevor concentrated his attention on the pot-holed road over which they drove.

The man's taciturn manner did not go unnoticed. Rob's thoughts swirled in his head. Did the man not want anything to do with a possible Sydney gangster or at least a fugitive from the law? Who could blame him for that? Yet he did not feel inside himself like someone who would do bad things. If only he could remember his past. Where did he come from and why were these people after him? It was all too much for him right now. Despite the discomfort of the wounds on the back of his head and his left shoulder, his body slipped into sleep.

In the back of the truck, Billy and Steve rocked back and forth between the nest of swag rolls they had built. Their hats were pulled over their faces to filter some of the dust as it flew up from the road at intervals when they passed through areas of bulldust. Bluey lay spread out across their feet.

"What did you make of those notebooks of Greg's – oops – I mean Rob's?" Billy moved his feet to get comfortable. "I mean who writes like that? All that stuff about the train journey and the country descriptions."

"I didn't really get to read anything properly. We were in too much of a rush but it sure was a heap of writing – more than Edith or Evie ever wrote in their diaries."

Laughter rang out between the cousins. "Geez, don't ever tell them we peeked. They'd kill us and if they didn't, Ma sure would." Billy's white teeth shone in the night.

"Do you remember how soft his hands were when he first started working underground? Sophie had to paint his blisters with iodine every night."

"You're right. I don't think he'd ever done too much physical work."

"No, but he never shirked the work. He always done his share."

Inside the cabin, Trevor's attention focused on the road. The truck lurched and slid along the deep gutters left by horse-drawn wagons, bullock wagons and the occasional motorized vehicles during the earlier rain season. He kept alert for kangaroos taking a sudden inclination to leap across the track. In the dim light of the vehicle's headlamps, his eyes strained to see the outline of cattle seeking the warmth of the road on which to rest as the night cooled. When able to do so, Trevor glanced over to take in the shadowy profile of this stranger.

In the back of the truck, Billy's and Steve's sultry conversation and grumbles at the odour of Bluey were short-lived. They dozed.

It was the change in the sound of the engine which brought Rob's head upright. Water splashed up over the bonnet as they drove across a small creek and up the other bank. Trevor pulled over in a cleared area in which many others had stopped previously, judging by the number of old campfire sites seen in the dull headlights.

"It's about two o'clock. We'll throw our swags out and catch a nap for a bit. Billy has a swag for you in the back."

Something big rushed off amongst the trees nearby, disturbed by the screeching sound made when Rob opened his door. He felt every one of his muscles make a similar complaint as he lifted his legs up and out into the night. His body followed slowly behind.

Thud. Thud. Thud. Thud. The four swags landed on the ground at the side of the truck. Bluey made a silent landing on top of a swag. She sniffed each of the swag rolls in turn. Even in the feeble starlight, Trevor recognized his swag and began to open it up beside the front wheel. He dropped down onto the internal blanket. After an inspection of the area, the dog took up guard position at Trevor's feet. Billy and Steve recovered their swags and began to throw them open a short distance away.

"Here, Rob. This other swag's for you." Steve began to arrange the canvas and blanket beside his own. "You might want to bring out your kitbag to use as a pillow."

"Is the water in the creek alright to drink? My mouth is a dust bowl of its own."

"You don't need to go down there with the snakes. You'll find a pannikin hanging on the gear stick. Fetch it out and I'll show you where the waterbag hangs on the front of the truck."

Gradually the noises of the night returned to normal as each man drifted into slumber. The occasional groan as Rob disturbed one of his wounds went unnoticed amidst the snores and snuffles of his camping partners.

The quarter moon slipped away. On the eastern horizon, a faint light hinted at a picaninny dawn. A family of kookaburras heralded the day with their chorus in the trees beside the sleepers. In the taller gum trees on the other side of the creek, the white cockatoos squawked their greetings to the promise of a new day.

"Geez, the day's half gone. Come on, you fellows. Shake a leg there. We should have been on the road an hour ago." Trevor jumped up and rolled the swag into a small bundle and secured it with a strip of leather hide all in one smooth movement. He tossed it up on the load before moving over to water the nearest tree.

Both Steve and Billy made similar quick and efficient risings. Rob found it impossible to jump up and out of his swag. A slow roll over onto his hands and knees was all he managed this morning. A long slow groan accompanied his creaking joints as he lifted upright. He felt a hundred years of age. The thought hit him. *I have no idea how old I am. When was I born? Where was I born?*

"Don't suppose there's a chance of any breakfast to be had, Trev?" Billy asked.

"A dingo's breakfast, brother. A drink of water and a look around. We'll be home in a few hours you can get Mum to cook you a feed then."

"Geez, it'll be dinnertime by then."

"Well, won't you be lucky? You can have breakfast and dinner together. If we have any trouble on the way, we may not get there before teatime tonight. Then you'll really have something to whinge about." Trevor threw his brother the keys. "Here you can drive for a bit – keep you awake."

Trevor and Steve realigned their swag rolls into comfortable positions and settled back with Bluey scratching for position near Trevor's shoulder.

"Your friend doesn't talk a lot, does he?" Trevor nudged Steve's shoulder.

"I guess he's still far from well although, now you mention it, he never did talk a lot."

"Are you sure he can be trusted? I don't want to take a thief or worse into our home – particularly with the girls home on holidays."

"I wager my life, he's as honest as any man I know. Even though he did travel on the train with false names and now we find the gangsters in Sydney want him dead and the cops are after him, I'm sure there'll be a good reason for him doing so." Trevor went to speak but Steve continued, "Remember, the Sydney bloke only wanted him dead because some broken-hearted tart down there told him to."

In the flickering shadows made from the lantern on the desk, Doctor Neatley dipped his pen nib into the ink and continued to write his report on the final hours of the woman they had treated during the night. Gratitude warmed his eyes as Matron placed a cup of strong black tea on his desk. With a sigh, she sat in the chair opposite to sip at her own teacup.

"Thanks, Matron." He stood up and removed a silver flask from the pocket of his coat hanging on the hatstand in the corner of the alcove behind the filing cabinet. "I think a nip of something stronger might be called for after such a marathon as tonight has been. Can I tempt you with a drachm?"

She held her cup across the desk. "Please, Doctor. Yes, it has been a marathon. I think the end was a relief for the poor woman. You did all you could, Doctor."

"Hmmm." He drank deeply.

At that moment, Nurse Bates appeared at the entrance to the alcove holding a lantern with its wick turned down low. Strands of hair had escaped her cap. Her drawn face told of the emotions experienced in the loss of a long-term patient of whom everyone had grown quite fond. But the news she had to impart now stirred her emotions in a different manner.

"Are you alright, Nurse?"

"Er … Matron, it's Mr. McInroy."

The doctor's eyes lifted from his report. "What's wrong with the man, Nurse?"

"That's just it, Doctor. He's gone."

"Gone where?"

"I'm not sure. The night wardsman and I had just delivered the body to the storeroom and dropped the soiled linen in at the laundry tubs when we found Mr. McInroy gone."

"The poor man's probably just gone outside to relieve himself, girl." The doctor dropped his eyes back to the words on the page in front of him.

"It's unlikely, Sir. He has made up his bed with pillows covered with the sheet. It looked very much like he was still asleep."

Doctor Neatley leant back in the chair. "Hmmm. I guess after such a head injury as he suffered who knows what has been shaken up in his brain."

"Nurse, you'd better ask the night wardsman to check the staff quarters upstairs to make sure he is not up to mischief there. In fact, you go with him while he's at it."

"Yes, Matron." As a new surge of adrenaline rushed through Nurse Bates' veins, her footsteps lifted and she ran towards the back stairs of the building. The faintest of light was seen in the eastern sky.

The chairs on both sides of the desk scraped back as the doctor and matron rose to investigate their patient's disappearance. The teacups stood half full on the rough-hewn timber desk.

In the dull yellow light of the lamp, the pair stared at the bed empty of a human body. The sheet had been drawn back to reveal a line of four pillows. Matron reached into the locker beside the top of the bed. Confusion clouded her face.

"The man has taken all his personal items."

"Well, I guess we can rule out mental confusion post-injury then. This has been a planned departure but for what reason, I cannot fathom. He always seemed an intelligent man and his medical condition was progressing nicely." The doctor mumbled more to himself than the matron at his side. "It's unlikely he'll be stumbling and lost out in the bush then. I can't see any reason to call the police." He turned about and as he moved away, he asked, "We do have his notes from the mines' office don't we, Matron?"

"Yes, they were sent over after his accident."

"Good, I'll write a letter to his next of kin and outline the circumstances of his leaving. No doubt he may be home before the mail."

Rob opened his eyes when the truck pulled up at double wooden gates attached to two enormous strainer posts. The late morning sun reflected off the new bolts on one strainer post where a wide plank carried the name, "Far Horizons", burnt into it.

"I got it," Billy yelled as he jumped down from the back.

Steve was behind the steering wheel when the truck made its way through the gate. Billy threw Rob a casual salute as the vehicle drove past to wait for him to shut the gate and climb on board.

"Only another fifteen miles to go." With a smile, Steve turned to his passenger. "How's the war wounds holding up?"

Rob gave a short laugh. "They said they'll be glad to get out of this torture rack, thanks."

"You, okay?" Worry walked in the furrows of Steve's forehead.

"Yeah, mate, nothing a good stretch won't fix."

Grassed plains spread as far as Rob could see in any direction with only an occasional gentle rise and fall of the land. Cattle were seen dotted throughout the landscape while others lay resting in the dappled shade of the scattered trees.

After some time, Rob sighted the homestead on a distant rise. The sun reflected sharply off the metal roofs of several buildings. Smoke drifted up from a chimney.

Twenty minutes later they pulled up beside an unpainted two-story timber building with top and bottom verandahs on all sides. Expectation animated the face of a middle-aged woman waiting to greet the arrivals. Her hands patted her hair into place before stripping the apron from around her waist. Not waiting for it to stop completely, she rushed over to the vehicle waving away the dust with a shake of her hands.

"Hello, Steve." A work-hardened hand reached to stroke the cheek of the driver. Moments later she was swept up into the arms of her youngest son. "Billy, my boy, it's so good to see you home safe and sound."

"Yeah, I know, Ma, what with Trevor and then Steve driving it was a life-threatening trip." He laughed.

"Next time, I'll leave you to walk." Trevor jumped to the ground and hugged his mother.

"Aunt Minnie, we've a friend here I'd like you to meet. The fellow saved my life and Billy's on the train out from the coast several weeks ago." Steve gently drew his aunt to the other side of the truck where Rob, amidst protests from the door and his stiffened body, slowly extricated himself from the cabin.

"Aunt Minnie, Mrs. Jackson, I'd like you to meet Robert – Rob – Bains."

Rob dragged the cap off his head. And made a gesture to bow. "Pleased to meet you, Mrs. Jackson."

Her smile lit up the tired face. The lines multiplied. "You'll have to tell me how you saved the lives of my boys but first we must feed you. Come in. Come in. A friend of Billy and Steve is a friend of the family."

She led the group into the shade of the verandah and followed it around to the back of the building where a narrow covered-way from the main house joined a large kitchen and pantry area. A long table with a wooden form on either side sat under the verandah beside the walkway.

"Do you mind eating in the kitchen, Mr. Bains? If you prefer, I can serve the meal at the table on the verandah or in the dining room inside the house proper."

"In the kitchen sounds great to me, thanks, Mrs. Jackson."

"How's the muster going, Ma?" Trevor asked his most pressing question.

"Good, I think. Your father and sisters are down working with the men today. They finished bringing up the herd from the south paddock yesterday. Today your father said they'd be drafting, spaying, branding, and castrating before the men go out to bring up the herd from the eastern paddocks."

"They've been busy then, it seems. Can I get a bit of bread or damper and salt beef and I'll head off down there to give a hand?"

"You'll not leave here until you put a decent lining on your stomach, son. I'm not going to ask how long since you've eaten. The workers will be eating in the camp kitchen at the yards. I have some fresh beef here – they killed yesterday – so sit yourself at the table and I'll do you some eggs and steak. I made fresh bread this morning to go with it." Minnie Jackson almost pushed her eldest son into the chair at the head of the table. With one hand she pulled the kettle and frying pan into the heat of the wide wood-fired stove while the other hand swept in a circle towards the others in the room to encourage them to be seated.

"Thanks, Ma. I'm starving."

"Aunt Minnie, I could eat a horse and chase the rider," Steve confirmed his agreement.

Mrs. Jackson lifted the lid on a wooden barrel in the corner and produced two loaves of freshly made bread. She placed these and a heavy wooden board with a large knife on the table. The knife-edge glinted in the light from the window.

Rob took in the kitchen with its stove of two ovens around which pans of various sizes and shapes hung from hooks on the walls. A solid rough-hewn timber table centered the room. Bush-built timber chairs lined its sides. Trellised vines outside the eastern and western windows cast shadows in the room. Cupboards and shelves lined every wall except that adjacent to the house. Here sat several vats in which Rob assumed they kept the brine solution for salting the meat. *Why would that come to my mind? What do I know of salted meat?* He pondered.

Rich aromas of meat cooking filled the kitchen as the steak sizzled in the pan. Trevor cut slices of bread and served them around on plates from the pile on the end of the table. Knives and forks were sourced from the tray sitting beside the plates. Mrs. Jackson turned her back to the stove.

"Now, Billy, I want to hear of this story on the train. How could anyone be in fear of their life on the train." She gasped. "Oh, you didn't jump the rattler, did you. You did have enough money to pay for a seat?"

Steve and Billy laughed. Billy started the tale. "It was more Steve's life he saved rather than mine, Ma."

Mrs. Jackson turned back to attend to the four generous steaks in the frying pan while Billy related the story. During this time the cooked steaks were heaped onto a tin plate on the edge of the stove while the eggs spluttered and spat in the pan.

As she handed the heaped plates to those around the table, Mrs. Jackson offered profuse thanks for Rob's action in saving her youngest son and her favourite nephew. Rob's face reddened to match the bougainvillea flowers growing on a bush in the garden seen through the window a short distance from where they all sat.

"It was no more than any man would have done, Mrs. Jackson. They have since helped me in return – in more ways than I can say. As I understand it, Steve and Billy were responsible for saving my life when I was trapped down in the mines."

"When did that happen?"

"Six days ago," he looked to Steve for confirmation, "or was it seven?" He took the plate offered, "Oh, Mrs. Jackson, I'm sure I can't eat all that food."

Mrs. Jackson smiled.

"Seven – today," Billy answered Rob's question around a mouthful of bread, steak and eggs.

"Billy, what does your father tell you about talking with food in your mouth?"

Billy laughed. "He says, 'Don't eat with your mouth half-full – fill it right up'."

"Billy Jackson, he does not. It was your grandfather who used to say that, despite my chastising him each time. We don't want our guest to think you've not been taught any manners."

Steve, Trevor and Billy exchanged knowing grins. Billy turned to Rob, "Don't mind Ma, Rob, she fusses a bit."

"I'm not fussing. I'm looking at a man who has obviously learnt good manners. Your mother must have taught you well." Mrs. Jackson smiled at her guest again.

Once again, a flush ran across Rob's face at the attention. "Mrs. Jackson, I don't really know. Since the mining accident, I can't remember anything about myself – where I came from or if I have any family – nothing."

Shock widened Minnie's eyes. "Goodness me, that must be terrible for you. What does the doctor say? Will you recall your past in time?"

"He said it's possible."

Trevor threw his fatty scraps to his blue dog lying in the doorway. He then wiped the empty plate clean with the last piece of bread before he stuffed it into his mouth.

"I'm off, Ma. Come on, you two." He indicated to Billy and Steve who were cleaning their plates with the fresh bread. Each of the departing men dropped their plate into the tub of hot soapy water on the bench against the wall. "I'll leave the truck outside. Will you ask Hoppy Davis to take it over to the storeroom and unload it when he can?" Trevor referred to the handyman who helped around the garden and house. Trevor spoke to his mother again, "Do you know if they've left any horses in the house-paddock, Ma?"

"Yes, your dad said the three of you would return sometime today. I'm not sure which horses are there, though." She turned to her guest. "Will you be joining them, Rob?"

It was Steve who spoke up as he stood in the doorway. "Rob will have to take it easy for at least a week or more. He still has stitches holding his wounds together."

"Oh, my goodness. I'll show him to his room." Mrs. Jackson shooed off her boys then turned to her guest. "You'll be ready for a lie down after such a long journey, Rob."

"Can I help you clean these things up first?"

"Absolutely not. The men are only allowed in my kitchen to eat. I don't expect them to do the dishes. Now come along and I'll show you where you can camp. Have you got anything with you?"

"Yes, Mrs. Jackson. I'll just get my kitbag from the truck."

Once Rob had been shown to a small room on the verandah outside Billy and Steve's room, he could not wait to delve into the kitbag they had packed for him. As much as he tried, he could not remember the boarding house they spoke of in Mount Isa.

As Mrs. Jackson's footsteps descended the stairs, the sound of galloping horses faded into the distance. The boys were on their way to the cattle yards.

Fingers hardened with recently acquired callouses in the mine struggled to untie the rope knot at the throat of his bag. Once he gained entry, he emptied the contents which, it appeared, had been packed in great haste. He was most interested in the large hard-covered notebooks, one red and one blue, which had been digging into his shoulders throughout their journey to Far Horizons. He placed them on the bed but did not open them. His gaze kept returning to the books as he found a leather belt with a pocket knife secured in a pouch on one side and a watch pouch on the other side – but no watch. These he lay on top of a pair of trousers and a shirt. Once dressed in his own clothes, he felt almost human again. The pair of socks holding his pay packet was stashed deep in the kitbag beside a razor and strop once again. The last thing in the kitbag was a leather enveloped pencil case with several pencils, rubbers and a pen. New pen nibs were discovered in a screw-top vial. He checked inside the bag again but there was no sign of a bottle of ink.

Eventually, he sat on the bed and lifted the first book. He flicked through pages and pages of writing. Curiosity built to such a level he could not resist pausing his page flicking to read in detail some of what had been written. It appeared to be a diary of sorts with descriptions of scenery or events he had witnessed. He did not know how or why he knew but he did think the writing style was pretty good. He opened the second book. This seemed to be made up of lists of dates and reminders of things. The letter R was repeated often and the letter K. Were these people or things or places? Weariness brought his thought processes to a close. He placed the books on the floor beside the bed against the wall. His eyes drooped.

The sun was well into the west when Rob Bains awoke. His hand stretched down to retrieve the two books from beside his bed. He opened the one with the blue cover, the one with lists and dates. His forefinger once again gently touched the letters R and K. He hoped just the sight of them might eventually trigger something in his memory. He did notice within the lists, words that appeared to be in code. Was this some sort of code or shorthand of his own making?

His memory remained blank. There was no sense sitting here getting more frustrated. He eased himself off the bed. His shoulder was particularly sore this afternoon. It was a struggle to drag on his boots. Downstairs, silence filled the house. His bladder led him on a search for the dunny. Every house had a dunny, didn't it? He found the little house, sitting slightly askew, in the shade of a huge mango tree behind the kitchen and near a bathroom of several shower cubicles. In this cluster stood a water tank on a frame of high poles beside a windmill which intermittently creaked and groaned with any little breeze coming its way. Tentatively he stepped inside the lavatory. His automatic response was to check all the corners for snakes or spiders. Where had he learnt to do that?

Outside once again, he paused and looked out past the buildings. Dust rose into a clear blue sky from somewhere to the south. The muster yards, he presumed. Curious feet led him towards a large corrugated iron building with a rusting roof. The rectangle building had the walls on the long sides made up of several large doors hooked back to allow airflow. One of the narrower ends was open to the elements while the other had been enclosed around a wood stove and kitchen accessories. Two lines of stretchers ran the length of the building. A swag roll lay at the end of one bunk. One of these beds was currently in use – the residence of the man named Hoppy, perhaps – he pondered.

Next to this building, he discovered the stables which housed racks for saddles. Tools for leatherwork and leather hides covered one of two benches. A double bail to milk the cows filled one side of the opening leading into a large wooden railed pen while the other side was made up of six horse stalls. When he walked through to stand in one of the stalls, he could see at the far end of the enclosed yard a wooden gate opening into a larger paddock.

Rob noticed how the house, shower, dunny and men's quarters ran parallel to the stables and to this building which he now approached, and beyond it to a farm shed. Each wall of this corrugated iron building, the size of a small house, was made up of push-out iron windows. Currently, all were open in a vain effort to tempt a little breeze. Rob heard Mrs. Jackson's voice call to him from inside.

"Hello, Rob, come on in. Do you feel better after your nap?"

He made his way to the front of the building and poked his head through the doorway. "Hello, Mrs. Jackson. Yes, a bit stiff and sore but I'm ironing out the kinks with a walk. I hope it's alright to wander around."

"Of course, Rob. I'd take you on a tour but with our bookkeeper suddenly retired I've been caught up with this inventory at the moment."

"What is this place?"

"This is the storeroom. We keep enough supplies of hardware, farming needs, work clothes, soft furnishings and nourishment to keep an army going."

"Can I help? Are you preparing the inventory for the end of year financials?" Rob's speech came to a sudden halt. The question was loud in his brain. *How did he know anything about inventories and financial records?*

"How's your counting skills?"

"I don't know … and yet … I think I can do it quite well."

Three hours later, it was the sound of galloping horses, laughter and cooeeing of the riders which lifted the concentration of the pair in the storeroom.

"Good heavens, is that the time? They'll all be looking for a good feed. We'll close up shop now and hopefully finish it tomorrow. Thank you so much, Rob, for your help."

"You're more than welcome, Mrs. Jackson."

CHAPTER TWELVE

Their immediate work in the storeroom was completed by the time they were ready for a morning break. Minnie Jackson and Rob sat on the verandah drinking from their cups of tea.

"Do you feel well enough to come with me in the truck to see what's happening at the cattle yards, Rob? We can have our lunch down there in the camp kitchen with the ringers. I'll bring a basket of the fresh biscuits I cooked yesterday."

"I would like that, thanks, Mrs. Jackson."

"Now, Rob, do I have to scold you again? I've already told you to call me Minnie. Goodness me we're not all that much different in ages. How old are you, anyway?"

Rob gave a rueful smile. "I've no idea."

"Sorry, of course. I forgot. Anyway, you look to be in your mid-forties, or thereabouts, I would think. William and I are only fifty-five years of age."

Rob smiled. He had met Minnie's husband, William Jackson, and their daughters, Edith and Evie, last night at the tea table. Hard work had taken its toll on the man who had stood tall and lean. Billy's earlier description of his father came back to him as he had noted the gammy leg, the result of a broken bone when horse breaking. William's left crooked forearm had been crushed in a cattle-yard gate by an uncooperative bull. A large scar buckled his right cheek where a run-a-way horse had kicked him many years before. Smaller scars were numerous upon both his hands. Thin grey hair barely covered his scalp.

At the cattle yards, Hoppy Davis approached the truck.

"Can I help you there, Mrs. Jackson?"

"No, I'm alright. I'll take these biscuits over to the camp cook. Will you show Rob about?"

"Yes, of course." Hoppy turned to Rob; they had met yesterday when the man had been pruning the roses in the front garden. During their evening meal, William had explained to Rob how Hoppy smashed his hip up in the Gulf country when throwing a maverick bull nearly twenty years ago. He had been a fraction too slow and the bull had taken its revenge. Hoppy had worked some years as camp-cook on a few droving trips with William, but it became too much for him and he lived here at Far Horizons – now semi-retired.

"They've just finished most of today's drafting. Trev's just started castrating the young stuff and if they put their hearts into it, they should get the old cows spayed too, before dark."

Mrs. Jackson ran over. "Here Rob, you'll need this if you want to breathe over there at the yards." She handed Rob a cloth from her basket. He quickly learnt what she meant when he noticed all the ringers had neckerchiefs over their noses and tied firmly at the back of their heads. The ringers and animals often disappeared in thick balls of dust as they rose from the scrambling feet of the bellowing stock, the working horses and the ringers themselves. The noise assaulted his ears. Cattle bellowed their fear and frustration. Hoarse calls of the men pitched across the pen between the roped beast and the small fire in which the branding irons lay red hot. Thin smoke puffs quickly vanished within the dust. After each completed treatment, the beast was up and away with a resentful swing of its head and a flying back foot or two before it tore through the gateway opened for its departure. From another pen, the next calf, hemmed in between two men on horses, was edged into the working pen where the riders dropped onto the beast and threw it to the ground. A short length of rope in the hands of one rider secured the beast's legs. At least six or seven animals had been through the process before Rob realized the ringer branding the calves was not a man. This worker was Trevor and Billy's sister, Edith. The other ringer, throwing and tying the calves, was the other sister, Evie.

After the initial surprise passed, he examined his feelings at seeing the girls taking part in the work on their father's property. He felt sure girls in the towns and cities might not approve but it somehow felt right happening out here in the bush. When he had met them last night, the girls presented as attractive young ladies in calf-length skirts worn by the women of late teenage years or early twenties, based on pictures he noticed in Minnie's magazines in the storeroom. They had entertained the family with solo and duet pieces played on the piano in the sitting room. Today, in men's clothing and layered with dirt and grime, they could have been men or women of any age. Minnie said last night they were home on holiday from their nursing training at the Townsville hospital and were due to return there within a few weeks.

Trevor's arms and clothes dripped with blood by the time he called a mid-day break. Hoppy and Rob followed the workers across to the unwalled, roofed shed under which three long tables were lined up parallel to each other. A rainwater tank stood at one corner of the building and it was here the ringers made their first port of call. Dust-dry throats drank greedily from the cool water. With their thirst quenched and further water tossed over their heads, faces and hands, they lined up to collect a tin plate heaped with salt beef and fresh damper. Minnie's biscuits sat on trays in the middle of two tables, each beside a large pot of strong tea and a tin of sugar – the surface black with flies.

Hoppy drew Rob over to a table where William and Minnie Jackson sat. He began to regale them with stories of his days working in the Gulf country. Laughter and jeering bounced around under the tin roof. Some of the men ate the food and took their pannikins over to sit with their backs against a roof post where they proceeded to drink their tea and doze. Others, after eating, just dropped their heads upon the table in front of them and shut their eyes. They had heard the yarns before.

A hush filled the empty rooms in the solicitor chambers. Business hours were long finished and everyone but Jim Sullivan had departed for their homes. The long dark velvet drapes had been pulled across the windows throughout the office building. A lamp with the wick turned up, standing on the desk beside his hand, cast shadows along the walls. In this hand, he held the correspondence received from Mount Isa this afternoon – his eyes seeing but his brain not wanting to understand. Once more he adjusted the glasses upon his face as if they might change the news written upon the page.

Dear Sir,

It is my sad duty to inform you as recorded next of kin to Gregory McInroy, an employee at the Mount Isa Mines Ltd, of his involvement in a recent accident at the mines.

Mr. McInroy received injuries as a result of this accident and has been conveyed to the Mount Isa Hospital.

We have received communication from the Medical Officer that Mr. McInroy's wounds were treated and he is as well as can be expected. You will be receiving correspondence from the doctor shortly as to Mr. McInroy's progress.

Sincerely ...

The letter had the signature of the mining manager beneath.

Jim removed his glasses and placed them on the blotting paper on his desk. A soft squeak of timber under strain fractured the silence of the chambers as he leant back in his chair. His legal mind began to pick out the main points in the letter in his hand. His friend, Robbie MacBurnie, who had changed his name to Greg MacBurnie and then to Greg McInroy in his madcap scheme to protect his family, had since had an accident at the mines. He threw the letter onto the desk and unwound his glasses from his ears to set them on top of the correspondence. As one of Robbie's best friends since childhood, the emotions stirred his heart rate. Like bubbles in soapy water, questions rose to the surface of his mind before they popped out inside his head. What on earth happened? Why did Robbie need to change his name the second time? What wounds were treated? Did his brother Greg's Sydney connection have anything to do with this? What the hell happened? And what did 'as well as can be expected' really mean?

The chair landed with a thump followed by a scrape on the polished timber floor as Jim jumped up. He began to pace the room. Long fingers trailed through his hair. His hands wiped down his face but failed to iron out the furrows in his forehead as he did so. Suddenly his expression cleared. He rushed back to the desk. Trembling hands sorted through the once tidy heap of personal mail that had built up over the several days he had been away working at the courthouse. He replaced his glasses on his face and began the

128

search for another Mount Isa postmark. It was the last one in the heap. He threw himself back into the chair and tore open the envelope.

Dear Sir,

As the Medical Officer of the Mount Isa Hospital, I wish to inform you of the admission to our establishment of Mr. Greg McInroy who, according to the notes provided by the Mount Isa Mines Office, has claimed you as next of kin. Mr. McInroy received several wounds following an unfortunate accident at the Mount Isa Mines.

The healing of Mr. McInroy's physical wounds made normal progress but the patient found he had no memory of his life before the accident. This memory loss may slowly recover over time or it may remain permanent. After five days in our care, Mr. McInroy discharged himself from the hospital taking all his personal belongings with him.

Sincerely ....

An indecipherable signature covered the remainder of the page.

Jim stared at the letter. "I bloody told him nothing good would come of all this. It was a crazy idea in the first place. Oh, mate, what the hell kind of fix have you got yourself into?" His hair stood on end as he dragged his fingers along his scalp. "Geez, how on earth do I tell Rhylla?" Once again, he stood up and began pacing his office.

He placed his hands on the desk and hung his head while the problem and possible actions to be taken spun in the butter churn of his brain. His weight leant forward on his hands while his feet rocked from toe to heel.

He snapped to attention and once more spoke to the empty room. "Okay, I'll need to chew on this overnight. By morning, when my head's clearer, I'll drop in to see Rhylla on my way to work."

After a crisp clear sky to begin the day, the sun had started to dry the dew on the grass when Jim Sullivan stopped outside the gate at Rhylla MacBurnie's house. Even after swallowing the breakfast his wife Mabel, insisted he eat, Jim felt nausea rising in his gullet. With a heavy arm and heavier heart, he lifted the latch and swung the timber gate inwards. He had only just shut the gate and turned to make his way along the garden path when Rhylla's voice called from the top verandah.

"I'll be right down, Jim."

The ornate front door opened to reveal Rhylla's wide smile above a floral belted dressing gown.

"You've got news of Robbie? He's on his way home, at last?"

Damn, I'd rather cut my throat than have to do this. When Robbie does get home, I'm going to give him a belting. The thoughts broke through the ice block in Jim's head.

"Hi, Rhylla. I'm sorry, I have news but not exactly what we expected."

Rhylla's hand reached through the doorway and grabbed Jim's arm. "Well, come inside and tell me what news you do have." She almost dragged him into the sitting room. "You can tell me now. Mrs. Barnes won't be over for a while yet and Kirsty is asleep upstairs."

"I think you'd better sit down, Rhylla."

Her face fell. Tears shimmered on her eyelids. A soft moan filled the room as she fell into the nearest armchair.

"Oh no, Jim, what's happened?"

Jim struggled to gather his thoughts as he settled into the armchair opposite his friend's wife. After several attempts, the story came out.

The tears now ran unchecked down Rhylla's cheeks. Her head moved from side to side in disbelief.

"B ... b ... but what does this mean?"

"According to the doctor's letter the wounds he received are healed or at least healing alright but he has a memory loss that may be a big problem for him."

"H…h…how will he know where to come home?"

"The doctor did say this memory loss may not be permanent."

Jim felt like crying himself. Robbie MacBurnie was more like a brother to him than his own brothers. Apart from his dear Mabel, this woman sitting opposite him, he admired above all others. The children of Robbie and Rhylla MacBurnie had called him 'Uncle Jim' from the first day they talked.

"Jim, I can't just stand by, waiting here. I'll have to go and find Robbie – wherever he is."

"Rhylla, to do so may place him in more danger. He may have suspected a threat to his safety and escaped to – who knows where. None of us really know what danger that poor-excuse-of-a-brother may have brought with him."

"What do I tell Kirsty? How do I tell her what has happened to her father? She will feel so guilty."

"How is little Kirsty, by the way?"

A gentle smile softened the tension on her face. "You and Robbie are as bad as each other. Kirsty is not a baby anymore. She is a young woman – a young woman who has decided to face the town gossips – to keep this baby and care for it herself."

"If Mabel and I can help in any way you must let me know."

A comfortable silence settled in the room. Shuffling footsteps in the room upstairs stirred them from their individual musings.

"Rhylla, I've been thinking, I might take a couple of weeks off and travel out to Mount Isa and ask a few questions. I know a solicitor out there; he was in my year at university. He may be able to point me in the right direction."

'Mabel won't be happy for you to travel without her and it may be too unsafe to take her with you."

"If necessary, I'll explain the situation to her. I'm sure she would not say a word to anyone else if I asked her not to. She has kept many secrets for me over the years. Would you be agreeable for me to tell her why Robbie is away?"

"Of course, Jim. I don't know anyone who I would trust more. The situation has exploded into much more than was planned for."

Jim lifted his watch hanging by its silver chain from his fob pocket. "Is that really the time? I must away. There'll be a few things needing to be sorted at the office if I'm to be away within the next few days."

"Are you sure I can't make you a cuppa before you go? I'm sorry, I should have thought of that earlier."

"Thanks, Rhylla, no. I must be off."

It was later in the morning when Rhylla sat at the kitchen table opposite Mrs. Barnes who smiled proudly at her latest creation of small decorated buns.

"My best, I'm sure."

"Yes, Mrs. Barnes, they are."

A thoughtful expression replaced Mrs. Barnes's smile as she poured the tea into the two delicate china cups.

"Mrs. MacBurnie, has young Kirsty been feeling off-colour lately?"

Rhylla bit her lip. Knowing this discussion was inevitable and probably long overdue did nothing to make the subject any easier. Mrs. Barnes would have had to be deaf not to have heard Kirsty vomiting each morning over the past two months. Mrs. Barnes was not deaf – nor was she dense.

"Mrs. Barnes, some weeks ago, well months now, I guess, Kirsty was drugged and raped by an unknown man." She composed her conscience – the man had been unknown to Kirsty and herself. "It appears the worst outcome has descended upon our girl and she has been left pregnant." Rhylla took up the silver teaspoon and stirred her teacup in unending circles. "Robbie and I chose not to report it to the police knowing how the law treats the victims in such instances. As you are no doubt aware, the girls involved are nearly always put through such an uncivilized grilling – not to mention being painted as the guilty party." Rhylla sipped at her tea. She struggled to contain the threatening tears. Mrs. Barnes reached her arm across the table and held her employer's hand.

"I'm so sorry, Mrs. MacBurnie. If I can help in any way, you only have to ask."

Rhylla gave her a wan smile.

"Robbie is away on his research trip but he is also hoping to trace the whereabouts of the man." She felt her face flush at this blatant lie told to a good friend of many years. But how could she tell Mrs. Barnes, Robbie had killed the man right in this very house and disposed of the body at some hidden site. No, those that need to be told including Mrs. Barnes and Mr. Evans – although he need not be told until much later – should only be told the bare essentials, similar to the information given to Kirsty herself. Having told Mrs. Barnes, she must now tell her parents as soon as possible – but how? Rhylla craved desperately to tell her father everything. He had always been her tower of support before her marriage to Robbie. But now Robbie was missing and his situation unknown. She needed the common sense and strength of her father. On the other hand, what was she to do if he insisted the police were to be involved?

Rhylla stroked Mrs. Barnes's hand in a silent gesture of thanks.

"Mrs. Barnes, I'm sure there is no need to remind you that what we have discussed within this house must always remain within this house."

"Of course, Mrs. MacBurnie. My lips are sealed."

Mrs. Jackson, Hoppy Davis and the man they knew as Rob Bains stood at the front verandah watching in the distance the three hundred head of bullocks and spayed cows being led out by Billy and corralled closely by the head drover, Trevor, with two of his regular ringers on one side and Edith, Evie and Steve on the other. This herd was off to the railhead at Cloncurry on their way to the Townsville meatworks. Edith and Evie were to accompany the cattle on the journey east before they had to return to their duties at the hospital. Dust rose around them in a long cloud. Occasional flashes of the bright colours of the drover's shirts and neckerchiefs caught the eye. Splitting cracks of the whips were heard at irregular intervals as the riders attempted to control any noncompliance within the herd not happy at being pressured into a controlled journey like this. The short sharp barks of the two dogs they had with them lifted in the dust cloud as they also imposed their will upon the beasts.

The camp cook with his team of packhorses loaded with supplies for this relatively short trip had left earlier along with the horse-tailer and spare horses. Between them, they were to prepare a mid-day campsite and hobble the horses in feed.

"Minnie, if you don't need me for anything around the house here, I'll get down to the yards to give the Boss a hand. Trevor will be back within two weeks and if we don't shake a leg those cattle going down to the Darling Downs will not be ready to leave."

"Yes, Hoppy, you get along."

Rob rubbed his shoulder as he turned around.

"How're your wounds doing, Rob?"

"Good thanks, Minnie. Much better since you took the stitches out the other day." He rubbed his hand over his head. "I've even grown a pelt on my skull. Billy says it's a lot greyer than it was though." He laughed.

"Do you feel up to teaching me more on those book-keeping systems we started yesterday?"

"Yes, of course, but I'm not sure if I'm right. I don't even know how I know anything about book-keeping. Perhaps you should wait and talk to your accountant first."

"That will take forever. He lives in Cloncurry and we only get to see him come the end of the financial year – which may end up being the beginning of the next year. He has a wide area of business."

"Well, of course, I'll help where I can."

"William says you must have done similar work wherever you come from. He says you're not the everyday miner-bloke. He told me you always open the newspapers at the business reports and share-prices pages. He believes you have book-keeping or business in your background somewhere."

"Hopefully, one day, I'll open my eyes and I'll remember everything." His unseeing gaze flowed over the plains. "While Trevor's away, I'd better forget riding the office chair and get a bit of practice in riding a horse if I'm to go on this droving trip with them next month. I see a raw butt and many aches and pains in my future."

"I'm sure William would be glad to offer you a position as bookkeeper if you wish." Minnie Jackson went off to the kitchen laughing.

CHAPTER THIRTEEN

It had been ten days since Jim Sullivan received notification from the Mount Isa Mines and the letter from the hospital Superintendent regarding his friend's accident and outcome. He sat in the private bar of the Mount Isa Hotel sipping a whiskey and reading a local newspaper he had picked up off the table.

He looked up when Bryan Berryman, his friend from his Sydney University days, arrived. Matching grins flashed across the room. Jim stood and walked over to shake the hand of his visitor.

"Can I get you a drink?"

"No, thanks, Jim. I have the girl bringing one in for me."

Jim placed the paper on the next table and both men sat. They talked for half an hour catching up on each other's news since they had last met. It was Bryan who dragged the conversation to the business at hand.

"So, Jim, the letter you wrote has me intrigued. I spoke to the staffing officer, Turner, Barry Turner, at the mines and he is willing to talk to you if you make an appointment. Based on the little I could tell him, he seems to think the man you spoke of, McInroy, recovered from the wounds received in his accident and departed from the hospital nearly a week later – before the doctor had officially discharged him."

"Thanks, Bryan. I presume there's a taxi hereabouts I'll be able to hire tomorrow to go to the mines office to organize an appointment."

"Well, I've done one better for you. After receiving the telegram sending notice of your arrival time, I have already made you an appointment for tomorrow afternoon at three o'clock."

"Many thanks. I appreciate that, Bryan."

It was several minutes before three when Barry Turner ushered Jim into his cubby hole of an office in the Mount Isa Mines complex. Even though the night had been quite cool, Jim now found himself perspiring under his suit coat in the warm Western Queensland day. The man matched Jim in height. He wore a hard-wearing material shirt and trousers and leather boots covered in dark clay soil.

"Can I offer you any refreshments? Cup of tea or something cooler?" Barry Turner pulled out the visitor's chair at his desk.

Jim sat resting his dark tailored hat on a knee. "Thanks. A glass of water would be a blessing. I appreciate your giving up your time like this to help me in my endeavours, Mr. Turner." Jim pondered the inflection of an accent in the man's speech but thought it might be impolite to ask his origin.

"Always pleased to help. I had the office girl bring out Mr. McInroy's file. I understand you're a solicitor yourself, is that correct?"

"Yes, I have a business in Townsville."

"This has been a long journey for you to make in your search for McInroy."

"The man is a good friend. I need to locate him for his family."

The discussion of McInroy's employment at the mines and the subsequent accident revealed little more to Jim than what Bryan Berryman had told him last night. The man did have one snippet of information which interested Jim – the address at which Rob

MacBurnie as Greg McInroy had stayed during his employment at the mines.

"The boarding house where McInroy stayed belonged to the miner who was killed in the incident alongside him," Barry Turner went on to say.

Jim felt a cold shiver run down his spine. He had been unaware that anyone had been killed in the same accident. *How close had Robbie come to dying too?*

"Will you be able to give me the address of the boarding house?"

"No trouble." Turner was already scribbling a note on a piece of paper torn from his notebook. "Now, there is one more thing, Jim." Barry turned the pages in the file in front of him. "Our Pay-master delivered some wages owing to your friend while he was in the hospital. There will be further money coming his way in the not-too-distant future. As we have no other address but yours, will you see he gets it when he turns up again?"

"Yes, of course."

The men said a cordial farewell. Mr. Turner invited Jim back if he thought there was anything else to be gained from further discussions.

Outside in the grass-bare landscape in front of the mine's office, Jim stood in the feeble shade of a lone stunted tree. The noise of the mining machinery pounded inside his head. Dust and smoke hung in the air clogging up his nostrils. His taxi driver had promised to return at four o'clock which was only fifteen minutes away. He contemplated the option of walking down the gravel road and across the unsteady footbridge over the Leichardt River near where further dust billowed up from the bridge-works in progress. He shucked off his coat and hung it over his forearm and prepared to wait.

During his short stay in the town, he had noticed how the people were more relaxed about time and he was not surprised to find it was nearly half-past four before the taxi rattled up beside him.

"G'day, mate. How'd yer go? Get everything you wanted, hey?"

"Would it be too much trouble to take me to this address?" Jim handed over the note but was not too sure if the driver could read the words. He repeated the address aloud himself.

"Yeah, of course. It's only just over the town, hey."

Jim's grip on the door threatened to bend the metal as the vehicle made a furious attack on the detour across the river. Water splashed up over the bonnet and the sides of the car.

"What happens in the wet season. Will the creek flood?"

"That's a river – the Leichhardt River. The mines have big vehicles to get their supplies across but the workers cross over the walking bridge nearby." The man lifted his hand from the bouncing steering wheel reflecting every rock on the track over which they drove. He waved it towards the fragile-looking footbridge. Jim cringed. "The Council says the bridge's almost finished which will be a good thing."

Dust spurted out from under their wheels when the taxi pulled up outside a two-storied unpainted timber structure.

"That's the place, Mister. Mrs. Bonanno runs the show, hey. She's a widow – a right dragon I understand. Runs it with the help of two Chinee men, hey." The taxi driver appeared ready to offer further information on the administration of the place but paused when Jim made to exit the car. "Do yer want me to pick yer up later?"

"No thanks, Driver. I can see my hotel just over there. I'll walk back."

Sophie Bonanno's thoughts wandered as she moved the broom back and forth across the floor. The same thoughts which had kept her awake at night for weeks. *What had happened to the nice Mr. McInroy? Did Uncle Matt complete the task she refused to take on? Had he killed the man? But then what had he done with the body?*

How long would it be before Molly Lynch sent a new man to end her own life? The movement of the broom ceased as her hand rested on the swelling of her abdomen.

"Little baby, believe me, you don't want the life your father and I had and I don't know if I can protect you on my own."

Sophie's head lifted at the sound of the screech of the front gate. *The Lings can't be back from the shopping yet? I wonder what they've forgotten this time?* She rested the handle of the broom against the wall and moved over to lift the curtain aside, just a fraction, to peek out through the front window. She watched the stranger as he walked towards the front door. This was not the usual applicant who came knocking on her door seeking board and lodging. Her usual customers were men from the mines or shop assistants from the town and sometimes the railway or council workers or postal workers. This middle-aged man of medium height and build was dressed in an expensive dark suit with a matching hat. Despite the dust on his shoes, one could see even at this distance they were accustomed to a regular polishing. Her heart began to thud inside her chest. This man looked very much like a city man – maybe from Sydney. *Had Molly Lynch sent her henchman already? It had been less than a month since Uncle Matt had left.*

When the knock rattled the front door, Sophie froze. Her hand once more fell to curve around her abdomen. The broom fell with a clatter to the floor. The curtain dropped back into place. A hand slapped across her lips to prevent the scream. She whimpered. The knock sounded again. Sophie drew herself up to her full five-foot-five inches and pushed the strands of hair back under the black scarf on her head. Her hands whipped off the apron at her waist before they swept down the black smock she wore. She moved to open the front door. It opened with a squeak to match the front gate.

"Can I help you?" She was thankful to hear her voice did not quaver even though her heart pummelled against her rib cage.

"Good morning, Missus. I'm Jim Sullivan. I'm a solicitor from Townsville. I'm here looking for my friend … er…Greg McInroy. I understand he boarded here while he was working at the mines – before he had the accident."

Sophie leant heavily against the door frame. *Was this really a solicitor from Townsville or was this Molly Lynch's man? If it was Molly Lynch's man, was he really here for Greg or her?* She stared into the visitor's eyes for long minutes. With more years than she wanted to remember of living in the world of men, she had learnt to sum up a stranger. The name Jim Sullivan flashed in her head. The name she had read on the stamped envelope found hidden in the curtain-hem in Greg's room after he had disappeared. The letter which had convinced her Greg and his belongings did not leave of his own free will. If so, he would have taken and posted the letter he had concealed so well.

"Are you all right, Missus?" Jim's gaze ran over the woman slumped against the door. He took in the swollen belly partly concealed beneath her dark loose dress. "Can I help you?" The woman continued to stare at him without saying a word. He stepped back away from the door. "Will I get you some help?"

With a noisy drawn breath, Sophie dragged herself upright. "No. I think you'd better come in out of the hot sun, Mr. Sullivan." Sophie had still not decided whether to hand over the letter or not but she wanted to hear more about this man and about Greg McInroy.

After she said goodbye and shut the door behind Mr. Sullivan, Sophie pondered her reason why she had not mentioned the fact that two other boarders had left the same day as Greg McInroy. Steve and Billy were infrequent but welcome customers of her establishment and had been friends with Greg, but they had left early on that particular day to return to their father's property. Greg did not disappear until late the same night as she understood it. Maybe it had been a coincidence, but on the other hand, maybe there was a connection. One she wished to keep to herself just in case this Mr. Jim Sullivan was not who he said he was. If Greg was still alive then she was not going to be responsible for aiding his demise. Look at the curse such action had brought upon her last time.

On his return to the hotel, Jim rushed into the bathroom where he sponged his sweaty body. The clean shirt felt cool upon his skin. He looked at his watch. It was time to meet the doctor in the hotel lounge. As he walked down the stairs, he patted the envelope in the top pocket of his coat. It would have to wait until after this next interview.

A rotund man in his late fifties with greying hair arrived just as Jim settled into a chair. He stood again and shook hands in greeting. "Jim Sullivan, thanks for seeing me, Doctor."

The man smiled revealing stained teeth beneath an untrimmed moustache. "Yes, Doctor Neatly, but call me Ben, son."

Before they sat the barmaid arrived with the drinks. "I presumed you'd be wanting your usual, Doc?"

"Thanks, girl, I will."

"And I've brought the same for you, Mr. Sullivan. Is that okay?" She placed a glass of whisky in front of each of the men.

"Thanks, yes. Put them both on my tab, please."

"Yes, Sir. Will you gentlemen be eating with us tonight? Cook does an Irish stew on Thursdays"

Jim looked over at the doctor. "Will you join me for tea?"

"I certainly will, Jim. The cook here is renowned for his Irish stew and he makes a loaf of bread to curl your toes – many people eat here for his bread alone."

"Thanks, Miss. We'll have two meals. What time will the dining room open?"

"It's open at the moment if you'd like to make your way there."

Later after the two men had eaten and the doctor had been called away to a hospital emergency, Jim sat sipping the last of his drink. As he went through in his mind what Ben had told him regarding Robbie's accident and treatment, Jim realized there had been little new in what the man had said. The doctor had stressed he had felt quite confident Greg McInroy had been of sound mind and not acting on a decision made with a damaged brain when he exited the hospital. He found some reassurance in this sliver of information.

Jim made his way upstairs to his room. As he removed his coat the crinkle of paper reminded him of the envelope awaiting his attention. He drew it out and used the pencil lying on the bedtable to help open the seal. As he did so, goosebumps flittered across his skin. These words had been written a short time before the mine accident. Was Robbie now alive or dead? It had been over two weeks since Robbie had disappeared. Are these words the last Robbie was ever to write? Two smaller envelopes were extracted – one with Rhylla's name on the top and the other with Kirsty's name on the front. He spread out the sheet of paper written to himself.

Dear Jim,

I was pleased to collect your last note at the Post Office. It was great to hear you have been able to catch up with Doug Hampson. How is our good Sergeant doing these days? I don't know if I'll ever be able to look our friend in the eyes again after this shemozzle. Even better news to hear the police are convinced my brother Greg has caught a train west.

With that news at hand, I am planning on finishing up at the mines at the end of this week and heading back home. I'm sure the blisters on my hands will be pleased. I'll need to take a circuitous route home which may take an extra couple of days but it will be worth it to ensure the family is safe.

Jim if I live forever, I'll never be able to repay everything I owe you for these past six weeks.

Forever in your debt
Robbie

CHAPTER FOURTEEN

Four weeks had passed since Robbie MacBurnie, now known as Rob Bains, had stood at the front of the house seeing off the herd of cattle for the Cloncurry railhead. Today, layers of dust settled upon his head and shoulders as he tailed the mob, with Trevor Jackson in charge, bound for the Roma area. His body swayed with the gait of the horse. His gaze took in the wide plains towards a range of low hills far to the east. Anxious fingers adjusted his blue neckerchief more firmly over his nose and lower face. A vague twitch of pain pulled at the muscles along the back of his neck and shoulder but he felt comfortable in the saddle. The past few weeks of exercising a few of the horses had built his confidence enough to believe horse riding was not something altogether new to him, but no amount of searching his mind revealed any answers.

A smaller cloud of dust hung over the horse-tailer Eddie Burkett and his off-sider, the magical black man they called Puffer, leading a mob of sixty horses to be used by the ringers over the next few months of droving.

Rob understood why everyone called Puffer, the magic man with horses. He had witnessed the man breaking in a horse only a few days ago. Puffer stood barely five foot six inches tall even if put through a clothes wringer and stretched to his limit. Wiry, was the only term to describe the lean chap whose skin was pure black velvet. He always dressed in black clothes. With his black felt hat pulled low on his head only the occasional glint of the whites of his eyes was seen. Rob recalled his shock at seeing the large patch of snow-white hair above the man's right eye when Puffer had lifted his hat to scratch his head.

Two ringers had hazed an outlaw horse into the round yard where Puffer was to teach the animal some manners. Muscles rippled along the body of the grey beast when it tossed its head and mane sending up a snort of anger and frustration. Dust puffs rose from the restless feet as the horse trotted backwards and forwards across the far arc of the yard. A sudden crash of the back hooves against the timber filled the air each time the horse struck out in protest and fear. Puffer remained perfectly still and straight on the opposite side of the circle about four yards in from the rails. He appeared not to be even breathing.

The outlaw horse paced. It snorted and kicked out.

Puffer stood unmoving.

Men outside the ring walked across softly to peer through the rails. Not a word was spoken. This was not the first time most of them had seen Puffer in action but the awe on their faces filled the gaps in the panels of the stockyards.

The grey outlaw stopped its pacing. It swung to face the silent man on the other side of the round yard. It snorted and tossed its head before standing for long minutes – watching. It threw up its head again and snorted with venom before standing silently, once more – staring at the black man.

But the black man did not move a muscle. A hot sun burned down from an unrelenting blue sky.

A grey offside front foot stamped at the ground. Thump, thump, thump, thump, thump. Dust puffs rose and fell quickly. The grey mane flew up into the air when the animal shook its head. This time without the trumpeting call of defiance. A rumble sounded deep inside the grey barrel of a chest. The outlaw feinted four steps forward in the direction of the immobile Puffer. The black man in black clothing did not flinch. The whites of his eyes remained hidden within the surrounding black of his skin and the shadow of his hat.

The horse feinted again – further this time – nearly halfway across the round yard. It stopped. The grey coat quivered. Wild eyes glared at the black shadow sharing the round yard.

Rob had not heard the black man's soft singing at first. The voice seemed to come out of nowhere. A quiet dirge of music. A repetitive range of only a few notes. The black man did not move his stance.

The grey horse retreated a few steps towards the far rail. It then rushed forwards – six fast steps before skidding to a halt. The music remained unchanged. The man remained unmoved.

Inch by slow inch, with stiff-legged steps, the horse moved closer to the man in black.

The music flow mingled with short sharp puffs of air from the black man's mouth.

The horse stopped moving forwards. As the regal head swung back and forth, the mane created a halo around the skull. A soft snicker shuffled the velvet muzzle.

The music and short puffs of air from the black man continued.

The outlaw's neck stretched forward to its full length but the four hooves of the large animal remained planted.

Slow whistles of puffing breaths flowed over the animal's nostrils.

One by one the legs moved the animal closer to Puffer who, between his musical notes, continued to blow his breath into the wide nostrils.

The equine head moved in close to smell the man of magic. The grey skin shivered across the animal's body.

The music, the air puffs and now gentle hands caressed the sides of the horse's face.

As Rob recalled the moment, a smile dislodged the dust resting on the neckerchief over the lower half of his face. It had all been so different from another type of horse-breaking he had witnessed the previous week. Three horses had been bagged down in the stockyards one day before being left bridled there overnight to think over their options. The next day everyone came out to witness the impromptu rodeo exhibition when each horse was saddled in the crush and let out with a rider on its back. This was repeated each morning for three days. On the fourth day, the horses with the riders once more in the saddle raced through the sandy bed of the creek nearby until the backs of man and horse were white with sweat. This process was repeated for another three days before the horses were declared ready to be ridden for mustering. Dust fell from the neckerchief again when a grin broke across Rob's face as he recalled the further impromptu short-lived rodeo displays each morning for several days after.

The yell of a rider drew Rob's attention to the even smaller dust cloud which hung suspended above Spud Murphy, the camp cook, who with his offsider, a native boy of about fifteen, named Sunshine, guided the dozen packhorses carrying the droving camp necessities.

These two smaller clouds of dust above the horse-tailer and the camp cook travelled faster than the grazing mob of seven hundred and fifty bullocks – passing them to the east between the herd and the distant low range of hills.

"How's it going, Rob?" Steve slowed his grey horse beside the brown gelding Rob rode. He patted the animal's wither. "Well, we're on our way. It'll take about three or four months to deliver this lot to Rosebud Flats – that's my Dad's place south-east of Roma."

"G'day, Steve. I'm okay, thanks." Rob lifted his hat and raked his fingers through hair wet with sweat. "Trevor was saying the horse-tailer had just returned from checking the state of the waterholes along this stock route we're to follow."

"Yeah, we're a bit late this year taking these boys to Roma for fattening up before catching the southern sales. We do the trip every two or three years and we like to get away before June but with one thing and another, we're a bit slow off the mark. Trevor was concerned about the state of the usual waterholes so late in the season and what grasses, if any, were left on the stock route. Eddie seems to be happy with everything. He says they've had average rainfall this year down that way."

Many interruptions filled Rob's first night of sleeping out under the stars. He watched the progress of the waxing moon across the sky for long periods. The ground over which his thin swag spread seemed to develop lumps and bumps as the night progressed. Not only did the unfamiliar earthy mattress digging into his back keep sleep at bay, but also the lumps of questions and bumps of possibilities swirling within the hollow echoes of his empty memory which refused to allow his mind any peace.

When and where in his life had he developed a familiarity with horseback riding? Probably not in a droving camp or he'd be snoring like the other bodies strewn across the ground nearby.

The constant question first posed at Far Horizons returned to hound him. Where and when had he learned to understand the bookkeeping and accounting process his knowledge of which had become apparent when helping Minnie Jackson in the store?

After a hot day, the night air drifted in cold and calculating. It penetrated deep into Rob's lungs and under any gap left between the one blanket and his body. He wrapped the swag canvas around himself, his blanket and his kitbag pillow. He draped his newly acquired Bluey coat over his head and shoulders. Muscles unused to working constantly in the saddle screamed their protest. The recent wounds acquired at the Mount Isa Mines set up a constant ache.

The cattle kept the guardians on the alert as the first two, two-hour shifts of ringers circled. The stock craved their own familiar cattle camps and were not content with this strange unknown country. Small half-hearted rushes of the animals threatened but soon passed over.

The quiet sounds of the midnight shift of ringers moving around the herd, one singing and the other making soft music with a mouth organ, fell upon the campsite before Rob's eyes fell shut. It seemed only a moment later they opened to the sound of Eddie, the horse-tailer, shoving a log on the fire to re-heat the billy of stewed tea leaves. Three-thirty in the morning with no sign of the picaninny dawn and it was time for Eddie and Puffer to bring up the fresh horses for the new day.

The next sounds were those of Sunshine, the cook's helper, kneading the flour and water to make the dampers for the day ahead. Spud Murphy, the cook, dragged the pot containing the salted beef, which had been simmering in water overnight, onto the flame where it would finish its cooking process. Meals to feed the hungry men in the day ahead.

Liberal amounts of plum jam or syrup softened the leftover damper toasted over the coals for the four o'clock shift of two ringers before they headed out to take their turn around the grinding circumference of the still resting herd. Thick black sugared tea helped it on its way.

The aroma of the freshly cooked damper next stirred Rob. He struggled to unwind his body from the knotted binds of his swag. The billy of tea had been freshened.

"I'll have a top-up of that too, Rob." Trevor held his pannikin up for a refill of tea. "How'd you like to ride up in the lead with me this morning? We don't want your lungs to fill up with the dust, do we?" He laughed.

A glimmer of light edged the eastern horizon.

Curiosity filled Rob's eyes as he watched and followed Trevor riding a dancing brown gelding. Trevor's loyal cattle dog followed interesting odours nearby but never too far away from the heels of the horse on which Trevor sat. Firstly, they rode back along the track on which they had come into camp the previous night. The man's eyes searched the ground around them.

Eventually, Rob had to ask. "What are you looking for, Trevor?"

"What do you see?"

Rob stared down at the smooth dust scattered with patches of browned grasses. "Nothing."

"That's right. We haven't had any cattle sneaking out this way during the night. We run a few branches over the ground where the cattle arrive into the camp and then in the morning, we look for hoofprints heading back to where we have come from."

Rob took several moments pondering the simplicity of this logic until Trevor began to speak again.

"We'll take a wide sweep around the herd to see if there are any tell-tale signs in either direction before we take up the lead and move things along." He nodded towards his dog. "Bluey there will likely pick up the scent of a wandering beast before we can see any hoof signs."

Rob nodded. His eyes widened in surprise – not only at the knowledge imparted. He had never heard Trevor speak so much in one day before.

In the cool morning, the cattle shuffled to their feet. Dust lifted from their coats as they shivered themselves awake. Occasional bellows erupted in protest at the disturbance.

The sun exploded over the horizon and the day's journey began.

It was mid-morning before Rob noticed the mob of horses with Eddie and Puffer in close attendance passing in the distance. A short time later Spud Murphy and Sunshine appeared on either end of the line of packhorses loaded with the camp supplies.

Kirsty's eyes opened. Something had disturbed her sleep but she did not know what. As her heart pounded in her chest the breath caught in her throat. A soft mewing sound escaped quivering lips. Her panicked gaze discovered nothing out of the ordinary in the faint glow of the moonlight within her curtained room. And then Kirsty heard it. She froze. Her ears strained to hear the noise again. After some moments, she realized it had been the sound of sobbing coming from her mother's room.

She threw her dressing gown around her shoulders and slid her cold feet into the slippers beside the bed. Kirsty stood paralyzed with shock to see, in the moonlight streaming through the gap in the front curtains, the body of her mother drawn up into a tight ball wrapped around two pillows which served to stifle most of the noise from Rhylla's gut-wrenching sobs.

Kirsty's tentative hand reached over and held her mother's shoulder. "Mum, oh, Mum, whatever is the matter? Please don't cry. Please tell me how I can help?" The young woman sat on the bed and threaded her arms about her mother. "Please, let me help?" Tears choked her entreaties.

The sobs ceased on a drawn breath. Rhylla began to unwind herself. "Darling, I am sorry to have disturbed you. I'm fine, really. Just having a weak moment. I'm sorry."

Kirsty lay down beside her mother and drew the covers up over them both. She held the older woman tight. "Are you missing Daddy? It'll be alright, you'll see. It's been over three months since he left on this research trip and he doesn't usually stay away longer than that. He'll be home soon."

Rhylla hugged her daughter in return. "Of course, he will, my darling." Her one hand slid under the pillow to touch the letters delivered by Jim Sullivan almost a month ago on his return from his search in Mount Isa. "Of course, he will." She rolled over to look at Kirsty. "What are you doing up and about in the middle of the night? Can't you sleep? Will I make you a warm cocoa drink?"

Later, as Kirsty snuffled in sleep on the bed beside her, Rhylla once again reached under her pillow to touch the letter to herself and the one to Kirsty. The last letters written by her beloved Robbie before his mine accident, hospitalization, memory loss and now disappearance.

With one hand unconsciously stroking the old scar on her right leg, Rhylla recalled the words tattooed in her mind, never to be forgotten.

My Darling Rhylla

Have received a very welcome letter from Jim who reports the police are convinced Greg MacBurnie has headed west towards Mount Isa via train. Tomorrow will be my last shift in the mine before I leave to make a convoluted pathway home. Home to my family – to those I love most in this world.

Sweetheart, I have missed you more than words can possibly describe. If I haven't told you before, I love you more than life itself.

The next couple of days until we can hold each other again will drag but knowing you are waiting for me will give me the strength to carry on.

Your ardent slave forever
Robbie

The clock ticked the hours away as Rhylla struggled with the decision of whether she should give Kirsty the last letter from her father. It seemed cruel for her to be told he was heading home and then to be told he was possibly wandering lost and alone out in the spinifex of the Queensland bush.

Her thoughts replayed repeatedly her conversation with Jim Sullivan when he returned with the correspondence which had been so full of hope for an ending to Robbie's journey. Should they tell the police of his dilemma or not. She strove to organize her rambling thoughts.

She must remember Robbie's reason for going to Mount Isa in the first place. He had wanted to divert the police attention away from the dead body of his brother, Greg.

Rhylla recalled Robbie relaying to her the conversation he had with Doug Hampson on that dreadful morning after Robbie's brother's body had been dispatched to the bottom of the quarry. Doug warned Robbie of the news he had received via the police grapevine. It was not only the New South Wales police and the Queensland police who were searching for his brother Greg MacBurnie but also the Sydney gangsters who wanted the man dead.

The doctor had told Jim Sullivan the patient he knew as Greg McInroy appeared to be organized and in charge of his senses when he left the hospital.

Fear clenched her heart as she remembered it was her Robbie who had spent the last few months living the life of Greg MacBurnie and laying himself out like bait on a plate for all interested parties.

Her mind clung to the knowledge that Robbie was doing what he believed to be the only way to protect her and the family. She knew he was not a killer by nature. In fact, he was the gentlest of men she knew. A tentative smile rested briefly on her lips. Well, perhaps not when he was playing the tennis finals – then he was out to win at all costs.

She also clung to the thought that the doctor believed Robbie was rational when he left the hospital. If so, Robbie must have had a plan in his head and he should make it home soon.

No, they must not tell the police of Robbie's circumstances.

To tell the police meant everything Robbie had attempted would be all for nothing. Within the blink of an eye, her husband could be locked in a jail cell for murder.

Rhylla massaged her pillow into submission and rolled onto her side to attempt sleep once again but her mind about-faced and begged the question. *What if the gangsters have taken Robbie, thinking he was Greg?* Common sense, even though unwanted, told her if such a thing were the case, Robbie would already be dead.

Rhylla shoved her fist into her mouth to silence the sob as it struggled to escape. She lay still hoping her restlessness had not disturbed her daughter.

CHAPTER FIFTEEN

They were nearing the third week of the trip. Rob's sleeping pattern had improved. Having taken an occasional turn relieving the others during the night shifts, he found his eyes slammed shut and his brain turned off as soon as he rolled into his swag. Rob once again ended up riding in the lead beside Trevor. He felt pleased to find the man not as prickly as he had first thought.

"Trevor, how come we've not had any problems with the cattle stampeding? I've heard the men talking of trips they've been on where the cattle were forever giving them trouble."

"Bullocks and spayed cows are the worst at that, for sure. We're lucky with this lot because they've only ever been on Far Horizons and have been handled a fair bit. I always keep them moving the first couple of days though – until they settle down into the routine. Some of the stuff we've taken out of the Northern Territory and the Gulf have been trouble from day one. They've come straight out of the scrub country, you see. They rush at the least excuse, day or night. We had to tell Spud he wasn't to fart anymore. It sounded like cannon fire. After one night's rush, we spent days searching for the damn animals."

Rob looked at Trevor not knowing if he told the truth or not. "You're kidding, right?"

Trevor shrugged his shoulders. "You know, I don't think a copper asks as many questions as you do, Rob?" Trevor grinned as he removed the hat from his head and belted it on his thigh. Dust fell to the ground. The horse beneath him flicked an ear but judged the noise nothing to get excited about and continued its brisk walk ahead of the herd. "You sure you're not a copper?"

Rob gave a wry grin in return. "Trevor, I'm not sure of anything but for some reason, the thought of possibly being a copper does nothing to stir my instincts."

"Well, it won't hurt this crew to think you might be. I've never known them to be so well-behaved and I've known them all a long time. Eddie and Spud worked as horse-tailer and camp cook with my father in his last couple of years on the track. Billy and Steve, you already know. Brother and cousin, they may be but I wouldn't put it past them to break a few minor rules, nothing too eye-watering, if the urge took them."

"They're only young yet. Isn't trouble what all young'uns get into occasionally?"

Trevor grinned again. "Yeah, you're right there. Struth, if my dad had known all we got up to in our teens, not one of us three would have escaped a kick in the bum until our noses bled on more than one occasion." Trevor stared off into the distance for some moments savouring his memories. "The blokes are dead curious about what you're writing in those books of yours every spare minute of the day, too."

Rob rubbed the back of his neck. A flush rushed across his face beneath the layer of dust. "I just write about stuff I see each day. Mostly about the country we pass through or the things the cattle or horses get up to. I'm always hoping for things that may lead me to remember who I was and where I came from. That sort of stuff mostly." He did not mention how he found this urge he had to write and his style of writing stirred his curiosity. Had he been a writer or journalist for a newspaper? He laughed to lighten the moment before asking another question. "See those hills way off to our left," Rob pointed with his arm, "Are we heading in that direction?"

"We'll follow them around to the south a bit. We'll water on the Hamilton River a few days and then head east on the Boulia-Winton connection track. Near Winton, we'll turn south towards Longreach."

"Back at Far Horizons, your father was telling me the government is in the process of reviewing the stock routes in Queensland with a plan to improve facilities and watering sites."

"Yeah, I believe so. But if it's all the same to them, I'll trust the instincts of someone like Eddie Burkett before I'd take much notice of someone who hardly ever sees the sunshine or a cloud of dust."

Trevor clicked his tongue and encouraged his horse to break to the right. Three large bullocks had moved away from the general herd. With heads down and heels more in the air than on the ground, they set up a determined show of argy-bargy. Their bellows rose on the air along with the dust ploughed up by their hooves.

"You keep going straight ahead, Rob," he called back. With a minimum of effort, Trevor and his mount along with the blue dog returned the recalcitrant trio back into the mob.

Rob watched the gradual appearance of a tree-line some distance ahead. The sun hung high in a clear sky. He thought this might be a sign of water or at least the midday campsite.

Rob's assumption had been right. The tree-line did become the dinnertime campsite but the creek bed held no water. Patches of short green grasses still flourished much to the delight of the stock. A large flock of galahs exploded out of the tree branches, their grey and pink plumage colourful as they protested loudly at the intrusion when Eddie and Puffer pushed the spare horses away from the green grass and out onto the drier flats before settling them down with their hobbles in place.

Having no designated chores assigned to him, Rob helped Spud serve out the meals to the ringers as they dribbled in after settling the beasts to rest in the heat of the day. As usual, the meal consisted of corned beef and damper. Today they were treated to dried apricots boiled in a thin custard. While the men were eating, Rob helped Spud collect firewood from around the trees. Some of the wood went back to be used on the current campfire. The cook tied several bundles of wood with thin strips of greenhide. Spud explained to Rob how he liked to carry a few bundles of wood on the packhorses when traversing the plains country.

"Sometimes the wood can be as scarce as hen's teeth out on the treeless plains." He explained.

To date, Rob had little to do with any of the others except Billy, Steve and Trevor but as he worked in the camp, he met the three other ringers working this trip.

Snips was a man said to have escaped the goldfields of Western Australia just ahead of the law. Who would be foolish enough to question a man who spent his spare time sitting with his wide shoulders and muscled arms that tapered to long fingers, hunched over his barber scissors and whetstone? Scrunched up beetled eyebrows above a mouth clenched over the tip of his tongue while his blades scraped, scraped, scraped, on the stone, did not invite curiosity.

It was Snips whose tenor voice serenaded the stock during the nights. He shared his shifts with Turkey, a wiry man with skin sun-hardened to almost the colour of bronze. Black eyes peered out on the world without expression. Billy had warned Rob never to ruffle this man's feathers. His words were few but his grunts were many and his skill with the mouth organ was a joy to hear. The third man, who shared the shifts with Trevor, had been named by his fellow workers as Streak – a tall, skinny bloke whose appearance belied the strength and endurance of the man. His hands were never still except when sleeping and that was only for brief moments of day or night. His leathercraft was a delight to examine and told of a man who gave attention to detail.

The whistle of a kite hawk drew Rob's gaze to the western sky. The magnificent bird drifted high on the thermal currents with only a minimal twitch of its body to maintain balance and direction. Rob stood enthralled. Black sauce dribbled from the salted meat lying limp on the slab of damper in his hand – forgotten. The dark liquid ran down his fingers.

The quiet voice of Puffer spoke at his side. "Before he die, my father say the whistling hawk carry messages – sometimes warnings. My father spirit now fly with the hawk."

Puffer and Rob stood in the scant shade of a lonely tree – the uncovered skin of the deeply suntanned white man only a few shades lighter than the skin of the black man standing at his side. They welcomed the brief relief from a sun blazing down upon the dried grasses.

Both men continued to chew on their food while their gazes remained fixed on the majesty above them.

"How do you know if the hawk brings a warning or a message?"

"The old people know."

When the heat of the sun began to ease, Trevor had the men and herd back on their feet leading off in a south-easterly direction. Tonight, there would be no water for the cattle. The men were on alert expecting complaints from within the herd. It was to be a dry night camp and no waterholes until lunchtime the following day.

Eddie and Puffer, with the horses, made an early exit with Spud and Sunshine and the loaded packhorses, not too far behind. In the faint glow of the promised morning light, Trevor watched them move out. They were to reach the next waterhole with time to water the spare horses and packhorses and bring them back away from the waterhole area to set up a camp.

With any luck, the entire herd would have slaked their thirst before the winter sun dropped below the horizon. He planned on bringing the cattle to the water in mobs of twenty or thirty head allowing the beasts to drink without danger of being drowned or bogged by the weight of the complete herd behind them. Snips and Turkey had been allocated the task of controlling the freshly watered cattle in an area not too far from their night's campsite. Trevor, Streak and Steve had the chore of drafting out the smaller numbers for Rob and Billy to take at a steady pace to the water. While Rob and Billy played nursemaid to the smaller group, Trevor, Streak and Steve had to hold the remaining thirsty cattle back in an area about two miles away.

From within the mob of spare horses grazing on the plain well away from the watering stock, Eddie and Puffer selected spare horses for the men working the cattle. They were mindful of how each ringer had his own string of horses and did not take kindly to being handed an unfamiliar animal. For many, this might seem an impossible task but this pair of horse-tailers knew every horse in their charge, their good points and their faults, their colours of every shade, their brands, scars, lumps and bumps.

With their selection complete they mounted their own animals and led the bridled horses towards the cattle herd still waiting to drink. The cattle churned around in circles. The clouds of dust their hooves stirred up swirled away to the north. Their bellows of protest rolled across the land drowning out all other noises. Trevor, Streak and

Steve rode back and forth across the face of the mob cracking their whips above the heads of the determined leaders.

Trevor was the first to gallop across to join Eddie's and Puffer's small group of relieving horses. With the smoothness of a ballroom dancer, he jumped to the ground, turned, and released the saddle lifting it in his arms ready to slip on the back of the horse Puffer led over in a trot. Effortlessly the saddle was secured and Trevor swung up onto the back of his fresh mount. His one hand patted the animal's withers while calm words steadied his gait as they galloped back to take up deterrent duties across the face of the herd. Streak and Steve replaced their flagging mounts with no less grace and speed.

The horse-tailers caught up with Billy and Rob as they returned to the larger mob to collect the next twenty beasts. Rob's speed in the change of horses did not match Billy's but his grace did not shame him in any way either.

Leading the five dusty and sweating horses, Puffer made his way further up the creek to where a small deep waterhole big enough for a few horses to access lay half-hidden beside the bole and exposed roots of a large tree. The trunk and upper branches of the tree hung out over the dry creek bed. Puffer wiped water over the coats of the exhausted animals.

Eddie continued with the final fresh horses to the watered cattle grazing contentedly on the plain. Snips and Turkey wasted no time mounting their fresh rides before Eddie watered the tired animals and led them to the remaining mob of spare horses. Like Puffer, he removed their bridles and settled them with their hobbles in the pasture of the plain.

The two men examined the sweaty dusty bridles for any weakness in the leather or buckles. Any not meeting Eddie's high standard were put aside to be repaired after their meal tonight before either man hit his swag.

Kirsty's eyes snapped open. Her fingertips stroked her abdomen. The moonlight draped her bed revealing the young girl's face aglow with a mixture of surprise and excitement. What just happened? Was it a dream? No, it had been real, this strange sensation inside her belly. Kirsty lay quietly wishing to feel it again. After some moments without a repeat of the sensation, Kirsty sat up on the side of the bed and sipped from the glass of water on her bedside table. Sleep had deserted her. She tiptoed into her mother's room.

"Mum, are you awake?"

Rhylla rolled over slowly. "Hmmm yes, Kirsty." Her eyes opened wide. "Kirsty, are you alright?"

A tangible tingle of excitement ran through Kirsty's body. "Mum, I think I felt my baby move. I know you said it would be a couple of weeks yet but I felt it like a tiny mouse running over my skin."

Rhylla laughed softly as she dragged herself higher on the pillows. "I do hope we have not got mice running around our bedrooms. Should I get Mr. Evans, the handyman, in here tomorrow laying mouse traps?"

They both giggled. Rhylla reached out with her finger to touch the dimples in Kirsty's cheeks glowing in the moonlight.

The following weekend, Rhylla stood at the open doorway of the music room. A smile lifted her lips and shone in her eyes as she watched her mother and her daughter playing a duet on the piano. Light fingers flew over the keys in harmony appearing to communicate back and forth in music. The pianists' eyes, filled with laughter and light-hearted enjoyment, sparkled. Pride and contentment filled Rhylla's heart to see Kirsty at peace. But it was nearly time to share their secret with the grandparents. As the music came to a lively ending Rhylla applauded.

"That was wonderful. The pair of you play as one. It's a pleasure to listen to you both together."

Kirsty jumped off the piano stool and ran to hug her mother.

"When you two have finished, afternoon tea is on the table. Go on into the dining room. I'll just collect Father from the office."

"Will Mrs. Barnes not be joining us today, Rhylla?" her mother asked.

"Not this time, Mother, it's her weekend off. She went over to stay with her niece last night. I believe Mr. Evans will collect her and bring her back here after the tennis match this afternoon."

Rhylla poured the tea adding a dollop of cream to both her mother's and father's cups. She stirred in a teaspoon of sugar to each before passing the cups across the table. The knife slipped through the sponge cake. With a slice of cake on each small plate, Rhylla slid them across the tablecloth to join the steaming teacups. Rhylla filled teacups and added cake to plates for both herself and Kirsty. Even her father noticed the scraping of the spoon in the cup that went on for much longer than was necessary.

"Planning on wearing a hole in the china, Lass?"

As much as Rhylla wanted to defer the telling of the news to her parents, she knew this was something that could not be put off a day longer. Her hand snaked over to hold Kirsty's hand firmly.

Rhylla began. "Mother, Dad," she paused. A lump in her throat almost choked her words. She coughed and started again. She glanced at Kirsty. When she saw the trepidation and tears filling her daughter's eyes, she went on firmly. "There is something we have to tell you which will come as a shock to you both." She squeezed Kirsty's hand gently. "Several months ago, an unknown man made his way into the house when Robbie and I were away. This man drugged and raped Kirsty who was here alone for an hour."

The sudden intake of breath from both parents whistled in the quiet room.

"Oh, Kirsty, you poor darling. How dreadful for you. Why did you not tell us at the time?" Mrs. McNeven jumped up from her chair and walked around the table to hold her granddaughter. The tears from both ran freely.

Mr. McNeven's look of disbelief travelled across the table searching for an answer in Rhylla's expression. His head swivelled towards his wife's face; his confused gaze then fell upon his granddaughter.

"Little Kirsty, my dear, I'm sorry."

Both grandparents realized the potential of the ugliness of this news. It flashed in their eyes at the same time.

"Oh, Kirsty," Andrew McNeven began to speak as his glance swung, a pendulum between his daughter and granddaughter. "Rhylla, are you telling us there has been an unwanted outcome to this shocking news?"

"Yes, Dad, Kirsty is pregnant."

The gasp of shocked response filled the room again. Mr. McNeven took a deep breath. Mrs. McNeven sat on the spare chair at the end of the table beside Kirsty.

"What are you going to do?" Beryl McNeven asked.

"Have you found out the man's name, yet? Have the police been told? Are they searching for the rotter?" Her husband asked questions as they formed – his brain in shock.

Rhylla swallowed more than once in an effort to clear her throat before she told the barest of news similar to that having been told to Kirsty. The man drugged and raped their granddaughter. Robbie has gone in search of the man in question under the guise of researching one of his novels. They had not chosen to report it to the police because of the attitudes held by the courts, the public and the press.

Little of the fairy-light cake was eaten. Mangled crumbs remained on the plates.

"Is it too late to have an abortion?" Mrs. McNeven nearly choked on the word.

"Mother, Kirsty believes the baby is not at fault here and Robbie and I agree with this. She plans to have the child and we will bring it up together, here."

"B ... but it will be so hard. People can be very cruel, you know."

"That is one reason why Kirsty has chosen to leave her school. We have the art teacher and music teacher calling here weekly to give lessons."

Kirsty allowed herself to be gathered into her grandmother's arms and led into the sitting room next door. Rhylla, with the help of her father, cleared the remnants of their afternoon tea before they made their way out through the back doorway. A brisk walk along the bridle path which led around the circumference of the long and wide gully behind the property had always helped set the world of Andrew McNeven and his daughter in order. A released valve when stresses mounted.

The winter sun struggled through the foliage of the native trees nudged by a mild sea breeze.

"Have you told the full story, Rhylla?"

Rhylla looked up into her father's face. Her eyes watered. The tears were heard in her reply. "No, Dad, it's not – not by a long shot. I cannot confide in you until you promise me under no circumstances will you repeat what I say – not to anyone – not even to Mother." She sucked in a noisy breath. "Not even the police if they ask. Absolutely nobody."

Father held Rhylla's eyes in his steady gaze. "As you wish, Rhylla, as you wish. You and I have held secrets before within the company business. I'm sure it will be no burden to keep faith with you again."

At this point, rivulets of tears flooded her cheeks. Her father clasped her hand. She held on tightly to what seemed an anchor in an unending storm. Rhylla sucked in air and swiped the moisture from her face. Walking slowly with her eyes downcast she began to tell her father everything.

"On that night when Kirsty was raped, Robbie and I came back from the train station well after dark. We assumed Kirsty was upstairs. I made my way to the kitchen to make a cup of cocoa for us and Robbie ran upstairs to ask Kirsty if she was going to join us. I heard an exclamation and a loud thump and ran up the stairs to find out what had happened. Robbie stood frozen while one hand rubbed the knuckles on his other hand. He stared at the body of a stranger lying beside the chest of drawers in a pool of blood. Robbie's mouth opened and shut, but he could not speak. When I turned to the bed, I discovered Kirsty sound asleep in disarray on the bed."

Andrew McNeven whispered. "Are you saying Robbie killed this man? I don't think I've ever seen him lose his temper, but if it was my daughter, I couldn't say I wouldn't do the same thing."

"Yes, Dad, he did. To make things worse, the man was his brother – the elder brother, Greg. The one who the family never speaks of. All Robbie ever told me – and this was years ago – 'My elder brother is nothing but a troublemaker and a ne'er-do-well.' The last the family had heard of him; he had joined the Merchant Navy a long time ago."

The two walked on for some moments each with their thoughts for company. Rhylla felt the tightened clasp of her father's hand around her own.

"What did Robbie do with the dead man? I guess the police were never told?" He asked.

Strands of loose strawberry-blond hair bounced around her face as Rhylla shook her head. "Robbie dropped his brother and his utility into the deep waters of the quarry. The only one who knows is Jim Sullivan. As far as I know, no one has ever found it since."

Again, silence hung between father and daughter as Andrew analyzed what he had been told. Their steps plodded softly in the dust of the bridle path.

"Am I to assume Robbie is not away on a research trip at all?"

"No, he doesn't want to be here to shame the family when the body is discovered. It was a coincidence on the afternoon before Robbie left, Doug Hampson, Robbie's policeman friend, I'm sure you've met him, spoke to Robbie about his brother Greg. Doug had received word through the police channels. Greg had been thought to be making his way north with the Sydney gangsters and police, from Sydney and Brisbane, on his trail."

Andrew shook his head slowly trying to digest all this information. "So, where did Robbie go?"

"He disguised himself as his brother and caught the train to Mount Isa. He hoped someone would report seeing Greg MacBurnie on the train and divert them away from the dead body."

"Good heavens; that means Robbie would most likely have the police and these Sydney rascals chasing after him."

"Dad, it gets worse. We had been corresponding through Jim. The last we heard from Robbie was some time ago when he, having heard from Jim that the police believed Greg may have been going to Mount Isa, wrote to say he was finishing up at the mines and would be making his way home."

"Where is he now then, Rhylla?"

"Eventually, we received letters from the Mount Isa Mines and the Mount Isa Hospital doctor saying there had been an accident at the mines. A local man was killed and another known as Greg McInroy, who left his next-of-kin information as Jim Sullivan, was badly wounded and has sustained memory loss." Rhylla's voice faded to a choking sob.

"I presume this Greg McInroy is the Greg MacBurnie who, in fact, is our Robbie MacBurnie."

Rhylla could only nod her head in assent.

"So, is he still in the hospital? Can we go and visit him?"

"No, that's the rub. After several days, he walked out – in the middle of the night. No one seems to know where he might be. Jim took a week off and went to Mount Isa to see what he could find out. That was how we received the last letter. Robbie's landlady had found it and gave it to Jim when he called."

"And what did Jim find out?"

"Nothing new. The doctor believes Robbie must have regained his memory because his leaving was quite well planned, it seemed."

"What do you think, Lass?"

The tears flowed freely once more. Rhylla struggled to control her speech.

"We know the police have not found him or Jim would have heard or it may have been in the papers. I believe he is dead." Several loud sobs broke into her story. "I think whoever from the Sydney underworld wanted Greg MacBurnie dead has killed Robbie in mistake for Greg."

"We cannot just assume that, my girl. Robbie would want you to keep positive, I'm sure – at least for Kirsty's sake – particularly now she's pregnant. Robbie might be travelling out west with his memory loss. I've heard of people losing their memory and then for some reason it just all comes flooding back. This is what we have to hope for."

"Oh, I have told Kirsty none of this. She knows no more than I told you and Mother earlier. I don't know if that has been right or wrong. She now resents her father, believing he has deserted us when we needed him most. How can I tell her any different? Robbie does not want her or the rest of the family to know him as a murderer." Rhylla's blue eyes, awash with not only her tears but a plea for his understanding, held her father's eyes. "If only I had not come home on the train that day. If only I had listened to you and caught the plane. If only Rob had not left the house to collect me. If only Kirsty had not been left alone in the house that evening."

Her father held her tightly. "It's no good wasting your energy on the 'if only'. What is, is. You have carried a heavy burden on your shoulders, my dear. I'm glad you've told me. My lips are sealed, of course. And don't forget, if things become too much, please call on me for support."

Andrew McNeven placed his arm around Rhylla's shoulders as they walked the last hundred yards to the back gate of her garden.

CHAPTER SIXTEEN

Like a predator cat, the rusty cloud now spread across the western horizon waiting to pounce. It teased the drovers, daring them to make a move before it sprang and devoured all within its path. Since early morning the anxious eyes never left the west for more than short periods at a time. Puffer, the magic horseman, had warned Trevor the evening before – long before the eyes of the white men discerned any signs of a long low cloud of dust driving in behind them. Within the camp, all but Rob had previous experience of the devastation a full-blown dust storm could impose upon a mob of beasts and a droving camp.

At Puffer's first warning, Spud and Sunshine had busied themselves preparing for a cold camp the following day. In the faint light of the challenged moon, while the ringers took their shifts watching the restless cattle, the cook and his helper baked several extra dampers. A fresh lump of salted meat was rehydrated and simmered overnight in the coals of their campfire. Water panniers were to be topped up at the first waterhole in the morning. Trevor had instructed everyone to ensure their canteens were full and with them at all times. The enjoyment of sipping on a pannikin of hot tea would be gone once the storm made its move. The winds of a dust storm on a campfire posed the added risk of a raging grass fire.

In the haze of the new day, as the cattle drank their fill before an early midday rest, wariness tightened the gut of the experienced ringers. They watched the approaching threat. Curiosity bedecked with streamers of fear threaded through the body and mind of Rob as the skies darkened. He jumped at the sound of a hammer on steel when Spud and Sunshine pegged the heavy canvas over a flattened camp. Eddie secured the last set of hobbles and unclamped the horse bells on the spare horses while Puffer wandered amongst their nervous charges whispering words of comfort.

At first, the still heat stole the air from Rob's lungs. Sweat ran down his arms inside his bluey coat, worn at Trevor's suggestion. His whole body vibrated when a tremble ran through the horse beneath him. The animal's brown head with the white star prominent upon its forehead tossed its unbrushed mane. A soft whinny introduced the first flurry of wind and dust. Rob did not need to swing the horse around to place its rump to the weather. The horse shuffled itself until satisfied.

Rob gasped at the suddenness of the attack. The wind and dust howled across the plain. One moment he watched a handful of nervous cattle picking the grasses spasmodically to his left and the next there was nothing to see but a wall of dust blocking out everything more than three or four inches away from his nose. Despite the neckerchief across his lower face, he tasted the dirt on his tongue. The horse shivered and snorted and stamped its feet.

Trevor's last warning to them all echoed in Rob's head. "Don't go moving around in the thick of the dust unless you want to be lost forever and buried." Rob swung down from the saddle and moved close to the horse's head. Holding the bridle short with the one hand, his other hand ran over the white star to the left of its forehead. Rob spoke quietly. The wind pulled at his coat. The sting of the dust bit at his neck and his ears. His trousers provided small protection for his legs. He shrugged his coat up and across his hat pressing it in tight upon his head. He removed one arm from the sleeve to assist him to wrap part of the coat about the horse's head, as best he could. His face snuggled in upon the animal's neck.

The shriek of the wind, the choking wall of piercing dust went on and on and on. Leaves, small twigs and branches of trees slapped against his back. How far had they travelled across this plain of little timber? On several occasions he felt the heavier thud of a bird when it crashed into his body, driven by a force beyond its strength to fly. The feathered body slipped down his legs to the ground.

Was it minutes or hours or days in this hell-hole of noise and discomfort when Rob felt his body sag? He felt his weight in the arm across the horse's neck. The animal stood hipshot in an apparent trance. Almost asleep on his feet, Rob felt as if he were drowning in the aloneness of it all. If there was a world out there, he could not see it. Would they eventually find him and the horse buried in this infernal dust?

His body tensed. A vision seeped into his head. A vision of a small boy – about ten or eleven-year-old – and a pony sheltered in a ramshackle stable. A fierce wind rattled the corrugated iron sheeting threatening to peel it from the wooden frame of the shed. In the vision, it was not dust driven by the wind but horizontal rains. Large tree branches crashed against the iron walls. Rob's conscious mind forgot the current storm as it scrambled to corral and solidify this vision which quickly unravelled and disappeared from his head. Where had it come from? Who was the boy? Maybe himself or someone near and dear to him? Was the vision real or just a dream? Was the vision an event from his unknown past? His questions swirled like the dust around him. In place of the boy and the shed in his head, a kite hawk filled his mind.

At first, the sound of the winds fading went unnoticed. A shudder through the horse nearly sent Rob to his knees. The creak of the saddle leathers and the bounce of the stirrups surprised him as his ears had become so attuned to the wailing winds. He unfolded his face from the coat to notice cattle appear in the thinning haze. Bellows of their fear lifted with the dust still in the air. The same dust clotted his air passages. His mouth felt as dry as the desert sand it harboured. His tongue felt too thick for the space available. The sting of the sand against the back of his legs reduced to a dull burning sensation. It seemed as though there was not a muscle in his body without an ache. Like the horse before him, he stood straight and shook the clouds of dust from his hat, coat, clothes and body.

A late afternoon sun hung blurred on the western horizon when he heard the hail of a voice coming at him from his left. He struggled to reply but all he was able to do was cough. When he coughed the once, it set him off. He coughed until he dry-retched.

"You okay there, Rob?"

Steve's voice pushed its way through the dust in Rob's ear canals. He shook his head and slapped his earlobes. "Yeah, mate, I'm fine. How're the others?"

"Whinging and moaning, but none wounded or lost."

"What about the cattle? I suppose they've all gone to billyo?"

"Ah, well, that could be another matter. Trevor and Streak are checking the perimeter at the moment. It's too late to attempt a count now. They'll wait until the morning when they have better light. We'll know then if we can move on or spend a couple of days searching for lost stock."

"I reckon even Puffer and Sunshine would have the devil's own job of tracking any beast after that lot."

"Puffer's out now chasing the sounds of the horse bells. Eddie's trying to organize fresh horses for the night riders."

"I could kill for a pannikin of tea. Do you think Spud and Sunshine will light a fire tonight?"

Steve laughed. "Spud's already been asked that question more than once. He's getting a bit prickly. I wouldn't say a word if I were you. He's stomping about and swearing something fierce at all the dust in his cooking pots. When I left him ten minutes ago, he already had the tarp up off the gear and Sunshine was nursing a campfire. He even had a pot of potatoes on the boil to go with the cold meat and damper."

Rob laughed at the picture Steve had drawn. "I'll keep out of his way then. I guess all our swags will rain dust for days to come too."

"No doubt."

Rob began to notice the sound of the shuffling hooves of the herd and an occasional bellow coming from their midst.

When Rob arrived at the camp, he noticed Trevor in deep conversation with Eddie the horse-tailer and Billy. Trevor called Rob over. "I see we've got a few missing cattle. If they don't find their way back to the herd by morning, Puffer will go with Streak to track the runners. They'll leave as soon as it's light enough. I'll want you to work with Eddie tomorrow, Rob." Trevor turned his attention to his brother. "We'll take a full count after the cattle water in the morning. The boys can push them through that jump-up across the creek. You and I will be on either side to do the count as they come up onto the bank. We'll take it steady tomorrow to let Puffer and Streak bring up the strays. We're only a day or two out of Winton."

Eddie grinned at Rob. "You'll enjoy the peaceful quiet of a before-dawn start, Rob. We'll bring the horses in closer to the camp before we hustle out fresh mounts for the morning shift."

"Will I need to open my eyes or can I do it with my eyes shut?" Rob smiled in return.

"Listen for the direction of the horse bells during the night. I'll kick your foot before first light."

A black night fell early. Rob shoved the notebooks deeper within the kitbag under his head. Any notes on the storm must wait until tomorrow's mid-day camp. As the events of the day rolled through his thoughts like sheets of newspaper on the press rollers, he calculated they'd been travelling for just over a month.

Excitement kept Rob restless in the early hours of the night. He was being trusted to help the horse-tailer. Qualms of inadequacy tempered the thrill. Could he do the job? What background experience had he to be doing this work? He had no idea.

When he eventually drifted off to sleep, his dreams ensured his sleep provided little rest. The boy and his horse returned – walking behind a herd of dairy cows and calves – along a muddy track between a thick forest of trees: black bean, maple, kauri pine were some names that filled his dream. Little sunlight penetrated the forest canopy. The boy shivered in the cool of the gloom. Rob struggled to rouse his conscious mind. Deep inside his head, the desire to understand how he knew the names of these trees tormented his sleep. The more he tried to focus, the more the dream faded until the fragile pane of his vision shattered like a glass window through which a cricket ball has been belted. Dread replaced the peaceful bucolic scene. Cricket balls and glass windows meant pain – a leather strap and pain.

Pain like the pain in his shoulder grasped in a firm hand and shaken. He woke with a start to the hushed voice of the horse-tailer.

"Geez, Rob, wake up, will you? No way you've been listening for the tinkler bells on the horses then, I guess. I doubt even the big bells right beside your swag would have stirred you from your rest. Time to rise and shine, mate."

Rob crawled out of the swag. He shook out his boots and drew them onto his feet before looking about him. The blackness of night remained. Two small red glows were visible from the campsite. One was the fireplace stirred up when Eddie shoved a fresh log under the billy of tea stewing in the coals. The other was the glow on the end of the cigarette the horse-tailer sucked on. Before his brain was completely awake, Rob had his bedding rolled and stacked for travel. Faint noises of the cook and his offsider drifted across the camp along with the aroma of breakfast gruel and remnants of the dust of the evening before. He reached for the saddle which he had stashed under his swag canvas along with his boots during the night. A trick Steve had shown him to prevent dingoes sharpening their teeth or appetites on the leather. With an effort, he ignored the grumble of his belly demanding tea and damper. Instead, he satisfied his thirst on a quick drink from the canteen attached to his saddle. A shiver ran through his body as Rob followed Eddie to the picket line near the campsite where the night-horses were secured. Cold fingers tightened the saddle on his mount.

"Can you hear the bells yet?" Eddie rode up beside Rob.

Rob cocked his head and listened intently. He picked up the sound of the heavier cadence of several Condamine bells interspersed with the musical tinkler bells. They seemed to be coming from different directions. He identified these and pointed. A hint of picaninny dawn glowed on the eastern horizon. In the chilly morning, the animals were in fine buckle after a good rest. The two men gathered up each of the several groups of horses removing their hobbles and hanging them from each animal's neck. Once united into one large herd, Rob tailed the horses and was fascinated to watch Eddie wend himself and his mount in amongst the animals, working chosen horses out of the main herd and into a small group, separate but within the bigger herd.

Spud's packhorses followed at the rear keeping close to chosen companions.

With the campsite only half a mile away, Eddie had his group of twelve horses standing grazing apart from the larger herd. He signalled Rob to help guide the morning's selection of horses over to near the picket line where they were bridled. Eddie inspected each of the night horses' backs for saddle sores and the shoes on their hooves were secure before releasing them to the main herd grazing nearby. Several of the flightier horses had thin green-hide ties around their necks to allow easier catching if needed. While they worked together Rob's admiration for the horse-tailer's skills rose just as his own shortcomings threatened to shatter any confidence he may have developed over recent weeks.

The murmur of voices drifting out of the next room where the art teacher discussed Kirsty's project did not register in Rhylla's mind. The distant water splashing in the laundry tubs where Mrs. Barnes worked at the washing was also unheard. Rhylla sat procrastinating at her desk. A writing tablet sat open on the blotter. The freshly nibbed pen lay at rest beside the inkwell.

She had planned to write to her older children, Tim and Bronwyn, to pass on the news of Kirsty's situation. But now, sitting here, it did not seem the ideal way to deliver the news. She tapped her fingers on the desk running other options through her mind. She stood and moved to the cabinet with the glass doors where her husband's published novels were displayed. Inspiration remained unresponsive. Her fingers fiddled with the hair about her face as seen in the glass reflection.

Waiting for the end-of-year holidays from the university would have been ideal. They always came home for Christmas, but the chance of them finding out through mutual friends and idle gossip left her horrified. No, she must either write or make the trip south to speak with them personally. The lack of privacy within the developing telephone service did little to inspire confidence. Besides speaking on the telephone was far too cold and impersonal to discuss such a sensitive and emotional subject. The thought of flying in a noisy and uncomfortable aeroplane was beyond consideration.

Rhylla returned to her seat at the desk and reached past her pen to take up a pencil. Her fingers also wrapped around the adjacent rubber. This correspondence was not going to be completed in one simple attempt.

Dear

Was she to write two identical letters? The two recipients could hardly be further apart in nature. Tim, the eldest, blessed with such a pleasant personality. Bronwyn, only a year younger, was a moody girl whose life had left a horrendous trail of tantrums. A girl who seemed happiest when picking on someone else.

With the end-of-year assignments weighing on your mind, I would have given anything not to have burdened you with the following information. I felt it best to apprise you of the situation at home personally, rather than you receive a distorted version of gossip through another channel.

I cannot think of a gentle way to tell you what has happened so I will dive right in.

Late in April this year, your sister Kirsty was drugged and raped by a stranger in this very house while she was at home on her own waiting for your father and me to return from the railway station. If this was not terrible enough for her, she has been left pregnant – due in February of next year.

Your father left immediately after to search for this evil man. We are unsure of your father's whereabouts at the moment.

Kirsty and I have discussed the situation and the options available for her. Kirsty has chosen to keep the child which we will care for together.

I appreciate this news will take some time to come to terms with and for you to comprehend. Your sister could well do with your strength and support during this time and beyond.

With love and faith

Your Mother.

As Rhylla read her first draft, the pencil scratched and inserted with great flourishes. In the end, the letter remained little changed from the original. She lay the pencil and eraser down and reached for her nibbed pen at the moment Kirsty spoke from her doorway.

"Mr. Bellingham has left, Mother. He did call a goodbye but you were engrossed in your work and he did not want to intrude."

"Oh, I'm sorry, dear. How did your class go?"

"If you have a moment, will you come and have a look at what we were doing? He has such a creative flair. I think I will learn much from him."

Rhylla replaced her pen and turned the writing pad over as she stood to follow Kirsty.

The pair discussed the art teacher's suggestions until the call from Mrs. Barnes in the kitchen interrupted them.

"Lunchtime, ladies," she called.

CHAPTER SEVENTEEN

Winton lay several days behind the herd. Once more Rob had been allocated the task of working with Eddie Burkett and Puffer. In the pale light of the new dawn, after the ringers had all eaten and moved out to begin mobilizing the bullocks, Rob herded in the line of packhorses. Spud fussed over the line-up of his packsaddles and pack bags. As he drove Sunshine to greater efforts, his voice rose above the bellowing cattle now being nudged into movement by the men on horseback. Woe betides Sunshine if one packsaddle or pack bag did not stand in the exact spot it should be. Rob stumbled into his firing line when he brought up the line of packhorses. Each specific animal had to arrive in the order of the packsaddles set beside the loads they were to carry.

"No bloody good you put Sarah ahead of Nitbite. She won't carry flour bags in a million years. She'll turn herself inside out trying to reach the flour, silly old cow she is. And you know that stubborn old Wizard's Pot, he won't carry anything but the water canteens. 'E's not silly you know. 'E's had a few long spells between drinks and knows full well where the water' be kept." Up and down the line he went poking and prodding – checking the two beef packs, the salt packs, the sugar packs and tin tucker, as well as the spuds, onions, and cooking gear, were all where they should be on the correct packsaddle of the correct packhorse. Spud paid particular attention to the balance of the load on each animal. The packhorse named Angel – and not for her nature – carried the responsibility of the dinner-camp load. She and Spud remained with the herd during the mid-day breaks to see the ringers were fed. When satisfied with their morning's work, Spud flattened the fire one last time with the blade of the shovel before it was secured on Angel's packsaddle beside the axe in its sturdy canvas bag.

Like the cook and Angel, Puffer, bringing in the fresh horses for the afternoon work, arrived at each mid-day camp a couple of hours ahead of the herd. Eddie continued on another three or four miles with the main bunch of horses to water them and settle them on feed with their hobbles and bells at the proposed campsite for the night. Sunshine and the packhorse team followed after Eddie to set up the cook's night camp.

Guided by the ringers, the cattle herd munched their way along the track for five or six hours until the heat of the day and the sight of the dinner camp signalled them to settle and rest.

Every five or six weeks the horse-tailer replaced the horseshoes on those animals with overgrown hooves. Each afternoon for several days, after the mob of horses arrived at the night's campsite, Eddie, Puffer and now Rob too, worked at this task until all the hooves had been inspected and shoes changed as necessary.

When horseshoe-changing was on the list of jobs for the day, Rob joined Eddie and Puffer with the horses while waiting for the cattle herd to arrive. Having only two sets of tools, the men worked in rotation while the third rested his back. Without really thinking, Rob stepped up to work on his first horse. Eddie Burkett paused in what he was doing to watch the new bloke on the team. With smooth strokes, Rob's hands ran down the length of each limb in turn as he inspected the feet. Without conscious thought, his hands reached for each tool required and proceeded to remove the nails holding the current iron horseshoe in place. Some shoe nails were broken, some had fallen out and others wedged by the growing hoof. Eddie's comment on his skill using the blacksmith tools refuelled Rob's curiosity. Where and when had he learnt how to care for a horse's feet? When, after completing the hooves of the first animal and the liquid fire of pain seared along his spine, Rob knew full well it must have been some years since his body had applied itself to such work.

Puffer arrived after watering and settling the morning horses. Eddie's call to Rob fell on grateful ears.

"You can take a break now, mate."

A sigh of relief added to Rob's groans when his body creaked into the upright position. After the first afternoon attending the horses' hooves, Rob was sure he'd never be able to sleep on the hard ground again, but his snores provided unappreciated music for the camp occupants before the two men on the first night-watch set out on their rounds.

At the end of the fifth day only one horse, Striker, remained to be manicured. Eddie glanced up at the sky where the afternoon light faded fast.

"Okay, you fellas," he spoke to Puffer and Rob, "Head over to camp and have your tea. You've done a good day's work today. I'll just finish this cranky blighter off before I join you."

"You sure we can't give a hand, Boss?" Puffer laughed. "Show you what to do or something, hey?"

"Bugger off, smart aleck."

Laughter filled the cooling air as Rob and Puffer picked up the spare shoeing hammer, rasp, pincers and hoof knife before they headed for the camp. Within twenty yards, a roar of pain spun them around. Curses went unheard as Eddie backed away holding one arm in against his waist. Striker snorted. The wide eyes flashed and the long mane flew when he tossed his head. Dust rose into the air and the earth shook when his front feet struck at the ground. Magnificent muscles writhed as the horse bucked. Its body twisted at impossible angles. Leather reins swished back and forth in the air over his head. Rob and Puffer dropped the tools they had in their hands and ran.

When they neared the crazed horse, Puffer's silent feet approached the animal. Whispered sing-song words gentled the horse. Rob moved over to help Eddie. He discovered a river of blood saturating the front of the horse-tailer's shirt and trousers. It ran down the front of his leather chaps.

"Geez, Eddie. What happened?"

"Arrrh … bloody horse – bloody stupid me. I should've left this beggar until we'd a better light in the morning. Something spooked him. Maybe he sniffed a dingo hanging about. He caught me off guard – kicked out at the wrong moment and the hoof knife slipped. Bloody hell that smarts. Can you see in this light, Rob? Feels like I've cut the whole arm off."

Rob stared at the sliced flesh from the base of the left thumb and halfway up the forearm. In the gloom, his face paled. He felt his legs wobble beneath him. The ragged sleeve hung down dripping blood into the dry ground. With the neckerchief from his pocket, Rob padded and pressed on the wound. Eddie groaned.

"Struth, that's not good news." Eddie offered up his own neckerchief to the blood bath. "Let's get over to the campfire to get a better look. Spud's got a first-aid kit somewhere amongst the gear."

It was Trevor who took charge of the wounded horse-tailer when they arrived in camp.

"Spud, get out the Vet box, will you? Streak," he called the ringer who stood watch with him most often, "hold a lantern up here so I can see what Ed's done to himself." The reassuring smile for Eddie went someway to masking his own fear of seeing the wound more closely. Trevor's throat clenched at the sight. He swallowed noisily. He turned to Spud as he arrived holding a small wooden box.

"Have we got any kerosene or something to disinfect this with, Spud?"

Spud's fingers, black with ingrained soil of the Queensland plains, dug through the contents of the medicine kit. "Here, Trevor. Here's a bottle of brown stuff. I think it's iodine. Will that do?"

"Yeah, I think so. Smell it. Does it smell like a hospital?"

Spud sniffed at the opened bottle. "How should I know – I've never been to a hospital."

"Give it here. It should do."

Trevor turned back to where Eddie's body began to sag. He and Spud reached out and guided the wounded man to the ground. Rob rushed up with a swag roll which he shoved in behind Eddie's back. Trevor eased the tattered shirt off the damaged arm. A circle of wide eyes glistened in the flickering light of the lantern. Their gasps joined the moths as they circled the flame. Eddie's blood pumped out of several smaller vessels with no sign of letting up. Fat and muscle tissue were visible where the skin edges gaped.

Trevor glanced up from the wound to the spectators. "Geez, I hope someone's watching the cattle?"

"Yeah, Trev," Streak spoke up, "Snips and Turkey are out on watch."

Trevor nodded his head as he poured the disinfectant over the raw tissue. Sympathetic groans from the audience joined the one released through Eddie's gritted teeth. Despite Trevor's attempts to drag the skin back together, it appeared reluctant to oblige.

"Isn't there something to sew this up with, Spud?" Trevor pressed a pad of clean white material retrieved from the medicine box against the worst bleeding points of the wound.

It was Spud who offered the first suggestion. "Me old grandpa bred pigs years ago. Those porkers could really do damage to each other when they took a mind to. Grandpa had us all out fetching every cobweb we could find. He mixed them with flour into the wound. They usually healed up okay. The ones that didn't, we ate."

"Ha, I hope you're not suggesting I'm on the menu for tomorrow, Spud." Eddie managed to spit out between his teeth.

"Ahh, here we go." Spud held up an old tobacco tin giving it a shake as he did so. The rewarding rattle of something small and metal fell upon their ears. "You know, I do remember me Gran saying her father made a mixture of a teaspoon of beef fat and a drop of kerosene to rub on wounds." His grunt heralded the separation of the tin and its lid. An array of needles lay in the bottom.

"They're bagging needles." Streak offered.

"Not all of them," Trevor reached in and chose a two-inch curved cutting-edged needle. "Now is there some sort of string or thread?"

Once more the grubby fingers of the cook shuffled through the contents of his box. "You know," he said, "It might have been the eaten-out sores around the horses' eyes."

"What?" Streak asked. "What about fly-eaten horse eyes?"

"The beef fat and kero. She was born in the Gulf – me mother. They have a problem with the flies in the Gulf."

As Spud explained the treatment to Streak, Trevor selected one of the two reels of black strong cotton thread. He unrolled a length and used the pocketknife from the pouch on his belt to cut it off.

"You know, Trev, if you'd provided us with sheets for our swags, we could've torn off strips to use for bandages," Billy piped up.

Lines fanned out from the outer corner of Trevor's eyes when he frowned and smiled at the same time. "I suppose you'll be wanting a lady in fine clothes to come with that, brother. You could always tear strips off her petticoats for bandages, too."

Trevor's roughened fingers struggled to pull the skin edges of the wound together while the men continued with their jovial remarks endeavouring to distract Eddie. Streak obliged by cutting the thread when required.

A week passed during which the flavour of the days changed little. The moving dust cloud above the grazing herd led off with the sunrise, while Spud and Sunshine cleaned up and packed the cook's camp. After watering the horses, Rob and Puffer moved them out on an arc to bypass the cattle. Eddie hung back out of the way cursing his arm in its sling, His impatience was seen in his every frown and his twitching shoulders.

With a final push to water, the droving plant arrived on the common lands outside Longreach. Under the tutelage of Puffer and Eddie, Rob's confidence lifted along with his knowledge of horse mobs and ability to identify individual animals.

Trevor escorted the reluctant patient the ten miles into the Longreach hospital where intelligent eyes peered out from amongst the doctor's grey whiskers and wrinkles. He was a man of few words and waited quietly while the matron removed the bandage stained with old blood, iodine and a good layer of western plains dirt. When Trevor's sewing skills were revealed, his frown and head shake spoke volumes.

"Matron, have we any of those new Tetanus vaccines left?" He queried the white-veiled nurse at his side.

"Yes, Doctor, there's one left. Will I jab this patient?"

"Yes, hopefully, it's not too late. Having been sewn up like a bullock, in a herd of bullocks and horses inundated with tetanus spores, it seems impossible he has not succumbed to the disease already." The Matron turned to attend to his orders when the doctor added to her responsibilities. "Oh, and can we have a clean bandage on this wound, Matron?" The doctor turned back to the patient without pausing, "Make sure you drop into the Roma or Toowoomba hospital and have your second injection. You can't work with that arm for a month, at least."

"B…b…but…"

A month at least," the doctor reiterated.

Rhylla sank back into the soft cushions of the armchair near the window of her bedroom. Matching blue curtains billowed on a breeze hinting at a warmer than usual spring. Maternity dress wear of several designs was spread across her bed. In front of the full-length mirror, Kirsty, dressed only in her underclothes, cradled the now visible bump of her abdomen.

"Gran suggested I should wear corsets to hide the pregnancy for as long as possible. What do you think, Mum?"

Rhylla swallowed. Her mind struggled to find a suitable answer. But she was saved a reply when Kirsty went on.

"I don't think I want to. According to Doctor Gleeson, this bulge is now a fully developed baby only four inches long. How could I squash this tiny creature under a pair of tight corsets?" Arms, hidden from the sun for too long, held up one of the maternity-wear creations.

Pleasure, tainted with a tad of horror at the thickening form of her daughter, evoked a wave of guilt like a school of piranha fish in Rhylla's soul. Along with Rhylla's constant anxiety for Kirsty's and the baby's future, their gnawing teeth added to the already burning in Rhylla's belly.

"What do you think, Mum? Which dress do you like best?"

Rhylla sat up taller on the cushions and struggled to bring her mind back to the subject of choosing clothes. "You'll need a set for good wear – suitable for town and maybe three house frocks, Kirsty, dear."

"Mum, I have no plans for venturing outside the front door. Why do I need a town frock?"

The knife of her words slashed into Rhylla's heart. Her once out-going, sports-loving daughter locked away inside the house. She jumped upright and moved to peer through the edge of the curtains wiping the tears from her eyes as she did so. Her dreams of grandchildren never entertained such a development as this.

Rhylla turned back and went to join Kirsty at the mirror. Her arm pulled her close. "Darling, I do hope you're not planning on deserting me on our daily walks. The doctor did say gentle exercise was very good for you and the little one. The Park behind the house is so pleasant and seldom do we meet anyone there."   Rhylla acknowledged her empathy for Kirsty. Having been snubbed on more than one occasion herself, when her supposed friends had crossed the street to avoid a meeting. She fully understood Kirsty's choice. Only three of Kirsty's once-many friends had continued to visit after it became known she was pregnant. Those visits gradually trickled off altogether – possibly under parental pressure.

Kirsty hugged her mother. "No, Mother, we will continue to walk in the park each day. Sometimes I find it hard to accept the failings of human nature, but I know I'm not responsible for this predicament and I know it's not the baby's fault. I try to remind myself of these things when some of those I once called my friends avoid me."

"Now, a little less of the chatter. This is not trying on dresses, my dear. The dressmaker will be here soon to make any adjustments if necessary." Rhylla stepped away and passed across a skirt and a blouse which had been gathered on a yoke, for inspection.

While Kirsty made several choices, Rhylla's thoughts continued to follow the theme of a moment before. She found herself going to the office less and less these days. Having sensed the awkwardness of dealing with some of her regular customers, she completed most of her work at home. Her secretary, Alice, under her father's supervision was fully capable of keeping things up to date.

The voice from the doorway surprised both Rhylla and Kirsty.

"Oh, I think that looks so nice on you, Kirsty." Admiration shone from the eyes of Mrs. Barnes. The smile continued to light up her face when she turned to her boss. "The policeman is downstairs, Mrs. MacBurnie – Sergeant Hampson. I have put him in the sitting room and told him you'd be there shortly."

"Thanks, Mrs. Barnes, I'll be right down. And yes, I agree with you, that dress is my favourite too."

Rhylla followed Mrs. Barnes down the stairs. "Can you bring in a pot of tea, please?"

"Of course, I have the kettle on the heat as we speak."

Rhylla paused at the doorway into the sitting room and sucked in a deep breath. The perfume of Mr. Evan's fresh roses in their vase on the corner stand did not disguise the hint of furniture polish despite the regular airing Mrs. Barnes gave this seldom used room. Rhylla rearranged her facial expression before entering. Doug Hampson jumped up.

"Rhylla, it's good to see you again. I was hoping to catch Robbie, actually."

"I'm sorry, Doug, but Robbie's still not back from his latest research trip. Can I help in any way?"

"Goodness me, this next book of his is going to be a saga by the sounds of things. What, he's been away nearly four months?"

Rhylla had no intention of correcting her guest to inform him it was closer to five than four months. "I'm sure it will be a best-seller, as usual, Doug," she commented seating herself on a corner chair. "Please sit, Doug."

"No doubt. No doubt. He always had the knack with words, our Robbie."

Mrs. Barnes entered and placed a large tray on the centre table. Rhylla shuffled forward in her chair.

"Thanks, Mrs. Barnes, I'll pour." She turned to Doug. "The usual for you, Doug – black and two sugars?"

"Thanks, yes."

"And a scone?"

"Please."

With the dregs in the teacups in front of them both and the scones now only crumbs on Doug's plate, he began to explain his visit.

"When you next write to Robbie, will you tell him his brother fled to Mount Isa and has since disappeared again? He'll be using another false name, no doubt. He has used several false names already that we know of."

Jumbled thoughts beat through the whisk of Rhylla's mind. *Why had it taken Doug weeks – no months – to come and tell her this himself? He'd have known Jim had already passed on this message to her. Why was he really here?* Rhylla stared in silence at the cup in front of her. She most certainly was not going to tell Doug that Greg MacBurnie was lying at the bottom of the quarry lake only a few miles from this very house. She was not going to tell him that it was her Robbie who had fled to Mount Isa and since disappeared.

"I'm sorry to hear you have not been able to catch him." A small frown crossed her forehead as she acknowledged the feeble attempt of her mind to conjure up something more profound to reply.

"As far as we're aware it's not only the police forces of Queensland and New South Wales who are on his trail. We're sure the Sydney Underworld haven't forgotten him either."

Rhylla felt her heart clench in fear. A pulse raced in her neck. As her hand went to her paled face it came away moist with perspiration. A dry mouth and frozen tongue denied her speech – not that she intended to tell Doug she believed in her soul that her darling Robbie, masquerading as Greg, was already dead. Probably killed by the people from Sydney. The ball of emotion stuck in the back of her throat allowed nothing but a strangled "Oh," to escape.

"Anyway, more pleasant things. How's Robbie, by the way? How's the family?"

Rhylla reached over to refill her cup. "Can I get you more tea there, Doug?"

"No thanks, Rhylla, I'm fine."

"The family's fine. Tim finishes his university studies at the end of this year. Bronwyn still has a year to go." Her voice box closed over. She was unable to mention Kirsty.

Doug watched Rhylla closely as she spoke. Concern filled his eyes. "Rhylla, I've been Robbie's friend since we were kids on our parents' farms in Atherton. I've known you since the pair of you were married – how long ago was that – must be nigh on twenty-five years. If there is something you need support with or advice on, you know you only have to ask."

Her head nodded. The only part of her able to move. *Did Doug know Robbie was missing? Did Doug know everything?*

"Rhylla, I'm not deaf to the word around town. I believe young Kirsty is pregnant and has left school. Is there anything I can do?"

Ice settled in her chest. How was she to reply to this? She could not repeat the storyline told to Kirsty and all the family. If she said Kirsty had been raped, Doug would play the heavy-handed policeman and that was not acceptable. She most certainly could not tell him Greg MacBurnie was dead, killed by his brother Robbie – a copper's mate. Tears welled in her eyes.

"Oh, Rhylla, I'm so sorry. Where is that damned Robbie? He should be here looking after the two of you."

The defence of her beloved Robbie released her voice. "Doug, Robbie and I discussed our options and what we should do. We decided we must go on with life as normal. Robbie will return when he has finished what he has to do."

"Okay, then I won't trouble you anymore today, but will you please remember my offer to help out, if I can, is there." He rose slowly and looked down at his host.

Rhylla felt the intense gaze of his dark eyes. Her voice sounded hollow in her own ears. "Thanks, Doug. You're very kind. I appreciate your support." With her insides tumbling like an ocean's whirlpool, Rhylla escorted Doug to the front door where she again thanked him and said farewell. When she closed the door behind him, the tears flowed freely down her cheeks. Smothered sobs exploded behind her hands. She ran back into the sitting room and hid her face in one of the sofa cushions.

CHAPTER EIGHTEEN

A pair of underpants riddled with cobbler-peg prickles would not have caused Trevor as much irritation as the sight of the hawker's wagon set up only a stone's throw from his own campsite. The sun hung low on the horizon. A blanket of chilled air draped around Trevor's and Eddie's shoulders. Following close at their heels, plodded the black packhorse they called Inkpot loaded with supplies collected while in Longreach. Trevor released and reclasped his cramped fingers on the lead rein.

Eddie did not see the frown or hear the soft curse from his friend, but he knew from experience Trevor's dislike of a tinker camped so close to the herd. They were both burdened by nightmares of a cattle stampede in the Northern Territory – cattle already skittish at the time as they travelled across an area of drummy ground on the Murranji Track. A stampede triggered by the sound of a drink-crazed hawker clanging pans to chase off the demons of his imagination in the middle of the night. Two good ringers were wounded that night – never to work again.

With a short nod of the head and a humourless smile, Trevor returned the greetings of the men at the camp. He passed the saddlebags to the cook.

"Don't let these beggars pull those papers apart until I've finished with it." He passed Inkpot's lead rein over to Sunshine. His hand slipped inside his jacket and dragged out several folded newspaper pages. He called Rob over. "Here's the business reports and share prices. Dad said they were the first thing you looked at when reading the papers. No good me leaving them in the newspaper for this lot. They'd wipe their bums on them before you could blink an eye." Without further ado, Trevor swung his mount around and cantered over to talk to the new arrivals at the tinker's camp.

A grey-haired, whiskered man who appeared as round as he was tall, greeted Trevor in a rich Irish accent.

"Evening, Sire."

Behind the man, a covered wagon stood with both side awnings up and open. Within the limits of their hobbles, two draught-horses grazed nearby. In the flickering light of a hurricane lantern hanging on a nail at the back corner, a large swag roll peeped out from under the wagon. Nearby a tall, slim woman, dressed in black from the tip of her head to the taped-up shoes on her feet attended a small fire. Her long fingers sprinkled a small handful of tea leaves into the water bubbling in a billycan. She picked up a bent spoon and tapped it three times on the side of the metal can before removing her tea brew to the edge of the fireplace.

"Will you sit? Can we offer you a cup of tea?" Once more the Irishman spoke, his voice gravelled with acres of dust.

As he dismounted, Trevor bit down on his impatience. "Trevor Jackson." He reached out his right hand. Trevor flinched at the strength in the hand he shook.

"Shamus O'Leary at your service, Sire." A stubby finger flicked towards his female companion. "My wife."

Trevor nodded in her direction but received nothing but a black-eyed stare in return.

"Och, don't mind her. She saves all her speeches for me."

The men squatted on their haunches near the fireplace drinking their tea from two chipped pannikins. The verbose Shamus O'Leary poured out what seemed a life history to Trevor who regretted having asked the man where he'd come from. In fact, he began to regret having made the effort to be polite. The dregs of the tea leaves dried in the bottom of his pannikin and he had not had an opportunity to say what he had come here to say.

Three hundred yards away, at the drover's campsite, Rob swallowed a hasty drink of his tea, washing down the dry damper stuck in his throat. He turned to Billy who whittled wood in the light of the fire. "Where's Steve? I haven't seen him tonight."

Billy grinned. "He's out on watch with Snips. He lost a bet today. Now Steve has to do all of Turkey's shifts tonight as well as his own."

"Should I ask, what bet?"

"You know how that pair like to think they know more than each other. Today Turkey knew more about the English castles than Steve did." Billy lay down his whittling and dragged the tobacco tin from his top pocket. He lifted out the sheaf of small white papers removing a single one, placing the corner on his moist lip. His fingers returned to the contents of the tin and sorted out a frugal heap of the shredded tobacco leaf. Not being a constant smoker, Billy's hands were not as supple as some Rob had watched when they spread the tobacco along the edge of the paper and rolled it up into a thin cigarette. Billy stretched over to lift a burning stick from the fireplace and lit his smoke. He inhaled deeply. He continued on the subject of Steve's bet. "Think I'll buy him an encyclopaedia for Christmas."

"That could be a bit heavy to haul about in his swag."

"Yeah, it would." Billy grinned again. When the cigarette had disappeared in smoke he jumped up. "Well, come on, Rob, we'd best go rescue my brother from the dreaded hawker-man. You heard the fella this afternoon when we went over to sticky-beak. He can talk underwater with his mouth sewn up."

"He can at that – we could be there all night." Rob finished the dregs in his pannikin. "Trevor did not look too happy when he arrived back from town this evening. What's biting his bum?"

"He hates tinkers of any kind. It's a long story; I'll tell you one day."

The arrival of his brother and Rob Bains released Trevor from his purgatory just as the Irishman was diving into the financial depression having befallen everyone. While Shamus was distracted by the new visitors, Trevor jumped to his feet.

"Must go." He grabbed Billy's shoulder and mumbled. "Tell this old coot not to make any sudden noises that might spook the cattle or the bloody horses, will you?" He strode to his horse and threw himself into the saddle.

While Trevor and Eddie had been away at the hospital most of the day, the men had killed a beast for fresh meat. The smell of frying liver and sweetbread vied with that of ribs and fillet. The ringers hopped about impatiently while Spud parried their advances with a long cooking fork.

"You lot ain't starving. Just hang on a tick until the meat's done."

Following the aromas from their own campsite, Billy and Rob were not long in returning from the Irishman's wagon.

"How'd you get away so easily?" Trevor queried his brother.

"I told him you shot the last fellow who camped near our mob." Billy could hardly speak for laughing. "I also told him this herd had already stampeded every other night since we started and we were concerned for his safety."

Rob interrupted. "We promised him a slab of fresh meat if they scarpered first thing in the morning and in the meantime, they must keep very quiet." Chuckles floated around the fireplace along with the hiss of sizzling beef.

Billy continued, "I'll just run a bit of meat over to the tinker's wife. I think it might have been a while since they've seen a good feed."

After they had eaten and the men on the second watch wiped their mouths on the sleeves of their shirts before making a move to relieve the first watch, Trevor declared the following day to be a day of rest.

"Not much of a bloody rest," Spud whinged. "I've still got all this beef to salt."

After tying his horse in the picket line, Steve threw his opinion into the ring while he stood warming his fingers over the fire. "Poor you. Us ringers still have to continue watching the cattle and horses – day and night."

Trevor looked up from the still sizzling, fresh ribs on his plate. Smoke rose into the night air. "You can have Rob tomorrow to give you a hand, Spud, and you'll have Sunshine." He tried to take small bites of meat from the bones but his burnt fingers dropped them immediately. They clattered onto the tin plate.

Around a mouthful of the pancreas, his favourite treat, Steve warned. "Keep that noise up, Trev and we'll start our own stampede."

"Up yours," was the terse reply.

Rob waved the tinker off at the first sign of morning light. Eddie stood at his shoulder with his almost white bandage seen stark in the glow.

"Rob, you'd better go check he's put the fire out properly. Trevor will track him to hell and back if he's left us a grass fire," Eddie warned.

At some stage during a rare day off, everyone revelled in the opportunity to swim in the river where they washed the dust of many miles from their bodies and their clothes. All except Spud, that is. Spud grumbled his way to the water with Trevor's threats and the unpleasant promises made by several of the men buzzing along with the flies around his ears. For long moments he stood on the bank staring with anxious eyes.

"For Pete's sake, just jump in, Spud. There're no crocs here. They'd have eaten Snips first if there were." Billy offered encouragement.

Filthy hands gripped the fallen log hanging from the bank as Spud edged into the water. At waist level, he stopped and bent his knees to let the water lap his chin. There was Buckley's chance of either threats or encouragement dragging him into the deeper water.

Books covered her desk in the home office. Rhylla's pale fingers stroked the shiny covers of her husband's published novels. Idly a cover was lifted and pages flicked. She knew every word in every one of his novels. She picked up her favourite and held it close to her chest. Tears drizzled unnoticed over her rouged cheeks. They blotched her face powder. The sobs took her by surprise. Choking, gasping sobs dragged every breath of air from her lungs.

"Oh, Robbie, my dearest, Robbie, where are you?" The words of her watered whisper melted together. "What am I to do?" Her hand dragged through her hair wrecking the tidy knot pinned at the back of her head. "I know you would never willingly have stayed away this long." A drawn rasping breath filled the room. "They have found you, haven't they, those Sydney murderers?" She threw her hand over her mouth to mute the sobs ripping through her throat. "What do I tell Kirsty and the others? Kirsty already thinks you've run away because of her predicament. Resentment is building up in her and I don't know what to do to help her. Many, and I think this includes Doug Hampson, think you and I have parted." Rhylla's hands once more attacked her hair. "Perhaps I should tell Kirsty that is what we have done – separated. I could say it was something we both agreed upon and had nothing to do with what happened to her. I could say the timing was just coincidental. Whatever I say, I cannot tell her the truth." Rhylla's tears flowed without control. "That's how this started – to prevent anyone, particularly the family, knowing you murdered your brother." She reached across and began to pile the books into a heap on her desk. At that moment, after a quick tap on the door, it was opened to reveal Kirsty.

"Sorry, Mum, I heard you talking. I thought Granddad must be here. Why, you're crying. Whatever is the matter, can I help?"

Pulling out the handkerchief tucked inside her sleeve, Rhylla attempted to restore some order to her face. She removed all the pins from her hair and raked her fingers through the strawberry-blond tresses now streaked with grey. Fumbling the books, Rhylla gathered them into her arms. With a heavy tread, she walked around the desk to replace them in the glass cabinet where they were usually stored.

"I'm sorry you had to see me at such a low ebb, my darling. Everyone has weepy times now and then."

"It's Dad, isn't it? It's all my fault. He only left because of me."

"Kirsty, your father never for one moment believed the rape was your fault. It was never your fault."

"Then why did Dad leave? Why hasn't he come back? You said at the time he'd gone to find the man, but that wasn't true, was it?"

Rhylla bit down on the truth as it threatened to blurt out into the room. "Darling, ..."

"How could he run off like that? It wasn't my fault. I hate him. I really hate him for deserting us. It's been five months so we know he's not coming back."

Rhylla bit her lip. A determined hand reached over to rest on Kirsty's folded arms. "Kirsty, your father never for one minute blamed you for what happened – neither of us did." Her head struggled with words that might comfort and ease Kirsty's pain. Her mind writhed with thoughts she did not want to think about. After a deep sigh, Rhylla took what she could see as the only way out. "Kirsty, you're right. Your father will not return. He and I had been going through a difficult time in our relationship before your unfortunate incident. We have separated." Sour bile threatened to rise up her gullet and explode from her lips on the tail of those words. Bouncing off the walls of her skull the words churned, *Sorry, Robbie, my darling, sorry. It's better our daughter should think you a deserter rather than a murderer.*

Kirsty stood with her mouth agape. Her grey eyes widened. "I don't believe you."

"I'm sorry, darling." But Rhylla could not be sure if she apologized to her daughter or to the man she loved above all others.

"Why didn't he tell me before he left?"

"Maybe he did. You never read the letter he left, did you?"

Tears welled in the four grey eyes within the room. Horror echoed in the voice of reply. "I burnt it in the stove fire." Her hand flew to her mouth. "How could you let him go? I don't believe you. You and Dad never argued."

"It is not civilized to argue in front of others and particularly in front of one's children, Kirsty."

"Oh, Mum, I'm so sorry. I still blame Dad for leaving when he did. He should have stayed around to help you."

"Even adults make mistakes, my dear. We don't come with instructions on life written on labels on our little fingers."

Rhylla finished tidying the books on the cabinet shelves, shut the door gently and turned to hold her daughter. "You know, my sweet, I was thinking we should take a holiday. Go to a place where no one knows us. Now, before Tim and Bronwyn return for the end-of-year holidays and before it gets too close to the birthing time. You have never visited the Bowen beaches. Mrs. Barnes often talks of the blue sea and wonderful sandy coves. We can hire a cottage for a month. I'll drive us down there in my car. We can take some of your father's fishing lines and catch our own fish." Rhylla held Kirsty away and peered into her eyes. "Come on, what do you say?"

Two small lines crossed her forehead. "I don't know, Mum. I feel safe here."

"I promise you if you don't like it down there, I'll drive you back immediately."

Kirsty fell into Rhylla's hug. "Yes, Mum. It sounds wonderful."

CHAPTER NINETEEN

The morning sun through the gum trees cast a dappled shade over the man calling himself Rob Bains. He sat on a log by the waterhole and watched the horses as they slaked their thirst. Sandy dust rose into the air where several of the animals rolled in the dry bed of the creek. The night horses, jubilant to be freed of their riders, saddles and bridles, revelled in the freedom. Rob's brown mount, held on a loose rein, pawed at the sand, impatience filling its dark eyes. The black mane flew into the air as the horse tossed its head. In the early morning light, a flock of budgerigars filled the air with colour and noise as they darted between the branches above. Amongst their numbers, pairs danced their springtime call of nature.

Creaking leather heralded the arrival of Eddie. It was time to move the horses away from the water and push on with their journey towards Blackall. Rob stood. His soft voice soothed the horse before he mounted smoothly into the saddle. The horses climbed the banks of the creek to move out through the scattered timber. Rob's glance flicked along the necks and feet of each animal, checking all had the clappers on their horse bells clamped and the hobbles removed from their fetlocks and tied safely around their necks.

"Fill your canteen at every opportunity, Rob. We'll be in for several dry camps ahead. A few of the waterholes we come across on the way to Charleville will not be the best. The horses will need water every day but the cattle will miss out some days." Eddie's horse moved restlessly under him.

"How long can they go without water?"

"On the Canning Stock Route in Western Australia, it's not unusual to go without water for three or even more days. They use camels to carry water for the horses and drovers. That's one track I haven't been on and I can't say I'll be in a rush to do so."

"I imagine the mob becomes restless when they're thirsty?"

"A bit impatient at times. Sometimes, at those waterholes we have to dig out, it can take all night to water a mob this size when the soak is slow to refill. Besides the digging, the hardest thing is keeping the thirsty mob back while we water a few at a time. You'll see, Rob."

"Worse than the time about a month ago when they only missed one watering, you mean." Rob encouraged his horse up the creek bank with a flick of the reins.

"Oh, yes, they can become quite spiteful when very thirsty." Using his one good arm, Eddie turned his mount. "I'm off to give Trevor a hand with the count."

Rob raised his hand in salute.

Billy, Steve and Eddie led a small group of bullocks towards where Trevor and Streak rested on their horses about fifty yards apart facing each other. The small mob passed through the laneway between the two waiting counters. Slowly the main herd dribbled behind them pushed along by Turkey and Snips. Eddie and Steve had broken away from the herd to stand, one behind each of the counters. Their job was to call out any number of cattle that may have bypassed the counting lane.

The counters, Trevor and Streak, steadied their horses with their knees and quiet voices. They each held their whip in their hands.

When they counted one hundred beasts, they called out to each other, "One hundred!" and they both tied a knot in their whip's long lash.

The voices of Eddie and Steve called intermittently. "Two on the north side or three on the south side," whatever the case might be.

Most days, the count was agreed upon by the four men. This day was no different.

After reaching the drier section of the route and almost two weeks of little sleep, obstreperous cattle and shortened fuses of exhausted men within the drover's camp, Rob felt the heat of the day burrowing deep into his head. The rhythmic sway of the horse hypnotized his soul and rocked his body. Ahead, the cattle blurred and writhed in the distorted perception of a weary brain. He felt himself sinking into a world of darkness, unable to raise the will to fight the lethargy. His head nodded on sagging shoulders. Hands holding the reins rested on the pommel of the saddle. High in the sky above and hidden in the rays of a blazing sun, a kite hawk whistled.

Strawberry-blonde hair swung out behind her head from under a pale pink scarf. A miniature replica, a small girl of perhaps three or four squealed in delight and danced around in circles as the lady held the tiny hands. Pink skirts swirled about their legs. The sound of their song hung sweetly in Rob's ears. "Here we go round the mulberry bush, the mulberry bush, the mulberry bush …"

Concentration furrowed the foreheads of the dark-haired older boy and girl engrossed in a game of chess within the shade of a large tree.

Lines deepened in Rob's brow as a thought gelled in his brain. *They only looked to be about six or seven-year-old. How could they be playing chess?*

The man at his side spoke three times before Rob shuddered in the saddle. Glazed eyes peered across into the white-toothed grin on the black face of Puffer where he sat as if one with his muscled grey horse.

"You counting sheep there, Rob, not cattle, I think? You watch you don' fall off the horse and sleep forever time."

Rob blinked his eyes and shook his head. "Just resting my eyes, Puffer. Just resting my eyes."

"Looks like you givin' them a damn good rest, Boss." The grin widened nearly swallowing his ears.

Rob's smile flashed – a dampened version. "Don't you and Eddie ever sleep?"

"We'll get enough sleep when we dead." The whites of his eyes flashed above the teeth.

Lying in his swag that night, Rob struggled to remember what his earlier vision had been about. A woman and children – but his brain had buried the finer details. *Who were they? Should he know them? Where are they?* Instead of answers to the questions playing in his head, only the sound of the Condamine bells and the smaller tinkler bells on the horses reached his ears, telling him where the animals grazed.

During those periods when all hands worked day and night to ensure the cattle were watered, men worked, ate and slept in cat naps, when they could. An uneasy silence reigned in the camp. Frayed tempers were revealed occasionally in short-lived frowns and frustrated grunts but seldom taken further. What little excess energy each man might have had was spent plumbing the depths of his character for strength. When he fell into the luxury of his swag, Rob wasted little time worrying about his grubby clothes, the stench of his body, or the dirt in his hair and the length of his whiskers. No one complained – everyone smelt the same. Bloodshot eyes peered out of inflamed eyelids. A brief thought of admiration flowed Trevor's way.

The man worked as hard as everyone else but he appeared not to flag. He remained steadfast. Each night, it took all Rob's strength to remove his boots from his feet before his eyes shut and exhaustion stole his mind.

The sour blanket of silence lifted when they entered the country with a permanent water supply near Charleville. Men laughed and joked. They bathed and shaved. Turkey played his mouth organ and Snips' tenor voice mellowed them all. Snips, the barber, cut the men's hair. A beast was killed to replenish their meat supply; a chore avoided in the waterless situations when their time was spent urging cattle forward to the next waterhole and the men lived on a diet of damper, jam and dried fruit. A happy reprieve from the need to coat any remaining salt beef with curry powder to disguise the taste and smell of tainted meat.

"Don't get too relaxed there," Trevor admonished the ringers playing a game of cards and telling yarns around the firelight one night. "The easterly track through Morven, Mitchell and Roma to Miles has many creeks but some of them may have less than the anticipated supply of water for the stock. The one good thing is, my uncle will send out a couple of lads from Rosebud Plains to help us out over the last week or two. They'll know the best watering places."

A few people still walked the street of Bowen in the fading light of day. Light shone through the open doorway of The Grand Hotel and out into the gravel road as Rhylla stopped the car within its glow. She drew a deep breath savouring the salty taste of the sea breeze as it drifted in through the open car windows until overtaken by an aroma of corned meat and cabbage cooking. She looked out at the facade of the two-story building and identified the room on the top floor corner where she and Robbie honeymooned all those years ago – twenty-three to be exact. The wash of nostalgia moistened her eyes.

Rhylla reached across and nudged Kirsty's shoulder. "We're at Bowen, dear." She unlatched the door but remained seated. "Thank heavens we took the time out to have lunch at Home Hill. We'd be starving by now if we hadn't. I'd forgotten how far it was from there to Bowen." She disentangled her body stiffened with inactivity and struggled to exit the vehicle. "I'll go and see the proprietor and collect the keys to our room. We only need to bring in our overnight bags."

"Don't forget to ask for a mud map to find the cottage, Mum." Kirsty's voice mumbled – heavy with exhaustion.

"We'll have plenty of time to do that in the morning, dear. We'll enjoy a sleep-in first and then begin our adventures after breakfast."

With the morning sun gleaming on the bonnet of the newly-washed car, courtesy of the hotel handyman, Rhylla and Kirsty waved a farewell to their host.

"You have got the mud-map with you, I hope, Kirsty."

The wrinkled fingerprinted paper with its smudges and scrawls waved in front of Rhylla's face. "Of course, Mum. Do you think you'll be able to make head or tail of it?"

"I'm sure I will but preferably not while I am trying to drive, dear." Rhylla eased up the clutch and they were away.

After three wrong turns, the blue car bumped along the narrow dirt track leading to their holiday cottage.

"I hope my baby doesn't get a fit of the hiccups on this road, Mum." Both ladies' bottoms lifted off their seats at a particularly deep pot-hole.

"That may be a distinct possibility, Kirsty."

The laughter of both women turned into a gasp of delight as the track they followed hugged the edge of the beach at Grey's Bay. Rhylla braked gently until the car came to a halt. They looked out to where the crystal-clear blue water swallowed the morning sunlight to reveal a sandy seafloor and the glitter of small fish.

"It's not far now to our destination, according to this map," Kirsty frowned as she studied the paper held tight between her two hands.

The track led them firstly to a fisherman's hut of slab timber with push-out wooden windows. Rust coloured the corrugated iron roofing. A man stood at a bench held up by two large rocks near the back of the hut. The sun glinted on the steel of the long knife he wielded with such speed it blurred the eye to see as he reduced a large fish into fillets and bones.

Rhylla's eyes took in the curtainless dwelling as she stopped the car. A large woman appeared at the doorway. Flour puffed from the hands she brushed against the stained apron tied around her waist.

"You be the tenants for Seaview Cottage, I'm guessing," she called. Gaps split the three teeth left in her top gums like tarnished lighthouses. "I be the caretaker, Mrs. White. I be Beryl Barnes's cousin. I'll just be getting you the keys."

Rhylla had opened her door and stood close beside the car left with the engine idling until Mrs. White re-appeared dangling three keys tied on a plaited piece of fishing line.

"Me 'usband Dennis'll meet you at the cottage. It's just around the corner there." A well-fleshed arm pointed along the dirt track. The man rinsed his hands in a bucket by the bench. He looked up at the mention of his name and nodded his grey matted hair.

Rhylla returned to her seat and whispered to her daughter. "These people are our new neighbours, it seems. The woman looks nothing like her cousin, our pedantic Mrs. Barnes." The two passengers grinned.

The track led in from behind the Seaview Cottage. Rhylla felt her hopes drop into her shoes as she pulled up near a rusty corrugated shed beside what was surely the outhouse. The cottage itself appeared to be a replica of the caretaker's hut. At some time in the past, this dwelling had received a coat of white paint, but it appeared sun, wind and weather had left little but a few strips of peeling paint over most of the timber slabs. She looked across at Kirsty who sat with her eyes and mouth open wide.

"Kirsty, at least it does have curtains at the windows, or at least these we can see, have." She struggled to produce a wry grin beneath the worry lines across her forehead.

Kirsty began to laugh – her dimples joined in. "Oh, Mum, this is wonderful. We'll be able to imagine we're true pioneers living the hard life."

Rhylla's eyebrows lifted. "Are you sure, Kirsty? Are you sure you don't mind?"

"Of course, I don't. Come on, let's investigate."

They shut the car doors with a sharp push and endeavoured to find grass stubbles to walk on to keep the sand out of their shoes.

"We'll need to wear our canvas shoes when outside, I should think, Kirsty."

As they rounded the corner of the building, both ladies gasped in surprise to see, opened out before them, a glistening blue bay protected by headlands of rocky boulders and shrubby bushes. She-oak trees cast a mottled shade along the edge of the sandy beach. The peaceful swell of the Pacific Ocean spread for as far as the eye could see.

At the moment Rhylla slotted the key into the lock of the front door, Mr. White appeared from a wallaby path through the trees. A little white and brown dog of dubious breeding followed at his heels.

"The Missus, she opened up the windows earlier to air the place out a bit." Mr. White explained as they entered a neat and clean large single room with the kitchen and living area at one end and a double bed and a set of double bunks at the other.

Rhylla's hopes began to lift when they discovered the inside of the cottage had recently received a fresh coat of paint.

Mr. White continued, "I'll be over each day to check the ice block in the ice-box." He opened the lid to reveal a plate heaped with fish fillets. "You'll be finding spuds in the basin under the sink if you want to have fish and spuds for your tea. Each day, I'll check you've enough fuel for the lamps and wood for the stove. I go to Bowen on Mondays, Wednesdays and Fridays and will fetch ice, bread, and the newspapers or anything else you might need." He turned to leave but swung around once more. "Don't forget you be on rainwater only. You don't want to be wasting the water. When the tank's empty we can't just order up the rain – pity."

Mr. White went to walk away towards the track through the forest and boulders when Rhylla noticed the little dog remained seated on the top step.

"Oh, Mr. White, don't forget your little dog," Rhylla called.

"That's Patch. 'E's not my dog. 'E's nobody's dog now. 'E lived 'ere with Old Joe Gavin until the family took 'im away. Like us all, 'e got too old for the fishing." Mr. White stood staring out over the sea. He sniffed long and hard. "'E was a good'un, Joe Gavin. Now, don't you worry none about the dog, it won't 'urt a fly and comes visits me Missus for a feed each night. It just waits 'ere at the hut 'opin' for Joe to return."

Mr. White disappeared along the track. Rhylla and Kirsty looked down at the dog. The dog looked up at the women – he wagged his tail.

"Oh, Mum, he is delightful."

"Hello, Patch," Rhylla smiled, "Seems you've won my daughter's heart."

Early next morning the sun sparkled on a blue sea lapping soft upon the sands of the calm bay. Sunlight shone in through the front windows. Rhylla peered out to where three fishermen baited their hooks before throwing their lines into the water. Often, they waited in vain for a response from the fish. When they trawled the lines back to the sandy beach an occasional shout of joy spread out across the sea while a fisherman challenged the determination of a scaly body to dislodge the hook from its mouth. Rhylla stroked the photo frame she held to her chest, lost for the moment in the idyllic scene.

"Would you like a cup of tea, Mum?"

Rhylla dragged herself back to the present. "Yes please, Kirsty." She held the frame away from her chest and stared at this picture which Robbie had treasured so much. When packing her clothes' port back in Townsville, common-sense had told Rhylla the photo's presence with her at all times was not going to make an ounce of difference to her lover's fate, but she slipped it in beside her beach towel anyway. He had taken the photo with the camera given to him for Christmas when Kirsty was only a four-year-old. Bronwyn would have been seven and Tim nearing nine years of age at the time. It never failed to fascinate her every time she studied this photo how the characters of her three children were so simply portrayed: Kirsty, the lover of dance and music, while the other two held more serious interests. Bronwyn's need to compete was highly developed even at that young age. Rhylla placed the frame back on the table and turned to join Kirsty.

"Anything specific you want to do today?" she asked.

"I guess at almost six months pregnant clambering over those boulders might be out of the question. We must bring the baby here when it is old enough to enjoy this magic place."

"You can climb the rocks after the little mite is delivered. I'll be happy to babysit. A few years back I'd have been happy to play rock wallaby with you but I think those days may be over." Rhylla sipped from the cup of tea placed in front of her. "Will we try our luck fishing?"

"Without any lines? Might be a bit difficult."

"There are lines in that little shed out back next to the outhouse. I'm sure Mr. White will oblige with bait. The locals certainly seem to enjoy the sport. In the meantime, we can walk along the sand."

By the time Rhylla and Kirsty restoked the fireplace and eaten porridge for their breakfast, the fishermen had left, leaving only their footprints in the sand.

"Take your shoes off, Mum." Kirsty sat on a fallen log and removed her canvas shoes. She wiggled her feet in the soft sand. Her blue dress swirled against her legs as she ran towards the shoreline.

Their laughter rippled over the waves as Rhylla wasted no time in joining her daughter. She hitched up her skirts to her knees and stepped into the shallow water. She gasped with pleasure at the coolness against her skin.

Mother and daughter stood, each with one arm holding their skirts. Their second arm threaded about the waist of the other. They stood in the shallows for long moments, both deep in their thoughts, while the ebb and flow of wavelets vacuumed the sand from under their feet.

With her eyes closed, Rhylla felt again Robbie's arms about her waist holding her steady as the sand disappeared from under their feet at another deserted Bowen beach, on their honeymoon. A soft smile tweaked at her lips. She recalled how they spent as much time exploring the treasures of their young bodies as they spent exploring the treasures washed up along the shoreline.

"Mum … Mum," Kirsty's concern leant an edge to her voice. "Are you alright? Your face has gone all funny – soft, like a marshmallow – and why the silly grin? And you should have your hat on. The sun's reflection on the sea has made your eyes water.

It took several seconds for Rhylla to bring her mind back to the present. "Marshmallow – you say my skin is like a marshmallow. You get to cook our fish and potato scallops for tea tonight for that remark, young lady." Both women smiled. "You are right about the sun hats though. The sun has a definite bite to it. I think I'll go up and read my book." Rhylla turned to her daughter. "You're a little sunburnt yourself. Would you like me to bring your hat down to you?"

"Thanks, Mum, no. I'll come up to the cottage with you. I want to sketch those boulders out on the point over there."

CHAPTER TWENTY

Noise! Noise, heat and dust! Thirsty stock! Whips cracked above the pounding hooves of bellowing cattle. The smell of water teased their nostrils and lent promise to their thirst. The riders yelled their orders. Whistles pierced the wall of dust and noise. Determined beasts feinted repeatedly against the equally determined men on horseback. Dirt swirled up from the shuffling feet to reduce the ringers' vision. It sifted through the neckerchiefs worn across their noses.

Lying low across the horse's neck, with the sweat and dust mixed to mud across his face, Rob rode on the left-wing. Billy's shouts came to him from behind. Trevor, Eddie and Streak worked the front swinging the leaders around upon themselves. Only the sound of their working whips and whistles reached Rob's ears. Their voices were lost in the cacophony of noise. Similar sounds struggled across the herd from the right-wing where Snips and Turkey fought the same battles.

As the cattle began to turn, Rob sat up in the saddle. The wind had risen picking up the dust and herding it away from his position. At first, he planned only to glance behind, but his head froze at the sight he beheld. Way back on the horizon, a lightning strike streaked from the sky. Its light fenced the blue-grey of the distant hills from the black-grey of a heavy sky. The horse beneath him tossed its head.

Rob turned further in the saddle searching for Billy. A wide smile and a pointing arm told him Billy had already seen the threatening storm.

Exhausted cattle began to stir at this new agitation. Nostrils flared with the promise of rain in the army of clouds charging across the plains towards them, darkening the sky as they approached. The riders circled the perimeter of fearful flesh speaking softly to horse and bullock alike, striving to settle the terror of a savage thunderstorm bearing down upon their defenceless position. The crack of whips now silent, outgunned by the ear-splitting claps of intermittent thunder. A dark world lit up with each lightning flash as it struck the earth.

Riders turned their attention to their jobs – to keep the cattle calm against impossible odds. Each man stilled the whirlpool of rising fear within his guts, refusing to consider his own vulnerability.

The wall of water crashed to earth around their heads. It swallowed the dust in one mighty gulp. Stock stilled – shocked into submission. Beaten, they stood heads down with their rumps into the weather. Thick dry tongues lapped at the water running down their noses. Men pulled the neckerchiefs from their faces and stuffed them into their saturated pockets. Heads lifted into the stinging rain drops savouring the moisture on their lips.

There followed an uneventful three weeks as they made their way east from Charleville after the bounty brought by the electrical storm. Horizons closed in with the occasional hills. Trees often provided shade at the midday camps, while creeks and streams ran with water.

"Welcome to the easy life, Rob."

Rob lifted his drooping head. With a smile wide upon his face, Steve rode up on his near side. "It's amazing what a bit of water will do to a man and beast."

They rode in silence occasionally nudging a grazing beast forward. When Steve jerked straighter in the saddle, Rob lifted his head, his eyes alert.

"Do you see that?" Steve's arm stretched out towards a line of trees in the distance ahead.

From their position at the lead, Rob stared but did not see anything of note. "Looks like another creek in front of us."

"No, not the trees. The two men on horseback."

Again, Rob stared ahead. "What? You don't mean those two black dots at the edge of the trees – they look like tree stumps been struck by lightning?"

"If I'm not mistaken, one of those burnt tree stumps will be my older brother, Mark. The other may be another brother or one of Dad's station-hands."

"We can't be too far from Rosebud Plains then, I take it."

"No, not far now. Maybe four days – all going well."

Five days later, a herd of travel-weary cattle, horses and men were diverted onto Rosebud Plains Station where Trevor and his cousin, Mark Whittle, rested their horses on either side of the open gate, counting the beasts as they passed through.

Rob hung back with the droving team when three riders approached to greet Billy and Steve.

It was Eddie who quietly informed him. "The old fellow is Tom Whittle, he's Minnie Jackson's brother and Steve's father. The fellow on the grey horse is Stewart Whittle. He's Steve's brother after Mark who led us here over the past few days. The sourpuss on the black horse is the next brother, Davey." They watched as Steve and Billy rode over to meet the family members. "Come on then, Rob. You can give us a hand to take our horses and Spud's packhorses up the back to the stockyards. We'll set up camp in the men's quarters."

Rob worked with Eddie, Puffer and Sunshine all afternoon as they checked the horses, removed the bells and hobbles from their necks and released them into the horse paddock as directed by an old dark-skinned man they called Blinkers – one of the station-hands on Rosebud Plains. With a mouthful of orders and flapping arms, Spud directed the unloading of the packhorses near a two-sided corrugated iron-roofed shed with a lean of enough degrees to make Rob think twice about entering.

"Don't come in here with your knees shaking, boys – you might bring the place down around our ears." Spud directed Sunshine and Rob as to where they were to place everything within his campsite. "We're having fresh meat tonight, I've been informed. They killed a beast this morning for us." The remainder of the ringers approached preparing to settle in but Spud had other ideas. "There's nothing for you here, just yet. You can help Sunshine clean up the leathers on the packsaddles."

Snips opened his mouth to grumble but was cut off with Spud's tone, "Don't go playing ladies here young'un. If you're wantin' the sweetbread tonight you can help clean the leathers."

The cool of night had been devoured by the heat of the early morning sunshine. Laughter, shouts and cooees from the stockyards drew Rob across the flats to investigate. Men were lined up along the rails offering encouragement to a local stockman who held on grimly to the reins of a piebald horse determined to remove him and the saddle from its back. Encouragement and instructions filled the air beneath the shade of the tall trees but were ignored by the otherwise occupied rider.

Rob rested his elbows on a rail and peered between two rails above. The snorting, bucking animal raced past his position sending up a cloud of dust. Rob jumped back. His face reddened as he coughed and spat until he nearly vomited.

"You right there, lad?"

Rob looked up into Tom Whittle's eyes crinkled with laughter. "It's a long time since I've been called a lad." He found it a struggle to find his voice lost amidst the dust in his throat.

"I guess it's all relative. I still call my son and nephew, lads, besides a few other names at times. You're their friend, I understand."

Rob stood back from the stockyard fence. "I reckon I might be nearly old enough to be their father."

"They told me how you rescued them on a train trip a while back."

"They've rescued me from a mine collapse since then. We're even."

Tom Whittle smiled and nodded his head. "As they should have too." He moved in closer to peer through the rails to watch the final act of rebellion by the horse. Sweat frothed on the hides of animal and rider. Cheers and whistles split the air around them.

Rob stood watching the cool demeanour of the rider. "Geez, that was some ride but look at him sitting there as if he'd just rode a kid's rocking horse."

"Don't be fooled, Rob. I bet you anything you like his heart is pounding like six horses were kicking on a stable door inside his chest. And that silly grin covers the fact he's sucking in air like the intake valve on an engine. The water dripping from his shirt will be all sweat but I bet some of that below the waist is piss. And I bet his arse cheeks are clenched so tight he won't be able to part them for several days."

"Well, he's doing a damn good job of covering it all up."

"The chaps call that young bloke, Glue. You can see why. He should be pretty chuffed with himself. The Piebald Bucker has a history of beating more experienced riders than that little fella."

The two men watched the rider dismount and lean heavily into the horse for some moments.

Tom turned his head towards Rob again. "I had a letter from my sister Minnie Jackson and her husband William. They speak very highly of you. William's words, if I remember, went something like this, 'He may be able to milk a cow and ride a horse but this fella's experienced in more cerebral pursuits'."

Rob's eyebrows lifted. "That was kind of them."

"Minnie wants you back as a bookkeeper. She can't praise your work enough."

"I'll send a message back with Trevor. I plan to move on."

"Is that because you're a natural wanderer or because of your memory loss. Minnie told me about your mining accident. Remember, with this financial depression, work is hard to come by, you know."

"Yes, I read the papers when they come my way. It's a worry right now, I agree. As I see it, things will not get better in the short term."

"Well, I'd like to test Minnie's opinion. If you can tidy up my account books, I'll speak to a friend in Toowoomba next time I'm down that way – he's an accountant. He's always whining he can't find bookkeepers for his office. What do you say?"

"Can I think about it for a bit?"

"Of course, but I do have time restrictions. I usually head off to Toowoomba in the first half of each November to place our Christmas orders. My housekeeper, Mrs. Paisley, has a list a mile long for me to have filled and then the mailman will need to deliver them to Rosebud Plains. The station-hands like to have a bit of a knees-up down there for a couple of days."

"How bad are your books? How long should it take to sort them out?"

"They're not too bad really – as long as you can read my writing, I guess. And my bookkeeping system leaves a lot to be desired, I'm told." Tom jumped back as one of the men came tumbling from the top rail. "You okay there, fella?" He turned again to Rob. "No more than a couple of weeks, I shouldn't think."

"Can I think on it overnight?"

"Of course."

Two days later, Rob looked up from the desk in Tom Whittle's office at the sound of footsteps approaching along the verandah. Trevor, Billy and Steve arrived at the doorway together. Their wide grins filled the gap.

"I can see you won't be joining us on the return trip to Far Horizons," Trevor spoke first.

Rob looked over the dusty books piled high on an untidy desk. He returned the grin. The task had seemed almost insurmountable on his arrival here but since then he had identified what books held what information.

"No, lads, I'll not be going back with you. Will you pass my regards and thanks on to Minnie and William?"

After a little argy-bargy, the three men burst into the room with hands outstretched. Rob shook the hand of each man while they wished him the best for the future. "And if you're up near the Far Horizons, don't be a stranger. Mum and Dad will be offended if you don't drop in," Trevor stressed.

"I most certainly will," Rob replied.

Rob followed them out of the house. From the shade of a pepperina tree, he watched as they mounted their horses and swung them around to follow the droving plant returning to Far Horizons.

Snips and Turkey were not with the group. They had left the day before to spend a little time and all of their pay, no doubt, in the big smoke of Brisbane.

A feeling of aloneness and despondency washed over Rob as he walked back to attack the account books in Tom Whittle's office. *This must be what it feels like to watch your family leave*, he pondered. *Have I left a family behind somewhere in my past?* Within minutes, back in front of the work crying out for attention, these feelings were overtaken by concentration on the work at hand.

His sneezes spilled out through the window when he used a rag, released from under a stack of novels on a chair in the corner, to wipe over all the account books and the desk. He lined up six errant pencils, one rubber and a ruler beside a heap of old envelopes to be used as scribble paper. The pen and inkwell were pushed aside for later use. Rob stretched his body upright in the seat, griped and released his fists several times before he reached over to place the first ledger open in front of himself.

The ten days it took him to wrangle and tie the hit-and-miss accounting system of Rosebud Plains, left Rob with a grumbling back pain, an aching head and red-rimmed eyes. The days spent explaining things to Tom and Mark Whittle left him thinking he was going to lose his mind.

Any discontent disappeared as he joined them and the others travelling by train to Toowoomba a week later. All travelled on Tom Whittle's coin.

A rowdy bunch of ringers with swags thrown over their shoulders ambled along Russell Street from the Toowoomba Railway Station towards West Street. They all stood back to allow Tom Whittle to pass through the partly opened sagging gate leading into a medium-sized cottage set back on an allotment with the lawns recently scythed.

"Davey, duck over and get the key off our merry widow, mate." Tom's pointing finger directed his son to the large house next door. "Don't dawdle about yapping, either. We don't want the merry widow to get her claws into you. She'll swallow you up in one bite, boyo."

"Aww, Dad, do I have to?"

"Stop complaining. Get the bloody key."

Rob noticed the outside of the cottage could well do with a coat of paint but inside appeared to have been recently introduced to a broom and dust cloth. Besides a kitchen and living area, the building consisted of two bedrooms and a closed-in verandah. He followed the example of the other ringers as they dropped their swags onto the floor of the verandah. Tom Whittle laid claim to one bedroom while his sons, Stewart and Davey, settled into the second bedroom. Mark had been left to supervise Rosebud Plains. His brother Steve had returned to Far Horizons with his cousins Billy and Trevor Jackson.

Within half an hour, the younger men had left in dribs and drabs to explore the city, its food and nightlife. Tom Whittle sat on the back steps with Rob. The men drank whiskey. Rob held his glass towards the fading light. He thought their glasses may have been crystal.

"This place has a woman's touch, Mr. Whittle. Is there a Mrs. Whittle hereabouts?"

The man sat in a despondent slouch. "No, Rob, not anymore. She died a few years back. She always had a delicate constitution. That's why young Steve lived up at Far Horizons from when he was a toddler. My wife could not cope with four small children on land miles from a city and with no women to help." The man sat staring out into the night closing in upon them. After long moments his body shuddered. He jumped up.

"Come on then, Rob Bains, I'm starving and I see the Merry Widow has left us a potato pie in the fridge. Let's eat."

While cutting two slices from the pie, Tom laughed quietly, "You can stay here when you get the job with the accountant. You'll have the scheming ways of the hussy next door to contend with, but the rent will be free. That's thanks for the help you've afforded the family."

In the dusk, as Rhylla drove in through the front gate of her home in Townsville, the depression hit her like a scud of rain slashing across the windscreen. Robbie's image filled her mind, but he was not going to come running out of the house to greet her as he used to do when she had been away. In those happy days, she had always felt the pull of desire just to see the laughter lines around his darkening blue eyes and felt his familiar warm hands on her body once again.

It was Mr. Evans coming from his flat above the coach-shed and Mrs. Barnes from the kitchen pulling the apron from her waist, who rushed out to greet the returning holidaymakers. Rhylla looked across at Kirsty – at her face blooming with health and her body swollen with child. A soft smile rested on Rhylla's lips as she watched her girl, no woman, she admonished herself, waddle over to hug the welcoming committee. Kirsty threw herself into the arms of Mrs. Barnes.

"It's so lovely to have you back. Your parents will join us for dinner shortly, Mrs. MacBurnie."

In the fading light, Mr. Evans began to unload the car. When sand flew up into his face from the rug he dragged out of the boot, he asked with a laugh, "What have we here, half the beaches of Bowen?"

Rhylla walked into her daughter's room where Kirsty was dabbing the finishing touches on the portrait of her mother developed from the sketch she had made when on their Bowen holiday together.

"Oh, Kirsty, that's beautiful. I can almost hear the lapping of the water on the beach. I'm sure you have reduced the grey in my hair and the wrinkles on my face, but I'm not going to complain."

"Mum, I paint what I see."

"Thank you, dear." Rhylla stepped back to view the painting from a different perspective. "It's very good. Is this what you plan on entering in the Art Competition next week?"

"I thought I might."

"It's a worthy entry, Kirsty." Rhylla turned to leave the room when she swung back to speak. "Kirsty, it's only a week until Tim and Bronwyn will be home for their Christmas break. Do you think I should plan some excursions for them?"

"Mum, I'm sure they'll have plans for their own entertainment with local friends. They're not children anymore."

"You don't need to remind me. Tim towers over me. I guess I'd better be prepared for the influx of untidy males, footballs, cricket bats and tennis rackets."

Kirsty laughed, "And their conversations will follow suit – when they're not talking girls behind closed doors."

Rhylla's laughter joined in. "And our Bronwyn sounds more like my mother every time I see her. It's galling to hear her telling me what I should and should not be doing in my life."

"I don't think she'll be on your back this time. I'm sure I'll be the one to get the rough edge of her tongue." Kirsty's eyes glanced down at her protruding belly and a wry grin twisted her lips.

An unexpected letter from Bronwyn arrived in the next mail. It announced she would be home for only the three days before

Christmas and three days after Christmas. She had been invited to spend the remaining holidays, including the New Year, with her friend on a property near Rockhampton.

After reading the words on the pale pink writing paper, Rhylla felt a rush of guilt swamp the initial feeling of relief. Robbie's words were loud in her head. "Don't let Bronwyn make you feel guilty, my Kitten. That girl can be like a bindi-eye in a saddle blanket at times."

Tim's body seemed to fill the complete door frame as he stood with laughter in his eyes and a wide grin on his face. Kirsty's laughter filled the room. "You're home. We didn't expect you until tomorrow." She began to waddle across to her brother.

"I caught the plane. Well, my little dimpled duck, give me a hug," Tim teased. "Are my arms going to stretch all the way around you two?"

Kirsty punched his arm before falling into his embrace. Tears poured down her cheeks.

"If you're going to make this shirt all soppy you can stand back, sister." Tim's deep laugh joined Kirsty's lighter tinkling laugh.

Rhylla rushed into the room. "Oh, Tim, you're early."

"My little duck here and I have already covered that bit. I caught a plane instead of the train. Bronwyn took the train to Rockhampton and will catch another train to be here before Christmas day." Tim released himself from Kirsty's grasp and strode over to wrap his arms around his mother. He lifted her into the air. "Do I get to pat you on the head like you were forever doing to me years ago?"

"Put me down, you … you big galoot."

Mrs. Barnes came across from her flat to see what all the merriment was about.

"My boy, my little boy – just look at you now." She moved in for her hug too.

Tim extricated himself from the women and asked, "Is Mr. Evans here today?"

It was Mrs. Barnes who answered. "He's gone to fetch some things from town. He should be only a moment. Come on into the kitchen and have a cuppa. I swear the man can smell the tea brewing and he'll pop right in."

Six days later as Rhylla crawled into bed exhausted having spent the day with Tim and Kirsty on Magnetic Island, pleasure and satisfaction overwhelmed her. Instead of her usual tears of sorrow when she crawled into her lonely bed, happy tears dampened her cheeks. Only Tim could have enticed his little sister to leave the house and Rhylla was so pleased to have him do so. Not once did he leave Kirsty's side. He stood tall and proud – a barrier for any curious looks or cruel comments. She lay listening to the music floating up the staircase as the pair of siblings played duets not heard for years.

Her smile dissipated with the thought of Bronwyn's imminent arrival on the morrow. Had the girl matured enough to leave petty jealousies behind or was she going to be the trigger to ruin everyone's Christmas?

CHAPTER TWENTY-ONE

"Oh, for Pete's sake, Grandpa, will you stop fussing about Kirsty like she's a living saint." Bronwyn's chair crashed backwards. The tone of her voice lifted in small increments with every word.

Rhylla's head rose from the Christmas card she was reading on the table in front of her. Mrs. Barnes tapped at Mr. Evans's sleeve and they both rose gathering up some dirty dishes from the table before making their escape into the kitchen. Mrs. McNeven's face paled. Tim frowned and rescued the chair. He tugged at Bronwyn's arm in an effort to draw her back down into her seat. She shrugged off his hand.

"She's responsible for this predicament she's in, I'm sure." She turned to her sister sitting with tears running down her cheeks and over her quivering lips. "Don't sit there like a bloated frog trying to look all innocent. You always encouraged the boys to hang around you at school with their tongues out and slobbering all over you. So, when one of them takes what you offered, you're all offended, and it's everyone's fault but your own."

Tim jumped to his feet. "Enough, Bronwyn. That's not true and you know it. You have excelled yourself in evil this time."

"Oh, shut up, Tim. Trust you to take her side. It's because of her, my father has left the house in shame."

"He's not only your father, Bronwyn, he's our father too – and Mum's husband. Have you no thought of anyone but yourself?"

Rhylla's chair landed with a crash behind her. Icicles dripped off her words spoken in almost a whisper. "Bronwyn, if you can't keep a civil tongue in your head, you can pack your bags right now. This is way beyond the pale. Your sister does not need stress like this so close to her confinement. I hope you can show better manners when staying at your friend's place."

Tears welled in Bronwyn's eyes as she stormed up the staircase to her room. "Nobody ever sees my side of things," she mumbled.

After the upheaval of emotions during the Christmas period with Bronwyn leaving in a huff and then several weeks later, the sad farewell to Timothy who departed to begin his training at the Brisbane office, Rhylla felt relief in returning to the relative normality of their lives. Kirsty struggled with her enlarged body in the suffocating humidity and heat. Her mood swings from depression to anxious anticipation of the birth of her baby strained everyone's patience. Not a day went by when Rhylla did not give thanks for the presence of the unfazed and dependable Mrs. Barnes.

"Mrs. Barnes! Mrs. Barnes!" Kirsty stood as if frozen to the spot. One hand held tightly to her enlarged abdomen, the other rested on the edge of the piano keyboard. Fluid dampened her skirt and dripped onto the floor of the music room. Pain ripped through her body.

The household had been functioning on a knife-edge for a week since the first of February when Kirsty's due date had arrived and passed.

Oh, why did Mother choose this morning to go into the office? rattled around somewhere at the back of her thoughts. *Or should I be saying why did you choose to come this very morning when my mother is not here, little one?* Kirsty amended her views. Relief washed over her at the sound of Mrs. Barnes's hurrying footsteps along the corridor.

"Oh, Kirsty, Kirsty, now don't panic. Remember what we practised." The housekeeper reached over and gave the young girl a gentle hug. "This is just your waters broken."

Kirsty's tears of fear and embarrassment saturated her blouse. "I'm so sorry, Mrs. Barnes, I've made a mess on your nice floor."

"Nothing a mop won't sort out, dear. Now, you have more important things to be thinking about. Let's get you onto the bed next door and then I'll ring your mother at her town office and the doctor."

Another pain grabbed her back while Kirsty sat in the chair watching Mrs. Barnes spreading the mackintosh on the bed and covering it with clean sheets.

Rhylla brought her car to a stop amidst skidding tyres and a cloud of dust. Doctor Gleeson arrived a moment behind her in a more sedate manner.

"Skidding tyres, Mrs. MacBurnie?" The words were accompanied by a wry grin. "I do hope you're not going to become overwrought on me. Kirsty and I will both need your steady hand and common sense this morning."

Rhylla took several deep breaths. "Your right, Doctor Gleeson. Sorry. Please come inside."

When Rhylla and the doctor entered the bedroom where Kirsty now lay in a restless doze, Mrs. Barnes turned towards the kitchen.

"I'll make a cup of tea for everyone then, shall I?"

Deep lines of worry eased somewhat at the appearance of the new arrivals. In the kitchen, her anxious hands prepared a mixture of dough. Within minutes a dozen scones sat upon a greased tray and were placed into the hot oven.

After his initial examination, Doctor Gleeson stood in thought outside the bedroom door. He sucked in the aroma of freshly baked scones as it wafted along the corridor. Tired feet led him to the kitchen.

"Mrs. Barnes, is it?" He addressed the housekeeper from the kitchen doorway. "That sure smells tempting. Mrs. MacBurnie asked if you might send a tray to her office for us both. And young Kirsty may have a cup of black tea if you will."

"Yes, of course, Doctor. Do you know the way to Mrs. MacBurnie's office?"

"Yes, I think so. I'll just follow this corridor around to the far corner, right?"

"Yes, Doctor. I'll bring the tray in a moment."

Rhylla's heart ached for her daughter as she freshened up Kirsty's face with a cloth wet with rose water. Her mind admired the girl's determination.

"I'll go and talk to Doctor Gleeson in the office. This sounds like Mrs. Barnes with a cup of tea for you, darling." Rhylla looked up as Mrs. Barnes swept into the room carrying a small tray with a cup of weak black tea sweetened with a spoon of sugar.

"Mrs. MacBurnie, I have left a tray in your office. The doctor is waiting there for you."

"Thanks, Mrs. Barnes," Rhylla nodded.

As she entered the office, she was pleased to see Doctor Gleeson sitting behind a cup of tea and a plate upon which sat two buttered scones.

"If only my wife and I had a cook like this." The doctor raised the scone in salute.

"Yes, she is a treasure. And no, you cannot have her. She is part of this family. Goodness me, she was here when I had my three children." Rhylla grinned.

"I'm glad to hear she'll not fall apart at this childbirth. However, I think I'll call in Mrs. Gleeson today, given the fact Kirsty is very young and this is her first birthing. My wife is a midwife and has helped with many of my deliveries. That is if you don't mind."

"We'll be very glad to have her expertise, Doctor Gleeson."

The day passed slowly for everyone – especially Kirsty. Mrs. Gleeson made herself useful yet inconspicuous sitting in the corner with her knitting when not otherwise occupied attending her patient. The doctor left on several other house-calls, now and then returning to assess the progress of the birth. Rhylla never left her daughter's side unless instructed by the midwife to move back to facilitate nursing care. Mrs. Barnes ensured everyone was catered for. Mr. Evans weeded the vegetable patch, pruned the roses and the front hedge as well as washed his own utility once and Mrs. MacBurnie's car three times before polishing it until it shone as it had the day it arrived on the train when new.

When Kirsty's contractions increased in frequency and compressed squeals fought their way past her tight lips, Mrs. Gleeson urged Rhylla to wait outside but she refused.

"You worry about that end and I'll look after the top end," Rhylla instructed the midwife whose eyes widened in surprise. Never had she been told to do that before at a childbirth.

Mrs. Gleeson looked anxiously at the watch hanging on the front of her uniform. Her eyes often drifted to the doorway. Rhylla held Kirsty's hand tighter and swabbed her brow continuously.

Through a crashing wall of pain, Kirsty almost laughed, "Mother, you're drowning me in rose water." But her weak smile was short-lived as a deep groan struggled up through her throat.

The midwife assisted the girl to roll onto her side and massaged the small of her back with olive oil. "It won't be long now, Kirsty." Again, her eyes lifted towards the doorway. At the sound of footsteps with which she was very familiar, relief lightened her expression.

The doctor swept into the room. "So how are we doing here?" Mrs. Gleeson moved aside while the doctor made his examination. "You two have been busy, I see. This baby is on its way."

The late afternoon sun crept through the curtains as the squall of a baby girl made her presence felt. The doctor and his wife busied themselves at the bottom end while at the top end of the bed, Rhylla's tears equalled Kirsty's streaming down their cheeks.

"Oh, darling, you have done it. Congratulations. You are wonderful."

"Thank you, Grandma." Kirsty's face glowed as the baby wrapped in a lemon bunny rug was lifted onto her arms. Her eyes sparkled.

In the kitchen, Mrs. Barnes and Mr. Evans laughed softly.

"We have a baby in the house again, how wonderful," Mrs. Barnes felt as proud as a grandmother herself.

"Well, we'd best look to our laurels. A young baby will keep us all on our toes, I should think." Moist eyes glistened above Mr. Evans's wide grin.

Back in the bedroom, Kirsty, cleaned and dressed in fresh clothing, sat on the chair by the bed nursing her baby.

"Thank you, Doctor Gleeson and Mrs. Gleeson, thank you so much." Kirsty smiled her gratitude as the pair left the room having refused refreshments from the kitchen.

Rhylla noticed Mrs. Barnes and Mr. Evans where they stood down the hallway. Anticipation painted their expressions.

"One minute," she called softly and pushed the linen for washing into the buckets waiting out in the corridor. Another bucket from the end of the bed with blood and afterbirth was covered with a cloth and placed outside the bedroom too.

"Can I let Mrs. Barnes and Mr. Evans in, Kirsty?"

A big grin and nod directed the first visitors to enter.

After all their adulation was exhausted, Rhylla asked, "Have you decided on a name for my grandchild yet, Kirsty?"

"Skye-Marie, Mum – Skye for my great-grandma and Marie for your second name."

"Skye-Marie," Rhylla whispered. "Beautiful."

Rob Bains's merry whistle set the birds in the trees above his head into a frenzy of fluttering wings and musical notes. He enjoyed striding along this part of West Street each workday, morning and afternoon. The canvas satchel slung over his shoulder contained a crib box, a notebook and a pencil.

"Yahoo, Mr. Bains."

The shrill voice froze Rob in his tracks. Clouds stole the sunshine in his day. Guilt filled his mind at his intolerance for a woman who only tried to be helpful, after all. He turned his face towards the tree branches hoping she might think him engrossed and go away but there was little chance of such luck.

The vines growing over the neighbour's back fence were swept aside, left and right, as her not unpretty head poked over the top.

"Oh, Mr. Bains, have you had a good day? I've made a cottage pie for my tea and it will be way too much for me to eat. Can I entice you to join me in a meal?"

Rob bit his tongue on the rude comment pounding on the back of his lips. A cooked meal sounded all right, but there were complications attached. Her never-ending voice for one, not to mention the insidious suggestions for their future, another. Testosterone stirred in his blood at his memory of glimpses of the woman's body exposed on frequent occasions – purely by accident, of course. Yet he was a man and his body had desperate needs at times. But ….

"I'm sorry, Mrs. Leek, I'll be working tonight."

"You work too hard, dear man. I'll drop a slice of pie over shortly then. It will save you cooking for yourself."

How could he be so crass as to refuse?

Rob's legs almost galloped the last few yards to his gate. He raced up the three steps, opened the door, shutting it with a slam behind him.

"Damn, damn, damn."

He let his weight fall back against the door taking long deep breaths in and out. He slid the strap of his satchel off his shoulder and made his way into the kitchen where an old typewriter sat on the table amongst the debris of his breakfast and crib-making earlier in the day. Four ledger notepads sat in a pile on one side of his recently acquired writing instrument and a box of typing paper sat on the other side. Moving to the sink he filled a glass with water and drank it without taking a breath.

"What am I going to do about this pesky neighbour?" He asked the willy wagtail dancing on the bushes outside the window. Once more his loins stirred at the thought of the open invitation to take all her treasures along with her compliments. What was stopping him? But he knew quite well what was stopping him – besides that voice, you could make sirens out of. It was the visions he remembered having on the droving track – the beautiful strawberry-blond-haired woman and the three children. The vision of a boy with his horse sheltered from a storm in a stable and the same boy following cattle within a forest. More recently, here at Toowoomba, on those nights when depression fell upon him along with the dark of night. When the repetitive nightmare disturbed his sleep with its crowd of people without faces. The lone woman at the edge of the dream – he knows her to be beautiful but he cannot see her face yet his fingers sense every inch of her body. Every time this dream fills his semi-conscious mind, his roaming fingers stop at a scar on her right leg. Sometimes his dreams include two blond women, maybe a mother and daughter, dancing around a maypole. The pair twirl faster and faster when he approaches them until just as his hands reach out to touch one or the other, they spin off into oblivion.

The knock on the door returned Rob's mind to the present, still having found no solution to his problem. He opened the back door but did not invite Mrs. Leek in.

"The pie I promised, Mr. Bains." She lifted her foot as if to enter but Rob stood in the gap of a door partly shut. "I cannot hear the clicking typewriter yet."

"No, Mrs. Leek, I'm just gathering my thoughts. Thanks for the pie. I'll wash the plate and leave it on your back steps as usual." Rob was just short of grabbing the dish out of her hands. He took the door handle in his tight clasp and edged it closed on the still-talking visitor. As it shut with a soft click, guilt at his lack of manners struggled with the rush of relief for having escaped.

Christmas holidays found Rob tapping away constantly at his typewriter and deliberately ignoring the multitude of knocks on his back door. When his thirst and appetite interrupted the writing and he discovered a meal of cold chicken with salads and plum pudding in custard sitting wrapped in clean tea-towels on his back steps, guilt fermented in his conscience once again.

Boxing Day morning, Mrs. Leek was to be seen in her back garden cutting fresh flowers. Guilt travelled with Rob along with his canvas satchel when he set out for the cricket ground where he had promised to join his boss and fellow staff for a game. He assuaged his battered conscience by pausing for a moment to call, "Hello, Mrs. Leek, thank you for the lovely dinner yesterday. I hope you had a pleasant day."

Mrs. Leek's mouth opened. She dragged in a deep breath in preparation to apprise him of all her Christmas news. Disappointment sapped the anticipation from her expression when her target had disappeared across the street and through the trees on a vacant allotment.

His boss, Mr. Acton the accountant, dropped into the room where three desks accommodated the three bookkeepers he employed. "Can you pop into my office a moment, Rob?"

Rob pushed back his chair and stood. A slither of fear tickled his gut for a moment but common sense told him it would be unlikely for the boss to be about to discharge him. Rob knew his work was fast and accurate. If asked how this was so, he would be unable to say. Besides, the workload kept the three bookkeepers more than busy. He entered Mr. Acton's office.

"Good, good, Rob. Come in, come in. Sit." He pointed to one of the two seats in front of his writing bureau. Rob sat with his hands on his knees in the chair indicated. "Rob, how are you finding it working with us here?"

"Good thanks, Mr. Acton."

"You seem to a have a knowledge far above a simple bookkeeper's standard, Rob."

A cold hand clutched his heart. Was the boss going to throw him out in case he asked for more money or something?

"Tom Whittle mentioned a little of your unfortunate accident and its aftermath." He noticed the lines deepen in Rob's forehead. "Please, don't be angry. I have not and will not mention your memory loss to anyone else. What I'm trying to say is you've obviously had a good grounding in this business and I'm asking you if you'd be happy to take on more responsibility. Of course, there will be an increase in your pay packet at the end of the week."

Rob sat quietly for some moments. Even with the country's financial depression showing some signs of easing, this was a handsome offer for a lowly bookkeeper. He relished the thought of further challenges but he did not want to draw attention to himself until his memory returned and he had a better idea of why he had been travelling with an assumed name as Steve and Billy had told him back in Mount Isa. More money would not go astray if he wanted to keep writing this book – this novel – he felt he had rambling around in his head.

"Thank you, Mr. Acton. I'd be happy to help you out where I can."

"Right, that's settled then. Now," Mr. Acton reached into the tray on his desk. He passed across an envelope with Rob's name written on the front in a slanting scrawl. "This is from my missus. She has invited all the staff to a belated Christmas celebration at our house this Saturday evening. Can you come?"

At first, Rob's inclination was to refuse. He thought of several hours of writing missed but then he reconsidered. They had all been working hard in the past months and a good knees-up might be just the shot.

"Thanks, Mr. Acton. That does sound wonderful. Please thank your wife."

Most of Saturday Rob spent regretting having agreed to attend the boss's dinner party, but when Mrs. Leek arrived in the mid-afternoon trying very hard to collar him into attending an evening listening to chamber music, he gladly clung to the excuse of a boss's prior dinner invitation.

On the evening of the dinner, he and his fellow bookkeepers, Liam and Ernie, dawdled around the gate leading into the Acton's front garden waiting for the arrival of their part-time typist, Miss Duggan. Each man smelt of soap and hair oil. Their clothes were fresh and ironed or as in Rob's case the trousers pressed under the mattress of his bed for twenty-four hours.

"Bloody women, always late," grumbled Liam. His arthritic fingers smoothed the thinning grey hair on his head.

"I've six sisters and I learnt long ago never to get into a lather about their tardiness. As I understand it, they each have at least twice as many items of clothing to put on than a man wears at any one time. It behoves us to be patient," offered Ernie through a grin in a lightly tanned face.

"Spoken like a man with six bossy women," Liam snapped.

A utility pulled up on the other side of the road. A young boy jumped off the back and opened the door for Miss Duggan. She eased herself out.

"Goodbye, Dad. See you, Charlie." Her voice drifted across the road above the rattle of the utility moving off.

Rob opened the gate for the young lady and the group trooped up to the front steps.

Mr. Acton opened the door. His wife stood at his side. "Come in, come in, young lady and gentlemen, come in." He introduced Mrs. Acton to the employees and directed them into a formal sitting room. The smell of timber polish assaulted Rob's nose when he walked into the room. The glasses and bottles on the small table in the corner gleamed. Having spent recent months in a droving camp and some weeks in a men's-only dwelling, Rob's nervousness shone out in the sweat upon his brow. His fellow guests did not appear to be any more comfortable. At Mrs. Acton's insistence, they moved to the armchairs and began to take their seats.

"Can I pour everyone a drink?" Mr. Acton manned the drink's table.

Rob almost fell headfirst into his chair. The sight of the painting on the wall held his attention far too long causing him to stumble. He caught himself with his hand on the back of the chair. He pushed upright again and moved behind his chair to examine the work more closely.

"Are you interested in art, Rob?" Mrs. Acton asked.

"Er … I'm no expert, Mrs. Acton, but I find this piece catches one's eye."

"It does, doesn't it. I think it's those haunting eyes. Of course, that is only a print copy. The original is hanging in the Toowoomba Art Gallery along with the other prize-winning entries in the recent state competition. They're on tour and will be here for another five days."

"Who is this Kirsty Mak, do you know?"

"No, I've never heard of her but I understand she's a teenager from the north who won the emerging painter's award. I don't recognize the model but she certainly has a classical beauty which is only enhanced by the sadness in her eyes."

Rob stood in a trance sipping at the glass Mr. Acton had placed in his hand. He stared into the haunted eyes of the artist's model. Was he going mad? He felt the old wound on the back of his head and neck tighten. Bushfire heat travelled along the ridge of the thickened scar. This woman was a replica of the woman of his visions and nightmares. Behind her, the waves on a beach lapped gently against the sandy shoreline. Tendrils of strawberry-blond hair hung softly against the clear skin of her face having escaped from the severe hair roll pinned up on the back of her head. A glimpse of white teeth revealed through a tentative smile of soft lips.

Rob could feel it deep inside – tugging at him. He did not know how or why but he knew one day he would learn this woman had some connection to him.

"Rob, can we drag you away from your muse there?"

Rob realized Mrs. Acton had called his name more than once. With hasty apologies, he re-joined the conversation around the room. Silently he vowed to visit the gallery the following week and purchase a print copy of that painting if it took a week's wages or more to do so.

PART THREE

EMOTIONAL TIDES

1947

CHAPTER TWENTY-TWO

The garden gate slammed behind her. Skye-Marie leant back against the solid timber and sighed. Today, more than most, she appreciated the demarcation from the world outside provided by the tall wooden fence built after she had escaped, as a toddler, through the previous hedge. Captured fragrances of the manicured gardens, the song of the darting willy-wagtails and the rustle of breezes through the leaves of the low trees and shrubs enfolded her in a welcome peace.

A frown marred the smoothness of her young forehead. One day she was going to really let fly and tell the twins exactly what she thought of them. She sighed. To do so would hurt her grandmother's feelings and she was loath to have that happen. The bullying of her cousins, who lived next door, had a way of digging into her flesh like biting insects. Gran advised her on many occasions to ignore them. They were to be pitied. The boys did not have an easy life in a household with a mother only interested in her career. Their father, although a good person, was a weak man. *It takes all kinds to make a family, child*, was Gran's mantra.

With a shake of her head, she dismissed Gavin and Alistair Dennison from her mind. Long fingers released her hold on the handle of her school port to ease the weight of her lesson books. The more important problem of THE question revisited her thoughts. She so much wanted to ask her mother THE question. Today was the day to ask the question; Skye-Marie had promised herself.

Picking up her school port once more, she made her way along the garden path to the front door. The hand holding the door key paused in front of the slot. Maybe she should wait. Her mother had looked so ill this morning.

The key slid silently into the lock. The heavy ornate door swung back without a sound. She dropped her school port at the bottom of the staircase. Rolling her shoulders and stretching her arms, she followed the mouth-watering smells along the corridor to the kitchen. Her stomach rumbled.

"Hi, Gran." Skye-Marie stepped over to the stove. "That smells nice. What's for tea?" With one hand she lifted the lid of the bubbling pot on the stove. The other hand wafted the steam towards her nose endeavouring to absorb the full impact of the enticing aromas.

"Hello, darling, how was your day? And that is Irish Stew if you'll put the lid back on the pot and allow it to cook." The large knife in Rhylla MacBurnie's hand did not pause as she diced the carrots with the sound of a drum roll.

Skye-Marie grinned as she walked over to plant a noisy kiss on her grandmother's cheek. "School was so-so. Flossie had a full head of steam today about uniforms not being worn properly."

"I wish you would show a little more respect for your headmistress. It's not ladylike to show disrespect to your elders." Rhylla's eyes twinkled remembering how her own two daughters were forever giving the same teacher a hard time all those years ago.

Skye-Marie's face sobered. "How's Mum? Did she go okay at the doctors' visit today? What did they say?"

"Your mother found it all very tiring. She's sleeping at the moment. Darling, will you pop in and check her for me? If she's awake, you can take her a cup of tea and some of the vanilla sponge cake your friend Doris's mother brought over this morning. I swear that woman's sponges could float away on the lightest breeze. I wish I could bake so well."

Rhylla MacBurnie's smile disappeared in a puzzle of worry lines as her granddaughter walked along the corridor towards the small bedroom adjacent to the studio room. Her artistic daughter, Kirsty, now occupied both rooms, painting her wonderful canvases when able and resting on her bed as exhaustion from the terrible disease overtook her. Rhylla slapped a hand over her mouth to cover the loud sob as it sought to escape. It all seemed too hard to have to tell Skye-Marie that her mother was not responding to the treatment as well as the doctors had hoped. She found it all too hard to accept herself. How was a thirteen-year-old daughter expected to cope with such terrible news? Kirsty had promised to give Skye-Marie the devastating news herself, tonight. Rhylla turned sharply to the stove. Blinded by her tears as they spattered onto the stove-top unnoticed, she stirred the stew vigorously.

Skye-Marie passed the laundry and a bathroom on her right and the staircase leading to the upper floor on her left. She stood in the doorway of her mother's bedroom for some time watching her sleep.

"Please, God – please, God – please, God – make her better. I'll do anything You want if You make her better."

Her mother's chest rose and fell rhythmically as she lay in the room lit only by the slivers of afternoon sunlight at the edges of the heavy drapes. Skye-Marie wiped at the tears spurting uninvited from her eyes. Years of weekend tennis had kept her mother tanned and physically fit. In such a short time, the tan had faded to a sickly pallor and the muscles retreated to someplace unknown. Knobbly joints stuck out awkwardly. Her once bright smile with dimples in both fleshy cheeks were now only a memory. In its place, a grimace of fragile skin was drawn taut across sharp-angled facial bones – a virtual stranger. Where had her mother gone?

Skye-Marie pulled her shoulders straight and wiped her face roughly. She was just about to enter the room when she noticed her mother's eyelids flutter like the wings of a broken butterfly. The eyelids lifted revealing an echo of once-sparkling blue-grey eyes. They blinked several times before the eyes focused.

"Skye-Marie, my darling, you're home."

With a rush, Skye-Marie hurried to the bedside. She held her mother's shrunken hand with its faded roadmap of peripheral veins. She dropped light kisses onto her mother's bony cheeks but resisted the urge to fold her mother in a bear-hug for fear of hurting her.

"How was school today?" Kirsty pulled back the bed-cover inviting her daughter to lie alongside her.

"Good thanks, Mum. What did the doctors say?" Skye-Marie slipped out of her shoes and snuggled onto the bed beside her mother. She again took her mother's hand; holding it as tightly as she dared. Even so, the bones felt as though they might snap.

A silence filled the room for some moments. A cold hand scrunched Skye-Marie's heart. Were there unpleasant tidings to come? The young girl bit her lip – she held her breath. Kirsty adjusted the pillows struggling to sit up a little. She placed a hand on her daughter's cheek.

"My most precious girl." Kirsty stopped. A muted whistle echoed along Kirsty's throat as she struggled for air. "The doctors say my body is not responding well to the treatment. The chance of getting on top of the disease is much less than we had first hoped."

Skye-Marie swallowed hard. Her mouth felt parched. She tasted fear in the back of her throat like a cup of dry sand. Dread threatened to steal her breath away.

"What does that mean? You will get better eventually, won't you?"

Feeble arms hugged her only offspring. "My dearest girl, we have to face the possibility that I will not recover."

"You mean … you'll stay like this from now on? We'll look after you, Mum. I'll spend my whole life caring for you. You'll be okay." Stuttered words fell from Skye-Marie's lips.

"Skye-Marie," The tears running down her mother's cheeks were too much for the young girl. Her daughter sobbed. "Skye-Marie, you and Gran may have to go on without me."

"Mum … you mean you might die? You can't. I won't let you. Gran and I will make you better. We have to."

With arms entwined mother and daughter sobbed quietly.

On silent feet and with reddened eyes hidden under a fresh layer of face powder, Rhylla entered the room. She placed a tray carrying a pot of tea, three fine-china cups with saucers, sugar and a small jug of milk upon the small table near the windows. From a crystal vase, a red rose-bud hung over the plate on which sat the cream and strawberry-topped sponge cake. "I know none of us feel like eating today, Skye-Marie, but it's up to you and me to encourage your mother to do so. Would you like to get up and pour the tea, dear?"

"Yes, Gran, of course." Skye-Marie's legs felt like diving weights were attached as she dragged them over the side of the bed. Removing the handkerchief from her uniform pocket, Skye-Marie wiped her face before turning to help her mother up and into the armchair by the side of the bed. Rhylla walked across to the windows and swished the lilac curtains aside. Light suffused the room enhancing the soft pink of the walls. Steam rose from each cup as Skye-Marie poured the beverage. The girl paused for a moment to admire the large landscape painting on the wall behind the bed. It reflected perfectly the parklands seen through the open windows opposite. Pride filled her heart as she gazed at her mother's signature in the lower right-hand corner – Kirsty Mak – her artist's signature. How many more canvases would her mother get to paint? She then turned towards the open double doors leading into the studio. The large canvas of her grandmother, her mother and herself stood partly finished on the easel. Would this ever be completed? *God give her strength. Give us all strength.* Skye-Marie knew today was definitely NOT the day to ask THE question.

Later, as they worked in the kitchen, Rhylla watched the mixture of expressions flitting across her granddaughter's features. Agony and sorrow, she recognized and understood, but there was something more. Something she could not put a name to.

"Want to talk about it, Skye-Marie?"

Rhylla watched as Skye-Marie frowned and bit her lip. Full lips opened and closed several times as the answer formed in her young head.

"Gran, I'd planned on asking Mum an important question today, but I can't worry her at this time. Will you answer it for me?"

Rhylla felt as if the blood had been sucked from her heart. Her mouth felt dry. She had a fair idea of what the question might be. Even though she knew Skye-Marie was old enough to learn the truth, Rhylla dreaded hurting her beautiful granddaughter. She poured herself a glass of water and watched as Skye-Marie shuffled some cutlery around on the table.

"Gran, can you tell me who my father is? And where he is, right now?" Once Skye-Marie began to speak her mouth spilt a flood of questions released from somewhere inside her. "Why hasn't he been in my life for the past thirteen years? Why does no one talk about him? Why are there no photos of him in the house?"

Rhylla drew a long sip of the water almost choking herself in doing so. She fought back a coughing attack.

"Are you all right, Gran?" The girl reached over to touch the older woman's hand. "I'm sorry if this upsets you."

When Rhylla caught her breath, she held Skye-Marie's hand. "Darling, this is your mother's story to tell you – not mine. Would you like me to talk to your mother tomorrow? Maybe she'll be a little stronger. I'll ask her when she plans on telling you all this." She leant across and dropped a light kiss on her granddaughter's cheek. "You do know we love you very much. You have grown into a beautiful, intelligent and kind young lady. We are so proud of you."

Rhylla watched as disappointment shadowed and moistened the blue eyes. The round cheeks swallowed the twin dimples. She drew the girl into a hug.

Later, when Rhylla lay in the expanse of her lonely bed tossing and turning in the summer night's heat, her mind refused to retire the memory of the blood oozing out around the dead man's head. Her ears rang with the thunk, thunk, thunk of the man's skull on the stairs as she and Robbie struggled to support his weight. An involuntary shudder ran down her spine every time the slam of the outside door echoed in her mind. A strong wind had caught the door when the body was dragged out into a dark uninviting night. Once again, the muscles of her arms and shoulders screamed for release from the pain as she had helped lift the man into the strange utility truck.

At least Skye-Marie had not thought to ask the question of where her grandfather might be or why he was not here with them. What was she going to tell the girl about that? Certainly not the truth. Only Jim Sullivan and her father, when he was alive, knew the truth of that dreadful night. Like the rest of the family, Skye-Marie would be told Robbie and she had separated a long time ago. Jim Sullivan had come to believe his best friend had been murdered by thugs from the Sydney gangland just as Rhylla had come to accept it.

She had not cried for her Robbie for such a long time. Tonight, she sobbed until long after the moon passed across the house.

In the darkness outside, Kirsty heard a mopoke owl's insistent call from the trees of the park. A burning fire in her belly hauled Kirsty up from sleep. Untangling her feet from the knotted sheets she sat on the side of the bed. In the glow of her nightlight, shaking hands removed one of the white tablets prescribed by her doctor. The bottle of antacid mixture beside the tablets trembled when she took a good swallow to wash down the tablet which threatened to stick halfway along her gullet. Her toes searched for the slippers on the floor. Leaning heavily on the walking stick she stood up and stumbled to the toilet next door.

Two more pillows from the chair were added to those at the top of her bed. Kirsty eased herself back to lie almost upright. Her thoughts jumbled inside her head. She refused to consider her death a foregone conclusion despite her words to Skye-Marie earlier. Even though she wanted her daughter to be prepared for the worst, Kirsty herself was happy to live in a bubble of hope.

Skye-Marie remained her primary concern, as she had for the past thirteen years. From the dreadful night of her conception, a daughter to be proud of had evolved. How could she leave forever this love of her life? Tears began to fall. She didn't want to say goodbye to her mother either; the stalwart pivot on which to lean during trying times. Kirsty's comfort was in the solace of knowing they'd have each other.

Her thoughts refused to gel – a regular side-effect of her medication. They swished and swirled around inside her skull like detritus in a whirlpool. But concentrate she must. She vowed to talk to Skye-Marie tomorrow. She must answer the questions often seen in her daughter's eyes in recent times – shadows surfacing like hidden currents. But what could she tell the girl when she knew so little about the night herself? How strange such a conversation will seem when her mother and she had barely mentioned the dreadful night – ever. And Rhylla was the only one left who might know more of the events than she.

The pale eyelids closed. Blond eyelashes rested on flushed cheeks. Try as she did to focus, her mind remained lacking any memory of that dreadful night. Only a spinning mass of emptiness featured.

Skye-Marie's question sat like a burning ember inside her head for two nights before her mother's condition improved enough for her to sit out of bed and answer her daughter's curiosity.

Kirsty sat on the padded armchair near the window with cushions around her fragile body and a knee rug crocheted by her grandmother over her legs. Bony fingers fondled the rug.

"This was the last thing your great-granny made before her final heart attack. Do you notice the colours, Skye-Marie? Each one is for each of her girls as she called us. As you can see, they are our favourite colours. Blue for my mother, lilac for yourself and pink for me."

From her position on the wooden chair at her side, Skye-Marie watched her mother's face as her mind drifted off into another thought or another time.

"Great-Granny created some wonderful patterns," she offered.

"Yes, my dear, she did." Kirsty's lips stretched into a caricature of a grin and a sharp cough sounded in her throat. "My granny gave up trying to teach your grandmother the craft but she felt more successful with her efforts on me."

A silence fell upon the room until the sound of children playing in the park drifted in. Kirsty's body tensed at the sound of one, particularly, noisy squeal.

"Mum, can I ask you a question?" Skye-Marie made a tentative beginning on her quest.

Kirsty sighed. Her shoulders lifted. "Yes, darling. Go ahead."

It was Skye-Marie's turn to pause as she gathered her thoughts. "Mum, will you tell me who my father is? And where he is? I am thirteen now and I think I should know." She bit her lip, worried she may have been too abrupt, but she ploughed on. "There is no photo of him anywhere in the house. Why is that?"

Kirsty closed her eyes. Her chest rose and fell several times. Her eyelids lifted and she looked into the eyes so like her own.

"I have not told you before, my dear, because the night when you were conceived is not something I wish to dwell on. The only good thing from it has been my lovely daughter of whom I am so proud and love so much." Kirsty drew several shallow breaths. She slipped her handkerchief from her gown pocket and wiped her lips. Skye-Marie's body remained still; her eyes fixated upon her mother's lips. Kirsty wriggled herself in the chair seeking relief from the pressure on her unpadded buttocks before she took up the tale. "I was fifteen at the time and home alone one evening. My father had gone to the station to collect Mum. On their return, they found I had been drugged and raped. I do not remember anything of it." Kirsty's hand went to her lips to prevent the sob from escaping.

Skye-Marie reached across and held her mother's hand. Mother and daughter remained quiet, busy with their thoughts.

"But Mum, do you know who he was? Does Gran know who he was? Did they catch him?"

"Darling, I don't remember anything of the night. It was Mum who told me what had happened the next day. The man was never seen. No-one knows who he was." Kirsty's chest sucked in air. Her face mottled as she strained to breathe. "I'm sorry, darling, that is all I know." She gasped before trying to speak again. "The important thing in all this is you. We love you. You're very precious to us." Kirsty could not go on.

Skye-Marie jumped up and ran to her mother's side. "Gran!" Anxious eyes turned to the door waiting for help. "Gran!"

Eventually, with Rhylla's help, Kirsty returned to the bed. The strident breathing settled. Her eyelids fell upon her cheeks. Sleep crept in.

Skye-Marie dropped a light kiss along with several stray tears on the forehead of her sleeping mother. Her first question had been answered.

"Sleep tight, Mum, I love you." Skye-Marie smoothed the sheet on her mother's chest with the help of the dull glow of the nightlight at floor level. A rough sweep of her hands brushed the remnant tears from her cheeks while standing at the doorway reluctant to leave. "Please keep her safe."

Leaden feet followed another light streaming out into the hallway from her grandmother's office.

"Night, Gran, sleep tight." Skye-Marie walked around the desk to offer and receive a kiss and a hug.

"Good night, my precious one. Is your mother settled? Did she answer your questions?"

"Only that she does not know who my father was. As you saw, she became ill after telling me that. Will she be alright?" Before Rhylla could frame an answer, Skye-Marie frowned. "How could someone drug and rape my mother. This was my father – a man who can drug and rape a young girl. What does that make me?" She threw her hand over her mouth to contain the revulsion inside her.

"It makes you a person who has overcome great odds to become a young woman of character, strength and beauty. Someone to be proud of. Now, my darling, you slip up to bed. Tomorrow is another school day. I'll be up to bed shortly, myself."

The moonlight danced across the floor as it filtered through the breeze-driven branches of the tree outside her bedroom. Skye-Marie lay back on her pillows and stared up at the ceiling while twiddling the ends of her long strawberry-blonde hair – only a shade darker than her mother's.

Skye-Marie's thoughts drifted on the current of tears within her soul. *Why is this happening to my mother? What has my mother ever done wrong? Is this some kind of punishment for having a baby when she was sixteen? Why should that matter? Why should the woman be blamed if she was raped? It was not her fault. This is the twentieth century after all. This is 1947 not 1847 for goodness' sake. How many women were raped and worse, murdered – treated like they were nothing, during the war? And who is my father? It seems hard to understand how no one knew who he was. Asking to see the birth certificate might be seen to be a sign of a lack of faith.* A groan rolled up from deep in her throat as once again her heart trembled and her hands shook as they had when, at eleven years of age, she had searched her grandmother's office seeking the document – all to no avail. *Am I really a bastard like the rotten cousins, Gavin and Alistair Dennison, keep saying? Even if I am a bastard, I'll not care, as long as my mother doesn't die. And who says the doctors know everything. Sometimes they're wrong.*

As sleep approached Skye-Marie realized her mother's story raised another multitude of questions she wanted to ask. Where then is her grandfather, for one? Nowhere had she found a photo of him when she searched the house for the birth certificate and photos of her own father. He and Gran may have separated but surely there must be one photo of him around – somewhere.

The typewriter keys rattled under the onslaught as Rob Bains' fingers struggled to keep up with the words flowing from his brain. His fifth novel neared completion. The writing had been kind to him. He now owned a cottage on the outskirts of Toowoomba. A small truck waited patiently under the awning at the side of the building for his need of groceries, writing supplies, intermittent work and communication with the outside world. Occasionally, Rob earned extra money helping his friend, Mr. Acton, when the accountant's workload threatened to overwhelm him, particularly nearing tax time. Everyone made the last-minute rush to have their accounts brought up to date.

At least once a year he caught up with Tom Whittle from Rosebud Plains who usually left a message for him at the grocery shop. The two held a belated wake for Tom's youngest son, Steve, who was killed at Dunkirk during the war. Rob wrote a letter to Billy Jackson when he had heard of his return with only one leg. Billy had not replied to date. Guilt chewed at his insides at these memories of his younger friends, particularly as he did not participate directly in the war himself. The doctors refused him on three occasions when he approached them for his medical fitness approval.

"With your history of head injury and ongoing memory loss as well as those fearsome wounds on the back of your skull and your arm, there's no way I could pass you fit for service." The three doctors must have been reading from the same hymn book. But the third medico dug the knife in when in January 1942, he added the declaration, "Your age is against you too, Mr. Bains. I would assess you as being over fifty years of age, maybe fifty-five, which is a bit beyond the requirement to join a fighting unit."

Today, Rob's eyes were blind to the expanse of the lower country spread out as far as the eye could see from his eagle's view at the top of the range. His ears were closed to the music and squabbling of the busy birds enjoying the nectar of the flowering trees outside the wooden window pushed open to its extreme. His busy brain ignored the message from his senses saturated with the perfumes of the blossoms. Hunger did not raise a concern – neither did thirst. Only the pounding of his fingers on the keys held his passion.

Notebooks, pencils and papers were in disarray upon the rough-hewn table upon which his new typewriter sat. On the ledge at his right, his three published novels ruled over everything else he owned. He awaited news from the publisher on his fourth manuscript. A kerosene fridge rumbled in one corner beside the bench with a bucket of water and a basin. The warmth from the now damped-down wood stove in the other corner raised the temperature in an already hot space. His narrow bed with its horsehair mattress and two blankets stood in the third corner. Hanging from a nail in the wall a glass-fronted ornate frame shouted, 'Out of place', in this humble shack. A portrait print, signed by Kirsty Mak, of the woman with strawberry-blond hair and haunted eyes, stared across the room. In the fourth corner, at his writing-table, he sat working. Next to the windows in one wall several fishing rods and lines were gathered neatly together. Near the opposite window, a canvas curtain protected the row of shelves holding his clothes, including his one town suit. A larger wooden table with two chairs filled much of the space in the middle of the room.

Today, his mind was in a frenzy to drown out the nightmares thought forgotten but which had returned to ruin his previous night's sleep. He had watched from above as the faceless crowd raced down the streets. The woman with the blond hair floated on the edge of the crush. A fearful face now sat upon her shoulders. A face of terror. He had only just extricated himself from this dream to fall back into the horror of the twirling maypole. The older woman's strawberry-blond hair was thin and grey. The younger woman clenched the ends of scarlet ribbons as the maypole spun her in wider and wider circles – screaming – out of control.

The sight of a whistling kite hawk which hung in the sky above his cabin when he walked outside to drink his first pannikin of tea for the day, filled him with foreboding. The words of Puffer, the aboriginal magic horse-handler he worked with on his droving trip, flooded Rob's mind once more.

"The whistling kite carry messages – sometimes warnings."

CHAPTER TWENTY-THREE

Rhylla sighed and rubbed her face. She reached across the desk to kill the light. Weariness filled every bone in her body as she pushed her chair back to stand. Her footsteps took her over to stare through the windows at the bed of roses with their blooms smiling up at the full moon. Tonight, her position as chairman on the Board of Directors of the family company held little pride or interest for her. The work, which usually excited and challenged her, now seemed a sodden bore – much less important than the imminent loss of her youngest daughter. It all seemed to be too much for her since Mrs. Barnes handed in her notice as housekeeper to take care of an ailing sister. Rhylla acknowledged this was something she was going to have to address in the near future.

Tonight, Kirsty had told Skye-Marie of the rape. No doubt there would be more questions once she had processed such devastating news. The girl would need support on that front as well as facing the approaching death of her mother. Rhylla's knees felt ready to fold. It was up to her to help them both. It all seemed a mammoth task without her husband's love and strength by her side. Every year she missed seeing the first rosebud of the season lying on her pillow. She sucked in a noisy breath blocked by unshed tears. A grunt burst from her throat as she felt again the pain of her heart ripped from her chest cavity. The sound was echoed by the slamming of the windows as Rhylla prepared to lock up for the night.

Thick carpet silenced her approach to Kirsty's room. A wave of relief flowed over her to find her daughter asleep. Tonight, they all struggled to accept the predicted prognosis. Something would need to be done for her daughter's care as she became weaker with the passing of time. Rhylla was determined to nurse her daughter here, in this house. The house in which Rhylla, Kirsty and Skye-Marie had been born, as had her firstborn, Tim and first daughter, Bronwyn.

Changes will need to be addressed, but not tonight. Tonight, she must sleep herself.

"How's your mother, Skye?" Doris's dark eyes watched anxiously as her friend stretched her right foot across to the offside pedal and pushed off on her bicycle. The head with the plaits of strawberry-blonde hair tied up in loops near her ears bowed against the wind. The contents of the school port tied to her bike carrier rattled as the wheels bounced on the gravel road.

"She's so weak, Doris." Tears glistened in the blue eyes.

Doris Seibel had not missed the dark shadows under Skye-Marie's eyes or the tremble of her chin. Her friend was barely holding herself together. At that moment, she espied Skye-Marie's cousins dawdling under the trees at the corner, doing twists and turns with their bicycles. She knew this was not a good sign. Those two would be up to some mischief and Doris guaranteed Skye-Marie and herself were going to be the butt of some weird joke only the lads could comprehend. Gavin and Alistair Dennison, attending a class two years behind the girls, were born bullies and Doris knew she and her friend were a prime target for their amusement. Most days their mother, Bronwyn Dennison, dropped the monsters off at school on her way to work. The other days, when she did not, they hung around waiting on their bicycles presenting a nightmare for their cousin and herself.

"Mum seems a bit brighter this morning. She ate a little breakfast and began work on her latest painting before I left." Skye-Marie noticed the boys. "Trust those two to be looking for trouble. Come on, Doris." Her bike shot forward when she pushed down hard on the pedals.

Doris's long brown fingers pushed the thick dark curls from her face then gripped her bicycle handles and followed suit.

"Skye, it must be a good sign if your mother's feeling able to paint then, mustn't it?" Her expressive black eyes spilled compassion as she gasped out her reply.

"I hope so. Oh, by the way, thanks to your mum for the sponge cake the other day. I think Gran is going to visit her this week. We enjoyed it. Pity you can't cook like that." Skye presented a wan smile as she stretched her arm out to pat her friend on the shoulder. With the boys behind them, they settled into a more sedate pace.

A flash of white as Doris rolled her eyes. "You'll never let me forget that disastrous cake, will you? Remember, yours on the day was not so great either. Miss Coburn said if she dropped it on the floor, it would make a hole through to the maths class below." They both giggled at the memory.

With great concentration, the girls pretended the boys were not hazing their back tyres and dropping their frequently used nasty terms like lumps of dog turd.

"Well, look here, Gavin, the two bastards."

"Yeah, brother – a pair of black and white bustard birds."

"Put 'em together and you get a magpie." Their laughter roared through the foliage of the overhanging trees.

Doris reached for Skye-Marie's hand. They rode side by side with one hand each on their bike. Both girls ignored the comments. Doris felt Skye-Marie trembling. The flush on her friend's cheeks glowed as it always did on those odd occasions when she was one step away from breaking her rule to ignore her cousins' taunts.

"Don't give them the satisfaction, Skye. What else can you expect from such a pair of screeky creepies?" Doris appreciated her own composure only came in the calming of her friend.

"Screeky creepies?" A grin filled Skye-Marie's cheeks to replace the fading flush. "Doris, how can you remain so unflappable. I find it much easier with you by my side when those two hurtle their insults."

White teeth and two sparkling black diamonds looked back at her. "You like screeky creepies?"

Both girls chuckled as they swung in through the school gate. They dropped their hands and jumped off their bicycles. The cousins flew past them. School children, off to have some time on the sports field, scattered in all directions.

"Do you want to go upstairs early?" Skye-Marie grinned.

"To the classroom? Are you telling me you haven't finished your homework? More like you're hoping a boy with initials D.B. may be doing his?"

Skye-Marie tried to look unconcerned but the brilliant blue eyes gave her away.

"Who? Oh, him; he's an egotistical show-off. I'm not interested."

"Who're you fooling?"

"Actually, I wanted to write a letter to Mr. Trimble at the grocery shop." Skye-Marie tried to look offended. "I want to tell him I won't be working for a while. I'm going to spend every minute with Mum while I can. You can deliver it to him this afternoon if you will."

"Oh, Skye-Marie, what will I do without you there to talk to while I unpack the boxes. Some of the ladies can be so rude to me when you're not there." Doris slapped her hand over her mouth. "Sorry, Skye-Marie, that is so selfish. Your mum and gran will like that."

Doris hardly took her eyes off Skye-Marie for most of the day. Worry filled her every searching glance. Her heart felt heavy with empathy and compassion trying to imagine how she would feel knowing her mother may die in a few months or maybe even weeks. She felt bile rising in her stomach. Doris only had her mother. There were other family members, but it was her mother, Janet, who was her mainstay. It did not bear contemplating.

As the two girls stood at the school gate with the afternoon sun hot on their backs, they said goodbye.

"I hope your mother's okay this afternoon, Skye-Marie. I'd better shake a leg if I'm to get to the shop in time."

"Thanks, Doris. If I have trouble with the maths homework tonight, will you help me before school in the morning? I'm not sure if I took in anything today."

"That'll make a change, me helping you."

"Rubbish, who absorbs history like a sponge absorbs water?"

Doris waved as she headed to the city centre while Skye-Marie turned her bicycle towards her home "Bye, Doris," she called.

Skye-Marie made the journey home from school alone. One conciliation prize – she had noticed her Uncle Bill loading the cousins' bikes onto his utility outside the school gate.

Once into McNeven Lane, Skye-Marie dismounted from the bicycle and shuffled along pushing it beside her. A war waged inside her head. She wanted so much to hurry home and see how her mother was feeling but the fear for what she might find held her back like an anchor chain around her feet. Why did it have to be her mum? Why couldn't things go back to the way they were?

The lane led between the houses of 244 and 248 Park Road West down to number 246, The Heather, situated on the edge of the parkland. The original owners, her great-grandparents had named the house after their family estate in Scotland. Skye-Marie had lived here with her mother and grandmother all of her life. She kept to the footpath closest to number 244. She always did. Her Aunt Bronwyn and the rest of the Dennison family lived in number 248. Thirteen years of experience had taught her to avoid them as much as possible. As she opened the vehicle access gate into number 246 her feet crunched on the gravel driveway which led off to the right and the three-bay garage. Her grandmother called this the coach-shed. Above the garage were two flats. One had been for Mrs. Barnes, the recently departed housekeeper. The other, now a storeroom, had been where Gran's previous handyman lived.

"Hi, Gran, are you home?" Skye-Marie called. Her grandmother was not to be found in the sitting room, the living room, or the kitchen. She ran to her mother's bedroom – no one. She checked the Studio – no one. The group portrait stood on its easel. Some progress had been made since she had seen it this morning before going to school. A good sign, surely. Skye-Marie followed the corridor around and poked her head into the spare bedroom and large office but there was no sign of anyone. Her heart fluttered. Where was her mother? Had she taken ill? Skye-Marie dropped her bag and ran back to the bottom of the staircase. She called out as she took the stairs two at a time. "Are you upstairs, Gran?" Silence her only answer. Her feet were flying now. She opened every door into the four bedrooms, sewing room, library and bathroom but only the dust motes floating on the sun rays through the gaps in the curtains were there to greet her. Just as she reached the bottom of the stairs again, she heard Gran's voice.

"Is that you, Skye-Marie? We're out in the garden."

Relief washed over her. Her knees felt weak. "Coming," she returned the call. "Do you want anything out there?" Skye-Marie found her mother and grandmother sitting in the shade of the house enjoying the cool afternoon breeze blowing in off the sea. New buds of spring draped the park trees in yellows, reds and blues. Sweet fragrances along with the voices of children playing cricket somewhere on the other side of the park drifted through the foliage.

"Here, dear, you sit by your mother while I make us a cuppa." Rhylla kissed the top of Skye-Marie's head in passing.

Kirsty turned her face for her daughter's kiss. "How was your day, Skye-Marie? You're home early. I thought it was your afternoon to unpack boxes at the grocery shop in town."

"School was okay. I wrote a note and sent it with Doris to give to Mr. Trimble. I told him I won't be in until you're better. I want to be with you more."

Kirsty reached out her hand and touched her daughter's cheek. "That's lovely dear, but only if you're sure. I know you like saving up your pocket money."

"The one thing I want more than anything, I cannot buy with all the pocket money in the world, Mum." Skye-Marie reached up to cover her mother's hand.

A companionable silence fell between Kirsty and her daughter. This was broken by the sound of hushed voices arguing in the kitchen.

"That sounds like Aunt Bronwyn. Should I go rescue Gran?" Skye-Marie's eyes rolled.

Kirsty's whole body began to shake, her heart pounded in her ears. She recognized the voice immediately. God knows she had had enough vicious arguments with her sister over the years. Why did the woman have to take her spite out on their mother and Skye-Marie, she did not know, particularly at a time like this?

"No, darling, your Gran is quite capable of taking care of herself. She has been dealing with Bronwyn all of our lives."

Bronwyn's rising contralto voice was unmistakable as it drifted out onto the patio. "You mark my words, Mum. You may be Chairman of the Board but I will stop you at every turn if you think you're going to make that little bastard child a director when my sister dies. We don't even know who the kid's father is. Kirsty says she was raped. What an excuse. She flirted with every damn boy in high school."

Rhylla's voice snapped in return. "Enough of that language. None of us need to be reminded of that dreadful night. Anyway, what would you know? You and your brother were away at the university when it happened."

"Well, it's probably true. My father left us for the shame of it. Kirsty was always your favourite; you always stick up for her."

"Enough! You are acting like a spoilt child – or is it just the drink talking. Your father did not leave for shame because Kirsty was pregnant. He left for another reason altogether."

"Don't think I'm going to believe your story that he left you for another damn woman. He was a good man."

"I told you before to mind your language." Rhylla bit her tongue. She wanted so much to spit out all she knew but to do so would hurt those whom she loved most. And that included her troubled elder girl. "You stink of whiskey. Don't come here making wild accusations against your sister. Now get out of my house and don't return until you can keep a civil tongue in your head."

Out on the garden patio, Kirsty's heart wept as she watched her daughter's face fill with horror. There was no doubt Skye-Marie had heard every word. She reached over to take her hand. Both their faces were as pale as the chrysanthemums bordering the path. Tears trickled down Kirsty's cheeks. She could not bear to see her daughter's pain.

"Will you take me for a short walk in the park, dear? I do miss getting out and about these days." Her legs shook as she stood with Skye-Marie supporting her left arm. Kirsty reached for her walking stick leaning against the back of the chair.

"Will I get the umbrella? The doctor told you not to let the sun on your skin."

"No, Skye-Marie, we'll keep to the shady trees on this side. We won't go too far." The pair slowly made their way along the cobblestone path to the back gate and out into the forested parklands.

"My darling, Skye-Marie, I'm so sorry you had to hear how malicious your aunt can be."

"Oh, Mum, why is she so cruel to you?"

Concern for the guilt she could see in the depths of her daughter's eyes carved a frown through the sweat on Kirsty's forehead.

"Name-calling will not help things, dear. Just remember, none of this is your fault or my fault, come to that. I've listened to Bronwyn's tantrums since we were kids. She was forever demanding Mum's and Dad's attention. I keep reminding myself she is the one to be pitied. You must do the same."

They skirted the huge fig tree spread out over a wide expanse of land. A fallen log under the shady branches made a resting place for the locals who often strolled through the area.

"Perhaps you should have had an abortion before I was born. If I were not here maybe things would not be so bad for you and Gran."

"Hush your mouth, child. You are the most precious thing in my life. If you weren't here, your Auntie Bronwyn would find something else to harp on about. She is only happy when she's picking on someone. Besides what do you know about abortions at your age? Abortions were no easier come by in my day than they are today."

"Huh, a bit like Gavin and Alistair, you mean." Skye-Marie chose to ignore her mother's question and keep the conversation on track.

Many of the questions she had pondered in recent times were being answered without her asking.

"Yes, that pair grow more like their mother every day, sad to say. Mind you, their father is not a bad bloke. Trouble is, Bill lets Bronwyn walk all over him."

"Mum, if you could recall who raped you, we could tell Aunt Bronwyn. Maybe then she'd let up on you."

Kirsty patted Skye-Marie's face. "I wish, but as I told you, I was drugged at the time and can only remember vague shapes and movements."

"Is there nothing we can do to bring back your memory?"

Kirsty's feet paused. She remained still – trying to catch her breath. With a faint shake of her head, she forced out the words.

"Not in this day and age, Skye-Marie. Maybe in years to come, but not now. Anyway, if I'm honest, I probably don't want to remember that night." Her feet shuffled around to face back the way they had come. "Why do we want to know? Gran and I love you absolutely and you love us. What more do we want? And you know my brother Tim and his kids, Jack and Muriel, think the world of you." Once more Kirsty's feet stopped while she caught her breath. "Pity Brisbane is so far away and we only get to see them when they come up for the company's annual meeting."

Skye-Marie chewed her bottom lip for a moment. She so much wanted to ask more about what she had overheard but when she looked up at the shattered expression and the extreme pallor of her mother's face along with the struggle her mother was having to breathe, she desisted.

A shaky hand stroked Skye-Marie's head. "I hope your gran is all right after that upset with Bronwyn. We'd best go see if we can help."

After stumbling the last few yards along the garden path and into her room, an exhausted Kirsty flopped onto the bed. Within moments she appeared to have fallen into a deep sleep. Skye-Marie slipped quietly out of the room in search of her grandmother.

While Kirsty's body craved sleep, her mind demanded attention. On the rumpled bed in the darkened room skinny arms flapped at her body as if making feeble attempts to defend an attack. She felt again the drag of her clothes over the skin of her arms and legs. She felt rough hands invading every secret place of her body. Her heart pounded inside her chest threatening to pulverize an already fragile rib cage. Her gut clenched in fear. Screams remained strangled inside a throat slammed shut in a spasm of terror. Even when the void of blackness enveloped her in its grip, the physical signs of terror continued draining an already weakened body. Her eyes flew open. A rumbling sound of an argument nearby rolled in like a thunderstorm before a thunderclap of a human being's shocked yelp filled her ears. The face of her father filled her vision.

Sweat ran in rivulets from every pore of Kirsty's tortured frame. Fearful blue eyes were held open by determination alone. Gasping, quiet sobs sucked in air.

Winds swished through the trees above Rob Bain's head. Even the larger branches creaked. Dust puffs rose with each footstep and quickly disappeared on the strong breezes. The birds had given up fighting the air currents this afternoon. They fluffed their feathers and huddled up behind the larger trunks of the trees. He walked with his hat pulled down tight on a bowed head. Occasionally he jumped when his bare feet found a sharp stone on the track leading to the gate where the sculptured kerosene-tin mailbox stood near the roadway waiting for the mailman's visit once a week.

As he did each week, he stood back and peered into the depths of the mailbox. Redback spiders had been known to assume squatters' rights beside the infrequent letters or parcels. Twice a carpet snake had to be forcibly removed from his chosen site for a sleep after a tasty morsel. Today there was nothing.

Rob felt his heart drop. By his calculations, today might be the day for his publisher's letter to arrive accepting his latest book for publication. This could mean it was still sitting on an editor's desk, or held up on its journey, or dropped into a large office bin. To boost his morale, he reminded himself how, after his third book had been published, the manager had promised they'd accept any of his works with open arms.

Today there was not even a note from the accountant, Mr. Acton, wanting Rob's services to help with the rising workload at this time of year. He leaned forward and peered in closer – just in case something was hidden. He jumped when a kookaburra in the branches above his head laughed. Rob sat on the ground with his back against the kookaburra's tree as he came to terms with his disappointment. With a small twig, he patterned the ground between his feet, scraped the area smooth then repeated the process. His head lifted. Curiosity filled his gaze. There were no fresh tyre tracks of the mailman's utility. Nor were there any fresh boot marks near the box itself. The mailman had not arrived. He was late today.

The sound of the truck brought Rob to his feet. He found the sun fading into the west. He must have dozed. A smile lifted his face when the mailman came into view around the nearest bend. He struggled to contain his excitement. Today might be the day after all. A cloud of dust rose around the vehicle when Max brought it to a stop.

A head of unruly grey hair and whiskers hung out the window. "Sorry, I'm a bit late, Rob. I had a flat tyre and then another. I had to wrap two tyres together like my father used to do during the war years when rubber and money were not to be found. It makes for a slow and rough trip. I doubt I'll be seeing my bed tonight."

"You're sure welcome to lay your swag out in my hut if you want, Max. There's a pot of hot kangaroo stew on the stove and there should be a drop or two in a bottle of scotch if we're lucky."

"I think I'll take you up on that, Rob, if you don't mind. I don't fancy travelling in the dark with these lights. A firefly has better illumination."

Rob clung to the door and the dashboard of the utility as he bounced around on the drum with a folded bag as a cushion situated as a seat beside the driver. He remembered he had not asked Max if there was mail for him. Not wanting to sound too anxious he put the thought aside until the morning.

The men sat up late into the night, their conversation accompanied by the soft shuffle of low branches across the corrugated iron roof of the hut. The moonlight made its way in through the windows after Rob turned the wick down on the hurricane lantern. Max crawled into his swag spread out on the floor near the wall opposite Rob's bed.

As Rob lay stretched out on his back on top of the blankets, he contemplated questioning Max on the presence or not of his mail but the rising chorus of snores emanating from his visitor's swag changed his mind. His thoughts danced around all the possibilities for his future as a noted author but common sense and modesty brought him tumbling back to reality. The winds had settled outside when at last his mind closed for the night.

As usual, the birds alerted Rob to the arrival of the day. Their songs rang out over the mountain and across the flats below. He opened his eyes to find the mailman and his swag roll missing. He heard the vehicle door closed with a grinding thump. Footsteps approached the back door. The man had not left yet. Rob threw his legs over the side of his bunk.

As he stirred the embers in the woodstove, he called, "You want some porridge for breakfast, Max?"

"That'd be good, Rob, but I'd sure like a pannikin of tea first." The door shut with a soft slam.

Later, when Rob escorted his guest back to the mail truck, the man began foraging around the bins in the back.

"I know there was some mail here somewhere for you. Hang on." He turned, waving two small envelopes in a gnarled grubby hand and one large brown envelope which caught Rob's eye immediately.

The address had been type-written and a posted-in-Melbourne rubber stamp marked beside the postage stamp. Rob's smile widened. He bit down on the urge to open it there and then.

"Good news, then?" Max smiled too. "It's good to know one delivers welcome news to people sometimes. During the war, I found it depressing when people watched me with trepidation. They weren't sure whether to welcome me or not. Some days it was nothing but bad news."

Rob nodded his head, the grin hanging on firmly. "This is what I've been waiting for. I'm hoping it's good news." The grin disappeared. Reality hit him. Maybe this was not good news. Maybe the publisher did not like his manuscript and wanted nothing more to do with him. Rob could not get Max on his way quickly enough before he ran inside to tear open the envelope.

CHAPTER TWENTY-FOUR

Kirsty joined Rhylla and Skye-Marie in the kitchen for the evening meal. A satisfied smile passed between Rhylla and Skye-Marie when Kirsty accepted a small plate of shepherd's pie.

Skye-Marie regaled them with the news of the results of her essay homework completed last weekend.

"Mrs. Carter says she wants me to enter it into the school section of the Townsville Show this year"

Rhylla and Kirsty paused in their eating to congratulate Skye-Marie.

"You get that from your grandfather, my dear." Rhylla smiled before putting forward the next subject of interest.

"I plan on moving my things downstairs into the bedroom on the other side of the studio so I can be near you at night, Kirsty. I worry about you down here on your own. Neither Skye-Marie nor I would hear if you called for help, darling. Besides, it's next to my office and that has many advantages for me." Rhylla beamed at them both. "If Kirsty doesn't mind her mother checking up on her every night, that is."

A wry grin lifted Kirsty's drawn cheeks. "Twenty years ago, I'd have been most put out but now I think it will be very comforting. What about you, Skye-Marie? Will you be okay rambling around upstairs on your own? You won't be frightened, will you?" Skye-Marie shook her head. Her cheeks puffed out with the sticky-date pudding inside her mouth.

Rhylla turned to her granddaughter. "Will you give me a hand to make a start after we clean up here?"

Skye-Marie chewed quickly, swallowed and scraped her chair back. "Let the work begin."

Clothes, scarves, delicate nylons, leather belts and shoulder straps of handbags spewed over the edges of the range of assorted boxes and laundry baskets lined up on the double bed. Stashed in the corner of the room, an expanding pile of clothes threatened to topple.

"Do you want me to pack those things into a box, Gran?"

Rhylla ran her fingers through her tangled hair while she eyed the heap of clothes. "Not just now, my dear; I have no more containers. Those clothes are destined for the church fete stall. We'll need to unload some of these boxes first."

Skye-Marie lifted the lid of the large pink flat box on the middle of the bed. Tissue paper crackled as she lifted it aside. She gasped and held the soft silk to her cheek. The hint of perfume teased her nostrils. She breathed deeply.

"Oh, Gran, is this your wedding dress? It's as soft as ..." She paused, seeking a comparison.

Rhylla laughed. Her grey eyes sparkled. "As a baby's bum, is what your grandfather said when he first felt the dress."

"Gran, it is beautiful. Can I wear it, if I ever get married?" Parallel furrows marred Skye-Marie's forehead. "That's if I ever get married. Who wants to marry a bastard?"

"Dear, when Mr. Right comes along he will love you for yourself, not for your lineage."

"Did Aunt Bronwyn wear this dress when she and Uncle Bill were married?"

Rhylla's face fell – for just a moment. "No, Skye-Marie, Bronwyn wanted a modern wedding and as the bride, it was her choice." Rhylla's hand dug deep into the jewellery box on her lap. Her fingers emerged draped with a bulky necklace of patterned gold and precious amethyst.

" Skye-Marie, your birthday is a few months away yet but would you like this gift?"

Skye-Marie's eyes sparkled. She reached out and dangled the treasure from her slim fingers. "Could I? Gran, that would be wonderful. When did you buy this?"

A soft smile rested on the older woman's lips. Grey-blue eyes gazed at a blank wall seeing things only her memory could see.

"Your grandfather gave that to me when your mother was born. He had given me a similar one with diamonds when our firstborn, Tim, arrived and then one with rubies when our second child, Bronwyn, was born. They have those jewels now."

Framed photos slipped out onto the bedcover as Skye-Marie went to lift one of the boxes. As she replaced them in the box, a photo of a tall man caught her attention. A tinge of grey teased the temples of the man with the dark wavy hair and chiselled features. His pale eyes held her gaze.

"Who is this, Gran?"

Rhylla's heart missed a beat. Her mind froze. What should she tell her granddaughter? The truth, that's what. Taking a deep breath, she answered. "That man is Robert MacBurnie dear – my husband, your grandfather."

Skye-Marie ran her finger over the glass above the handsome face taking in every characteristic. "Do you miss him, Gran?"

"Yes, my darling, so very much." Moisture glistened in her eyes.

"Why did he leave? Was it because of me and the shame of Mum's pregnancy like Aunt Bronwyn says?"

"Absolutely not – your grandfather loved Kirsty more than his own life." Rhylla jumped to her feet. "Now, are we going to start carrying this lot downstairs?"

After her third trip down the staircase, Skye-Marie groaned when she lifted the large sealed cardboard box from off the chair in the bedroom on the top floor. "Gran, what on earth have you got in here, a dead body?"

"What?" With her back to the door, Skye-Marie did not notice the guilty look as it flashed across Rhylla's face. "Oh, you're joking, Skye-Marie. Er … no, it's just some stuff from the office. I'll have to go through it tomorrow."

As the Chairman of the Board of the family company, most of the office work came to Rhylla via hand delivery or post but occasionally boxes of documents arrived at the front door by a carrier. Skye-Marie's sharp eyes noticed what appeared to be published book covers through a small tear in the side of the box. Not something the clerks usually delivered for review.

"Gran, these look like printed books. I didn't know the family had anything to do with the publishing industry?"

With a wry grin, Rhylla spoke. "No, dear, we don't. Those are a couple of the books written by your grandfather. He was an author you know."

"Can I read them, can I?"

"In time, of course, you can. One day these will belong to you but I think some are a bit risqué for a thirteen-year-old."

Skye-Marie felt warm inside. A grin split her face. She tried to remain calm. This was the first time anyone had spoken of her grandfather except Bronwyn when ranting. She begged her grandmother to tell her more but Rhylla had other ideas.

"It's getting late, Skye-Marie, my dear. That might do us for tonight. Didn't you say you had homework to complete?"

Skye-Marie sighed. Later, as she walked up the stairs, she picked up a small photo on the carpet. It must have slipped out from one of the boxes. In the hallway light, she was able to recognize Robert MacBurnie, her grandfather, but the second face beside him was a stranger to her. She could not help notice the likeness of the two young men. She slipped it into the pocket of her dressing gown and went to turn back down the stairs but stopped. As much as she would like an explanation of who this second man was, she knew her grandmother needed a good night's sleep. She about-faced and climbed the stairs to her room.

The rising moon cast long shadows across the parkland as Skye-Marie stood at her corner window just above the studio downstairs. A glow of light lit up the garden towards the front of the house. Her grandmother must still be working in the office. Skye-Marie walked over to the south window but could not see any lights from her mother's room. She hoped her mother was sleeping comfortably. Her thoughts ran through the traumatic afternoon. It was impossible to dredge up any pity for Aunt Bronwyn. What makes her so jealous? How does Uncle Bill put up with her? The noise of the flying foxes feeding on the flowers of the forest drifted in on a gentle breeze. Distractions come all too easily when doing mathematics. If her homework had been an English essay, she would be in her element. A determined step took her back to her desk where her books lay spread out waiting for her attention. One last sigh and she focussed on the maths problem set for the night.

Rhylla's torchlight, aimed at her clock, revealed it to be two o'clock in the morning. She was not sure what had woken her. She lay unmoving, taking shallow breaths. Her ears ached with the straining. Her curtains billowed in the soft glow from Kirsty's night light, next door. The wind rustled the branches of the trees outside. A rattle of timber came from the garden.

"Oh blast, I forgot to ask Mr. Bingle to fix the bush house trellis when he was here yesterday. I mustn't forget when he comes back to mow the lawn on Monday." Mumbling to herself, she slipped her legs over the side of the bed. Her head lifted. Strangled sobs drifted in from her daughter's bedroom. Rhylla forgot her slippers. She ran. In the glow of the night-light, Kirsty tossed back and forth on the bed. Terrifying choking sounds gurgled from her throat.

"Kirsty, Kirsty, are you awake, darling. What's wrong? What's the matter?"

The gurgling noises stopped. Kirsty's breathing paused.

"Wake up, darling, wake up. You're having a nightmare." Rhylla took her daughter into her arms.

The frail body dripped with sweat. Kirsty dragged in ragged breaths.

"Oh, Mum, something was shaking me and shaking me. There was blood everywhere – all over everywhere. A face hung over me. But there were no features to the face." She began shuddering.

Horror held Rhylla's heart but she knew she must remain calm. "The first thing is to get these saturated clothes off you, darling, and change the sheets. Do you feel able to walk to the shower or would you like me to sponge-bath you here?"

"I'd like to have a shower, thanks, Mum."

Rhylla looked up from where she helped Kirsty put on her slippers. Skye-Marie stood huddled at the doorway with her arms tight around her middle; her un-brushed blond hair hung in disarray around her head.

"It's alright, dear, your mother has just had a dreadful nightmare. She's covered in sweat."

Kirsty's shaky voice whispered, "Sorry to disturb you, Skye-Marie. It was only a nightmare. The doctors said the treatment gave some people nightmares." Kirsty then reached up and took Rhylla's arm.

Skye-Marie shook herself and jumped out of the way. "I'll get some fresh linen and make up the bed." She turned and made her way to the linen cupboard under the staircase. With the bed refreshed, Skye-Marie went to the kitchen to make a pot of cocoa.

The following morning, Skye-Marie heard a conversation coming from downstairs. Doris was early.

"Can I make you a fresh cup of tea, Doris?"

"No thanks, Mrs. MacBurnie. I just wanted to tell Skye-Marie what happened to Mrs. Turner last night. Mum is so upset. Mrs. Turner had a fall. She became confused in the shower and tried to walk alone while Mum was getting her clothes."

"I'm sorry to hear that, Doris. Did she hurt herself?"

"They've taken her to the hospital."

"How terrible, Doris. Do you know how bad she might be?"

"Mum's waiting to hear from the doctor. Mrs. Turner's family came to the house in the middle of the night and they blamed Mum. They were very loud. All the neighbours heard. They said they'll take their mother home with them and give Mum the sack." Tears began to run down the ebony cheeks.

"How dreadful."

"They said they'll sell the house." Doris's words were barely distinguishable as she choked back her sobs.

"Goodness me, it all sounds a bit rushed when the doctors haven't even made a diagnosis."

At that point, Skye-Marie's feet whispered down the staircase.

"I'm ready." Her words were cut off when she noticed her friend's tears.

"Why don't you two girls sit for a little while in the living room. I'll bring Doris a drink of orange juice."

After fifteen minutes the girls left through the side door to collect their bikes.

"Doris, I'll go and visit your mother later this morning to see she's okay."

"Thanks, Mrs. MacBurnie."

The rattling bikes moved through the double gates and out onto the roadway.

Rhylla felt weary. After the disturbed sleep last night and the trip into town to deliver Kirsty to the hospital for her treatment before dropping the car off for service this morning, she looked forward to a sit-down and a cup of tea. The mechanics were due to complete the car service before two o'clock this afternoon – just in time to collect Kirsty.

As soon as she stepped through the garden gate, Rhylla knew something was amiss. She stood perfectly still. Lorikeets squabbled in the grevillea trees. The morning sun felt hot on her uncovered forehead. Sweat trickled down her face after the short walk from Park Road West where she had asked to be dropped off. The lace curtains billowed out through her open office windows on a gentle breeze. That's odd, she was sure those windows were shut when she closed up before leaving this morning. Then she heard it. A mumble of voices floated out into the garden along with the smell of cigarettes. Her heart echoed in her ears as she tiptoed around the rose garden and between the shrubs from where she peered into the room unobserved. Bronwyn's twins, Gavin and Alistair, sat with their feet up on her desk. The little rogues were drinking her best Jamieson whiskey from her crystal tumblers. Both boys puffed strongly on the cigarettes which were always kept in the bottom drawer of the desk for guests and occasionally for herself. One of her husband's earlier books lay open on the desk. She had been re-reading it last night before going to bed. Instead of fear, fury increased her heart rate even further.

Rhylla retreated to the back of the house where she let herself in silently through the laundry door. She stood outside the office for some time listening to their conversation.

"Listen to this bit," Gavin asked his younger brother by twenty minutes. He did not wait for a reply and began to read. *"David's finger traced the outline of Sareena's lips. They stared into each other's eyes. He brought his mouth gently down to kiss her sweet smile. Soft arms reached around his neck and pulled him tightly into her embrace. A willing mouth opened to receive his deep kiss. Their bodies blended into one. His heart pounded against his ribcage. The core of his soul throbbed in rhythm."* Gavin sighed. "God, I'd like to deep kiss Miss Harrow's lips. Did you see her nipples sticking through her shirt yesterday?"

"He's going to do her, isn't he?" Alistair asked wide-eyed. "What do you think it'll be like to deep kiss a girl?"

"I can't wait to find out what it'll be like to fuck a girl."

"I want to know why Gran reads this stuff; she's a bit old isn't she?"

"She must do, look she has at least ten or twelve books from this writer."

"Why aren't you boys at school?" Rhylla strove to appear nonchalant leaning with her shoulders against the door frame. Her grandsons need never know it was their grandfather who wrote those novels.

It took all of her self-control to prevent a grin from breaking the severe expression she had presented to the pair as she watched their reaction. Gavin slammed the book shut. The boys scrambled to their feet. The office chair tipped over in the rush. The boys endeavoured to stub out their cigarettes and cover the glasses all at the same time.

"Er … um … why aren't you at the hospital?" They spoke in unison.

Rhylla chose to ignore their question and posed another. "Don't you think, at eleven years of age, you might be a bit young to be making decisions on smoking or drinking and adult reading?"

"It was music and choir practice this morning. Only sissies do that stuff." Gavin offered an excuse.

"So, you thought, 'Gran and Auntie Rhylla will be at the hospital. We'll play hooky in Gran's private office, did you?'"

"We had nowhere else to go where it was comfortable." They both had the decency to at least look guilty.

"Now you have made the mess you can clean it up."

"But Gran we don't do housework or clean up," Alistair offered.

"No, we have Mrs. Taylor to do that," Gavin finished for him.

"Come with me. I'll show you where the cleaning cloths, the polish, the brush, and dustpan are kept and how to use all four."

"Ooooh, Gran, are you serious?" The boys asked in unison.

"Nevermore," was Rhylla's stern reply.

Rhylla felt like a prison warden supervising the boys' every move as they emptied the ashtrays in the outside incinerator and washed the glasses in the kitchen sink. They wiped the outside of the bottle and the desk with a damp cloth and then swept the floor.

"You won't tell our parents, will you, Gran?"

"Why shouldn't I?" Rhylla's curiosity stirred.

"Dad will use the strap around our legs and then Mum won't talk to him or us for days or longer. It's murder living in the house when that happens."

"I'll think on it."

"Please, Gran, we won't do this again, please?"

"You can leave the novels there on the desk. I'll put them away myself."

As she watched the lads head out to their bikes hidden under the camphor laurel tree, she pondered the goings-on in her daughter's household.

Was Bronwyn no different to most mothers on these occasions? Feels worse than the children at the time, but doesn't know what to do better.

Kirsty slept on the car seat beside her. Rhylla's mind pondered the events with her grandsons earlier in the day. Her thoughts revisited an idea she had considered last night when unable to sleep – a live-in housekeeper. And her discussion with Doris Reibel this morning presented a perfect possibility. While one side of her mind listed the advantages of having such a person, her inane need for privacy rejected the thought of a total stranger living under the same roof as herself. When it had been Mrs. Barnes here, it did not seem to matter. She had been an essential part of the family. With her living in the flat over the coach-shed they maintained privacy for the family in the house. Common sense reminded her the house had three spare bedrooms on the top floor, beside Skye-Marie's room. Space was not an excuse. Plus, there were still the two flats above the coach-shed, used only for storage now. On the other hand, with her company commitments, she did not have the time to offer Kirsty the attention she deserved, particularly if she was to maintain the household by herself. With her mind still at a stalemate with itself, she pulled into the front driveway reaching over and touching her daughter's hand lightly.

"Home, sweetheart."

Rhylla's smile lifted at the sight of Skye-Marie rushing out to greet them.

Skye-Marie sank into the pillows on the chair beside her mother's bed. Her sleeping mother lay with the light azure blue rug drawn up over her shoulders and over the back of her head. Only her translucent white face was visible in the artificial light. Skye-Marie felt the weight of a cement block in the place of her heart. It dragged at her chest wall; her shoulders sagged at the pull of it. Her soul had been sucked up into it. No more tears were left to fall; her eyes were dry. It was the fall of the soft hand of her grandmother on her shoulder which drew Skye-Marie from her reverie. Her fingers reached up to intertwine with those of her grandmother.

"Come, darling. Your mother will sleep tonight; she is exhausted. We must keep our strength up. Let's try to eat something."

In the kitchen, silence hung heavy between the intermittent soft clatter of cutlery on the china until both plates were pushed to the middle of the table with much of the meals remaining. Both of the diners sipped at their teacups.

"Gran." "Skye-Marie." They spoke together.

"You first, Skye-Marie." Rhylla reached over to touch her granddaughter's hand.

Love radiated between the younger blue eyes and the older grey eyes.

"Gran, have you considered hiring another housekeeper to replace Mrs. Barnes? There's a lot more work to do here now and you have been looking very tired lately."

Rhylla's smile lit up the room. "You must have read my mind, Skye. Or should I say, you and Doris have been collaborating?"

A shade of guilt flashed across Skye-Marie's face along with her smile. "Whatever do you mean, Gran?"

"It just happens your mother and I talked on this very subject on our way to the hospital this morning. Your mother supports having a housekeeper, wholeheartedly. I went over to talk with Janet Reibel after lunch. I thought she may have known someone who might be interested in work. The poor woman was in a state when I arrived. Mrs. Turner's family has given her and Doris until this weekend to evacuate the house. The relatives are keeping their mother in their own care. They plan to sell or rent the property."

"How can we help, Gran?"

Rhylla sat in thought for some moments while her mind once again rationalized her need for help and the need to protect her secrets.

"Janet walked back here with me and I showed her what her responsibilities would be. I explained to her how you look after your room and I will care for my bedroom, office and your mother's room and studio. Janet will cook our meals, do the laundry and care for the remainder of the house. She will have weekends off, unless in the event of an emergency. Janet agrees to all of this. I told her I want to discuss this with you before making a final decision."

Skye-Marie's face glowed. "Oh, Gran, where will they live?"

"I have offered her accommodation in the bigger of the two flats above the coach-shed. You must remember, Skye, having a live-in housekeeper and daughter means twenty-four hours a day, seven days a week. They become part of the family. Any disagreements have to be resolved peacefully within the unit."

"Gran, no problem. Doris and I have been friends since we started school and we've never argued yet."

"Can I leave you to clean up these dishes and I'll take a quick drive over to Mrs. Turner's house to tell Janet the news?"

In the morning, before her breakfast, Skye-Marie helped her mother to freshen up and dress. She used a soft brush to smooth the thinning hair on Kirsty's head.

Rob Bains had been too excited to sleep. The typewriter keys clattered away, from the time he had read the acceptance letter and saw the advance cheque from the publisher, through the night in the dull light of the lantern until the morning glow of a cloudy sky announced the promise of a sunless morning. His fingers raked his hair before rubbing the reddened eyes. His stomach rumbled. The question of when did he last eat became a difficult one to answer. Stiff muscles in the back of his neck made themselves felt. He pushed the chair back and attempted to rise. Legs almost paralysed with lack of use, trembled. They threatened not to oblige. Ingrained dirt stained the hands he thrust out to grab at the table edge. He paused to regain his balance and stretch his limbs.

His feet, alive with pins and needles, stumbled across the hut to stir the fire in the woodstove where he found not a skerrick of hot coals. Rob sighed. If he wanted a cup of tea, he would need to start the fire from scratch, restock the wood box near the stove and fill the water bucket from the tank outside. By the time a fire danced in the stove box and he returned with his water bucket, the rising wind gusts slammed the door shut behind him. The strong breeze whistled through the open windows. Sheets of writing paper swirled off his desk. He scrambled about shutting the windows and rescuing his night's hard work lying about the room.

Rob stood at the small open window above the bench near the stove to eat a bowl of porridge. Wariness filled the blue eyes watching the erratic footsteps of lightning strikes as they marched across the land from the coastal strip towards his home. The storm hit with a crash on his roof. There was no point trying to see out through his peephole any longer. Impenetrable sheets of water filled his view. Trees bowed to the power of the storm, their limbs and smaller branches thrashed wildly. Cracks of thunder overhead threatened to split his eardrums. The temperature plummeted. He lifted his jacket from the nail behind the door and wrapped it tight about his body.

At the table, he sat examining his kingdom. What if the roof should lift or worse still, his whole hut be demolished? The thought propelled him into action. The sea chest standing at the end of his bed bounced across the rough-hewn flooring timbers as he dragged it over to the writing desk. He threw it open. Clothes were tossed aside. His typewriter, writing papers, blank and filled, were placed inside. All the many books in the room were collected and added to the water-proof store. The latest correspondence and his cheque were included in his treasure. With a flick of his wrist, Rob pulled a blanket from his bed and folded it over everything before he secured the trunk's lid.

As he sipped from his steaming pannikin, his eyes roamed the room. He jumped up again and strode to the wall where the portrait print by Kirsty Mak hung. A gentle finger traced the face of the woman and her haunted eyes. He lifted it down and added it to the trunk contents.

Hail, branches and winds punished the roof of the hut and its awning. His heart raced to the beat of the swish of leafy branches against the iron roof. A thud of something heavy landed above his head. Fear settled in just below the surface of his mind as he considered the threat imposed by the constant noises and the thought that at any moment a large tree may come crashing down upon his cabin. Any noise he could not identify, his imagination filled the void with vivid scenes. And then, there it was. A sheet of iron torn loose clanged against another. It did not sound like the hut roof. It must be the roof of the shelter under which he parked his vehicle which was attached to the hut.

Rob sat listening for long moments weighing up in his mind the need to secure the sheet of iron and the risk of facing the elements if he ventured outside. He thumped the table and stood up. An empty thick hessian feedbag was removed from a hook in the wall beside the door. He pushed one corner of the closed end of the bag into the opposing corner of the closed end and placed the peaked point over his head pulling the sides of the bag down around his body as far as it would reach. He gathered up two of several rolled ropes hanging from neighbouring hooks. As he lifted the latch, the wind nearly sucked the door out of his grasp. Rob's body stumbled forward several steps before he steadied himself. Water splattered up from his bare feet at each step as he examined the loose sheet of iron on the awning. The lightning had eased somewhat which was a blessing knowing he was going to be working near the sheets of iron on the roof of the shelter.

Water flowed down his improvised raincoat. It trickled inside, cooling his body rapidly. A fist cleared the water from his eyes. Using the rope, he tied a knot at the base of one outside corner post and attempted to throw the remaining rope diagonally across the length of the awning. It was not until his third attempt that the rope slithered to the ground at the other end of the shelter and close to the hut wall. Goosebumps rose on his shivering skin as he sloshed his way around to the untied end of the rope. Putting his weight into the pull he tightened the hemp rope and struggled to secure it to the base of the house-post. With the second rope, he repeated the process from the other two corners of the awning roof. Once satisfied he had done the best he could, he fought the wind and rain to walk over to look out through the swirling trees growing at the top of the cliff face, but the grey cloud of rain made it almost impossible to define where the edge of the clifftop was.

He shivered and again rubbed the water from his face. Rob turned and with the wind at his back, he ran towards the cabin. A loud crack of thunder vibrated through his body – he jumped. On its tail, a flash of lightning and another crack of thunder split the air close by followed by the sound of timber falling. A large tree limb plummeted to earth. Rob increased his pace but one of the bigger branches grazed the side of his head spinning him around and tossing his body into a small gutter filled with water from the rain and the overflow of the tank at the hut. The small stream rushed towards the edge of the cliff face where it fell as a miniature waterfall. Rob's body lay unmoving on its side with his head, shoulders and arms on one bank of the gutter. Blood seeped from the wound in his scalp and coloured the water pouring over his face and into the dirt. His lower body and legs lay twisted along the length of the gutter. Water banked up against his chest and abdomen before flowing over his legs.

Rob's head jerked – his upper arm reached out. One word filled the pause in the falling rain.

"RHYLLA!"

He fell back into the mud.

The rains persisted. Water rose higher on Rob's chest until it soon splashed over his neck. It threatened the tip of his chin and mouth.

CHAPTER TWENTY-FIVE

Where had the week gone to? Here it was Friday already and the flat for Janet was still in the process of being sorted. The casual handyman cum gardener, Mr. Bingle, had rearranged furniture under Rhylla's instruction and shifted many boxes including the box of Robbie's novels into the smaller flat for storage. At least those scallywags Gavin and Alistair won't have access to Robbie's books now they'll be under lock and key, Rhylla reflected. Janet Reibel, the new housekeeper, and Doris were coming over after their tea tonight to dust and clean the rooms of their new accommodation before her brother delivered their possessions in the morning.

Rhylla sat on a worn sofa in the spare flat going through the box of Robbie's books. Light fingers stroked each book in turn. Her mind recalled the story within each cover and every one of the plots and characters within them all. One by one, the books were placed inside a lockable cupboard held here in storage also. At the bottom of the box, she found the latest two books she had purchased. They were by an author called Robert Bains. Rhylla had discovered these works by this author recently and enjoyed them both so much she had a standing order at her favourite bookshop for any other books this man might publish. The shop had one currently on order and she had been led to understand another book was to be released very shortly.

Apparently, the author lived as a hermit somewhere in Queensland. A short spiel inside each cover explained how the author wished to let the work speak on his behalf. It had been the similarities in the style and genre of the writing her Robbie had used when he was alive which had captured her interest. A familiar pain ripped through her chest at her thought. She seemed to live every day wishing he were alive but refusing to let herself believe he could be anything but dead.

The clatter of Monday morning's breakfast dishes drifted through to the office where Rhylla worked. Skye-Marie rushed into the room and over to her grandmother's chair. She bent to drop a kiss on her forehead.

"Doris and I are off to school now, Gran. I have said goodbye to Mum. She's settling down for a nap. You have a nice day. I'll see you this afternoon."

"You too, darling." Rhylla lifted her head and called through the doorway. "'Bye, Doris, have a good day."

"Goodbye, Mrs. MacBurnie." Floated back.

Just then the phone on the corner of her desk jangled. She snapped it up to cut the noise which might disturb Kirsty.

"Hello, Rhylla MacBurnie speaking." As soon as she heard the caller's voice her face lit up. "Oh, Tim, it's so good to hear your voice. How are you and the family?"

There was silence within the room as she listened to her son's reply. "I'm sorry to say, Tim, our Kirsty is fading each day." Rhylla's voice caught for a moment in her throat. "Tim, is this a business or a social call?" She pressed the handpiece closer to her ear. After a short time listening, a cynical smile curled her top lip.

"That's very nice of Bronwyn to be so concerned for my well-being. No, I won't even consider stepping down from the position of Chairman of the Board. No, I'm not overworked here caring for your sister. In fact, I now have a live-in-housekeeper who has taken many burdens off my shoulders." Rhylla paused. A frown furrowed her forehead as she again listened to the voice of her son on the other end of the line. Anger boiled in her stomach. She swung around to stare with unseeing eyes through the windows. Her voice shook as she answered.

"Tim, you know very well not to listen to a word Bronwyn says on the subject of Kirsty or Skye-Marie and her parentage. I can assure you, as I have assured Bronwyn, on more than one occasion, your father did not rape Kirsty. He was collecting me from the railway station at the time when it happened. We discovered Kirsty emerging from a drugged state when we arrived at the house." While she listened again, Rhylla struggled to regain her equilibrium. One hand clenched the phone stand while the other pressed the earpiece hard against her head.

"Tim, you need to remember our Bronwyn always has her own agenda. She's determined to remove Skye-Marie from her rightful position on the company board when Kirsty passes on." Rhylla drew slow deliberate breaths as she listened until her son finished what he had to say.

"Yes, Tim, that is right. When the time comes, I will have Skye-Marie's proxy vote until she is twenty-five years of age; just as I have Kirsty's vote while she is ill." Rhylla chewed her lip and tapped her fingers on the large blotter on the desk as she listened.

Rhylla spoke slowly paying attention to her diction when she replied. "Tim, both the company solicitors and my solicitor, Jim Sullivan, have examined the details of the company by-laws and the statements in our wills. They are satisfied all is as it should be. If anything does happen to me, Kirsty has indicated, in her will, as have I, in my will, that you are to be the executor of both wills. You will have the proxy for Skye-Marie's vote until she reaches the determined age." Her head nodded as her son spoke at length.

"Yes, yes, Tim, I will endeavour to speak once more to Bronwyn and make her see sense although I don't hold out much hope for my success." She smiled at his further comments. "Yes, Tim, I will do that. Goodbye, dear, and love to you all down there in Brisbane." She hooked the earpiece and speaker back into place. Her body sat unmoving while her unblinking eyes stared into the wall. "That girl goes too far, sometimes," she mumbled. It was Janet's tap on the door which stirred her from her reverie.

"Mrs. MacBurnie, Kirsty is sleeping. I have the sheets boiling in the copper but will I start the washing machine now or wait until she wakes up?"

Gratitude shone in Rhylla's smile. "Thanks, Janet. Yes, you can start the machine. Are you familiar with how to use it?"

"Yes, Mrs. MacBurnie, it's the same kind as Mrs. Turner has … er … had."

"If you close the laundry doors, the noise doesn't reach Kirsty's room through the bathroom next door."

When Janet turned to go, Rhylla once more pulled her glasses down onto her face and straightened the papers out in front of her. A sigh escaped her lips as she realized some clarity must be brought to everyone's understanding of Kirsty's rape. A grunt followed the sigh. She acknowledged to herself how the full details of the dreadful evening could never be revealed.

After lunch, Rhylla stood in the connecting doorway between Kirsty's bedroom and the studio. She watched her daughter preparing a new canvas for her paintings. Gone were the usual strong sweeping strokes of the brush. Short weak passes of the white base-brush eventually covered the canvas before Kirsty leant heavily on the back of the chair near where she stood.

"Hello, darling, feeling a little better this afternoon?"

"Perhaps a little, but I do feel as weak as a kitten."

"Can I bring you a cuppa?"

"I think a break sounds wonderful."

Rhylla moved forward to assist Kirsty back into the bedroom where the small table had been set up near the windows. Mother and daughter sat drinking their beverage, nibbling on Janet's scones and enjoying the parkland views. After ten minutes, Rhylla sighed. She knew this unpleasant discussion could not be put off any longer.

"Kirsty, I had a worrying phone call from Tim this morning."

"Oh, Mum, is he alright? Has someone had an accident?"

"No, darling, it's closer to home. Bronwyn has been telling Tim that you think your father raped you all that time ago."

Kirsty began coughing on the sip of tea as it went down her air passage. Strident inhalations brought Rhylla to her feet. Fearing her daughter's ribcage may crack under the pressure but fearing more Kirsty was going to choke to death, she patted the bony back until normal breathing resumed.

"Oh, Mum, I'm sorry. I didn't want to say anything to you. It would have broken your heart. When I think back to that night, and barely a day goes by when I don't, I see his face staring down at me."

"Darling, this is all my fault. I'm so very sorry." Rhylla struggled to maintain her composure. She swiped at the tears on her cheeks.

"Mum, please don't get upset. How can any of this be your fault?"

"I should have sat down and made you tell me everything then and there. But when you became so upset and said you just wanted to forget it all, I encouraged you." Rhylla swallowed and took a deep breath as she remembered the waves of relief washing over her when

Kirsty had made it known she did not want to call the police. A strangled sob took her breath away. What had she done?

Both women sat deep in their thoughts until Rhylla spoke up.

"If only I had explained to you at the time how it couldn't have been your father. I knew it couldn't have been your father. He was at the railway station with me at the time the rape was committed. When we arrived home, we noticed the headlights of a car driving off across the park. They seemed to have come from our house. We thought it was young larrikins fooling about." At this point, Rhylla's eyes fell on her hands in her lap smoothing one over the other. Guilt niggled in her gut. In her heart, she knew this white lie would make no difference to the truth of the rape but may protect the innocent.

Kirsty's quivering hands reached out to her mother. She clenched her eyes tight and shook her head to remove the vision of her father looking down into her face. Her voice came out between gasping breaths. "You're right, Mum. Perhaps we should have spoken more at the time. I once told Bronwyn I didn't know if it was my father. But it was stupid of me to say anything to Bronwyn. Even as a child, I knew how she twisted any information to suit her own ends.

"Oh, Kirsty, my darling, if only we had talked about it all then. I'm so sorry. I could have put your mind to rest on that score." Rhylla paused. Her mind swirled within her head. How could she allay her daughter's fears? How could she reassure Kirsty that memories can become distorted? Lifting her hands to Kirsty's face, her fingertips traced the pale cheeks, with a whispered touch. "Will you come with me back to that night again?"

A thumping pulse began on either side of Kirsty's throat. She knew she had to do this if not for herself then definitely for Skye-Marie. Over the years, her mother had offered many times to go with her to the doctor for counselling but the thought of talking to outsiders had been too difficult to bear. Hard though it was to accept, she knew her time on this earth was lessening day by day. She must find the courage to look back on that night?

After a long shaky breath, Kirsty answered. "Yes, Mum, if you will help me think back on it now – together – just you and me."

Rhylla rose and closed the door to the hallway. It shut with the faintest click. She pulled her chair close to Kirsty's and held the two fragile hands in her own.

"Can we think back to just before it happened? What was the last thing you do remember? It was a night when I was due to arrive back by train from a meeting in Brisbane. Your father left the house at seven o'clock on his way to collect me from the station. You had been left on your own at the house. Can you remember what the two of you had for your dinner before he left?"

Kirsty sat dragging up vague pictures and memories which had plagued her repeatedly over the past years. "Yes, I think that was possibly the last thing I distinctly remember. I told you this before. We always had bread and sugar on the last meal before your return from business trips. It was his secret with all of us. You were such a stickler on making us eat good healthy meals. Even though it was only the two of us that night, we still had bread and sugar with lots of butter." A warm smile rested lightly upon her lips at the thought.

"Can you see in your mind, the moment when he left the house to get into the car?"

"This is where my head becomes crazy. I see his back walking across to the car shed, but then I see his face standing at the door at the same time."

Rhylla bit her lip and pondered for some minutes. "Do you think your mind may be recalling two scenes together? You say you know your father went to get the car. Where were you standing when you waved goodbye?"

"At the door, I think." Kirsty shut her eyes again, not moving.

Rhylla watched. Anxiety lined her face. Had she pushed Kirsty too far – too hard? She jumped when Kirsty began speaking again.

"No, no – I'd started working on my homework. I remember; Dad came over earlier and patted me on the head. He waved the sugary plates at me and laughed. Do you remember that wicked laugh he had at times? He said he'd better get rid of the evidence before you got home." Kirsty sat in silence with her eyes closed; her face muscles twitched with her thoughts. "The water splashed in the sink. Oh, and he cursed softly when a plate dropped into the sink." Kirsty paused. Her shallow breathing scarcely lifted her chest. "Then I heard the door slam behind him. He tooted the horn as he drove out of the garage." Her silence became prolonged.

Rhylla hesitated before asking, "Did someone come knocking on the door, or ringing the bell? We found no evidence of a break-in."

"No, Mum, I'm sorry. I can't remember. Oh, yes, I went over to pull the curtains on the front windows. I can't remember going back to my homework though. I can't think what may have interrupted me." Feeble hands wiped at the perspiration running down her face. "I just can't remember. I'm sorry, Mum."

"Darling you have done well. Now I'll tell you what I know. We arrived back just after the rapist left. You were still pretty out to it all. I went to the kitchen to make the cocoa and your father went up to ask you if you wanted some brought up. Within seconds his voice yelled down the stairway. Somewhere between his driving off and us returning home someone entered the house and attacked you."

Kirsty's headshake was barely discernible.

"Kirsty, do you think the second face you are recalling at the doorway might be this stranger upon whom your subconscious has imposed your father's face? In your mind, you have put the two men together one going and one coming? It would have been a short time between your father leaving and the stranger arriving I would think."

"You must be right, Mum. I kept remembering Dad's face as I drifted up out of the blackness. I always thought he must have done it to me. I could not believe such a thing was possible; he'd always protected us. I could not speak to you about it because that would have hurt you too."

"I'm sorry, my darling. Your father was in the room with me when we arrived home. I should have made the two of us sit down and add our memories together while they were still fresh, but I thought you might be better off if you just tried to forget everything and get on with life."

"Mum, it's not your fault. I'm to blame too. I just could not have faced going to court and telling everything to a whole room of people and reporters and everything." Tears rolled down her face to fall drop by drop into the deep hollows formed by the top of her shoulders and the protruding clavicles.

Rhylla stood up and took a small handtowel from the table and sopped up the moisture. She held her daughter in a gentle hug. Rhylla had to sink her teeth into her tongue. She so much wanted to reassure Kirsty. The rapist would never hurt another young girl. The man had been punished.

A soft tap on the door stirred mother and daughter from their thoughts.

"There's a Mr. Sullivan to see you, Mrs. MacBurnie. I've put him in the sitting room."

Rhylla jumped up and opened the door to Kirsty's room. She turned back. "Will you be all right on your own now or would you like me to send Janet in to sit with you for a while?"

"No, I'm feeling much better – sort of lighter inside – if you know what I mean."

Rhylla smiled. She then turned her face to Janet who had stood back to wait on the other side of the corridor. "Thanks, Janet. I'll go and see what Jim wants."

Rhylla found Jim Sullivan sitting on the sofa with his head in the daily newspaper. She paused for the moment taking in the signs of age which had crept up on him of late – especially since the death of his wife Mabel, last year. The once thick brown hair had thinned into a monk's cap on top surrounded by thinning strands of grey hair. The wide intelligent forehead remained with added lines of worry. The skin on the backs of his hands had wrinkled and the tan had faded. He looked up.

"Oh, good afternoon, Rhylla. Sorry to arrive unannounced – just passing your street. Besides, I don't want to go back to the office and listen to all the young fired-up solicitors making me feel like I'm an old man. I don't need them to remind me." He laughed and Rhylla joined in.

"Wisdom comes with age, Jim – or so my father always said when he reached fifty years of age."

They both smiled.

"I wanted to say hello to Kirsty too. I heard she was not doing too good." Jim paused when he noticed the tears welling in Rhylla's eyes. "I'm sorry, dear, have I come at a bad moment?" Usually, when looking into those blue-grey eyes, Jim revered the strength and compassion to be found, but today a deep sorrow also dwelled within. He could not help thinking how Doug Hampson, their friendly copper, never missed the opportunity to berate Robbie MacBurnie for having walked out of Rhylla's life. Jim knew if he hadn't been included in the scheme, he might agree wholeheartedly with Doug's opinion. Jim felt sure Doug held a candle for Robbie's wife but as far as he knew had never acted inappropriately. Come to think of it, every male within miles held a candle for the beautiful Rhylla McNeven, in the day, including himself.

"No, Jim, of course not. You're always welcome here at any time; you know that. Kirsty will love to see her Uncle Jim. Come, I'll have Janet bring us some afternoon tea."

"Janet?"

Rhylla turned back to her visitor. "Yes, Jim, with Mrs. Barnes gone I found it near impossible to do everything I wanted to do without some help. Janet Reibel's daughter has been a friend of Skye-Marie's for years. You'll be pleased to know she is a much better cook than I am so it won't be rock-hard scones or sunken cake for tea."

"That's the lady who let me in, is it?"

At that moment, they had reached the kitchen en route to Kirsty's room. Janet looked up from where she had been setting up a tray of sandwiches and a lemon slice with a pot of tea and cups.

Rhylla made the introductions. "Is that a tray for us, Janet?"

"Yes, Mrs. MacBurnie. Will I bring it into Kirsty's room?"

"Thanks."

Jim stepped forward. "Here let me carry the tray, Janet, it looks very heavy. Besides, I want to make sure I get the lion's share of that slice. I hear tell you're a great cook."

"Thank you, Mr. Sullivan. Truly I can manage, besides I'm just waiting for the billy to boil. I'll be there in a moment."

Rhylla poked her head around her daughter's door to ensure she was ready to receive visitors. "I have a lovely surprise for you, Kirsty." She stood back allowing Jim Sullivan to enter.

A soft broken voice attempted to squeal. "Uncle Jim, this is great." She struggled to rise.

"You stay just where you are, Miss. I don't want your mother hounding me with a whip." Jim walked swiftly to Kirsty's chair and took her gently into a hug. His face remained unchanged despite the shock and sadness he felt at the fragility of his expert tennis partner of several years.

At that moment, Janet entered with the tray.

"Thanks, Janet, can we have it on the table there? We can look after ourselves."

"As you wish, Mrs. MacBurnie." Janet smiled as she set the tray down as instructed and exited the room.

Jim praised the treats and drank deeply from the cup of sweet tea. When Kirsty's eyes began to droop, he stood up and made his apologies.

"I'll see you out, Jim." Rhylla turned back to pat Kirsty's hand. "I'll return in a moment, dear, to help you back to bed."

As they made their way along the corridor to the front door, Rhylla asked. "Jim, how are you managing to cope now without Mabel. I know how hard it must be for you. She was your rock."

"It hasn't been easy but work helps. The family is a great support but they do fuss a bit." He grinned. "Always telling me how to do things like I was the child and they the adult."

Rhylla laughed. "That happens, Jim. I know exactly what you are saying."

The half-moon lay on the water beside the still body. The light it cast exposed earth still wet from the earlier rains. Each light gust of breeze scattered drops of water across the ground from the drenched leaves of the trees. The silent footsteps of a prowling dingo approached. A bird, dead as a result of the storm, swung by its neck from its clenched teeth. At the scent of the human being, the dog backed up and made a sweep away to the west. The "woo-woo" of an owl hung on the air of the forest. After midnight, a bandicoot sniffed at the blood saturated in the ground near the unmoving head of the man.

The apricot glow of the early morning eased over the horizon strengthening with every hour until it lifted above the trees on the plateau. Steam rose from the damp earth and the man's wet clothing as it burned down upon the clearing. The tink - tink - clink of the expanding and contracting iron roof of the wooden hut marked the passing hours of the day.

When once again the half-moon lay in the water beside the man's still hand, the dingo returned but hesitated at the human odour. With numerous dead birds lying around on the forest floor since the storm, hunger did not rate high in its priorities. For the second time, the bitch bypassed the silent body.

Along with early morning light, the sounds of heavy machinery penetrated the forest. The government road employees worked to clear the district thoroughfares of the debris left by the storm of two days ago. Sam Nugent directed his men with saws and axes to clear the track leading up to Rob Bains's cabin.

With the cabin in sight, the tall giant they named Scotty called out, "Hey, Boss, there are no tracks around the cabin. No one has been here since the rain. The bloke's ute's here, though. It has a bit of a bend in it where a tree branch has damaged the corner of the awning.

Sam went over to join his offsider. "The fella must be here somewhere. I'll check out the hut, you look around the back see if you can pick up a footprint."

In only a few moments, Scotty's yell rang out. "He's here. He's down."

"Geez, he must have been there throughout the storm. Looks like the limb what took the awning collected him too. Look at the gap in his scalp. Is he alive?"

"Dunno, he's awful still."

Sam stood looking down at the man he thought most likely dead, trying to figure what best to do first.

"Scotty, go fetch McMillan, he was a medic in the army in New Guinea. Tell him to bring the first aid box and another man to help us get this body down to the road. We'll take him to the hospital."

A tarpaulin wrapped around two stout poles provided an improvised stretcher. A groan rolled out of the wounded man's mouth as his body was moved onto the frame.

"McMillan, I have to admit I didn't believe you when you said the fella was alive. Seems I was wrong."

"Don't get too excited, Boss. I won't guarantee he'll still be alive when we get him to town. It won't be smooth travelling in that springless old truck of ours."

Sister MacGregor's starched veil poked up from her head like a secret weapon – the expression on her face, another. Cowed, the junior doctor assisted the trainee nurse as instructed.

Sister MacGregor turned to the two men with dirt falling from their work overalls onto her clean floor. Her mouth turned down at the edges.

"Do we know who this gentleman is?"

"Rob Baines, Sister." Sam Nugent provided the information. He had been cleanly bowled out on more than one occasion at the monthly social cricket matches by this man. He knew him well.

The doctor's soft voice interceded. "How did you find him and do you know how long he has been out in the elements?"

"We think he was knocked on the head by a fallen branch in the storm two days ago, Doctor. That would explain the wound on his head and the tree limb on the ground nearby." Sam continued with the explanation refusing to be intimidated by Sister MacGregor's frown. Scotty had slunk out of the casualty room to wait outside in the work truck where he rolled himself a cigarette.

"Is he gonna be alright, Doctor? We was sure he'd carked it."

"Only time will tell us that." The despondent face of the doctor looked up at Sam. The man in white shook his head.

"Well, you do all you can for him. He's a top bloke."

"Of course, we always do."

CHAPTER TWENTY-SIX

It was night when he opened his eyes. A glow of light revealed beds lined the walls around him – a hospital. The murmur of voices emanated from somewhere behind him. He blinked his eyes. A scarlet wall of pain washed over him. It rolled down from his skull which felt as if it had been cleaved into two separate parts. His thoughts lay divided and burrowed into each part. Scenes flicked through his mind like watching the Saturday matinee movie.

On one side, the most prominent picture, Rob Bains sat typing at a desk inside a cabin. All around forest crashed about him as the thunder and lightning pounded his mountain. The din changed to the yells of stockmen and the crack of whips as Rob Bains rode in the dust behind a herd of cattle – cattle travelling from Far Horizons to Rosebud Plains. Steve Whittle and Billy Jackson, his constant companions … but no, Steve now lay dead somewhere on foreign soil and Billy left a leg behind in the same cold lands. Steve and Billy who had rescued him from the collapse at the Mount Isa Mines. They said he must change his name. People were after him – wanted to kill him – but why?

On the other side of his head, split open laying on the pillow, he watched a boy, Robbie MacBurnie, growing up with his family on a farm on the Atherton Tableland. Squeals of children diving off a home-built raft into a bottomless lake, the dark shadows of the deep waters enclose him as the pressure mounts against his skin. The teenager with promise sent off to university in Sydney – a world so large and crowded and busy and noisy. A hollow in the young man's gut as home-sickness took its toll until he began to adjust. The cheers of a crowd when his skill with the tennis racket won his team a point. The boos of another crowd when their favourite had been bowled out by his twisting cricket ball. A rolling stomach and raging butterflies in his belly when introduced to one Rhylla McNeven at a dinner party. Pride when standing in his robes on graduation day. Pride swallowed at the reminder of his mother's advice – 'Pride comes before a fall'. Pride without restraint as he stood in his best suit to say, 'I do', beside the keeper of his heart. Pride at the births of his son, his daughter and then Kirsty. The miniature of her mother. Horror replaced the pride filling his soul at the feel of his fist against the jaw of the man who raped his young daughter. The sight of the blood oozing out around the head of his older brother. The sound of the man's utility carrying the body bouncing down the cliff face at the quarry.

A long groan rolled up from his toes and filled the ward in which he now lay. He gasped shallow breaths and his heart pounded inside his chest.

Quiet footsteps approached. A fierce voice within his mind demanded his silence. He lay quiet as he slipped into the darkness.

"Is he dead?" A junior nurse asked.

"No, but his breathing is erratic." The senior girl reached for the man's wrist. "This pulse is pounding and all over the place." She leant closer to the patient. "Mr. Bains, can you hear me." But there was no reply. She drew the junior aside. "I want you to find the night sister. Tell her Mr. Bains seems to be having some kind of turn."

But when the night sister arrived the man's vital signs had returned to normal. "It looks like Mr. Bains has passed some sort of crisis. There is no point waking the doctor at the moment. Everything seems back to normal."

The next time he surfaced the fierce voice had not left him. The man the nurses called Mr. Bains lay quietly with his eyes shut endeavouring to make sense of the memories scrambled like eggs inside his head.

A week later, the doctor released Mr. Rob Bains into the care of Mr. Tom Whittle who had arrived in town in response to a message sent from Mr. Acton, Rob's friend and occasional boss.

"Now, Mr. Whittle, I want you to ensure Mr. Bains returns to see me in three days or sooner if you become worried about his condition."

"Yes, Doctor, of course."

Tom Whittle drove Rob back through the avenues of trees to his house in West Street in a car borrowed from a mate in town. With a cool breeze and a warm sun overhead, the two men waved to the merry widow standing on the front steps of her house next door. As the friends moved into Tom's house they spoke in unison.

"Not the merry widow anymore. Poor Kevin." Grins of relief lit both faces as they repeated their frequently quoted mantra of nearly ten years.

"I think I'll lie down for a bit, Tom." Rob rubbed his forehead.

"You, okay?"

"Yeah, fine. Not quite as spry as I used to be."

"Hear what you're saying, Rob."

Despite all Rob's pleas, Tom Whittle refused to drive him out to the hut at the top of the cliff.

"Not until you have your check-up with the doctor on Thursday," he kept telling him. "The doctor would have my guts for garters if I took you out there over that rough track, Rob. He put the wind up me, he did."

"What, the great Tom Whittle scared of a little city boy. I find that hard to believe. What about all the stories you tell us of facing up to brumby horses and mallee bulls? Are you saying they're bullshit?" Rob chuckled.

Tom chuckled with him. "Those doctor fellas are no better than magicians and wizards, young'un, just you remember that. They'd as soon cast a spell on you or stir you up a poisonous potion as shake your hand."

Rob laughed outright but grimaced when pain shot through his head. "It's that Sister MacGregor had me running for cover." He rubbed his forehead. "I think I'll go rest a bit."

No sooner had his head hit the bare mattress and its uncovered pillow when his thoughts began to churn. For days now, he had struggled to arrange his memories in chronological order. Until he was sure he had regained all his memories intact, he rejected any action which might serve to place him in a predicament from which he could not disentangle himself.

When eventually Tom dropped him at the hut on Saturday morning along with a box of groceries, they first extricated the utility from the fallen section of the shed and ensured it was still driveable. Rob then waved Tom off with a smile on his face and trepidation in his soul. What more mysteries and memories awaited him here.

Before going inside, Rob walked around the hut searching for damage. He pulled a few small branches down from the roof and off the top of the tanks. He cleared others from the track around the building. The imprints of many footsteps indicated the place where the roadworkers had found him. Small forest animals had been busy digging holes within the area.

The door scraped open. Having come from a hot sunny day outside he found it pleasant to enter the dark, cool room. He walked around the perimeter opening all the windows to let in the light and fresh air. His heart skipped a beat at the sight of the empty desk and bookshelf but immediately he recalled he had transferred everything to the sea chest in case the roof was taken in the storm. He unlatched and lifted the lid. A soft screech accompanied its opening. Sitting on top of everything else, Rhylla's portrait painted by Kirsty Mak looked directly into his eyes. Logic drew him to the conclusion the artist must be their daughter. After returning it to the hook on the wall, Rob sat back on the bed and gazed not only at the painting but the memory of the two women who had meant so much to him. A voice of guilt chewed at his ear reminding him they had another son and daughter too. He shook the voice away. Yes, he knew that and he loved them both and was proud of them but his baby girl, the image of her mother, pulled at his heart-strings.

"I'm coming home, ladies, I'm coming home." His eyes sparkled as he whispered into the silent room. But within a short time, a dullness seeped into the blue eyes. How could he return home if there was still a risk of his being discovered responsible for his brother's murder – where, in fact, the guilt did belong. Besides, Rhylla and the family will have made a new life for themselves after all this time. Rhylla may have married again. He threw himself back across the bed. Sorrow and regret, like a raging avalanche, threatened to overwhelm him. Maybe it was better when he didn't remember his previous life. The sun outside had reached its zenith when Rob pulled himself upright again. So, was he going to hang around here wallowing in self-pity? He had to find out. Kirsty had been raped, what if she had fallen pregnant. How did she and her mother get through that?

He must write to Jim Sullivan, the only other person who knew the full extent of that horrific night. Rob jumped up. Better still, he'd go to town and ring Jim from the phone box at the Post Office. He flopped back down onto the bed. No, he couldn't do that. The last instruction Jim had given him was never to talk on the telephone. They must always write. It wasn't hard for the police to learn details of phone calls made.

Rob scrambled around in the sea chest replacing all the things onto the writing desk and his books onto the shelf on the wall. The cheque and letter from the publisher came as a surprise – with everything else going on, he had forgotten. When he pulled the rough-hewn chair up to the desk and sat, he paused. His head ached; his vision blurred. As he stood to move over to his bed, his hands and legs trembled. With a thud, he landed across the mattress. He slept.

After parking his car inside his garage, Jim Sullivan sat for some time in the dark with his hands on his lap. A weariness weighed down his shoulders. Work relieved his loneliness but sometimes it became exhausting solving everyone else's troubles. Years of living with the guilt of not having solved his best friend's predicament swam like a grey nurse shark beneath the surface of his mind.

The car door shut with a sharp click. Jim walked over to the house without noticing the freshly mown lawn or the pruned hedges. He slipped the key into the door. When he walked into his house, the smell of furniture polish hung thick upon the air as it had when Mabel was alive. More pleasant aromas drifted out from the kitchen where his evening meal warmed in the oven waiting for him to sit down as it had when Mabel was alive. The bathroom gleamed, no evidence of his clothes upon the floor and a clean towel hung from the rack as it had when Mabel was alive. He expected the bed to be folded back and a clean set of clothes for the following day draped from the rack in the corner as it had when Mabel was alive. But Mabel was not alive. Only Mabel's well-trained house-help moved like a ghost to perform her duties. His bed was a lonely, lonely resting place.

His hat and coat he left hanging on the hat-stand before dragging the tie-knot loose about his neck. Several letters lay on the tray on the hall table but Jim could not raise the interest to investigate their origins. In the kitchen, he removed his dinner plate from the oven. It landed with a thump on the table beside his cutlery. Habit rather than appetite or interest inspired his hands to lift the knife and fork.

The mail remained untouched when Jim made his way to the bathroom and again on his way back to pour himself a glass of whiskey. Tonight, there were no folders of briefs from the office to study. He sat in the faint moonlight falling through the uncurtained window sipping from his glass. A crash of something outside brought him to his feet. When he found only the upturned bin his curse reached no further than his back fence.

"Bloody dogs."

With the bin reinstated and the back door shut he made his way past the mail on the hall stand. Jim retraced his steps and swept the few letters up into his hands. Only his personal mail arrived at his home. In the sitting room, he flicked a light switch and sat back in his well-worn chair. Idly he strolled through the envelopes in varying sizes. A letter from his daughter now living in his hometown on the Atherton Tablelands – married with four children. He cast it aside – he had heard all the well-meant lectures and advice before. Another, with a window, would be the electricity bill or maybe the telephone bill – they usually arrived in the same week. A third, from his brother, now retired, always welcome and always full of news of the family farms. But the fourth letter held his attention. A scrawl written by a hand using a pen in need of a new nib, it seemed. Yet there was something familiar about the scrawl. Curiosity consumed him. His hand lifted to tear the envelope apart and release the mystery when the jangle of the telephone called him away. He threw the partly opened envelope into the armchair from which he had arisen. Cursing inconsiderate callers beneath his breath, he went to answer the instrument of torture.

Rhylla watched as the sedan car rattled out onto the road. A niggle of worry flashed across her thoughts. Would the old car remain in one piece for the journey to the jetty where they were to meet the ferry? It was only a few miles away. The smooth rumble of a well-maintained engine gave her some confidence. Janet's brother, a mechanic, worked miracles to ensure his sister had a vehicle to drive. A wide smile lit up Rhylla's face at the sight of the two laughing girls in the backseat. Janet's one arm waved to her over the bonnet of the car while the other arm guided the vehicle out of the cul-de-sac.

It had been a good idea to send them off for a day's escape to Magnetic Island. They all needed a break from the shadowy depression of a house waiting for death; particularly young Skye-Marie.

Jim Sullivan had sounded so strange on the phone yesterday. It had been more than three weeks since he last visited Kirsty. But it seemed to her, Kirsty was not the primary reason for his visit later this morning.

After the day-trippers disappeared around the corner, Rhylla swung on her heels and returned along the driveway to the house. Her first port of call was Kirsty's room where she found her daughter lying awake staring at the wall. Rhylla's face fell as reality rushed upon her like a cloudburst over her head. She struggled to lighten her mood.

"Good morning, my dear. Are you ready for breakfast?"

A wan smile beneath the fading eyes looked up; her daughter's voice but a whisper. "Yes, Mum, but I think I'd rather freshen up first. Did Janet and the girls get away without any trouble?"

Later, with her daughter back resting on her bed, Rhylla answered the chimes emanating from the front door.

"Good morning, Jim." Age may have stooped the man and thinned the grey hair but his brown eyes sparkled when the boyish grin split his face. A worn dark briefcase hung from one hand while a cardboard box balanced in the crook of his other arm.

Rhylla stepped aside with a laugh. "Come in, come in. You come bearing gifts, I see." She closed the door behind her guest and turned to receive his chaste kiss upon her cheek before she led the way past Kirsty's closed door to her office. Relieving him of the box and placing it on the desk, Rhylla moved to the corner of the room where a tea tray sat upon a small table. "So, how have you been since we last saw you? Gosh, it must be a month since you were last here," she asked. "How's the family?"

As she turned to face him, Jim held up an item from the brown box. THE ACCOUNTANT'S CURSE stood out in bold print across the shiny cover of the newly published book. In a similar-sized print along the bottom of the cover, ROBERT BAINS stared out at the world.

"Oh, Jim, you've been able to find a copy of his new book. Mr. Dobbins in town told me I'd probably have to wait weeks before he would have it in the bookshop."

She turned the first page and was surprised to read a dedication written in longhand, something the author had not added in his previous two books she had read.

"To the keeper of my heart – my northern treasure." Her eyes moistened. *I wonder who he is, he certainly is a romantic. His northern treasure must be very special.* Rhylla placed the novel on the desk and moved back to prepare tea for both of them.

"Muffin or chocolate slice?" she asked.

Dregs whimpered in the bottom of the cups and the last crumbs lay defeated on the plates. Rhylla rose to check on Kirsty but she was only away for a few moments.

"Kirsty's still asleep. She sleeps a lot these days."

Jim Sullivan had exhausted his family news drawing a few laughs from Rhylla when he related some of the pranks his grandson had got up to while studying for the end of his first-year examinations at Brisbane University.

"Rhylla, I really came to talk to you this morning. I have some news which will come as a shock to you."

Her eyes snapped up. "What news? Who from? Not my grandchildren, I hope."

"If you finish with the questions, I may be able to tell you."

"Sorry, sorry, Jim. I just don't think I can take anymore bad news these days."

"This news, you may find good news."

"Well, out with it, Jim. Don't keep it all to yourself."

"I'll have another cup of tea if there's any in the pot there."

Rhylla began to upend the teapot. "I can make you a fresh pot, Jim."

"No, this'll be fine. I just want something to wet the whistle."

Jim sipped at the refilled teacup Rhylla placed in front of him. "I had an unexpected letter four weeks ago." Jim stopped talking. He had rehearsed his speech multiple times on his journey over here but suddenly he was unsure what to say first. "It came out of the blue. When I saw it, I thought the writing was familiar."

Rhylla's eyes lifted and stared at Jim's lips as if collecting every word coming out. Her mouth opened and closed but the question refused to be spoken. She held her breath. Her body remained still – waiting.

"Yes, it was from Robbie. He's living outside Toowoomba."

"He's alive – really alive?" Her hands clamped over her mouth. Tears spurted from her eyes unannounced. Her hands slipped down to rest at the base of her neck. "But why hasn't he let us know long ago? Why did you wait so long to tell me? The last thing I heard was after he'd received word the police were convinced his brother had travelled to Mount Isa back in 1933. He said he'd be home within days. It was the same week he received the wounds in a mine collapse and the doctor said he'd lost his memory. Do you remember, Jim? You went out there to see what had happened but couldn't find a trace of him." Rhylla's voice began to rise. She slammed her hands over her mouth again. Her ears pricked listening to hear if Kirsty may have been disturbed.

Jim took the opportunity to interrupt. "Two friends, Robbie had made there, living in the same boarding house, learnt of a plot to have him killed while he was still in the hospital. They spirited him out of Mount Isa."

"But where did he go? Didn't they know he came from Townsville? Had his memory returned by then?"

"No, his memory has only returned just over a month ago. As I understand it his friends took him to their parent's cattle station."

"And he's been there ever since?"

"Not exactly, but I think if you will let him back into your life, he'll tell it all."

Rhylla repeated her earlier question. "Why have you taken so long to tell me all this, Jim?" She bit her lip and dragged in a reluctant breath.

"I had to be sure the letter was genuine. That's why I never called last week to see Kirsty. I caught the plane to Brisbane and then a connection to Toowoomba. I found Robbie living in an old timber shack in the middle of a forest writing his books – a man the same but different. He has been through a lot, Rhylla." Jim pointed to the book on Rhylla's desk. "Robert Bains is our Robbie. He wrote the note inside the cover while I was there."

Her gaze fixated on the book sitting on the desk. Sobs almost choked her. A whispered voice asked, "What sort of things?"

"From what I gather the hardest has been living all this time not knowing who he really was. He does some work as a bookkeeper for a local accountant, Acton. Robbie didn't remember he was an accountant of note, himself."

"But he remembers now?" A tentative question.

"Yes, Rhylla, he thinks he has regained all his memory since being almost killed in a fierce storm recently. We spoke for two days non-stop. His memory was pretty much intact about both periods of his life. He and his friends left the property near Dajarra droving cattle south to another place near Roma. From there he ended up in Toowoomba."

Silence hung in the air for a long time as both explored their thoughts.

"He wants to come home? He hasn't forgotten us? He hasn't found a new wife?" Rhylla's questions burst from her lips.

"That was Robbie's first question. 'Has Rhylla remarried?' The answer, I think, is that his subconscious never really forgot you. He showed me a print of a painting he'd found in the Toowoomba Library. It was the portrait Kirsty painted of you at the Bowen beach. The one with which she won the Queensland prize. It hung on a nail in his wall above where he sat writing his books. He did not know who the lady was or the artist. He just loved the painting." Jim let Rhylla absorb this before going on. "Robbie told me of some dreams and nightmares he'd been having over the years. The children and you featured prominently in different ways but he didn't know why. The only thing that kept him from searching further was because he had been told by his friends how he had arrived at Mount Isa under a different name. He thought he must have had a shady past and kept his head down. When they, the friends, learnt someone was out to kill Robbie (when he was calling himself Greg) they changed his name again to Rob Bains." Jim drained his cup. "It was probably lucky they did because no one, not the police, the Sydney gangs nor we were able to trace him. They kept him safe."

"Should I go there … but I can't – not with Kirsty in such a bad way. Should I send him money?"

"Not just yet, Rhylla. Robbie wants to come home but he understands he's still under a cloud of course and cannot be seen as Robbie MacBurnie. I told him to remain Rob Bains for the moment until we can work out what he should do. He most certainly must avoid the police. As I see it, the ganglands may not be such a risk. He has had two name changes since Greg MacBurnie and they haven't discovered his whereabouts to date. Possibly whoever had put the hit out on Greg may have been killed when the razor gangs in Sydney disintegrated nearly ten years ago. I'll see what I can find out about that too. No, he does not need money. He showed me a cheque from his publisher. He's doing fine. In the meantime, I'm expecting a thick envelope to arrive in my mailbox with a letter for you inside."

Jim stood. Rhylla followed suit. "Oh, you're going already."

"Yes, I think so, Rhylla. You have a lot to take in and consider. I'll call back tomorrow. It's Sunday, and I won't have to go into the office. I'll visit Kirsty then if she is up for it."

Rhylla nodded. There was no chance of escape for her voice through a throat in spasm. Moisture welled in her eyes as she led Jim to the front door.

Rhylla sat opposite Kirsty at the small table under the window. They were eating the egg sandwiches Janet had prepared before leaving with the girls on their day out. Her subconscious noted the partly eaten sandwich now back on her daughter's plate. Anxiety burned her stomach as she watched the custard wobble in the spoon in Kirsty's hand, on its way from the plate to her dry lips. The other side of her thoughts churned with anticipation of a husband returned from the dead. What hurdles would they need to jump if they were to return him safely within the household?

With Kirsty back on the bed, Rhylla removed the potty from the commode chair. Sadness at the vision of her once-vibrant girl now reduced to hobbling only a short distance to a commode chair almost brought her to tears again. She forced a smile upon her lips as she left to empty the contents. By the time she returned, Kirsty's eyes were closed in sleep. Rhylla stood at the doorway watching. Every day it became harder to remember the beautiful Kirsty. Her daughter lay with little to no padding below the skin which draped her protruding bones. Would Robbie be home before their daughter was gone? What was he going to think seeing this caricature of his baby girl? Her footsteps dragged as she turned to make her way to her bedroom.

The sight of the book lying on the white linen quilt over the bedclothes emptied her mind of all but the excitement, laced with no small amount of fear, at Jim's news. She opened the curtains further to allow extra light into the room. With the quilt folded down and her pillows stacked, Rhylla removed her house shoes, climbed onto the bed and wiggled her buttocks into a comfortable position. Eager hands opened the book to the page where Robbie had penned his personal message to her. Soft fingers traced the letters.

The knocking on the front door seemed to have gone on for a long time before Rhylla's conscious mind registered.

"Oh, darn it." She dragged the handkerchief from her pocket and wiped her eyes. Reluctantly she sat up and slipped her feet back into her house shoes, dragged a comb through the tangled knots and dusted a layer of powder over her face. Her footsteps moved swiftly to the side door where the frustrated caller who had left the front door was now hammering.

When the door opened to reveal Doug Hampson, Robbie's and Jim's policeman friend, her knees threatened to give way under her as a flood of guilt sapped her strength. Rhylla's mind clung to the question like a dog to a meaty bone. *How does he know? How could he know? I only found out before lunch. How?*

"Can I come in?" Curiosity lay in every line of Doug's face.

"Sorry, sorry, Doug. I'm not myself lately, what with Kirsty's illness and all."

"Of course, how is your girl?"

Rhylla only managed a nod which shook the tears out over her cheeks. Her fists flung them away.

"Sorry, Rhylla, to bother at a time like this but I have some news you will find of interest, I'm sure." He took in the moist and haunted eyes. "Can I come in?"

"Yes, of course, Doug." Rhylla opened the door further and led her guest to a chair in the living room. "Can I offer you tea?"

"No thanks, I've just this minute finished my lunch." With another close look at his host, Doug was in two minds about whether he should have come here or should he have let Jim Sullivan pass on the word to Rhylla. He was the family solicitor after all. But Rhylla had always been so strong. He took a deep breath and ploughed on. "Do you remember the quarry out near our old fishing hole – near Davidson's old place?"

Rhylla sank lower in her chair. A weight of chains held down her heart. She nodded her head.

"They've been looking to develop the land around there. On Monday, a couple of surveyors went swimming during their break. They thought they'd seen a vehicle in the mud at the bottom of the quarry lake. Two police divers went out and eventually confirmed it was a utility truck. Yesterday afternoon they retrieved it."

Almost breathless, Rhylla managed to appear to be taking part in the conversation. "How on earth would a vehicle be at the bottom of the quarry?" Her stomach spasmed. She felt as though she were going to vomit. A scream threatened to escape. She knew. She knew very well. Did Doug know? How could this happen right now? Just when she had learnt her Robbie was alive and wanted to come home. How could the gods be so cruel?

"Not only a vehicle but a skeleton too."

Rhylla only just managed to convert the scream into a grunt of repulsion. She held her hand to her mouth. "Oh, Doug, who was it? Do you know?"

"Not yet, that will take some time. Everything has been taken away for investigation."

"How, gruesome. Why did you think it was of interest to me?"

"I have a feeling it may be Robbie's brother's vehicle. I plan to go through my old notebooks and see what information the Sydney police sent at the time. I heard one of the fellows say it could have been there between five to twenty years so the timing might fit."

She felt her white face turn even whiter. Her insides surged. *He knows. Doug knows. Why now?*

As he made his way through the front gate and out to his assigned police car, Doug Hampson's thoughts exploded from his subconscious like quail disturbed by a prowling fox. He pondered Rhylla's reactions. It was not the Rhylla he knew, but then with the worry of a dying daughter, it was understandable. Who knows how anyone would react in such conditions? His fingers paused on the door handle. Flashes of memory flicked across his mind like the changing patterns through a kaleidoscope. An old suspicion buried deep within his head had often chewed away at him over the past years. The vision of the last day he'd seen Robbie returning from a run with Jim Sullivan. Something bothered him about that scene. The clothes Robbie wore were not his usual choice of dress when out running. And Rhylla did not act like herself that day; usually, she behaved so uppity – her with all her father's money. Had it been nervousness made her beautiful eyes jump about like they did that morning? Robbie and Rhylla always seemed the perfect couple but who knows what goes on inside a marriage? Look at his own farcical existence. What really happened to Robbie all those years ago? We only have Rhylla's word he has a new life somewhere else. Now Robbie's brother's utility turns up with a dead body. Whose body is it lying on the cold slab in the morgue now? Did Rhylla have something to do with Robbie's disappearance? It does seem hard to believe.

He opened the car door and sat. With his hands resting on the steering wheel, he continued to analyse the ideas swirling in his head. Should he talk to Jim Sullivan? Probably not, he won't say a word against Rhylla; he had a huge crush on her when they were younger – probably still has. A frown deepened on his forehead. It's strange they never made a go of it after Jim's wife died but as far as he knew they hadn't. One quick flash passed almost before it registered. Were Jim and Rhylla together responsible for Rob's disappearance? He shook his head. No, that's impossible. He'd known Jim since the three of them, Jim, Robbie and himself, were kids in prep school. No way would Jim have any part of something bad happening to Robbie.

Impatient with the travels of his mind, Doug reached down and started the engine. He sat still as another thought demanded attention. If it was Robbie's body on the slab, what was he going to do about it? Was he going to do anything about it? If he hoped to be made the Inspector of the local area when the position became vacant next year, he knew he'd be advised not to make any waves.

Doug's growl at his thoughts became absorbed by the engine of the car as he drove off.

CHAPTER TWENTY-SEVEN

Skye-Marie sat in her room fingering the photo she had found on the staircase when helping her grandmother shift into the downstairs bedroom. They must have been brothers; they were so alike. If the one is her grandfather, as Gran said, the other must be a great uncle. She planned to ask her grandmother tomorrow.

She turned out the light and lay back on her pillows but as so often happened her thoughts returned to her discussion with her mother about the day she had been drugged and raped. Who might it have been who had raped her? Her mother had said she only remembered shadowy figures. Skye-Marie rolled over unthreading her legs from the tangle of sheets. Why should she care about a father who held no concern for her? She admitted to a wonderful and privileged life but sometimes she felt jealous when other girls at school showed off their fathers at school events. If she had a father the rotten twins could not call her a bastard. But then Doris would have to face them on her own. Doris can't remember a father in her life and it never appears to bother her. She seems content with just her and her mother. Sometimes she talks of an uncle who helps them out at times but Doris only sees him on odd occasions. Maybe she should listen to the minister at school assemblies who was forever telling them to 'Be thankful for all our blessings'.

In the mornings, after cooking porridge and setting the table for the MacBurnie family, Janet returned to her flat to do the same for Doris. Rhylla and Skye-Marie ate alone.

"Gran, did my grandfather, your husband, have an older brother?"

Porridge dripped unnoticed onto the tablecloth from the spoon paused in an unsteady hand halfway to Rhylla's mouth. Wide eyes stared at her granddaughter. She struggled to breathe. Slowly she set the spoon back into her plate.

"Where on earth did you get that from?"

"Well, no one talks of Grandfather. I know his people live on the Atherton Tablelands but we have only visited once I think since I was a baby."

"He had two younger brothers who run the family farm up there. You might have been too small to remember." Rhylla refused to let the sight of Robbie's older brother Greg, focus in her head.

"Oh," Skye-Marie felt sure the other man in the photo was older than her grandfather but the look in her grandmother's eyes hushed any other question on the subject.

The ticking of the kitchen clock sounded like a time bomb in Rhylla's ears. Spearheads stabbed at her conscience. Skye-Marie deserved to know her family – well those members deserving of knowing. Robbie deserved to be known even if not all of his story was revealed.

"Skye-Marie, would you like me to have the wedding photo of your grandfather and me enlarged and framed for you? You did say you liked the dress. I will do the one of the family group. We can sit down together and I'll try to tell you all I know of the family members on both sides." Rhylla's pleasure at Skye-Marie's excitement drowned out her relief knowing Greg MacBurnie would not need to be mentioned. "Now, I think I can hear Doris coming. You'd better hurry if you don't want to be late for school."

Janet answered the knocking on the front door. The westerly wind almost dragged the door out of her hand and into the face of the visitor standing on the step with his hat in one hand. "I'm so sorry, Sir. Oh, it's Mr. Sullivan, isn't it?"

"Yes, Janet, is Mrs. MacBurnie in?"

"She is, but at the moment she's busy in Miss Kirsty's room. Would you like to come in and wait?"

Jim Sullivan rubbed his forehead in thought or maybe disappointment. "Er … no … I have an appointment in half an hour. Um … Janet … if I give you this envelope will you make sure Mrs. MacBurnie gets it as soon as possible?" He dragged a crumpled envelope from the inner pocket of his coat.

"Yes, Sir, that will be no trouble." Janet stroked the mail smoothing out some of the kinks.

"Well, thank you kindly," Jim smiled as he turned to make his way out through the front gate with his head bowed and a hand wedged firmly on his hat. An exotic carpet of rose petals lay on the ground on either side of the path. Leaves from the large tree near the coach-house blew out across the street. He shut the gate behind himself and stood for a moment watching the miniature whirlwinds of dust dance along the roadway. The sound of the wind as it crashed through the trees in the forest behind the house reminded Jim of storm waves crashing onto the shoreline. A sensation not unlike his own hopes of a future with Rhylla as they crashed on the shoreline of fate.

Rhylla entered the kitchen with Kirsty's breakfast tray in her arms.

"Here, Mrs. MacBurnie, I'll take that." Janet took the tray and began to unload the dishes into the soapy water in the sink.

"Oh, Janet, Kirsty has hardly touched a morsel. A sparrow eats more than her these days." Rhylla struggled to prevent herself from giving way to her tears.

"I'm sorry to hear that. Perhaps I'll make her a strawberry junket for lunch – it seems to be her favourite."

"Thanks, Janet. It's so hard to know what may take her fancy on any given day."

"Mrs. MacBurnie, there's a letter for you on the hallstand. Mr. Sullivan left it while you were in with Miss Kirsty."

Rhylla's eyes brightened. "Thanks, Janet." It had to be a note from Robbie. Jim had said to expect one any day now. Her feet felt out of her control as she made her way to collect the letter.

Comfortable on the sofa in the sitting room, Rhylla stared at the front of the envelope where her name was scrawled across the paper in his handwriting. An attempt had been made to remove a smudge of dirt from the corner. Was she dreaming? Fourteen years of wishing, hoping, despairing, and now, when she was convinced of his demise somewhere, somehow, a letter to her from the only man she could ever love. Slowly, savouring the action, Rhylla slit the envelope and removed the single page.

Dearest Rhylla, my Kitten, my heart, my soul, my reason for living,

Where do I begin? What do I say? It would be so much easier if you were sitting opposite me and I could look into those enchanting eyes. Well, I can do the next best thing. I have a copy of the work Kirsty painted of you at the Bowen beach bought not because I had any idea of whom the model or the artist might be, but because when I first saw it, the face captured me and I could not understand why. It sits in front of me as I write.

I am so sorry to hear of Kirsty's illness. I cannot imagine your heartache. Jim is going to do everything he can to smooth the path for my return but only if this is what you want.

If you prefer that I did not return, I will try to understand. The past fourteen years must have been very hard for you not knowing where I had gone to or what had happened. I remember writing a letter advising of my imminent arrival home. I think that must have been on the day of the mine collapse when I was buried and lost my past. Jim said it was my landlady Sophie who found the letter and gave it to him when he went out to Mount Isa searching for answers.

In all this time I have felt an emptiness, an incompleteness, which I could not understand. I felt sure there must have been someone out there waiting for me but after my friends told me of my name changes before arriving in Mount Isa, I believed I must have had some kind of a shady past. I suppose that is not too far from the truth. I do believe, knowing what we both know (now) you might be more lenient to me than I was to myself. Since the mine accident, my nights have held many confusing nightmares but now, I think I understand where many of those were coming from.

I beg of you three things: To forgive me and love me like you always did. To welcome me home again. To see Kirsty one last time before she leaves us forever.

Believe me, when I say in the past fourteen years, I have never felt attracted to another – my heart held me steady even if my mind did not understand why.

With love, complete and eternal,
Robbie

The tinkle of Kirsty's bell disturbed her reverie. As Rhylla walked along the corridor to the sick-room she considered what Kirsty's thoughts may be on the possible return of her father. Until recently when they had sat down and talked it through, Kirsty had been convinced her father had been her rapist. Unless she knew of the death of Greg MacBurnie, her daughter would not understand why Robbie had not been able to return home. Even now with the death to be officially confirmed, Robbie's return might be perilous for himself and the family. Should she reveal this fact to a feeble Kirsty? Or should she continue with the misdirection and say her father who had left them without any warning now wanted to come home? As she stepped through the doorway, Rhylla was no closer to an answer to her questions.

The heavy shadow over Rhylla's heart lifted somewhat to find Kirsty sitting up in the bed with a sketchbook and pencil in her hand. When she viewed the subject of the work her heart rolled over. Robbie MacBurnie's face smiled up at her from the white page. She could not speak. Her throat refused to allow a word out. Her teeth worried her bottom lip.

"Mum, I do hope you like this. I know you have never stopped loving our dad and Skye-Marie wants so much to know him. This will be for you both when I am gone."

Through her tears, Rhylla's gaze followed the line of dark, wavy hair, his clean and chiselled features, the laughter lines at the edges of his twinkling eyes.

"Kirsty you have captured his likeness so well. Where did you find a photo of him? I thought I had buried all his photos deep in the storage boxes."

"His face has always been in my head and now since we spoke recently, for the right reasons."

"If you plan to do this in colour, his eyes were a pale blue which turned almost violet when stirred with emotion."

"Why did you hide away his photos?"

"It hurt so much when he … er … he left. I didn't want to be reminded of him continually. I thought it might help ease your pain of missing him if his photo wasn't a constant reminder too. I understand now, one doesn't need photos when a face is in your head forever."

"Would you prefer I hadn't done this sketch?"

"No, my darling, no. It's wonderful. I'm so glad you feel differently about him now than you had all that time not knowing of his innocence."

Kirsty dropped the pencil from her bony fingers and reached up to take her mother's hand. "I'm glad too."

"I've been meaning to tell you; I found the family photo taken at my wedding. It's quite large. Since Skye-Marie has been so interested in her family tree, I thought I'd see what they can do at the studio to improve the snap and make a decent frame for it. It will make a nice present for her – if you approve."

"She'll like that but be prepared for one million questions when you do?" Kirsty's dry and fragile skin pulled across the bones of her face in a poor imitation of a grin. Rhylla smiled and hugged her daughter gently.

"Now, it's lunchtime, I see. I know Janet has made a strawberry junket for you?"

"Could I have a boiled egg too?"

A smile lit Rhylla's face. If I can remember how to boil an egg. Janet has almost barred me from the kitchen.

When Kirsty slept after eating, Rhylla sat in her office for hours drafting out a letter to give to Jim for Robbie. Excitement ran like a raging flood through her veins but a niggling smouldering fire burnt inside her gut as she considered the enormous difficulties in reuniting the family. After all, the family and friends believed Robbie to have left her for another woman. How does one re-explain this?

She leant back in her chair. There was another major problem – Bronwyn. Tim never believed a word against his father but Bronwyn … well … who knew.

Robbie ran a brush through his unkempt hair which hung low on his neck. Impatient hands swept away the black and grey hairs lying loose on his shoulders. He flicked the brush over his salt and pepper whiskers and moustache before his hands dusted down the front of his navy shirt. He knew it was foolish to be going to all this trouble, after all, he had a long journey and days before he might get to see Rhylla. Even without the promise yet of her commitment he was determined to move closer to Townsville. He tossed his brush into the hessian bag with the last of his belongings: a coat, a few clothes and a toothbrush. Secured firmly in the tray of the utility, next to a wooden box with his remaining belongings, the sea-trunk held his precious writing equipment and books. His blue eyes hinted at violet as he took one last look around the inside of the hut which had provided some comfort to him over the recent years. He shut the door. He was ready to leave. From the front of the vehicle, he sat to peer, one last time, out through the gap in the forest trees looking towards the coastal plains. Yes, it was time to move on.

From Toowoomba, he made his way in an easterly direction to join the coastal road north of Gympie. After a day dragging the steering wheel left and right to avoid ulcerated pot-holes in the track his arms ached. On the banks of the Mary River, he camped overnight before heading north. Three more nights he camped out in his swag under the truck. Rain showers dogged his journey most of the way. After crossing the Burdekin River, excitement churned in his belly.

He felt her so close. Instead of the steering wheel under his fingers, he felt her soft face and cheeks, her slim neck, her shapely body. As much as he wanted to see again their home in Townsville, he resisted the urge to do so. Calloused hands gripped the wheel tight. Rob Bains, as he must remain, for the time being, concentrated on the road heading further north. He still had the family to protect. His resolve strengthened as he again remembered Jim's last letter which had arrived just before leaving Toowoomba. Excitement bubbled inside of him as he recalled the memorized words related to the news of his family. Nervousness diluted this thrill when he remembered Jim's report on the discovery of a body and vehicle in the quarry. At the time of Jim penning the correspondence, he had heard nothing more on the police investigation. Jim had invited him to use his isolated fishing hut fifteen miles north of Townsville. Far enough away to remain unseen and close enough to visit Rhylla when safe to do so. After stocking up on supplies at the last corner store out of town, he drove the last lap of his journey.

Clatter, clatter, clang! Robbie's eyes snapped open as his head swung up from the pillow. His eyes closed quickly as a sharp pain screamed from the old wound sites on his neck and head. He sucked in his breath and opened his eyes more slowly to peer around the fishing hut seeking the source of the racket.

Sitting on the edge of the wooden table near the stove, a grey possum tensed ready for immediate flight. It watched the intruder's every move.

"Hello, Possum." A smile crinkled the edges of Robbie's eyes. "Did I forget to put everything away last night?"

It had been late afternoon when he had arrived, exhausted. By the time he had opened the valve on the water tank, fired up the wood stove to cook some bacon and eggs bought at the Townsville store, he barely had the strength to eat his meal before he crashed onto the nearest bunk and slept. This early morning visitor had discovered the unwashed plate and utensils he had left on the table. The tin plate now lay upside down on the floor.

Idly Robbie wondered what other wildlife may have made a home inside the long-vacant hut. He had been too tired to investigate last night. There used to be a carpet snake found often in the woodshed built against the wall of the hut near the back door. It was inevitably found in residence when they visited in the early years.

The possum's gaze fixated on the newcomer.

Robbie's gaze roamed his spartan surroundings. A secure feeling of belonging eased over him in this place he knew from before his memory loss. As young married men and renewing their friendship in Townsville, Jim, Doug and he had spent irregular weekends fishing and exploring. When their sons had grown older, they joined their fathers on these peaceful get-a-ways – roughing it in the bush.

Robbie eased his legs over the edge of the bed and dropped his feet softly to the floor but the wary possum scurried through the wide-open window. Its claws were heard scratching their way along the branches of the casuarina tree. Robbie followed the possum outside using the doorway to exit.

He splashed water over his face from the tap at the rainwater tank before stretching his body and limbs. Wearing only a pair of shorts, Robbie followed the well-worn path through the trees towards the sea. Along with the various animals, a local Aboriginal family camped further along the coast in a grove of pandanus trees, maintained numerous pathways within the bush.

Robbie stood on a large boulder near the shoreline staring into the pristine clear waters in which he could see the baitfish darting and diving nearby. The heat of the sun draped his body like a warm welcome home. His body tensed. His memory of the dangers in this area lifted his awareness. His eyes darted left and right like the baitfish below the rock upon which he stood. He searched for signs in the sands and water for evidence of resident crocodiles. The sands remained smooth except for human footsteps since the last high tide. He assumed the food gatherers had been down to check their fish traps in the rocks near the mangroves. Relief washed over him when his search of the soft sands higher up the beach revealed no marks of the long sliding body and propelling footsteps of a crocodile. Robbie could see the seabed for quite a distance; therefore, he did not need to look for the wire-netting pattern on the surface of the water which usually indicated the presence of a crocodile watching from below murky waters. A smile lit up his face when a sea turtle appeared further out drinking in the air.

His eyes continued their restless search for wild pigs, poisonous snakes and crocodile nests as he made his way back to the hut. Robbie's heart pounded in his chest when a scrub turkey erupted up out of the grasses. He laughed at himself as he watched the bird make its awkward flight up into the branches of the trees.

After preparing his breakfast, he took his bowl out to sit on the stump near the front door to eat his porridge. He listened to the eerie whistling noise which had been a feature of this area since he first visited with his friends. At those times when they felt unsettled by the persistent noise, they debated its cause, but no one had offered up a satisfactory solution. Today this noise reminded him of the whistling kites he had witnessed when droving between Far Horizons and Rosebud Plains. Those birds had seemed to be around every time he had his nightmares and strange visions which now, he knew were reflections of his past and his deep-seated worries. Did this noise, here on the coast and so close to a reunion with his family, have a subliminal purpose relating to his fate?

The typewriter remained unpacked and forgotten. Only the painting by his daughter of her mother had been removed from the sea trunk. Every evening he gazed at the picture hanging on a nail in the wall until the light stole her image away. After darkness seeped into the hut, he wandered outside to watch the moon and stars on their journey across the heavens and he dreamt his dreams of hope.

CHAPTER TWENTY-EIGHT

Saturday, the fifteenth of November – she had waited for nearly a week for the day to arrive. Rhylla jumped out of bed and rushed to her mirror above the dressing table. Her fingers massaged the lines stretching out from the corner of her eyes, those which made their unwanted appearance across her forehead and the deepening ones around her mouth. Rhylla threw off her nightie and ran her pale hands down her body. What wasn't wrinkled, sagged. Her heart quailed. He won't want to see the damage the years have done. He'll expect the Rhylla of forty-four years of age with a younger face carrying only laughter lines and a body to be admired.

"This was all a mad idea. I can't bear to see the disappointment in his eyes." She mumbled as she rushed to cover up the damages of time, as best she could.

Skye-Marie's soft knock sounded at her door. "Are you awake, Gran?" Her voice hushed.

Rhylla opened the door. "Yes, darling, I'm just getting dressed. Is everything alright?" She noticed the uneasy blend of excitement and anxiety swimming in her granddaughter's eyes.

"Gran, do you think I really should be going to this tennis day with Doris and Janet? What if Mum becomes ill?"

"My dear, your mother would only worry if you were to sit at her bedside every minute of every day. She is happy for you to be having a day out. Only last night she said how pleased she was to see you back playing tennis. The exercise will do you the world of good and put a bit of colour back into those cheeks."

Skye-Marie threw her arms around her grandmother's neck.

"Now, it might be an idea to go in and see if your mother is awake yet. You will have time to give her breakfast."

In the kitchen, Rhylla found Janet working at the sink. "All ready for the big day, Janet?"

"Yes, Mrs. MacBurnie. All week, the two girls haven't stopped talking about the return of Saturday tennis."

"And you, Janet? How do you feel about going? I know some people can be cruel at times. Will you be alright?"

"Don't you go worrying about me. I can stand up for myself. I will admit it was hard at first when Doris was the only charity child at the school. Some of the mothers resented us. But with three others now attending most of the mothers are more accepting. The ladies from the church have always been supportive. In fact, they've invited me to a game of doubles with them."

"I'm pleased to hear that. I didn't know you played tennis."

"I never have but I've watched Doris over the years. We'll see. I'll give most things a go once."

Later as she shut the door behind the tennis players, Rhylla allowed the silence to wash over her. Today promised to be filled with her own challenges. According to Jim, Robbie was going to visit her. Her footsteps led her to Kirsty's room where she found her daughter asleep with the sketch pad on the verge of falling to the floor. She rescued the pad and scrambled around the floor seeking the pencil. Order had no sooner been restored when the knock sounded on the front door.

Rhylla's glance through the dining room windows on her way to the front door took in the strange utility parked close in under the camphor laurel tree near the coach-house. Its presence, at the very spot Robbie always said kept him away from the snooping eyes of the neighbours, did not register in Rhylla's mind. She had other things racing through her head; the imminent arrival of the husband she had not seen for fourteen years – her Robbie. At the door, she stopped. Her fingers patted her hair into place, smoothed the lines on her face and any creases in her frock.

Her hand reached for the door handle. She turned the knob slowly. Was she doing the right thing? With a deep breath, she swung the door open – paused – and gasped. She felt the shock cover her face like a cement mask. Her mouth dropped open. What was this stranger doing here just when she expected her Robbie to arrive? How can she get rid of him politely? She looked anxiously left and right out into the garden and then back again. Who was this man with his head and face covered in grey hair?

At that moment, her gaze took in the deepening blue almost violet of his eyes. Her stomach rolled like a ship in a gale. Hundreds of butterflies performed a frenzied dance inside her abdomen. They fluttered down into the very core of her being. Her legs turned to marshmallows. Moist eyes closed. Strong arms circled her waist as she felt herself slipping towards the floor.

Robbie shuffled them both into the hallway and closed the front door. He pulled Rhylla close and held her tight until the trembling of both their bodies steadied. She felt her strength returning with the long-forsaken touch of his arms about her.

"Robbie?" A whisper.

"Rhylla, my little kitten." He whispered her name in return, savouring the novelty of wrapping his tongue around the words he had only recently recalled. With one hand he outlined those wonderful eyes and mouth, retracing similar journeys of years long ago.

She clung to his shirt-front aware of his still-strong body beneath the thin cotton. "You've grown whiskers, Robbie. You said you hated whiskers." Her hand reached up to run across his closed eyes and down his nose and over the grey beard.

"The whiskers make a great disguise. Dare I say even you did not recognize me at first?"

She smiled a sweet smile. "No, I didn't. I thought you must be someone looking for work. I didn't know how I was going to get rid of you before my husband arrived."

Once again, their soft laughter caressed the corridor walls.

"Shush, we'll waken Kirsty. Come to my office."

As they made their way around to the office, Rhylla's one thought rose above the multitude of other eddying thoughts. *Should I have kissed him? I've never kissed a man with a beard and whiskers? Did he expect me to have kissed him?* She jumped when he spoke.

"How is my baby girl?"

"Robbie, she's not well." They paused at Kirsty's doorway. Rhylla watched the frail chest struggle up and down. "The doctor says she may not last until Christmas." Her voice deserted her as her throat choked on her tears. Robbie reached over and held her hand. Tears hung on his eyelids. They walked around to the office.

Rhylla rushed into the room and pulled the drapes across the windows. "I'll just go and bring us a cup of tea."

On the way back from the kitchen, Rhylla found Rob leaning against the doorway of Kirsty's room. Tears now ran unchecked into his beard.

"Come my dearest, come and have a cup of tea."

"Oh, Rhylla, I am so sorry. Maybe this is a punishment for my impetuous actions all those years ago. If I had never swung that punch maybe things would have been different." He drew in a ragged breath. "It may not have prevented Kirsty's illness but at least you might not have had to face this alone."

"Kirsty does not know it was her uncle who raped her. Nobody does but Jim. As far as she knows the rapist got away. Young Skye-Marie has been told the same story when she asked earlier in the year. And now, with the body in the utility discovered in the quarry, hopefully, they should have no reason to make a connection to the rape or you."

"Jim told me they'd found the body when he dropped your letter out at the hut yesterday. Doug Hampson had told him. Jim thought they didn't seem to consider me a suspect."

"Our Police Sergeant seems to get about a bit. It was him who came here to tell me. Do you think Doug might know? I had the feeling he knew more than he was letting on? He scared me, he did."

Rob put his arm around her shoulders. "Jim and I have kept Doug well out of this. He may have been our friend since we were kids, but he is a police officer and we didn't want to put him in an awkward position at the time."

Rhylla led her husband into the office and guided him to a chair by the window. She stood and poured the tea from the teapot on the tray at the small table close to his hand. She ran her hand over his beard once more.

As she turned to sit, Robbie called her name softly. "Rhylla, you have a visitor. It's Doug Hampson himself if I'm not mistaken. He has put on a bit of lard, hasn't he?"

"No, it can't be." She tiptoed to the window and peeped around the side of a curtain to see Doug Hampson walking down the garden path. "Good heavens, what am I to do?

"Get out of here and close the door. I'll not even breathe. Keep him over the other side of the house." He clasped her shaky hand. "You can do this, Kitten, you can."

Rhylla bent down and kissed Robbie's eyes, his nose and brushed his lips with hers. "How long it seems since I heard you call me Kitten? I shan't be too long."

Her feet flew around the corridor to the front door where she paused and took three deep breaths before swinging the door inwards.

"Oh, Doug, this is a surprise. Is everything alright? It's Saturday today don't tell me you're working today."

Doug Hampson took a step backwards to see a flushed Rhylla standing in the doorway looking in his opinion extremely guilty about something. Perhaps it had something to do with the utility parked out of the way near the car shed.

"Are you well, Rhylla? You look a little flushed."

"I am. I've been working in the office. I nearly didn't answer the knock but when I peeped out and saw you standing here, I ran to the door. Once upon a time, a short run like that wouldn't raise a sweat but I have to admit I'm not as young as I used to be."

Doug did not miss the fact she remained standing in the doorway so she obviously didn't want to invite him in. She might be working but then she might have a fancy man in there too.

"I heard you had a new housekeeper. Doesn't she answer the door for callers?"

"Janet, no, normally she would but she has taken the girls to the tennis fixtures on at the school today. Hence, I'm taking the opportunity to catch up on things."

"I won't keep you, Rhylla. I just wanted to let you know the preliminary report on the human remains found in the quarry came back this morning. We're convinced the skeleton is that of Greg

MacBurnie. The vehicle in which he was found is one Greg MacBurnie was known to be travelling in at the time, according to our reports. A gold pocket-watch was found amongst the bones. They were able to identify words engraved on the back as *"Greg MacB Forever Molly L."* After reviewing my notes at the time, I think we can safely assume the Sydneysiders may have done for him back then. The Brisbane investigators will be crawling all over the vehicle next week so we may find something more substantial then."

Doug's arm shot out when Rhylla swayed and grabbed at the door.

"Thanks, Doug, I'm alright. It's a little upsetting, I guess."

"Are you sure there is no way you can contact Robbie?"

"I don't think so. I'll ask Jim if he has heard anything but I doubt if he has. You do have Greg's family address on the Tablelands, haven't you?"

"Yes, they have been informed." He spun his hat around in his hand. "Well, I'll be on my way." On his way back to the car the oddness of Rhylla's behaviour held his attention. When he reached his vehicle, he could have kicked himself; he had meant to check out the number plate on the vehicle under the tree.

Before returning to Robbie, Rhylla went into Kirsty's room. She stood watching the eyelashes flickering on the translucent cheeks.

"Are you awake, darling?"

The eyelids lifted slowly. "Yes, Mum. I must have been dreaming. I thought I heard Daddy's voice."

"Do you wish to see your father, dear?"

"It's the one thing I wish I could do before I die, Mum. I know I'm dying. It has taken me a while to accept, I know. I want to tell you how much I love you. How much I've appreciated all you've done for me over the years." The whispered voice paused. The eyes closed. Rhylla held her breath. She thought her daughter may have breathed her last, but the whisper continued. "Our Skye-Marie has given my life meaning."

"Darling, you have given the world so much with your wonderful art. Remember that too." Rhylla paused considering the wisdom of her next words. "Kirsty, your father is here. He wants to see you. Do you feel strong enough to see him?"

"Please." Her eyes closed again.

Pulling the handkerchief from the pocket in her skirt, Rhylla patted the tears on her cheeks before she went into her office. Twice she opened her mouth to speak. The words did not come out.

Robbie jumped up from his chair and enfolded her in his arms. He cradled her head against his chest.

"Kitten, what has happened?"

"Kirsty knows she is dying. It's the first time she has mentioned her dying. I think she heard your voice or she was dreaming but Kirsty wants to see you."

Together they walked into the room and stood at Kirsty's bedside. Robbie sat on the edge of the mattress and took up a pale, brittle hand in his strong tanned fingers.

"Kirsty, my baby girl, it's your father."

The eyelids sprung open. The eyes widened. "Daddy." The word hung in the room – almost inaudible. "You have whiskers but I remember your voice."

Robbie swallowed on the tears built up like a dam wall in his throat. "Hello, sweetheart."

"Daddy, I wanted so much to talk to you. Skye-Marie wants to know who her father is? Who was there with you? I remember your face." The alabaster eyelids closed. Shallow irregular breathing spoke of continued life.

Robbie looked up at Rhylla sitting in the chair on the opposite side of the bed. He raised his eyebrows. The whisper interrupted their gaze.

"Lying here, I think I remember new things – or maybe I've been dreaming. Did I hear you swear that night? I had never heard you swear before. There was a crack sound and then a crunchy thud sound." Kirsty licked her dry lips. "Did you see who raped me, Daddy? Did you punch him?"

It felt like a horse had booted him in the chest. He was sure his heart stopped. He looked over at Rhylla, hoping for guidance. She shrugged. It was up to him.

"Kirsty, yes I did hit the man. I didn't know him." Unseen by his daughter who lay with her eyes closed listening to his voice, Robbie hoped she did not hear the lie. "The man's head hit the chest of drawers in your room. He died. I disposed of the body and then I had to leave. I could not have you and the family hurt by the police naming me as a murderer." He looked over to Rhylla for approval. Her smile and nod sent a wave of relief throughout his body.

"We don't need to tell Skye-Marie that bit, do we?"

"No, Kirsty, we don't. I think it's best she believes what you and your mother have told her already."

Kirsty shifted her eyes to her mother. "Mum, can I have a sip of water?"

"Of course, my love. Do you want to try a little custard for lunch?"

"Just water."

"Will I go now?"

"No, Daddy, please stay with me."

With Kirsty returned to sleep, Rhylla sat with Robbie in the kitchen. Neither was taking much notice of the egg sandwiches on their plates but they had both emptied two cups of tea. Bursts of desultory conversation dragged themselves across the table.

"I think I should ring Tim this evening, Robbie, and tell him how low Kirsty is."

Robbie nodded his head. "Does Bronwyn know?"

Rhylla sighed. "Yes, I have kept her abreast of Kirsty's health, but it's Bill who shows the most empathy. I'll phone them too."

"It sounds like Bronwyn has not changed a lot."

"Bronwyn is still our Bronwyn, I'm afraid. Thinks only of Bronwyn. Drinks too much. No matter what I say she blames Kirsty's pregnancy for your leaving – says you left because you were ashamed of Kirsty."

"Sounds like she still works hard at making her own life miserable. Poor darling, she has always cut her nose off to spite her face."

"Bronwyn's brain may be sharp as a filleting knife in business but she never took the time to mature as a person, I'm afraid. It has been frustrating at times."

Robbie reached across the table and took Rhylla's hand. "Kitten, I'm so sorry. It has been hard for you."

"Harder for you, I think, Robbie." Rhylla squeezed his hand.

Tea grew cold in the cups as silence lay across the table. Robbie looked up from where his gaze had locked onto their joined hands.

"What did Doug have to say earlier?"

"The remains from the quarry have been identified as those of your brother, Greg. Doug thinks the Sydney gangs are responsible, but the Brisbane investigators will be here next week."

"Hmm." Robbie's gaze glanced up at the clock. "When will Skye-Marie be home from the tennis?"

"Janet will bring the girls home after they finish their games."

"Do you think they'll mind if I stay the night?"

"Janet won't mind in the least – she has a pot of stew you can't jump over waiting in the fridge for our meal. Janet and Doris live in Mr. Evans' old flat. You may run into a barrage of questions from your granddaughter though."

"I think the hardest questions are over. Kirsty doesn't want her daughter to know any more than you have told her."

Squeals and laughter heralded the arrival of the tennis players. Janet's voice called several times.

"Hush, girls, Kirsty may be asleep."

A silence fell over the group trooping into the house through the back door when they looked up to see Rhylla standing at the kitchen door with a tall man, his head covered in untidy grey hair and whiskers, behind her.

Skye-Marie hesitated before rushing up to hug her grandmother. "Doris and I both won our singles' match and Doris and I won the doubles."

"Hello, Mrs. MacBurnie," Doris spoke softly, head held downwards.

"Congratulations, girls, well done."

"Hello, Mrs. MacBurnie, is everything alright?" Janet asked.

"Yes, thank you, Janet." Rhylla looked over at the group in front of her. "Everyone, I would like to introduce you to Mr. MacBurnie, this is Skye-Marie's grandfather."

Silence once more descended. It was Janet who spoke first.

"Pleased to meet you, Sir."

"Pleased to meet you too, Janet. Rhylla has been telling me how well you look after her. My sincere thanks."

Janet nudged her daughter's ribs.

"Pleased to meet you, Mr. MacBurnie," Doris knew what a nudge in the ribs meant.

"Pleased to meet you too, Doris. You are my granddaughter's best friend I understand."

The dark curls danced as Doris nodded her head.

All this time Skye-Marie's eyes examined the man in front of her. She took in his likeness to the man in her grandmother's wedding photo. It was hard to be sure with all that grey hair. She stared into his eyes. He stared back. She did not miss the hand on her grandmother's waist or the smile on her grandmother's lips which reached to crinkle the blue-grey eyes.

"Why have you come back?"

Rhylla gasped. "Skye-Marie, where are your manners?"

Janet took hold of Doris's hand. "We'll go to the flat and clean up." She almost dragged her daughter out through the back door.

Rhylla nodded her head at the departing pair. She turned to Skye-Marie and spoke – her voice like steel.

"Your manners, Skye-Marie."

Skye-Marie continued to stare at her grandfather. "I don't know if I'm pleased to see my grandfather or not, Gran. I have never met him before. I hardly knew he existed until recently."

Rhylla's heart sank like a ship holed by cannonball fire. This sounded like something Bronwyn would say. Her mind struggled to find appropriate words but she did not have to bother.

Robbie gently moved her aside and walked up to Skye-Marie. "Just as I have apologized to my wife and daughter, Kirsty, I feel I owe you an apology too; even though we have never met. To you Skye-Marie, I humbly apologize for any heartache caused."

Skye-Marie's mouth dropped open. A frown flickered across her brow and then her lips twitched. Robbie almost lost his balance when she threw herself into his arms.

"Oh, Grandfather, I've so much wanted to meet you. Will you be staying for a while? I have so much I want to talk to you about."

Robbie grinned. "How many questions? Have you made a list?"

Rhylla did not realize she had been holding her breath. A long sigh whispered through her nose.

CHAPTER TWENTY-NINE

Skye-Marie scraped the last pieces of meat off her plate before carrying her things over to the sink.

"Would you like me to wash these dishes, Gran?"

Rhylla lifted her water glass to her lips and sipped. After sitting the glass back on the kitchen table, she replied. "No thanks, dear. I'm sure your mother would like to have you sit in there with her for a bit. She has been quite low today."

Skye-Marie sucked in a sob. "You mean she's dying – now – already?"

"I think her time is getting close, darling." Rhylla held out her arms to receive her weeping grandchild.

"Go, my dear. Sit near your mother and hold her hand. Speak to her of all those things in life you have enjoyed, especially those things you shared together."

Rhylla's and Robbie's eyes followed their granddaughter along the corridor to the corner before she disappeared into Kirsty's room.

Robbie turned to his wife and lifted her hand into his own. "You realize Kirsty has very little time left, Rhylla, don't you?"

Rhylla nodded her head unable to speak. She felt the sobs deep inside her like rocks in the bottom of an ocean waiting to be spewed up by a tsunami wave.

"Do you mind if I stay tonight?"

A wry grin held her lips. "Robbie you must never leave this house again without me at your side."

His eyes crinkled above the whiskers.

Rhylla spoke slowly, planning as she did. "Will you sleep in my room downstairs tonight? I don't want Kirsty to be left without one of us by her side. We can take it in turns to sit with her."

A morning glow suffused the room when Robbie shook her shoulder gently. The thick porridge of her exhausted mind melted at his words.

"You might want to bring Skye-Marie down here. I think our daughter is taking her last breaths."

Rhylla threw her feet over the side of her bed. Toes shuffled about feeling for her slippers. Her arms tossed the sheets aside in search of her dressing gown.

Robbie returned to his daughter's side.

He strained his ears to hear the whispered words. "Glad, Daddy. Glad you came."

"Darling, I wish I had found out earlier." Her hand disappeared into his gentle fist.

He looked up as the hushed footsteps entered the room. He disentangled Kirsty's hand and stood to allow Skye-Marie to sit in his chair. He pulled up another chair from near the wall.

"Is she …?"

"Not yet, dear. Take her hand in yours. Let her know you are here."

Rhylla pulled the second chair closer to the other side of the bed. She took up the soft brush and began to brush Kirsty's thin hair with its streaks of grey through the strawberry-blond locks.

"Mum, we are all here together. You and me, Gran and Grandpa."

Kirsty sighed a long sigh and breathed no more.

The three around her bedside never spoke. Their eyes remained fixed on the face at peace. Each held their breath as if waiting to breathe when Kirsty took her next breath until only the three drew breath together and broke the spell. The silence continued – no one stirred.

It was Skye-Marie who eventually rose and closed her mother's eyes completely. Rhylla then stood and lifted the sheet over her daughter's head. A sob fell from Robbie's mouth as he pushed his chair back and rose to his feet. He held an arm about Skye-Marie's shoulders and stretched his other hand across the bed to join with Rhylla's reaching hand.

Shortly afterwards, Janet found the three unmoved when she came in to prepare breakfast.

"I'll make a pot of hot tea."

"Thanks, Janet. Don't make school lunch for Skye-Marie today. She won't be going to school for the remainder of the week."

"Yes, Mrs. MacBurnie, I am so sorry."

"Thanks, Janet." Rhylla released Rob's hand. "I'd best go and telephone the doctor, and Bronwyn and Tim."

When Rhylla returned to the kitchen she was pleased to see Robbie had enticed Skye-Marie to eat a little porridge.

"Tim has a seat on today's aeroplane from Brisbane."

She sank into a chair and took the cup of sweet tea offered by Robbie. He held out the tray of dry biscuits. Rhylla shook her head. The constriction in her throat made it impossible to swallow anything but fluid.

Robbie reached across the table to touch her fingers. "Do you want me to talk to the undertaker?"

"Yes, please, I don't think I could manage that. Hopefully, he can do the funeral tomorrow morning. Talk to Jim first. I think he has already made preliminary arrangements weeks ago." Rhylla turned to her granddaughter. "How about you go upstairs and get cleaned up and dressed. There'll be people here wanting to pay their respects today. You can go for a drive with your granddad to the airport to meet your Uncle Tim later."

Rhylla had not been wrong. Kirsty's friends from the church and the tennis club and the art world trickled in all day. Janet never left the kitchen. Pots of tea were made, emptied and made again. Trays of scones disappeared into the oven and reappeared fifteen minutes later, cooked. Trays of sandwiches were topped up frequently.

Tension built when Bronwyn and Bill walked into the house. Before Rhylla could take her to one side, Robbie walked up to them and spoke quietly to his elder daughter. Rhylla did not hear what was said but the woman did behave while in the house.

The clock in the hallway struck three in the afternoon when Tim arrived from the airport with his father and Skye-Marie. Rhylla sighed with relief to see father and son were getting on famously.

Between it all, Rhylla looked to prepare suitable clothes for her, Robbie and Skye-Marie to wear at the funeral the next day. It was while she was upstairs, she looked through the window and noticed Doug Hampson and his wife approaching the front door. Her feet flew down the staircase. She caught sight of Robbie heading towards the kitchen. With a multitude of apologies, she made her way between several people standing in the corridor talking and partaking of the treats served up by Janet. Robbie was just about to enter the kitchen when he felt himself being swept up into Rhylla's strong grasp. She half dragged him along the corridor and into her office.

"Pull the curtains and lock the door," she ordered.

"Why?" Robbie gasped.

"Please, darling, Doug Hampson has arrived."

It was Jim who had noted the slight kerfuffle between Rhylla and Robbie. His head swung around searching for a cause when he noticed Doug and Eileen enter through the front door. He marched up to them and shook Doug's hand.

"Hi, cobber, it's good of you to come." He nodded at Eileen Hampson. "And you too, Eileen. Come inside. I'm sure you know most of the people here. Can I get you a drink or something to nibble?" Jim held the Hampson pair corralled in the living room until he noticed Rhylla return to the fray minus Robbie who, no doubt, was secreted on the other side of the house.

Fixing a smile on her face, Rhylla walked towards Doug and Eileen. She held their hands.

"Thank you for coming. It means so much to the family to see you here. Please, can I get you something?"

"Jim is off scavenging for us at the moment, thanks, Rhylla." Doug smiled. "Rhylla, where else would we be when Robbie's family needs our support and our commiserations at such a sad time."

Jim returned with a whiskey for Doug and a lemonade for Eileen who had been taken off by one of the ladies from the church guild. He went to find her and deliver the drink.

Doug leaned down and spoke softly. "Rhylla, you can tell Robbie to get a haircut and shave those whiskers off. They do not suit him at all. If Rob is feeling guilty in any way, he can know the final report is in on Greg MacBurnie's demise. It has been ruled Greg was killed by the Sydney gangs over drugs. The Brisbane boys found a stack of opium sealed in containers in the panels of Greg's utility. You can tell Robbie he can come home. Now I must collect my wife – I have a mountain of paperwork on my desk to get through."

With her head swirling and jelly sticks in place of her limbs, Rhylla automatically played the part of a polite hostess as she guided

Doug and Eileen on their way. After she closed the garden gate behind them, she fell back hard against the timber. Not an ounce of strength remained in her legs. Her mind screamed at her. *He knows. He knows. He knows. How long has he known? He never said a word. Has he been protecting Robbie, but how did he know?*

Doug sank into the seat of the car. It felt as if a weight had lifted off his shoulders. The final summation including the essence of the reports from the Sydney police in 1933 and his own recommendations and knowledge had the coroner place the blame firmly onto the Sydney gangsters. He smiled at his thoughts. *I may not have Jim and Robbie's academic brains but I've a good cop brain. I understand human nature. What else was Robbie going to do to the man who raped his youngest? The Sydney gangs may not have killed Greg, but they have many other bodies lying about. It won't hurt for another to be placed at their doorstep.*

"Are you alright, Doug?"

"Yes, Eileen, my dear. Yes, I'm hunky-dory."

Somewhere in her busy day, Janet found the time to cut Robbie's hair.

"When I first started cutting my father's and my two brothers' hair, they had to put an upside-down bucket near the chair for me to stand on so I could reach their heads."

Robbie's dubious look was not lost on his female barber. She winked at Rhylla. "I only cut off one of my father's ears in all that time."

During the afternoon, Rob cleared his face of his whiskers. Standing at the door with her mouth agape, Skye-Marie watched the process as he stropped the blade and ran it in sweeping strips down his soaped-up face.

"How come you don't cut your skin?"

"If one doesn't want to have a face of raw flesh one soon learns to be careful."

As the night eased in upon the household, everyone climbed into bed red-eyed and exhausted.

CHAPTER THIRTY

When it was time to leave for the funeral, Rhylla could not be found. It was Robbie who discovered her in Kirsty's room. Very slowly she moved from one canvas to another. Occasional hiccoughing sobs caught in her throat as she looked at something that reminded her of a poignant moment in her daughter's life. On the table, by the empty bed stripped of all but the ticking-covered mattress, lay the final sketch pad with Robbie's face peering up at the ceiling. She picked it up and held it close to her chest. How were they going to manage life without their baby girl?

The clean-shaven Robbie who had stood at the door watching, now moved into the room.

"Come, my darling, this is the last thing we can do for our Kirsty. We must be brave."

The day matched the mood. Grey skies with scuds of drizzling rain accompanied the sombre faces and flowing tears. Big, black umbrellas protected the mourners from the miserable elements where they gathered at the cemetery. Rhylla glanced down at Skye-Marie. What must the child be feeling standing here waiting to see her mother's coffin disappear into the ground? Skye-Marie sucked in a sob. Pride filled Rhylla's soul for herself and for Kirsty. The youngster had held her head up high all morning. Rhylla's mind cast back to the church service which thankfully was not too drawn out. Maybe someone had spoken to the usually verbose parson.

Rhylla turned her gaze up to her husband on the other side of Skye-Marie. A soft warmth suffused her heart and drifted off into all corners of her soul. With all the excess hair consigned to the incinerator, she had her Robbie back again. Butterflies bumbled around in her belly when he looked over to her with a soft smile.

"Chin up," he mouthed.

Life is strange, she thought. *We lose our daughter but we regain our own lives. Now it is up to us to ensure Skye-Marie continues to make her mother proud.* The tears leaked out and onto her cheeks. How could she have any left?

THE END

Elizabeth Rimmington sincerely hopes you have enjoyed *Rhylla's Secret*.

Her plans for future novels:

Following so many requests for another book to follow *Shadow of the Northern Orchid* and its sequel, *Shadows on the Goldfield Track*, Elizabeth has already begun to research the pearling history on the seas above Cooktown, Queensland and the terrain and industry on land north of Cooktown.
In appreciation of the recent assistance by the Past Graduates Association of the Townsville General Hospital, Elizabeth has plans underway to centre a novel around the hospital in historical times.

Visit Elizabeth Rimmington at her website
www.elizabethrimmington.com.au
Take advantage of her FREE monthly newsletter, including a new short story every time, by joining the mailing list.
Find her on Facebook – elizabethrimmington.author